CHRISTOPHER, MOT AND FIDGIT

A story by
Michael Bread

Typeset in Buenard

Illustrations by © Andrea@kja-artists.com

Editing, design, typesetting and publishing by UK Book Publishing

www.ukbookpublishing.com

ISBN: 978-1-914195-04-4

MICHAEL
BREAD
BOOKS

CHRISTOPHER, MOT AND FIDGIT

Prologue

Thomas Burke was a thief aptly named because he had always been a Burke, but not always a thief. He left school at 13 because "it could do nothing for him and was a waste of time".

Some six years later he bitterly regretted his decision after seeing his school friends and fellow classmates stay on, qualify, and further their careers with well-paid jobs. "Not for nothing am I called berk," he would remind himself at least once a week. But he had a habit of blaming fate every time he got something wrong. "It was 'fate'," he would say, when in fact 99 times out of 100 he was firmly to blame. He could hardly read and write and after he was kicked out of the family home by his dysfunctional parents he slept rough and started to earn pennies and then pounds collecting discarded drink cans.

He stole a supermarket trolley to cart his cans around and to take them to the scrap merchant. He was doing fine until one day the scrap merchant suggested he steal more supermarket trolleys because the scrap value was better which he did until caught on camera, identified, followed back to the scrap yard and arrested with the scrap merchant.

The merchant went to prison; Thomas got a suspended sentence, a criminal record and became even more unemployable as a result.

He went back to collecting tins. The years flew by and he got himself a driving licence, a small truck and several regular customers in the building trade collecting their unwanted metal (it was cheaper to give it to him than pay to have it taken away).

And then again fate took a hand when Thomas took a wrong turn down a country lane and found an abandoned dental clinic. It had lain empty for some time obviously because of the state it was in, and at some point someone had broken a window to get in. Drawers and cupboards had been searched but none of the 'metal' had been taken.

Thomas spent the next few weeks stripping everything he could from the building until there was nothing left but a dentist's chair and all the equipment around it. He took a different route home every time he left the clinic because he was terrified of getting caught again. One of the different routes involved a steep climb up a forest road full of potholes which his old truck struggled with and down into the next village where he could dispose of his scrap.

Having cleared everything he could, Thomas viewed the chair and the other equipment with some apprehension. It had to be worth something, he thought. So, armed with a set of spanners he set about taking it apart. It was very heavy, and he knew it would take some time.

To the rear of the chair was a strange arm that cranked over the top of the chair with a strange pointy thing on the end. Having never been to a dentist before (his rotten teeth were proof of that), he had no idea what it was. At the bottom of the cranked arm was a large heavy looking box. It had lots of alarming looking labels on it, including a large yellow triangle with a black border and three more funny looking triangles in black with a black dot in the middle, and it was secured with a big lock. Having forgotten any reading and writing he ever attempted to learn he had no idea what the signs or writing meant.

So as far as he was concerned, locks meant something of value. The door therefore had to be opened.

He spent over an hour heaving and shoving with the biggest tools he had and slowly the door began to bend. It was starting to get dark and Thomas realised sooner or later someone was going to visit again and his luck would run out. As this was the only thing left of any value (he had already loaded everything else) he was desperate to get open what he thought was a safe. With one last almighty heave, the lock gave way and the room was suddenly bathed in green light.

The last effort had made him fall over when the lock gave way, but he got back up, dusted himself down and walked back over to the box.

The door was now wide open and mounted inside was a long glass tube with round ends that was the source of the green light. He was bitterly disappointed that there was no sign of the anticipated money, but he noticed that the inside of the box was lined with a thick layer of lead, as was the door. "Oh well," he thought, "not a complete waste of time," so he dragged the box with the tube out of the door and with great difficulty pushed it onto the back of his truck.

He tied it down as best he could but couldn't shut the door completely as it was bent out of shape.

It was now very dark, and the green glow was showing through the gaps in the broken door, so he hastily threw a sack over the box and for the last time drove away from the clinic he had systematically robbed for weeks.

Thomas didn't like driving at night, but he was in a hurry and very worried about getting caught so he drove as fast as he could – way too fast for the bumpy potholed road in the forest, and certainly too fast for his dilapidated truck.

Thomas was constantly looking in his rear-view mirror. It was completely dark and the green light lit up the trees behind him. If anyone came the other way he was in trouble. He pushed the accelerator pedal to the floor as he started to panic.

Unknown to Thomas the violent way he had opened the locked door and the bumpy journey was shaking the green tube away from its mountings so, just as he crested the top of the hill at a ridiculous speed, it broke free from its box, rolled down the back of the truck and bounced off. Thomas looked again in his rear-view mirror and

---

saw nothing. It was completely black. He slammed on the brakes and jumped out as soon as he stopped, just in time to see the glass tube disappear down the hill and into the undergrowth.

His shoulders sagged with a combination of disappointment and relief and he climbed back into his truck and hastily drove away. The tube bounced and rolled this way and that almost coming to a stop several times only to slip and start its downward journey again. It reached a lower road, rolled across it, almost slowed to a stop in the gutter, rolled over the edge and continued downwards bouncing from grass knoll to fern and back to knoll again.

At the bottom of the hill was a short road that led to a beautiful five-bedroom house. On the opposite side of the road facing the house was an old oak tree more than 100 years old.

Time had taken its toll and sometime in the past the tree had split in two just above ground level. Over a period of time the weather had worn away the tree beneath ground and it had filled up with rotting leaves. Several animals had come and gone but fortunately at the present time it was now vacant.

The green tube was nearing the end of its journey. As it rolled and bounced down the last hill it hit a rock, spun through the air, and landed right in the cleft of the old oak tree with such force it buried itself deep in the leaves and disappeared from sight.

One week after Thomas' last visit to the old clinic he became mysteriously seriously ill and was taken into hospital. He had a pretty good idea why he was ill as he had now seen the same warning labels he couldn't understand in the

X-ray department, but he knew if he told the doctors about the green tube he would end up in prison again, so fear kept his mouth shut as he got sicker and sicker, while the doctors puzzled over what was wrong with him.

chapter 1

The neighbour's cat lay on a branch that he had strategically chosen to view an upstairs window on the second floor. It wasn't his tree in his garden but as he had no natural enemies or otherwise, he considered he owned it.

There were no other cats or dogs for miles and, apart from the odd fox now and then which was late at night or early in the morning, he had the place and this tree to himself. He had had three fights with foxes — lost two won one — but decided the pain was not worth the victory. When I say neighbour, he lived in fact several miles away but cats being cats they love to explore and one day he had noticed a little cage by a first floor window. Having climbed the tree, he found it contained a small grey mouse. Now this cat, like most, liked to hunt and catch mice but this one posed a problem, in a cage and behind a window!

He had watched the little girl whose room it was play with the mouse. At first it stayed in the cage but over several weeks it became bolder and now ran up and down the little girl's arms. But mostly it liked to sit up at the window looking out and the cat licked its lips waiting in anticipation.

The cat knew spring was nearly over and with the warmer weather the windows began to open — that would be his chance. What puzzled the cat was why the mouse would sit for hours staring out of the window. Then, one day, he spotted why. About three branches up on the other side of the tree he spotted another little mouse. This one was brown. The cat was very surprised by the cheek of this mouse to come up into his tree! The fact that the mouse had been coming there some considerable time before the cat arrived counted for nothing it seemed.

The mouse was apparently completely oblivious to the cat's

presence. He was transfixed looking at the little grey mouse that in turn was looking at him.

"Argh," thought the cat, "two little sweethearts. Well, this is going to be very easy. First I'll get one and then the other." He slowly backed away from his perch. This was going to be easy, he thought again. After all, stalking prey was second nature to him.

He decided to climb higher, so he could then get above the mouse and jump down onto him. He moved slowly to prevent the new young spring leaves from rustling too much and just as he reached what he thought was the right place that magical moment he had been waiting for came, the window he had been watching for so long opened and the cage was placed outside!

He couldn't believe his luck! So much time and now caught in the wrong place, but he decided to go for the cage. The door was open, and the little grey mouse was inside. She was watching him and had nowhere else to go. Gathering all his strength he launched himself off the branch.

However, he had made one simple mistake: he had taken his eyes off the little brown mouse who had worked out exactly what the cat was going to do. The mouse had watched him go up the tree and as soon as he launched himself towards the cage the little mouse did the same. The difference was with no fear whatsoever he went for the cat. His tiny body hit the cat which of course made no change to the cat's downward course, but his little sharp teeth sank deeply into the cat's ear and he hung on because he knew the little grey mouse's life depended on it.

The attack was such a surprise the cat completely misjudged his aim and instead of landing on the cage, landed on the windowsill and hit the cage. Its little door slammed shut as it fell clean off the other the end of the sill. The cage tipped, bounced on a tree branch, and then fell from bow to bow turning over and over.

The little girl screamed, her mother came running and together they watched as the cage bounced downwards towards the ground. On the last turn the door burst open again and the grey mouse was flung from the cage, hit the tree's trunk, and fell to the ground. The little brown mouse had watched it all happen as the cage went down and as he clung to the cat's ear. The cat skidded to a stop on the windowsill, so the mouse let go of his ear and fell after the cage hoping for the best. The cat felt smug for not falling off, but not for long. When the little girl's mother attacked him with a broom, he too had to leap from the windowsill, but he was luckier as he landed back in the tree.

The little brown mouse rolled into a ball and landed on soft moss. He was up and moving in one bound. He had seen roughly where the grey mouse had landed and had to get there before the cat. He found her seconds later, but she was unconscious.

He tried to wake her, but she failed to respond. All the time he could hear the cat thrashing about in the foliage above him. It was only a matter of time before the cat calmed down enough to realise where he was. He had to get her to safety, but where?

The tree he had fallen out of, of course! Just at the base there was a tiny hole between the roots. He had never investigated it, so he was taking a big chance because if it was already inhabited it was all over.

He tried to pull the grey mouse towards the tree, but the moss made it impossible and she was too heavy to carry. He looked around for something to help. It was too early in spring for new leaves but there were plenty of old ones left over from autumn, although they were all too weak and rotten, so there were no leaves strong enough around to make something to carry her with.

And then he saw it. After all the bashing around in the tree a large leaf was still growing at the base of the tree, he had no idea why, but he seized his chance and although the stem was very big he chewed it off in seconds.

He raced back with it, placed it next to the grey mouse and with all the strength he could muster, rolled her onto it. At that precise moment, the noise from above stopped. The grey mouse looked up but could see nothing. He grabbed the stem of the leaf between his teeth and his paws and pulled. Nothing happened, but he heard movement from above. The cat was on its way down.

Spurred on by this he pulled again, and the leaf began to move. He pulled and pulled and the leaf began to move a little bit further and faster with each effort. The ground helped as it sloped towards the tree which was only a few feet away, but it felt like miles. The hole at the bottom of the tree was getting closer and bigger but was it big enough to pull the little grey mouse and the leaf through? And was there enough room inside to get out of reach of the cat? And was there anybody else dangerous living there? All these questions ran through his mind as he got closer but so was the noise the cat was making above. He was sure by now the cat could smell them and just as he got to the hole the cat burst out of the tree and landed just behind him.

Within seconds the cat was after him but with barely a moment to spare and with a last burst of energy he pulled the leaf with all his might and they both tumbled into the hole. The cat's paw followed right behind and caught the brown mouse across his back. It was only a glancing blow but it drew blood and a loud squeak.

The cat went into another frenzy having been cheated of his prey yet again, and he tried in vain to force his way into the hole whipping his claw around inside.

The brown mouse lay at the bottom of the hole in a heap with the little grey mouse right next to him. She fortunately had not woken up so did not have to witness the fact that they were just out of reach of the shrieking cat in a furious temper. It was truly terrifying. The cat appeared to have given up, but the brown mouse knew that it was just waiting for them to come out. It could not have known the little grey mouse could not move on her own and that the brown mouse would never leave her.

"I can't," he thought. "I fell in love with her the moment I saw her, and I think she feels the same." A feeling of sadness came over him to think that he might still lose her, and if she never woke up, they would never even have had a chance to exchange a single word.

The sun began to set, and he felt it getting cooler. He heard the little girl and her mother outside searching for her mouse. She was crying constantly and cursing the cat, "I hate that cat, I hate that cat," she repeated almost constantly between sobs.

"I know, dear, I know, but I think she's gone." This increased the volume of the sobbing. Chad heard the rattle as her mother picked up the battered cage and the little girl's sobbing faded away as her mother took her back inside.

He snuggled up next to the little grey mouse and wondered what to do. He would have to sit out the night and hope for the best. She was still breathing gently as he in turn drifted off to sleep.

chapter 2

C had was a field mouse, born and living in a hole in the ground by the river. And he hated it from the moment he first saw it. It had a menace about it. It rose and fell and swirled and gurgled. Sometimes it was calm and placid but at other times it rushed by at such speed he did not understand how something could move so fast. He watched it many times, on some days some mysterious force began to push the water back from down the river so that as the water flowed down it caused the levels to rise dramatically. Fellow animals assured him it had done this for years, but he had a sense of foreboding about it. His parents named him Charlie but from the day he could speak he would warn every animal in the neighbourhood who was polite enough to listen how dangerous he thought the river could become. Of course, the other animals found it all very amusing that one so young would prophesies about what might happen.

Then one day one of the older animals said, "Young mouse you are full of too much chat." Everyone laughed and said, "I think we will call you 'chat' not Charlie." Over time it became Chad and he adopted it as his name. Only his parents would call him Charlie, no one else. As with all field mice his home was a hole in the ground not far from the riverbank where he lived with his parents. He was an only child; he did not know why as all the other families around him had three, four or five siblings. One day he thought I will get up the courage to ask my parents why I am the only one.

He woke up one morning and announced to his parents he intended to find them somewhere else to live that was on higher ground away from the river. His mother smiled, and his father groaned, "Please Charlie, not this again."

"No, I mean it, Father, I talked about this until no one will listen so today I'm going to search for a new home."

"Whatever you say, son," said his father.

"Well, be careful," said his mother and their conversations were apparently over!

And so he bravely set off across the fields where they lived. They stretched for miles and the land was very flat but, in the distance, he could see trees and that's where he was headed. "Easy," he thought, "I can be there and back in one day."

The first day was not very successful. He walked for what seemed like days, but it couldn't be because the sun hadn't set or risen once, and he didn't reach a single tree. He realised quite soon to his dismay that this was going to take considerably more than the one day he had planned for.

He barely made it back home before darkness descended. His mother was relieved; his father just tutted.

The following day he got up just as the sun rose. He was better prepared. Well, mentally anyway, as he had decided no matter what he wasn't coming back until he found "his tree".

It was a chilly day but dry and he found that with a change of plan he was moving faster than yesterday. He knew this time there was no turning back, so he had to find shelter before dark.

The fields were easy at first but then the grass changed to wheat and it was hard to see at the bottom of all these stalks so every so often he would climb a stalk of wheat and take his bearings. The trouble was all this up and down and up and down every so often and so early in the morning was very tiring.

Not long after entering the wheat field he sensed he was being followed. He stopped several times to listen but whatever was following stopped too. Perhaps it was just the wind or his imagination?

He had not travelled much further when he heard the same movement sounds in front of him!

He stood stock still, the wheat swayed gently in the wind and the scrabbling came nearer.

Chad took off as fast as his little legs would carry him, ducking and diving around the wheat stalks over fallen branches around an old pile of bricks but behind him, he heard whatever it was giving chase. He burst out of the wheat field into a small bare stretch of land and he felt whatever was there was right behind him. Throwing himself into a ball he rolled over to one side, turned, and stood up to fight!

The creature that had stalked him through the wheat field and chased him out of it landed in front of him. It had a huge head and six legs and was over five times his size.

"Oh," thought Chad, "I've had it." It was a huge ant. Chad had never seen one this big before, but it didn't move forward it just stood still with its head rocking gently from side to side. For about a minute they stared at each other. Chad was just waiting for the inevitable attack and fight which he was sure he would lose.

And then, much to Chad's surprise, the ant spoke: "Hello old chap, are you by any chance lost?" Chad had seen many ants of course of a much smaller variety and whenever he was near them, they studiously ignored him, and certainly never spoke.

"Sorry?" said Chad, somewhat shocked.

The ant, thinking Chad couldn't hear him properly, said again a little louder, "I said 'HELLO OLD CHAP ARE YOU LOST BY ANY CHANCE?'"

"I heard you the first time," said Chad, "and I'm not lost; well, I wasn't until you chased me around in circles in the wheat field."

"Argh," said the ant, "you were certainly lost the first time you came out here and then went back home to your parents."

"What!" said Chad with surprise and then some embarrassment, "You followed me then? I didn't see or hear you."

"That," said the ant, "is because I didn't want you to."

"Oh!" said Chad falling silent for the moment. "So, what exactly are you doing here then?"

"What's your name?" said the ant, completely ignoring Chad's question as if he hadn't asked it.

"My name's Charlie, but everyone calls me Chad."

The ant didn't reply immediately but stood very, very still as if in deep thought. "Well Chad, I don't have any family — never did really, I was part of a colony." Chad went to raise his hand, but the ant raised one of his front legs and waved it slightly as if to say 'wait,' and Chad sat back on his behind and let the ant continue.

"We all lived under a tree in the woods."

This time Chad couldn't help himself. "I want to live in a tree; that's what my mission is!"

"Do you want me to continue or not?" said the ant, a little impatiently.

"I'm sorry," said Chad, "I promise not to interrupt again."

The ant sat back on his hind legs to make himself more comfortable and continued. "Now where was I? Ah yes, so, we lived under a tree hundreds of us with one queen. I was born a worker ant so that's what I did. But I knew I was different — I could speak, but no other ant could so although we could communicate in normal ant way not one single ant apart from me was interested in doing anything else except work or breed or fly away to form new colonies. All a bit boring," said the ant half to himself.

"Then one day something very strange happened. It was at the end of the day and was just getting dark when there was a huge bang in the tree above and something very heavy fell into the trunk. All pandemonium broke out. The news spread quickly — we had been invaded! The Queen instructed everybody to leave save the eggs and just me and five others were to remain and guard the old nest. Of course, we obeyed. The nest was evacuated very quickly and they were gone. As the days passed all the others except one lost interest and followed the rest of the colony, but I wanted to know what had happened, and what had entered the tree trunk just above us. One ant stayed with me for a long time and although we worked together alas, he couldn't talk but I realised later he did grow as big as me and we were like brothers. Then one day he went to get something which he did every day and didn't come back. I searched for him for several days but there was no sign of him. After that I was alone, I haven't seen or heard of him since. I think he must have died. A little sad really."

Chad felt sad too after hearing this part of the story.

"What I didn't mention," he said suddenly brightening up and as if just remembering, "was the green glow that was coming from the trunk above. I think that's really what made the queen decide to leave – it was so unnatural."

By now Chad was transfixed. He had absolutely no intention of interrupting because he was dying to hear the end of the story.

"I was to be disappointed. All I found was a green ball of sorts that glowed in the dark. Nothing else. No invaders, no rival colony trying to take us over. So, I went back to what was left of our nest and tried to repair some of the damage done by our queen's rapid departure."

"What happened to the colony?" said Chad, breaking his promise not to interrupt. The ant didn't seem to mind this time. "They live not far from here, but I'm not welcome any more. Well, not inside anyway. They don't seem to mind when I visit the colonies in the back of a cave, but I am only allowed in the entrance, no further than that."

Another question formed on Chad's lips, but he managed to bite it back.

"So, I stayed and then one day I went to go down one of the tunnels I hadn't been into for some time and I didn't fit I had grown so much! Curious to see by how much, I went out to one of the nearest ponds. I couldn't believe what I was seeing. I don't really know why I hadn't noticed as I realised I had been lifting much heavier things much higher than before. And then the biggest surprise of all: when it gets dark now, I glow green just like the glass ball. So you see why they won't let me back in the colony, too big and the wrong colour at night." The ant laughed at this and Chad joined in.

"Talking of night," said the ant, "it's going to get dark soon and we have been talking a long time. Well, at least, I have," he laughed again. "Do you have somewhere to stay?" he asked Chad, of course knowing the answer already as it was apparent Chad hadn't really planned anything.

"Er, no," said Chad now feeling a bit uncomfortable having to ask a stranger who he thought was some kind of monster out to get him when in fact he was just trying to help.

"So, what's your plan, Chad?" said the ant.

"Well I thought I'd take you up on the offer. Is it far?"

"I'm afraid it is for you, old chap, but if you jump on my back, we'll get there in no time." So the ant lowered himself to the ground and Chad jumped on the ant's back. He quickly raised himself to full height and set off at a fast pace.

Chad hung on for dear life. He had never moved along this fast before, never mind this high in the air! But he could see for miles. "You alright?" said the ant. "Yes fine," said Chad, which of course was not true. He was terrified he was going to fall off at any moment which would have been very embarrassing, "thank you so much for your help."

"No," said the ant, "thank you so much for being my friend, you're the first creature I've met who hasn't run away from me since I was small."

On the ant's back there were small hairs which Chad was using to hang on to. He was bouncing all over the place and thought at any moment they were going to come out, but the ant didn't seem to mind.

"What's your name?" Chad managed to say in between bouncing from one side to the next.

"I never had one," said the ant. "We don't have names in the colony just predetermined duties." Chad was quiet for a moment. He had no idea what the word predetermined meant and was too embarrassed to ask. Much later in his life he would learn that if you don't ask or seek to find out no matter what you will never learn new things and words. Having thought for a moment, he said "well I have to call you something."

"How about Ant?" said the ant.

Chad laughed, "Well okay, Ant it is. Hello Ant, my name is Chad."

Ant laughed too and said, "hello Chad" again!

They had left the wheat field now and had slowed down. Although they were travelling on open ground it was full of obstacles which Ant had to either climb over or go around, whichever was easier or quicker. As a result, Chad had to look where they were going just as much as Ant otherwise a sudden move could throw him off Ant's back. Chad was amazed at all the objects they passed: big round black things with holes, short oblong red things, white containers, big black balls and numerous big white objects of various sizes. "What is all this?" said Chad.

"Rubbish," said Ant.

"What?" said Chad.

"Rubbish," said Ant again.

"I don't understand," said Chad.

"Well, you have to be careful," said Ant, "all this stuff used to belong to creatures called humans, they are tall, walk on two legs, move around in big machines that make a growling noise and go very fast sometimes. And every so often they throw everything they have away."

"Why?" said Chad.

"I really haven't been able to work that out yet," said Ant, "but I will one day. Oh, one other thing you should know it's best to stay away from them on the whole they don't like insects and mice!" Chad went very quiet.

"For instance," said Ant, "those red things are called bricks. They build their houses with those." "So why had they thrown them away?" asked Chad.

"Like I said," replied Ant, "I don't know." So, for the remainder of the journey Ant gave Chad a running commentary naming all the things he could as they passed them and of course lots of things he couldn't.

Ant had begun to change direction slightly. Chad could tell because the line of the trees he could just see in the distance started to move to the left. Of course, he said to himself they weren't moving to the left therefore they had to be turning to the right.

They slowed to a walking pace when Ant said, "You will have to get off here for now and wait for me. If you turn up at the cave without me talking to them first, they will probably attack you." Ant lowered himself down and Chad got off. "Won't be long old chap," said Ant and disappeared around a pile of rubbish.

Chad was now on his own and realised he had put a lot of faith in his new-found friend. If he didn't come back, he was well and truly lost.

Curiosity and the fact he was hungry and hadn't eaten all day got the better of him and he started to investigate some of the "rubbish" that Ant was talking about. Besides there were some tasty berries growing next to the round black things with holes in called tyres.

He hadn't gone far when he heard a fluttering sound and a strange frantic cooing. He moved closer to the sound and knocked over some of the rubbish. The cooing and fluttering immediately stopped.

He poked his head carefully around a pile of old red things which he seemed to remember Ant called bricks and there, caught up in a green mesh was a white pigeon! The poor creature was terrified but when she saw it was just a mouse she relaxed a little bit. "Can you help me please?" she cooed.

Chad moved closer. "How?" he asked, immediately feeling silly for asking a stupid question.

"I foolishly came in here to find something to eat," she replied politely, not ridiculing Chad for what he asked, "and got caught up in this. The more I struggled the worse it got, what do think?" Now Chad had moved closer he realised it was not a pigeon but a very young dove.

"I can help you get free," said Chad and without thinking he jumped up onto the piece of wood that the dove was trapped by. If he had looked more closely, he would have seen that the net she was trapped under had been pinned to the board. This was no accident, it had been planned!

"I'm so sorry," said the dove with a voice of anguish, and suddenly looking very sad.

"Why?" said Chad, "it's not your fault you got stuck. Accidents happen you know."

"I'm so, so sorry," said the dove again this time looking really frightened.

"Don't worry," said Chad with a mouth full of plastic as he cut through the plastic mesh with his very sharp front teeth. "I'm not going to hurt you and I'm nearly done," he said spitting out pieces of the green plastic as he worked. Just one more! He felt the dove shiver with fear and then there was a loud bang and it went dark.

Chad was in shock. It took several seconds for his eyes to adjust to the dark but wait it wasn't completely dark. The white dove was now a pale shade of green! "You're green," said Chad before he could think of anything reassuring to say.

"No," said the dove, "you're the one who's glowing green."

Before he could reply the top of the box that had been slammed down over them opened and a large human face appeared. "Well, will you look at that, a bleeding mouse. I won't get anything for the fur you got." A huge hand came into the box to grab Chad. The dove cowered in the corner. Chad ran to one side, the hand followed.

Chad was soon cornered there was nowhere to run. "I'm going to feed you to my cat," bellowed the face. Just when he realised there was no escape the man started to squeal in pain. The hand withdrew so quickly it knocked over the box letting Chad and the dove free.

Chad could not believe what he was seeing. The man was dancing around screaming and beating at his trouser legs, "No, get out!" he screamed. "No! No! No!" He tripped over a pile of bricks, banged his head on a wall and fell silent.

The dove turned to look at Chad and for the first time smiled and then said, "I'm so sorry."

"Why do you keep saying that?" asked Chad.

"He has done this before," said the dove. "He uses me as bait to catch all sorts of animals then kills them and takes their skin or fur to sell. If I hadn't stayed still, I'm sure he would have killed me too." Suddenly the man's trousers moved, Chad and the dove cringed backwards and then from the left trouser leg out popped Ant!

"Didn't take you long to get into trouble again old chap, did it?" And then he laughed, "This biting bit is not to my taste, you know" and laughed again.

"Oh! Ant, am I glad to see you," said Chad.

"Hello," said Ant to the pretty dove, ignoring Chad completely, "nice to meet you. I think we better move along before he wakes up with a sore head and takes it out on us," waving one leg in the direction of the unconscious man.

"Where are we going?" said Chad trying to get some response from Ant who seemed solely interested in the dove and nothing else.

"To the ant cave of course," said Ant, "and now we have an extra guest. Come on quickly, only it is getting very dark and if you think it's dangerous now it gets a lot worse later."

"I'd fly," said the dove, "but he clipped my wings," she said nodding back in the direction of the unconscious man, "so I can't fly away and every time they started to grow back, he clipped them again."

"Never mind," said Ant, "it's not far so you'll have to walk. I can't carry you both." And then to Chad, "but I think I said that once before, eh chad?"

"So," said Ant to the dove, "you're very young, how did you end up in this pickle?"

"I was in our home; well, nest," said the dove shyly, "and getting ready to take my first flight when my parents were getting all excited about a new place they had heard about full of worms."

"Really," said Ant "where? What was it called?"

"I don't really remember," said dove. "I think it was called the worm hole."

"Oh," said Ant suddenly showing more interest. "Are you sure?"

"Yes, that's what it was called."

"And so, what happened?" said Ant

"They left to find it and they never came back," said the dove sadly. "I don't think I'll ever know what happened to them. Then after getting hungry I tried to fly, fell out of the tree and got caught. I never managed to fly so I guess I never will." The dove went very quiet.

"Don't worry," said Ant, wishing he hadn't started the conversation. "Once your wings grow back, you'll be fine. You'll see."

chapter 3

This time it seemed Ant was as good as his word. With some twists and turns around the rubbish piles and ups and downs on the other indescribable piles of something, they cleared the rubbish dump. In the distance was a small rock face. "That must be where the cave is," thought Chad, "but it's a long way away." Thinking Ant had once again understated the time it would take because he had six powerful legs Chad was about to comment when Ant disappeared down a large hole with the dove in tow. Chad had lagged behind and was thinking so much about how empty his stomach was and whether he would expire before his next meal he was completely unprepared for the sudden change in direction. Picking up his pace he hurried to catch up hesitating briefly before he too followed Ant and the dove down the hole.

Plunged into darkness he had to change senses. He could hear Ant and the dove up ahead and then he noticed a green hue emanating from the walls. But as he moved along, he realised it was coming from him – the green on the walls was a pale reflection. He had almost caught up and now he could see the same green hue coming from in front of him. "It's Ant, of course," he thought. "I rode on his back and somehow I have got some of the green in me!"

As he rounded the bend of the small passage he was in, he simultaneously caught up with Ant and entered a large cave. In front of them was a small group of ants. Chad had forgotten how big Ant was until he stood next to the members of his old colony. They parted to let him through either out of respect, awe or fear. "No, not fear," thought Chad again – ants weren't afraid of anything.

Ant came to stop in front of a small pile of berries and nuts. "I asked them to collect some food for us," said Ant turning around to face the dove and Chad who were now level with each other. "I didn't expect another guest," said Ant to the dove. "I hope this is to your liking?" The dove fluttered her eyelids at Ant. Chad rolled his eyes and looked away, embarrassed.

"Thank you so much," said the dove, "you're very kind." Ant sat back, and the others sat with him forming a vague circle.

The ants didn't move at all.

"Don't worry about them," said Ant. "We can stay tonight and then we will have to move on." There was a hole high above them that obviously led to the outside. The darkness had fully descended and a full moon was shining. Some of the light reached where they were sitting creating a circle of light on the ground diminishing Ant's green hue. Chad began to eat, and the dove pecked here and there at the food. She briefly looked at the ants and then wisely changed her mind!

Ant didn't eat at all.

"You," said Ant, looking at Chad as if announcing something of great importance, "should learn to read and write!"

"What's that?" said Chad with a mouth full of food.

"It's something humans use to communicate with each other. I found one of their books and taught myself but alas I can't write. No hands," said Ant waving his two front legs as if to demonstrate. The dove studiously showed no interest at all and continued to rake through the berries and nuts indiscriminately, much to Chad's irritation.

"What good is that to me?" said Chad, glaring at the dove. Ant got up, went to a corner, and brought over an old tired book with no cover.

The ants didn't move.

Ant placed the book on the floor and flicked open the first page. "Here," he said, "is their alphabet. It starts at A and finishes at Z. When you put them together in a different order, they mean different things. I have learnt a lot about the humans and the world we live on."

Chad looked confused. "I know," said Ant, "it is confusing, but I know you're different to other mice Chad, just as I am different from other ants."

The ants didn't move.

Something changed. The circle of light in the cave dimmed perceptibly, Ant appeared to glow brighter, there was a flash from above followed by thunder. Chad looked up just as it flashed and thundered again. This time the cave shook slightly. Chad looked nervous, the dove was sleeping. Ant was still talking.

The ants didn't move.

And then hundreds of ants appeared. They smothered the dove and started to move her further into the cave. In a flash Chad realised Ant hadn't been asked to leave the colony, he was the colony! He ran the colony. Chad turned and ran, guilt flooding through him. He couldn't save the dove; they would kill him if he tried. Ant wasn't his friend; he had been lured here just to be food!

He ran to the exit that he had come in from. Ant called after him, "Chad, wait, stay for dinner."

"So you can eat me too?" he shouted as he ran.

"What?!" said Ant.

Chad had never run so fast in his life. The passageway he came in from now had large puddles of water in it getting bigger by the minute. He was lucky there were no other tunnels so no other way to go but the way he came in. In minutes he was out into a strange changed landscape. It was very dark. The moon was gone, the ground was sodden and the rain was so heavy he could feel it stinging his back. He ran and ran. He knew the ants would not come after him in this weather.

Common sense told him to take cover but the thought of the ants catching him drove him on. Some friend Ant had proven to be. He had all but carried him into the nest to die.

A shiver ran through him. He ran, and he ran, and he ran.

The rain passed, and dawn was breaking, and Chad was nearing exhaustion. He knew he could go no further; he was sure that he had run far enough to get away. With the last bit of energy he had left he buried himself in a pile of leaves, digging down far enough until it was dry and then instantly fell asleep.

chapter 4

When Chad awoke the rain and wind had stopped and through the leaves he could see a little bit of daylight. Cautiously he crawled out of the leaves to greet the day, the terrible memories of the dove's death and Ant's betrayal still fresh in his mind. "What now?" he thought. "Well, back to the plan: find the tree I want to live in." Trying to put the past day out of his mind he realised he was lost and somehow he would have to find the right direction to head in. And then he heard a faint growl. Chad froze. Ant was truthful about one thing thought Chad, it is dangerous out here!

He heard the growl again this time fainter. "Odd," thought Chad, "now it doesn't sound so frightening." Surprising himself, Chad followed the direction that he thought the growl had come from. Now he was out of the leaves he could see how much it had rained. There were small and large puddles everywhere which he had to go around. "No time for swimming lessons," he thought, his sense of humour returning. He reached a small bank beneath a bush and heard the growl again but this time much fainter. In fact now it was more like a whimper. Even more curious, he carefully crawled up the bank and through the hedge preparing for a rapid departure if he found himself in trouble again and entered a small clearing. The sun was up now, and it was getting warmer. Small wisps of steam were rising from the ground as it warmed up.

There in the middle of the clearing was a small fox cub lying sprawled on the ground. Chad hesitated. One thing he had learnt from his last experience was never to assume anything is what it is until you're sure it is what it is! "Phew," he thought, "that sounds complicated." He moved a little closer, the fox had not seen him and then it growled again. Moving slightly it turned in his direction and their eyes met. Chad froze on the spot. At first the fox didn't move or say anything. It blinked once or twice and then, realising it was no longer alone said, "Can you help me please?"

"Why should I?" said Chad, instantly regretting the harsh and defensive way he had replied.

"I'm stuck," said the fox, "actually no I'm not. I'm trapped."

"What do you mean?" said Chad, cautiously moving closer fully understanding what trapped meant and making sure he wasn't the one being trapped! The fox moved slightly, and this time Chad heard a jingling sound. Now very curious he moved closer still, carefully circling the fox to get a better view but still leaving his options open for a hasty escape.

Now with a clear view Chad understood. The fox's front paw was caught in what looked like to Chad two rows of curved metal teeth. "What happened?" said Chad.

"It's a trap," replied the fox, "set by humans to catch animals like me. My parents warned me, but I didn't listen and got careless."

"I know about humans," said Chad. "I've seen what you mean first hand, something I'd rather forget."

Chad was now very close to the fox and felt comfortable in being so. It was obvious that he was in pain and needed help. He looked at the huge iron jaws. "What can I do?" he exclaimed, "I'm only small."

"No, you're right," said the fox. "They will come soon and then it's all over." Chad sat for a moment, thinking. The trap had closed on the fox's paw, but it had also caught a small tree branch at the same time which stopped it closing completely. If this hadn't happened Chad was sure the little fox would have lost his foot. It was obvious he had struggled to escape to no avail. He had lost a lot of blood and was fading away, his eyes had become glazed.

"I have an idea," said Chad. The little fox didn't respond. Chad went looking for what he wanted — a small branch similar to the one caught in the trap slightly thicker and slightly longer.

He scampered down a small hill and nearly ran into a pond, after looking twice he realised that it was slightly bigger than a pond perhaps a lake or a river but whatever, that didn't matter now. He looked around and piled up against a log was a small pile of branches that looked just right but he wasn't sure if he could move any of them. Gripping the end of one he started to heave at it. It moved a little bit and with all the travelling he had done he was now a lot stronger, so he heaved again, and it moved a bit further. He heard something moving from the other side of the log. A huge round face appeared with two long brown knives hanging from the front upper lip. Chad shrank back and let the branch go, more of the face appeared and then it spoke.

"Oi! What do you think you're doing my little friend? That's my wood." Two small hands joined the face and rested on the log and Chad realised at once it was a beaver. And the two knives were in fact his very big front teeth. Somewhat relieved that it wasn't a dangerous creature from the lake he hurriedly explained why he was taking the wood.

"My friend is in trouble he's caught in a trap and can't escape—"

"So!" said the beaver interrupting Chad in mid flow, "you have a friend, another mouse who's in trouble. A likely story, why would you need a big lump of wood bigger than you?"

"My friend is not a mouse," said Chad indignantly, "he's a fox!"

"A mouse has a friend who's a fox?"

"I just said that," said Chad, "and if I don't help him the humans are going to come back and—"

"What!" said the beaver interrupting Chad before he could finish, "humans, humans, you are having trouble with humans, what about their dogs?"

"I don't know what a dog is," said Chad.

"Well, you will and I'm sure your friend caught in a trap does," said the beaver knowingly nodding his head as if it was full of knowledge and he knew everything.

"Yes," said Chad, willing to say anything to get some help.

"Well, lead on," said the beaver, "we will have to see for ourselves."

Chad was puzzled. There was only one beaver, so where was the other one that made up the we? Chad led the way and the beaver clambered over the log to follow. He was much bigger than Chad thought and had a big tail like a tennis racket without strings. The fox was still unconscious, and Chad thought he was too late.

"I see," said the beaver, taking charge, "there really is a fox, and a trap." The beaver took one look and bounced back down the hill. "Oh," thought Chad "he's given up already," but before he could think anything else the beaver was back with a large branch twice the size of the one Chad was after. The beaver quickly chewed the end into a point, placed it over the existing branch and stuck it in the gap between the two metal teeth.

"I'll be back in a minute," said the beaver this time at least telling Chad instead of just disappearing. He seemed to be gone forever but when he returned he was pushing an oblong boulder. "Sorry it took so long," said the beaver, "but it's a little heavier than I thought." By now Chad was completely confused. He had heard about how beavers build things, but this was the first time he had seen it first-hand! The beaver rolled the boulder under the existing branch to stop it moving and then proceeded to pull down on the other end. At first nothing happened. Then Chad saw the metal jaws move a little bit. The fox woke up and moaned. Chad was relieved as he had thought the little fox had died while he was away because he had been too long. The bleeding had stopped but moving the metal jaws must have hurt and that's what woke him. The beaver pulled himself onto the end of the branch and the jaws opened some more. "Quick," he said, "push your friend's foot out of the way. I can't hold the trap open forever and I think this branch is going to break."

As if the branch had heard him it started to creak and groan. "Quickly," said the beaver again. Chad ran over to the trap and with all his might pushed the fox's foot out and fell through the jaws of the trap. At that moment the branch broke with an almighty crack. The trap slammed shut again with Chad right in the middle.

The beaver fell over the fox, sat up, and they both looked at poor Chad. The trap had come down right on his body. The beaver nodded his head from side to side, "No chance for your little friend," he said to the fox, "he gave his life to set you free." The fox looked devastated.

Before they could say anything more Chad quickly slid out of the trap surprising them both. "Ha!" said Chad, "you forgot about the branch that saved the fox's foot — it saved my life too! I'm much thinner than your foot and it stopped the jaws before they cut me in half."

"Well you are a lucky mouse," said the beaver, and then they heard the dogs.

"Quick," said the beaver, "dogs, dogs mean humans and humans are not good for us. We have to scarper. Quick, follow me." The fox was now looking more positive so took the beaver's advice and followed him down the bank with Chad right behind.

"Where are we going?" shouted Chad, which sounded more like a squeak than a shout.

"I hope you can swim," said the beaver. "I'm not a normal beaver, I've built something special which you can hide in, but you can only get to it through the water and you'll have to hold your breath to get there."

Now Chad knew what swimming was but not what was meant by holding your breath. The dogs were getting much closer now. They didn't have much time as the dogs would follow the scent. I'm putting a lot of faith in another stranger, thought Chad. I hope I haven't made another mistake?

They arrived at the water's edge and the beaver pointed at a big pile of wood in the middle of the lake. "That's my home," he said proudly. The fox and Chad looked at each other in dismay, the dogs would be on them any minute. Now, Chad knew he could disappear into the grass and the beaver could swim away, but the fox with his bad leg couldn't run anywhere until he got better. They both turned to look at the beaver with a "you must be joking" look on their faces.

"Come on, into the water now and follow me if you don't want to be ripped apart!" The beaver easily slipped into the lake and with one last look at each other and a shrug the fox and Chad followed the beaver into the lake. The water was cold, but it spurred them on. The beaver was fast, but of course he would be, he was made to swim. The fox was doing well and within a couple of minutes he reached the pile of wood with Chad not far behind.

"Now," said the beaver, "the tricky part. This is my lodge where I live. The entrance is underwater so hold your breath and follow me. The dogs can't follow us through water as they lose the scent." The fox knew what he was talking about being almost like a dog, Chad didn't, but having come this far they both took a deep breath and plunged under the water after the beaver.

chapter 5

C had surfaced inside the loft. The beaver was already there and the fox had just arrived and was shaking the water off his fur.

Chad was surprised by the inside. It was completely dry except where they had come into it from the lake. The sides and the roof were made from carefully bent and interwoven branches and in some areas they had been left open to allow light to come in, and it was surprisingly warm for which he was grateful as the river had been very cold. There were no other ways in or out so with dismay Chad realised he would have to leave the same way down through the lake.

There were small areas at the bottom of the structure where you could look out and not be seen. Chad moved over to one of these to see what was happening just as the dogs burst through the bushes down to the water's edge.

There must have been 20 or 30 of them all falling over each other trying to find the scent they had just lost. The beaver was right; if they had still been there the dogs would have torn them to pieces. Chad smiled to himself. The dogs were so excited they were pushing and shoving and creating such a melee that any scent that there might have been was completely lost in the churned-up mud. The fox and the beaver had joined Chad to look at what was happening. The beaver put his hand up and over his mouth to indicate to them both to be very quiet. "Sound travels very far over water," whispered the beaver.

Suddenly there was a shout. The dogs calmed down a bit and through the bushes a human appeared, but this one was different. He had on a big red coat, white trousers with black boots, a black hat and a big long thin stick in his hand. It sent a shiver down Chad's spine. Two of the older dogs were calmer and they were looking at the lodge.

"Be quiet," said the beaver in a whisper. "We don't want the man to hear us."

"What's a man?" said Chad as quietly as he could.

"Humans come in different types – men and women and boys and girls. The men and women are big and the children are small. This one is a man and he is in charge of the pack. Chad was about to ask what a pack was when the fox who had been listening quietly moved over next to them and said, "They are hunting me." As if he had heard, the man followed the dogs' gaze and he too was now looking at the lodge

Chad, the fox and the beaver moved back from the openings. They couldn't be seen, but it felt like the man was looking directly at them. For what seemed like forever he looked at the lodge and then turned away calling after the dogs to follow.

All three of them realised they had been holding their breath and let out a sigh of relief, perhaps too soon because no sooner had they done so, one of the older dogs who had been watching the lodge before returned to the water's edge and sniffed the air. He was called to again by the man and reluctantly left.

"That one knows we're here," said the beaver. "He can smell us in the air. He's older, calmer and more sensible. We will have to wait before you can leave."

"You can stay here the night and leave tomorrow if you are well enough," he turned and said to the fox. "I will go and get us something to eat."

"What?" enquired Chad, wondering how he was going to bring nuts or berries under the water.

"Fish," replied the beaver. "That's what I eat. Is that alright?"

"Fine," replied the fox.

"Yes, that's fine," replied Chad, wondering what on earth fish tasted like.

Just as the sun started to sink over the horizon the beaver

slipped out of the lodge. "He has been a great help to us," said Chad to the fox.

"Yes, I know," the fox replied, "strange he lives here all by himself."

Chad nodded in agreement. He was feeling very tired today. It had been an exhilarating day but a tiring one. There was a splash and a plop, and the beaver set a fish down in front of them and disappeared back into the water, presumably to get one for himself.

"After you," said Chad simply not knowing where to start.

The fox had no such problem and tore into the fish with ease. "Would you like me to get a piece?" said the fox, his mouth full of fish.

"Well I've never had fish before," said Chad, "but I'm very hungry I think I could eat anything." The fox dropped a small piece of fish in front of Chad just as the beaver returned with his own dinner.

They ate in silence for a while. Chad ate some of his fish until the hunger went away but he knew as soon as he got outside he would tuck into berries. The beaver cleaned up and everybody settled down for the night.

"How come you live on your own?" Chad asked the beaver.

"Well," replied the beaver, "I didn't always. We beavers partner for life you know, and I met my partner when I was very young. We were very happy and settled here to have our offspring. Then one day she said she had heard rumours going around the other creatures in the area that there was a wormhole somewhere nearby and she was curious to find out what kind of worms. The dogs unfortunately were out that day. She never came back so alas the dogs must have got her thinking she was a fox."

With the mention of wormhole, the fox sat up. "That's strange," he said. "I have heard that name before – my parents mentioned it and left very early one morning to look for it. They never came back."

"Chad," said the beaver, "you're glowing green!"

"Yes, he's right," said the fox in amazement.

"I know, I know," said Chad with a weary sigh.

"But how come?" said the fox.

"Well it's a long story but it's about a ride on the back of an ant."

"Very funny," said the beaver with a huff. "If you don't want to tell us that's alright."

"It's true," said Chad and he proceeded to tell them what had happened. It took him well into the night but with the green glow all around the lodge it somehow came across as more dramatic.

"And so that's how I ended up here," said Chad, finishing his story.

"Well, I have to say that is truly amazing. If it weren't for the green glow I would never had believed you."

"Neither would I," said the fox, "but we need to help you get back on your way if you're going to find those trees."

"You're right, fox," said the beaver. "We have to help. By the way what's your name?"

"I never had a name," said the fox.

"Neither did I," said the beaver.

"Well Chad, come on, now we are part of your adventure you can give us names what do you think?"

Chad was very surprised. "I don't know I just can't think. Wait a minute, Freddie the fox and Builder the beaver," he suddenly announced!

The fox and the beaver fell about laughing. "That's perfect," they both said together. And Chad felt the happiest he had been for a long time and very pleased. They all slowly drifted off to sleep.

chapter 6

C had awoke first, dawn had broken, and his green hue had diminished. He went over to one of the openings in the loft to the look out. There was a heavy fog and it had turned cold. He could see very little and the edge of the bank was only just visible through the fog. He had had a good day with his new friends, but he yearned to be moving again. The weather was turning and he had to get to the woods before winter set in. He turned around to find Freddie and Builder watching him.

"The fox can stay here," said the beaver, "I mean, Freddie" and he laughed a little bit. "Until he gets better. I know you want to move on. I'll show you the way to get back on track and don't forget to come and see me again."

"I will," said Chad, "when I come back to see my parents."

The beaver dived down into the water and Chad turned to wave goodbye to the fox before he too followed the beaver into the water. He soon reached the bank and the beaver guided him further round the pond. "If you go straight through here and follow the track you will avoid the path where the men usually walk. Good luck," and before he could say goodbye the beaver was gone. Chad turned to follow the track and the beaver suddenly reappeared: "If you ever get into a new adventure Builder the beaver wants to be part of it, okay?" He grinned from ear to ear and before Chad could answer he was gone again.

Builder's parting comment had raised Chad's mood as he was a little sad to be leaving, but he made up his mind that if he ever needed help this would be one of the first places he would come.

The fog was lifting and the sun was coming up. Chad set off at a fast pace – he was much fitter now. Runner, climber, swimmer there was nothing he couldn't do! Well, except flying of course, but who knows, he thought, who knows? In his haste to get going he hadn't really paid attention to where he was going and ran straight into a huge blackberry bush. Wonderful, breakfast! thought Chad, and it didn't smell like fish. Picking the biggest one he tucked in. He had just got started when a squeaky sounding voice said, "IT'S MINE."

Chad turned around quickly and there, standing in front of him was the biggest seagull he had ever seen. "IT'S MINE," said the seagull again.

"They can't be all yours," said Chad getting ready to run because he knew seagulls would eat just about anything.

"It's mine," said the seagull, "all mine."

"Don't you say anything else," said Chad trying to engage the seagull in a sensible conversation while slowly consuming another berry which the seagull had failed to notice.

"Yes, but mostly it's mine except when I don't," said the seagull.

Chad wolfed down another berry determined to fill his stomach before he made his getaway. Ignoring the fact that what the seagull had said made no sense at all he tried a different tack: "This bush was here before you came along, correct?" said Chad.

"Er, yes," said the seagull surprised by the non-confrontational question Chad was asking and a little confused that somehow he was engaged in a conversation with a mouse who was considerably smaller than himself and not expected to stand his ground and argue.

"Well," said Chad, "based on that information you cannot say that this bush is yours then."

The seagull tipped his head from side to side and smacked his beak together as if deciding whether to answer the mouse or eat him. "Everything is mine," replied the seagull with some deliberation. "That's the way all seagulls are brought up." This was said with the hope that Chad would have to accept this as fact.

"Well I don't agree," said Chad eating another berry and wondering whether he soon might explode as he had eaten so many.

"I have never had a conversation with a mouse before," said the seagull suddenly. "They always run away. So are you saying this bush is yours and not mine?"

"No," said Chad, "it's not mine, it's not yours. It's for everybody."

"Who's everybody?" asked the seagull sounding more confused by the second.

"Oh, never mind. I must go now," said Chad trying to back away into the undergrowth concerned he had pushed his luck too far.

"But I don't want you to go," said the seagull pleadingly with a complete change of tone. "I was just getting to know you. Nobody ever wants to talk to me; they either run away or want to fight over what's mine."

Chad hesitated and let out a little sigh. He felt a little sorry for the seagull. He knew from his home life what it was like to be surrounded by others who all thought the same and to think anything different was considered odd. He paused from eating for a moment, mainly because he was concerned that his fat belly for now full of berries might seriously get in the way of him making a quick escape.

The seagull noticed Chad had paused and smiled, clacked his beak several times which Chad hopefully took as a good sign and spoke again. "What's your name then and where are you from and where are you going and what's next and what's after next?"

"Goodness," said Chad, "that's a lot of questions."

"I have more," said the seagull settling down on his legs to make himself more comfortable, "lots more."

Chad thought before he answered. He knew that if the answer prompted a whole lot more questions he would probably be here all day. "My name's Chad, I came from the lake and I'm going to the woods to find a new home." Happy with that Chad waited to see the seagull's response. There was no immediate anything apart from the seagull tipping his head from side to side again as if he had water in his ears. "Because," continued Chad cautiously, "I want to live in a tree not in the ground."

"Why?" said the seagull.

"Why not?" said Chad, getting frustrated with the rate of exchange. "Anyway, what's your name?" said Chad having waited politely for no reply.

"I don't have one," said the seagull immediately and making Chad jump.

Thinking back to the last time he came up with something, he said "how about Sid the seagull?"

The usual extended silence prevailed and then the seagull said, "I like that, it's mine."

Chad started to laugh and much to his surprise the seagull started to laugh too. There followed a long silence between them and Chad took this as the perfect time to ask a favour.

"Have you ever carried anything heavy, Sid?" said Chad adopting the seagull's new name.

The seagull smiled. "Yes, I have. Some pretty big fish from the sea and a couple of times an eel from the lake." Chad didn't need a reminder about fish, but he carried on, "well the reason I asked is I told you I wanted to go to the woods and as I am now in a hurry I wonder whether you could give me a lift on your back? The usual silence prevailed and then Sid said, "you might fall off?"

"Well I thought about it and if you don't mind I could hang on tightly to a couple of the feathers on your back."

"Okay," said Sid without hesitation. "Hop on." A very surprised Chad said thank you and carefully climbed onto the seagull's back. "Ready?" said Sid.

"As ready as I'll ever be," said Chad full of excitement because he was going to fly.

Sid the seagull launched himself into the air with such force Chad nearly fell off before they left the ground. His arms felt like they were going to come off then the force of take-off pressed Chad hard into the seagull's back and Sid banked hard left and swooped down again and Chad was flying in the air hanging on with just two feathers at arm's length. Then Sid went up and down and left and right and then he climbed so high Chad could see for miles and whooped with delight, "Thank you, thank you so much," said Chad.

"You're very welcome," said the seagull diving downwards towards the woods. The seagull's wings were huge. Chad couldn't understand how something so big could be folded up against his body on the ground.

The wind was in Chad's eyes and he could feel his fur rippling along his back. He could see the woods approaching at breakneck speed and right at the front stood two tall pines. "There!" he shouted at Sid, "there, right there." Sid flew downwards at a steep angel and just at the last minute pulled up and dropped his legs to land. Chad thought right then he was going to explode, and all the berries would come bursting out. Fortunately, it was only Chad's vivid imagination at play and he slid from the seagull's back and landed on the ground giddy from the pleasure of it all.

"Thank you again," said Chad.

"My pleasure," replied the seagull. "I will come and see you again if I may, I have lots more questions."

"Of course," said Chad.

"One thing I will ask though," said the seagull, "I would appreciate if you kept this to yourself. I do have a reputation to keep." He winked once and launched himself into the sky and was quickly lost amongst a sky full of seagulls.

chapter 7

At last Chad reached the trees he believed he had come so far to find. He couldn't believe that had taken him this long, but what a journey and what things he had learnt on the way. Just two trees stood out at the front at the crest of the hill as he had seen from far above. The rest of the wood spread out behind them, but what appealed to him was that both trees had small holes about ten feet above the ground where branches had snapped off some time in the past.

"Ah," thought Chad, home and food storage – something very important that he had learnt from Ant. He quickly climbed the first tree and cautiously peered inside. A quick sniff confirmed nobody was home and hadn't been for some time. He checked it out for size and then scampered down one tree and up the next to the other one. Same process, no one was home either and this one was bigger than the other one and had a more concealed entrance from above.

So, decision time. Home on the left, storage on the right! For the next few days he worked very hard. First he filled both holes with straw to help stop anybody else moving in, then nuts, berries, anything he could find which wouldn't go bad quickly. After a week of hard work, he was set up.

He did however have to admit to himself that running up and down a tree was a lot harder than living down a hole in the ground. The days were getting shorter now and the weather was turning colder.

From the entrance to his new home he could see the river in the distance and imagined what his parents were doing and of course all his friends (such as there were) and neighbours.

"Well, if they could see me now," he thought. This was Chad's first autumn and winter to come, Beaver the builder had told him what to expect and maybe hibernate but there was so much to do and see he didn't want to waste a moment of time sleeping!

There was suddenly a rustle in the leaves above him, well those that were left anyway, and the sky began to darken. Chad looked towards the river, but he could no longer see it. There was heavy rain moving quickly towards him with more dark clouds.

"Finished just in time," he thought. It was time to snuggle up in his new home and wait for the storm to pass. He ducked inside just as a huge gust rocked the tree from side to side. The rain was torrential and the wind was increasing minute by minute as dark descended. Chad began to wonder whether living in a tree was such a good idea after all. The tree swayed and rocked and every so often something broke. The storm raged on and on all through the night and Chad was unable to sleep a wink.

Just as dawn broke the storm broke too and it stopped raining almost simultaneously. Some rain had got into Chad's home and the floor was a little wet in places but otherwise he was fine. Tired and sore from being thrown around and unable to sleep he climbed up to the entrance to see what damage the storm had done.

The clouds were gone and the sky was clear, but all Chad could see was water – the very thing he warned his parents about had happened! Everything he could see, where he had travelled with his new friends and where he had lived with his old ones was gone now, totally submerged under water.

He could no longer distinguish between the river and the flooded plains. With a heavy heart he realised that nothing on the riverbanks could have survived and of course it also meant he would never see his parents again. A single tear ran down his cheek as the enormity of his loss slowly sank in.

He crawled down into the straw in his new home and curled up into a ball. He had never felt as alone in his life as he slowly drifted off to sleep.

chapter 8

C had awoke with a start. It was late afternoon and he had slept nearly all day. At first he thought he had been dreaming, but a quick look around his new home reminded him he had not. He reluctantly crawled up the entrance to look out. The sky was clear and the sun, although beginning its descent as it neared the end of another day, still shone brightly and shimmered off the new lake that had formed. Chad looked across to his other tree where he had stored his food.

"Oh," he thought, "I'm here and the food's there and there's ten feet of deep water between. Well, I could wait for the water to go down which eventually it must, or I will have to swim to my food store! But I don't know what waits for me in the water!"

He decided to wait another day. Another sun rose, the skies were still clear and the water was still there. And now his stomach was grumbling, and worst of all his head still hurt from thinking about losing his family.

He waited one more day and as nothing had perceptibly changed he realised that he would have to swim between the trees to the food if he was to survive. He climbed out of his home and edged down the tree carefully watching out for birds of prey. He didn't expect it to be a problem as the colour of his fur blended into the tree. The water was full of rippling reflections, so it was impossible to see what was beneath the surface.

He edged his way around the tree to the shortest distance between the two and, closing his eyes briefly and wishing for the best, he launched himself into the water. Ten feet was not a great distance for a mouse on the ground but in water it was a marathon. Within seconds of diving in he realised he had made a big mistake. Whatever was in the water with him had heard the splash as he dived in and Chad could feel the vibrations in the water and a small splashing sound growing ever closer.

He was now more than halfway across but whatever it was, it was closing in fast and Chad realised he wasn't going to make it in time. All the things he had planned to do with his life were fading away, as was his energy as he swam for his life. A tree branch torn off in the storm drifted slowly past and in seconds Chad made a decision to try and survive. He turned to the branch which was just inches away and scrambled aboard. Seconds later the thing in the water hit the branch, missing Chad, but such was the force of the blow the branch started to slowly spin. Chad sensed the water was now moving faster which meant that finally the water was draining away. He quickly realised if he did not get off very soon he would not survive. He had no food and he would either drown or starve to death.

The branch was spinning and with each complete spin it got nearer to the tree. He had to decide quickly: which end to run to and jump off? The creature in the water hit the branch again. It was circling and trying to knock him back in the water.

Chad ran to what he guessed was the right end of the branch that would be nearest the tree. On the next turn it was his last chance. He knew that after this turn the tree would be out of reach and with the water now moving faster by the second he could never get back. He ran as fast as he could down the branch and launched himself back into the water just in front of the tree with a foot to go. But the creature in the water had followed him down the branch in the water and as he jumped, it attacked.

The tree was just a foot away. He was sure the thing chasing him was just behind him and then there was a huge disturbance in the water and in the air just as he was about to reach the tree. He braced himself for the pain when the creature behind grabbed him. There was a huge splash which caused a small wave and he was pushed the last few inches towards the tree. He grabbed it and climbed clear of the water with what was left of his strength.

He turned around to see how on earth he had escaped his fate. Climbing away from him was a seagull with a huge eel wiggling in its beak. "You are a very lucky mouse, Chad," called out Sid the seagull struggling to speak without opening his beak as he flew away chased by several other seagulls who were no doubt all saying, "It's mine it's mine."

"I didn't even have a chance to thank you," he thought. He crawled around to the front of the tree and into his store, collapsing in a heap and feeling too tired to attempt to eat. But of course, like all mice, his stomach ruled! So within a few minutes he had tucked into some nuts and his stomach was nicely rounded again. As he drifted off to sleep he thought, "I'd better stay with the food for now, I'm not going through that again."

Chad awoke in a more positive mood. He had had a very lucky escape thanks to his friend Sid the seagull. One day he hoped to see him again and thank him personally.

"Time to plan for the future," he thought.

chapter 9

O ver the next few days Chad watched the water slowly drain away. To the rear of his trees was a bank that the water had not risen high enough to breach so everything behind it, including the wood, had not been flooded. He looked both up and down the valley and as far as he could see it was the same in both directions. With hindsight now, he realised he could have swum to the bank and been on dry land a lot sooner. It was now very cold, and ice had formed on the tree branches. The last of the leaves had finally fallen and winter had truly arrived. Part of him wanted to continue his journey, but the instinctive side wanted to stay in the warm.

And then the final decision was made for him. It began to snow and snow and snow. It was beautiful to look at — the whole valley changed and it was now a continuous sheet of white with the odd tree or branch sticking out here and there. The wind had increased, blowing huge banks of snow into slopes. This was the first time Chad had seen snow. It was just magical the way it appeared out of the sky especially at night nothing one minute, a snowflake the next.

Chad realised it was time to stay put. He crawled back into his home and curled into a ball to wait for winter to pass.

chapter 10

Christopher awoke in his most favourite place. Bed! Not just any ordinary bed but the best bed in the world (he only thought that because he had made it himself). When I say made it, I mean he made it for himself! Not made it. Oh, confusion. Anyway he had never seen another bed, so he couldn't really judge if it was the best bed in the world, he just knew it was!

He had chosen the paper it was made from well. The outside was made from beautiful Christmas wrapping paper he had found wrapped around an old pipe. The inside was lined with the best quality newspaper and the bedding was a munched-up handkerchief that had been stuffed under the floorboards. The whole thing was rolled into a ball with an entrance at the bottom and top, so he could dive in or out of bed any way he chose.

Christopher lived with his mother and father and his two older sisters Mot and Fidgit. They lived under the floor of the dining room and kitchen of a very big house. Their space was divided into six by six long walls that supported the floors. At intervals along the walls were holes to allow air through. His family used these holes to travel back and forth. There were other areas at the front of the house that Christopher had never gone into; they were very dark and scary, so he had stayed away from them.

Christopher had been born in the house. He was the only one as the girls had been born in a tree just outside. Something had happened, and they had to leave in hurry, but his mother and father had never told him what that something was, and his sisters were too young to remember.

They met to eat each evening in the very centre of their living area. They never met to eat in the morning because their parents left every day very early to go and forage for food. There was only one way in and out of the house and Christopher's father had told him and the girls it was very dangerous. Where they ate there was a small table and six small chairs, and each mouse had their usual place around the table.

Christopher knew what his father meant about the dark and dangerous area he had warned him about so there was no chance he was going anywhere near it!

Their mother and father's sleeping area was right in the centre of the rear of the house and there were no holes connecting it to the other areas. It was in fact the only place that had a small door to get in and out of and none of the children had ever questioned why. It just never occurred to them.

The mice moved around in semi-darkness but here and there, there were small gaps in the floorboards that allowed light to filter down and sometimes wonderful smells of food cooking in the kitchen.

The right side of the house at the rear was where the girls slept, and Mot spent most of her time looking at herself in a broken piece of mirror she had found and doing little else but talking to herself about how pretty she was.

Fidgit liked to build things and spent all her time finding bits of wood or brick and creating strange objects and structures. Neither mouse showed any interest in each other's hobbies, if you could call them that.

Christopher had the left side to himself and so he spent a lot of time in his bed.

Just above his head all day and most of the evening there was continuous talking, sometimes music, but mostly talking. At first Christopher thought it was the people who lived in the house that his parents had told him about and warned him about. He had never seen them, but he did hear them moving about particularly early in the morning and in the evenings, and that was when the best smells filtered down to him from the kitchen.

Today he had woken up to the usual sounds of movement above his head and the talking when something very strange happened. The newspaper that made up a large part of his bed was right in front of his face and suddenly one of the words he was looking at matched a word he heard from above and he knew what it meant! At first it was just one word and then another and another. Christopher pulled the paper towards him and now the words he understood were coming at him so fast he quivered with excitement.

He jumped out of his bed and ran to the newspapers he hadn't chewed up since they were of course much easier to read. Page after page he read, amazed at what he could do and what he was learning. The sounds above his head now took on new meaning and he was puzzled as to why he hadn't paid more attention before. He now wanted to learn more but, afraid to speak to his parents or his sisters, he kept this new-found ability to himself. "But one thing's for sure," he thought, "I have to find more papers to read from somewhere."

Then one evening over dinner their father started to chat about the past. This was very rare. He had occasionally spoken of how he met their mother and some of the other animals he had met on his travels prior to meeting her, but mostly they would talk about what the children had done that day or their plans for the future. Their parents never mentioned where they had been the night before or what they had done but every day without fail they returned with fresh food for the family and everybody was happy and content.

"Well," said their father suddenly and unexpectedly to the children. "I remember when we first moved in here it used to rain food. Do you, dear?" he said to their mother. Their mother nodded silently, as surprised as the children by their father's sudden reminiscing.

"The house belonged to an old couple," he continued, and they lived alone. "There were lots of gaps in the floor above us where you sleep now son," he said, nodding at Christopher.

The children sat in silence. It was so rare for this to happen and they knew so little about their parents' past they didn't want to interrupt for fear he would change his mind and stop talking. "They would cook fresh bread and cakes, and some would drop on the floor and when they swept it up it would rain down on us. We lived here quite well and never had to go out. And then one day it just stopped." There was silence from the children while they waited for their father to continue. "Ah, but that's another story," said their father and left the table.

Christopher, now overwhelmed by the discovery that he could read and his need to learn yet more, had to say something.

"Father," said Christopher before his father had left completely and, unable to contain himself any longer, "where did the table and chairs come from?" he asked. Their mother looked round quickly at their father and exchanged glances. Only Mot saw this because she was older and more perceptive.

"Well that also is another story," said his father, carefully avoiding the question and hurriedly leaving the room.

That night as usual everyone went to bed, but Christopher couldn't sleep. He tossed and turned thinking non-stop about the table and chairs, where his parents went, why they had the only door, and what was hidden behind it.

So for the first time in his life he stayed up all night. He heard the movements stop upstairs and the voices stop. He heard the creaks and groans of the house settling down for the night and he waited and waited.

His parents moved very quietly as they left their room, passed his door and then disappeared around a corner into the darkness of the front of the house. Then there was silence. Christopher waited to make sure they were not coming back and crept out of his bed.

He left his room and turned around the corner he had seen

his parents go around. Much to his surprise, it was not dark. Actually, it was dark but for some strange reason he could see perfectly well the whole length of the house. At the very end was a small semicircle that looked like tunnel with a yellow and orange flickering light coming from it. Christopher hesitated very briefly, but any fear he may have had was now overwhelmed by his new-found determination and curiosity – so much so that he was even surprised himself.

He worked his way down the house towards the light where he passed more newspapers and coloured magazines that he knew he would have to come back for. It was amazing that all this had been here and he hadn't known. "Don't be silly," he thought to himself, "you only learnt to read yesterday!"

He reached the arch that the light had come from. Now he was nearer it was not as big as it seemed. He carefully stuck his head out to see what was beyond.

Directly in front of the arch was a huge table surrounded by chairs sitting on a large red and blue carpet with long red tassels along the sides. The room was dark.

To the left was a long hallway and on the other side of an arch there was a matching arch on the opposite side and that is where the yellow and orange light was coming from. Christopher carefully crept out of the hole he had come from. It was in fact in a wooden skirting that ran all around the room and the hole was a knot that had fallen out many years ago. He ran along the skirting to the first corner and then to the edge of the first arch. He was taking great care because he simply didn't know what lived up here.

Christopher was closer to the light now and noticed it was flickering. He scooted across the hallway over to the second arch and looked around the edge and there, right in front of him, was a huge fireplace with a big log fire. It was mesmerising; he had simply never seen anything like it before.

He looked left and right, ran over to the hearth in front of the fire and sat back to watch. The logs burned with a steady flame, but occasionally little spurts of fire would pop out here and there and sometimes with a hiss. So preoccupied was he with the fire that he never heard the attack when it came, and a huge paw came crashing down and pinned him to the floor.

Christopher could hardly see let alone breathe, but he heard a voice say, "Well, what have we here?"

In the blink of an eye he pushed up and threw the dog over to one side as if it weighed nothing at all. The dog rolled twice and landed on its feet. Christopher got ready for the attack. It never came. The dog lay down and started to laugh. "You," he said, "you are without doubt Chad's son." And he laughed some more. Christopher could not believe what he had just done. The dog was huge and he was tiny by comparison, but he had thrown the dog over as if it weighed nothing. The dog trotted over to Christopher and sat down next to him. "You must be Christopher, yes?"

"Yes," said Christopher nervously and somewhat surprised that the dog knew both his and his father's name.

"Hello," said the dog. "My name's Slippers and there's a cat around here called Blanket that doesn't like your father very much so probably won't like you either. I think he is out at the moment though." Christopher was stuck for words at first but after a minute or so while Slippers sat there patiently waiting for a response, he replied "Er, yes, you are right, but how did you know who I am and how do you know my father?"

"Here," said Slippers. "Come and sit next to me and I'll tell you all about it, or as much as I know anyway."

chapter 11

Christopher went to bed with more questions than answers spinning around in his head and awoke with the same questions still unanswered. For the first time since he had been born he had become curious about his family's origins.

"Strange," he thought, "yesterday I was content without a care in the world and today I can't stop thinking!" Where did his parents go every night to get their food and why sometimes did they come back with cuts and bruises? Surely just getting berries and nuts couldn't be that hard. But as he had never been outside before he had absolutely no idea what outside looked like.

When Christopher sat down next to Slippers he had no idea what he was about to hear and then Slippers began.

"Comfortable?" he asked Christopher. Christopher had nestled down next to one of Slippers' paws by the fire and just nodded in reply. "Well I'll begin," he said.

"Your father was here when I came and so was the cat Blanket. In fact, the cat was here before your father and unknown to them both they had some history. The tree that used to stand opposite the house was once where your parents lived until it was destroyed in a storm. Your father never told me much about how they came to leave in a hurry he just told me one day it started to fall down, and they had to get out. You weren't born then but your mother was expecting you and you were born shortly after they moved in.

"They settled in with no problem and chose to live where you live now in the back of the house. They never had to go out, which was just as well as the only way in is through the front door. There are no holes anywhere to the outside.

"Your father told me he didn't mind because at the back of the house was a kitchen and the old floor that was full of holes where over the years the floorboards had shrunk. The old couple who owned the house for many, many years lived here then and cooked three times a day. They were pretty careless when cooking, so a lot of food dropped onto the floor. Each day after cooking they would sweep the floor, but of course because of the gaps between the boards, Chad told me it 'would rain food every day' and they wanted for nothing.

"Because of the storm, the people who clear up old trees when they fall down were very busy and, as the old couple didn't have a car, and nobody else lived in this road they left the broken tree on the ground until someone could find the time to clear it."

There was a sudden rattling noise and the front door opened. Christopher buried himself under Slippers' fur. "Don't worry," whispered Slippers, "that's Mrs Smudgeit. She comes to clean every day for the people who now own the house. They go to work very early and come home late, so they leave the television on in two rooms with different things on. If I get bored I can go and watch it."

"I see," said Christopher, also whispering but not really understanding. He had never seen a television, so he had absolutely no idea what one looked like. "That explains the noise that my sister and I listen to. I would very much like to look at it too."

"Later," said Slippers, "you will have to wait until she is gone, and she lays out food and water for Blanket and me too. Blanket knows when she comes so he will be back soon." That could be a problem, or maybe not, thought Slippers, remembering how easily Christopher had thrown him over.

Mrs Smudgeit came over to Slippers and tickled his ears. He normally got up to say hello, but he didn't want to let her see Christopher. "Not feeling well today, boy," she said picking up a log and throwing it on the fire. "Chilly today," she said half to the dog and half to herself. She took a bowl of water off a small table and put it down for Slippers and went upstairs to start her cleaning.

Christopher came back out from under cover and said, "you were saying?"

"Ah, yes," said Slippers, "where was I?"

"The tree," said Christopher.

"Oh yes, that's right. Well, everything was fine until eventually the tree people caught up, which had taken months, and came to start clearing the tree away. Apparently they found a broken tube in the roots of the tree and the next minute there were humans everywhere. Blanket told me they were here for weeks cleaning up some dangerous mess they found and while it was being done, the old people had to move out temporarily. Once the work was completed, they felt uncomfortable living here and, with the tree gone, their view was ruined and so they decided to move somewhere smaller. The house became empty and that's when it became a problem for your father."

"Why?" said Christopher, asking his first real question.

"Well firstly Blanket didn't really live here. He was a wandering cat and used to come and go but after the old people went, he started staying here because they left the cat flap open."

"What's a cat flap?" asked Christopher.

"A small door in the front door to allow animals to come and go. In fact it was this door that allowed Chad to feed his family, but also started the argument."

"Argument?" repeated Christopher.

"Well, perhaps argument was the wrong word," said Slippers. "Confrontation. Yes, that's the word, confrontation.

"After the old couple moved out the food stopped falling through the floor, but it didn't have an immediate effect because there were so many humans around clearing up that tree I mentioned, and they threw so much away there was food everywhere. But to get to it your father had to leave his home, travel through the hall and out of the front door. He would do this every day, sometimes twice a day if the humans left early enough, and he occasionally took your mother with him to help."

Slippers suddenly got up and went over to his bowl for a drink. "Want some?" he said to Christopher.

"Thank you," said Christopher, joining him at the bowl and getting rather wet as dogs tend to slurp a lot when they drink. They both resumed their places and Slippers continued: "And then one day your father returned home and climbed through the cat flap as he normally did and made his way to the hole in the skirting you came out of – what you probably call your front door. Only this time, things were different. Sitting across your front door was Blanket with a big smile on his face. He knew the house inside out and therefore thought catching your father was going to be very easy. Your father put the food he was carrying down and advanced towards Blanket.

"This puzzled Blanket and he found it a bit disconcerting. No mouse had ever responded to his presence this way. Blanket arched his back and prepared to pounce, 'You don't remember me, do you?' said your father. Blanket hesitated for a second and then launched himself straight at him. He landed on him, or so he thought, but your father had deftly moved out of the way and Blanket had to content himself with sliding down the polished floor and hitting the skirting. Your father you see had recognised Blanket who had kept him and your mother trapped under a tree for several days. If it hadn't been for a heavy rainstorm and a friend called Ant he would never have escaped. Your father knew it was the same cat as before because he tore a lump out of his ear saving your mother." The thought of this made Christopher wince.

"Blanket of course did not recognise your father because he was brown before."

"My father was brown like me before?" said Christopher.

"Yes, apparently, so something happened to him in the tree that used to stand outside but he doesn't talk about that part of his life much."

"He doesn't talk about anything much," said Christopher.

"Blanket turned around enraged and without hesitation prepared to attack again. Cats like to play with mice before they kill them," said Slippers, "but any ideas Blanket had of playing were gone. 'I have never seen you before and you will cease to exist very soon!' said Blanket, and attacked again. This time your father just stood there waiting and Blanket screeched with glee. As Blanket landed, your father stepped to one side and grabbed his nose. Blanket somersaulted over himself, your father let go and he crashed into the wall.

"He got to his feet, aware now that this was not a normal fight. Your father advanced towards him. For the first time Blanket hesitated and your father said, 'you cannot beat me I am stronger than you, but I bear you no malice. You attacked me because of your natural instincts, but if you persist I will hurt you.' Before your father had finished, Blanket attacked again and this time, he picked him up and threw him at that wall," said Slippers, nodding in the direction of the front door. "You can still see the dent."

"Blanket ran away and didn't come back for weeks. He doesn't go near your father now, but he still harbours a grudge. He knows he has a family. When your father comes and goes he just watches silently. I think he is biding his time, so be careful."

chapter 12

C had was dreaming, he was dreaming about food! Nuts and berries and more nuts and more berries and berries and nuts and fish – yucky!! But he could hear something growling and rumbling. It was scary. And then he awoke.

Something had changed. He could hear it was raining and it felt warmer. He realised it must be spring, but what was the rumbling? Of course, his stomach was complaining again. He had eaten most of his stored food during the winter months and slept a lot. Then he heard something else – a bird cooing.

He crawled out of his bedding up to the entrance and carefully stuck his head out. There on a branch just outside his front door was a beautiful white dove. When Chad appeared, she didn't fly away but turned to look at him. For a moment she did nothing and then said, "hello, Chad, how are you?"

Chad was quite taken aback. "How do you know my name?" he enquired incredulously.

"You don't remember me, do you?" she replied.

"Should I?" said Chad.

"Well I was a lot smaller the last time you saw me, and I couldn't fly."

In an instant Chad recognised her. "But you're dead," he said, "the ants ate you." She smiled. "Ant said you would say that. When you ran out he called you back, but you kept going before he had a chance to explain." Chad went to speak and then changed his mind. It looked like he was going to appear very foolish, so why make it worse?

"The cave was about to flood," continued the dove, "and they all came out to carry me to a higher place within the cave, so I wouldn't drown. They let me stay until my feathers grew and before Ant left he made me promise to find you and tell you what happened."

"So how did you find me?" said Chad, still a little dubious, although he couldn't think why as she was here alive talking to him, so it had to be true.

"Ant told me you had a dream to find a new home in a tree in the wood so as soon as I could fly I looked around for something with a possible home for a crazy mouse." She smiled as she said this. "These two trees I found straight away but I didn't know you were sleeping, so I have been looking almost everywhere and today I just happened to stop for a rest when you popped your head out. Just lucky really because I was going to give up soon as I didn't know if you were still alive. It is a long way for a mouse to come on his own."

"Well," said Chad, smiling. "I did have some help." He looked towards the sky but there were no seagulls around today, least of all Sid.

"But you're right," said Chad, "I nearly drowned and almost got eaten by an eel so perhaps I'd better find a home a little nearer to the ground and more suitable for a field mouse."

"I've got to go now," said the dove, "I have fulfilled my promise to Ant as he arranged for me to be looked after well. Good luck, Chad," and she just flew away before Chad could say another word.

He was disappointed because he wanted to know what had happened to Ant. He guessed now he would never know. Chad looked down the valley from the entrance of his tree. He knew he couldn't go back now; there was nothing to go back for. He had found his new home, he had a magnificent view, plenty of food and he felt pretty safe up here. But he realised now it wasn't really what he wanted, which made decisions difficult as he didn't really know what he was seeking. Something was missing – he just didn't know what it was. So the search had to continue, which meant going further into the wood. It was dark and dangerous in there he knew, but he had come this far and wouldn't stop until he found what it was that was driving him.

He had a quick meal, finished off what was left of his food and didn't even bother going back to the other tree. He quickly scampered down to the ground. He had had so much practice now he could move as fast as a squirrel.

Unfortunately, he couldn't leap from branch to branch like they could but he was only a mouse, after all.

Today was a beautiful day but foggy and as usual the fog had accumulated in the lower parts including the valley and beyond.

The small bank where the two trees he had lived in stood was clear of fog but on either side, it was thick with it. Chad would normally avoid going out in weather like this but the itch to move on was overwhelming. He worked his way down the bank until he reached the edge of the fog and then, summoning up more courage – he was after all already a very brave and bold mouse – he entered the foggy mist.

One of the advantages of being a mouse was being very small and able to hide. Your nose and eyes were also very close to the ground. So, using his sense of direction and his memory of the land around the trees he used to live in and had just left, Chad made his way towards the bank at the rear leading to the wood. The fog was beginning to thin out and then Chad stepped onto a big flat slab of black rock.

It was wet and flat and smelt very strange, and he had never seen anything like it before. While he pondered what to do he heard a faint whining sound and it was getting closer.

Two white glowing things were appearing through the fog. They grew brighter as he watched, and they bobbed up and down and moved slightly from side to side.

Chad backed off the black rock into the grass to watch, scared, but dying to see what was coming towards him. The fog suddenly lifted and out of the fog appeared a strange box on black round things that Chad had seen before in the rubbish tip when he was with Ant. On the back were blue boxes full of little white bottles. He had seen those in the rubbish tip too, but they were clear, not white. And then he remembered Ant told him they were empty milk bottles.

The whole thing suddenly lurched to a stop right in front of him and out from the front stepped a young man. He had on blue trousers, a white jacket and a black peaked hat. He rubbed his hands together and then reached into his pocket for something. Chad tensed. Had he somehow seen him? Of course not, Chad was far too small. He pulled a small black object out of his pocket and poked at it a few times. It made some squeaking noises each time the man poked it. That must really hurt, thought Chad, and then the man lifted it to his ear and started talking to it.

Chad realised now he was looking at one of the vehicles that humans move around in that Ant had talked to him about. While the man was talking away and looking in the opposite direction, Chad came out of the grass for a better look.

He moved round to the back of the vehicle and then he picked up the scent of food. This puzzled him a bit because all he could see from down where he was were white bottles. He moved towards the rear of the vehicle and then spotted a chain hanging off the back. He could see others looped all round it but this one was hanging down very close to the ground.

Temptation, curiosity and a rumbling stomach overwhelmed his common sense and he looked round for something to stand on so he could reach the chain. Near the edge of the black stuff which Chad now realised was what humans called roads which they made to run their vehicles on was a boulder big enough for Chad to jump off and grab the chain, but he would have to move it closer to the vehicle. The man was still talking away to his little black box. Chad assumed he was apologising for poking it so hard that it squealed with pain.

Using the trick he had seen the beaver do to the man trap for the dove, he got a short stick and in no time at all got the boulder moving. Unfortunately and fortunately, in no particular order, the stone broke free from the mud but rolled very quickly onto the road with a clatter.

Chad froze! The man stopped talking. "Hello," he said, turning around, "is anyone there?" The man walked down the side of his vehicle, looked, and turned back. The stone meant nothing to him but everything to Chad. He briefly looked around then walked back towards the front of his vehicle and resumed his conversation. "Yes," he said into the little black box, "the usual driver called in sick, so I have to do all the deliveries today," as he walked back to the front. His voice faded away and he partially disappeared in the fog.

"I see," said Chad to himself, "this is a milk float and they are bottles of milk! I didn't know milk came in bottles — that would explain the empty ones I saw before."

The boulder had by luck landed just by the chain. With excitement, Chad bounced out of the grass on to the boulder and grabbed the chain. Unfortunately, at that precise moment the man decided to resume his journey. The sudden jolt nearly pulled Chad's arms out of his sockets. He was hanging on for dear life. The chain swung from side to side perilously close to the wheels. "This is it," thought Chad, "I've had it now." And then the milk float started to climb up a hill, so it slowed down which of course helped because there was less bouncing about and now the chain was hanging at a steeper angle and the wheels were further away.

Now though, there was another problem: as Chad got nearer the top of the chain the chain's arc as it whirled around got smaller and smaller which meant any minute now he was going to get squashed into the side of the milk float.

Chad clung on to the chain and each time now there was a bump he would use that to help him climb up to the next link. He knew that sooner or later the milk float would have to go downhill again and if he didn't reach the top by then he would be finished. He had to get hidden in the milk crates before the float stopped again.

Then fate and luck took a hand. The float went over a very big pothole and as it came out the jerk flung the chain up in the air with Chad hanging on, so he took a chance and as it hit the top of its arc, Chad let go!

Well, it had seemed a good idea. Chad had let go of the chain, but the chain didn't want to let go of him. They were both moving at the same speed and Chad could see the flat back of the float coming towards him at a terrible speed. Unfortunately the chain was right behind him and in an instant he realised that when he landed on the float no matter how quickly he rolled away the chain would flatten him and it was all over. He had simply run out of ideas.

But it would seem his luck had not completely run out. The float hit another bump just in the nick of time and changed the direction of the chain flying through the air behind him. He had just enough time to hit the flat wooden deck and roll away and the chain crashed down next to him, scraping lumps of wood out of the floor of the milk float.

Chad rolled onto his feet with Sid the seagull's words echoing in his head "you are a lucky mouse Chad." He ran over to the milk crates and hid in between them just as the milk float got to the crest of the hill and began to pick up speed. The float was bouncing all over the place and the bottles were bumping into each other and making a terrible din, he actually felt sorry for them!

As the float tore down the hill Chad looked out of the side to see where they were going. The black road twisted and turned left and right with the trees on either side and a ditch running between them and the road. And then, up ahead, Chad saw a fork in the road one left one right. The float turned left and immediately the road sloped downhill. Within a few minutes the float began to slow and stopped in front of a pretty house with a small front garden. It had to really because the road went no further, and this house was the only one. The man hopped out of the front of the float, came around to the back and grabbed four bottles of milk from a crate and put them in a smaller crate with a handle. He quickly went over to the front gate, walked up to the front door and put the bottles down on the front step. As he turned around to come back one of the bottles fell over. The man said something which Chad didn't understand, turned around, picked the bottle up and put it in a different place. Satisfied it was now going to stay there he turned to come back, bringing the empty crate with him.

Chad thought that the poor milk bottles must be very dizzy after that terrible ride. "I think it's time to get off before anything else happens or he finds me," and without thinking about the food he could smell but not see he ran over to the chain which was now hanging peacefully still, ran down it and jumped into the road. The float took off almost as soon as the man got in, it did a sharp U-turn and tore back up the hill, and then there was complete silence.

Within a minute or two the silence changed. The birds started to tweet and sing again — obviously they hadn't liked the man or the float, or both.

Chad checked his surroundings. "I need to find some food," he thought, "and somewhere to stay." Little did he know that something would soon happen that would change his life forever.

chapter 13

C had worked his way around the house. There was fortunately no sign of any dogs. At the back of the house there was a large tree which Chad knew would have some buds on it that he could eat. And as he was now a highly qualified tree climbing mouse, nothing was impossible! He circled the tree and quickly climbed up to the first branches and tucked in to some grubs he found.

He heard a noise coming from the house. Up at the first-floor window stood a little girl. She was really excited about something and was clapping her hands and jumping up and down with glee.

In front of her was a large box wrapped in pink paper. With mild curiosity and because he had nothing better to do, Chad watched what was happening.

Chad couldn't hear very clearly because the window was shut but the little girl was so excited he could hear her through the closed window. It was obviously some kind of gift because the little girl started to tear away the paper. Chad craned forward for a better look and nearly slipped off the tree. Much to his surprise what appeared from the paper was not a box but a cage. The little girl's excitement became even more obvious when Chad saw her mother's hands reach down, pick up the cage and place it on a table beside the window.

Inside the cage was a little wheel and a ladder leading up to a little square box with a round hole in it. Chad was still extremely puzzled as to what this was all about until out of the hole poked the head of a little grey mouse.

The little girl dropped some food through the bars and the mouse came all the way out. Chad was frozen to the spot. He had never before seen a grey mouse and never a mouse as beautiful as this. Shortly the little girl left her room and the grey mouse went back into her box. Chad waited all day, but she didn't reappear, and neither did the mouse.

From that day on every day Chad would climb the tree and wait for another glimpse of her, but for several days he was frustrated. She either didn't appear or the curtains were closed, or the cage was moved away from the window.

And then finally one day Chad had just arrived for his daily vigil when the curtains opened and right in front of it was the cage and the little grey mouse was up at the bars looking out waiting for something.

Chad's heart soared when he realised she had been looking for him. For the first time their eyes met, and Chad nearly fell out of the tree. From that day on Chad thought of nothing else and spent every waking moment in the tree just to see her. But he realised that no matter what he did they could never meet.

Although Chad was besotted with the grey mouse, after several weeks he became aware he was not alone in the tree. It was becoming warmer and the leaves were beginning to grow back. The little grey mouse spent as much time as she could when out of her cage looking out the window.

Several branches below a cat had appeared and was watching the window with anticipation. Chad pretended not to notice and then one day the cat changed positions and started to move up above him. Chad knew what this meant but he stayed still, still pretending he hadn't noticed. Just as the cat moved into position above for what Chad knew was an attack, the little girl's window opened and then everything changed...

chapter 14

Over the next few days Chad went over what he had done in his head and try as he might he realised there was nothing he could have done to change the outcome. The cat was still out there. From time to time a shadow would fall over the opening, Chad would tense up and then it would move away. He knew that cat knew they had no food and sooner or later he would have to go outside. He was at a loss as to what to do.

On the fourth day he knew they wouldn't last much longer and he would have to go out soon. Getting ready for what was probably the last thing he would do in his life he suddenly noticed it had become a little darker outside. There was the sound of the tiny patter of rain falling. It grew darker still and then the tree above him creaked and he felt it sway slightly. The sky grew black with dark approaching clouds and the rain heavier, Chad smiled. He knew the cat would not stay out in this weather and he would have a chance to get some food. There was a huge flash which lit up the sky and turned everything white briefly and then it was dark again. The sound of thunder followed. The rain was so heavy that some of it trickled into the entrance. Chad lapped at it gratefully. A little voice from behind him said hello.

Chad spun around. The little grey mouse had woken up! It must have been the thunder, thought Chad. He bounced over to her and she smiled. "Hello," she said again. Chad thought his heart would burst. He held her hand. "I thought you were going to die," he said shyly.

"Where are we?" she asked.

"Inside the bottom of the tree hiding from the cat, but he's still out there and trying to get us," said Chad sadly. The little grey mouse shivered and then sat up. She had a large bruise on the back of her head and said, "my head hurts."

The storm had now increased in strength and the tree above them creaked and moaned as the wind pulled it one way and then the other. "This storm will help us," said Chad, "cats don't like the wet."

"What's a storm?" asked the grey mouse.

"You don't know?" said Chad. The grey mouse looked him.

"I don't know any life outside of a cage you know this is all new to me."

"I'm sorry," said Chad, raising his voice as the storm and the noises from the poor tree had got louder. "What's your name?" he asked.

"I don't have a name," replied the grey mouse. "I was born with lots of other mice and never had a mother or father. We all lived in this big place with other animals next to a big window much bigger than the one up there," she said, nodding towards the little girl's window and then regretting it because her head hurt when she moved it. "Lots of people like the little girl would look in the window pointing at this and that and then one day they chose me. I was picked up, put in a box and ended up here. She looked after me very well but then I saw you," she said shyly.

Chad went a little red. "Well, my name's Chad," he said, puffing his chest out "and I am quite good at giving out names. Would you like me to choose one for you?"

"Oh, yes please, Chad," she said, using his name for the first time which Chad of course liked very much.

"Ah well," said Chad, hesitating as he had not really expected her to agree quite so quickly. Henrietta was the first name that popped into his head.

"I love it," she said without hesitation. She was obviously completely smitten with Chad.

"And I will call you Hen for short."

"If you say so, Chad," she said. "Thank you so much for saving me."

"Well," said Chad, "we have to get out of here as soon as the storm's over because the cat's bound to come back when it gets drier. Do you think you can walk?"

"I'm not sure," she replied, trying to sit up more. "It hurts a lot." The storm suddenly died as did the rain. It was so sudden that both Henrietta and Chad jumped at the sudden silence. All that was left was the drip and trickle of the remaining water left in the tree as it slowly found its way to the ground. The sky brightened which in turn allowed more light into the hole they were hiding in and then the shadow returned and stayed over the hole and they both held each other waiting, waiting.

chapter 15

The shadow moved closer to the hole and there was a scrabbling and rustling sound. Whatever it was, it was going to come in and there was nowhere to escape to. The creature entered the hole. Its huge head came in first and then a familiar voice said, "hello old chap, in trouble again I see." Ant pushed his way into the hole with a big smile on his face.

"Ant!" said Chad with relief and excitement. "How? How did you find me?"

"Aren't you going to introduce me?" said Ant, completely ignoring Chad's question.

No surprise there, thought Chad. "This," said Chad "is Henrietta my friend."

Ant smiled. "That's not what I heard," said Ant.

"What do you mean?" questioned Chad defensively.

"Well," said Ant, "I had been wandering around trying to find out about this wormhole that so many animals in the wood have heard about when I heard that a little brown mouse had been observed up a tree watching a little grey mouse." Henrietta laughed, and Chad went a little red again. "Well, I thought, there is only one mouse I know that likes trees that much, so I came to see you. Just in time again it would seem." Henrietta laughed again and then let out a painful sigh.

"Are you still hurting?" said Ant, now more serious. "We need to get out of here soon, that cat's going to come back. Even I can't take him on, I had to wait until the storm came. That drove him away, but he will be back. He really doesn't like you it seems."

"Can you move?" Ant said to Henrietta.

"I don't think so," she replied, "it's still too painful."

"Well this calls for a plan then, I will be back soon," and

without saying another word, with great difficulty Ant turned around and climbed out of the entrance.

He was back less than 30 minutes later with a ball of string and before Chad could say a word, he was gone again. This time he was gone for quite a while and, when he came back, he had with him the last thing Chad would have expected.

It was about the same size as Ant, silver in colour with red sides and had four wheels that were grey and shiny in the middle. "What on earth is that?" said Chad, coming outside to look at what he had brought back. "This," said Ant "is what humans call a roller skate." Chad looked at him as if he was mad. "Well we need to get Henrietta away from here before the cat comes back. She can't walk and she can't ride on my back, so we will have to pull her out of here, yes?"

"Well, yes," said Chad, beginning to understand what Ant meant. "Where did you get it?"

"Rubbish," replied Ant, smiling, and Chad nodded and immediately understood.

Cutting the string into short lengths Ant cleverly made a harness to fit round his body and with Chad's help he tied himself to the roller skate. They had dug away some of the soil at the base of the entrance so the top of the skate was level with it. Ant held it steady while Chad, with a lot of huffing and puffing and some painful groans from Henrietta, managed to get her into the skate.

With Chad pushing and Ant pulling they managed to get it onto the road where it rolled a lot easier. "This is the easy bit," said Ant, "we have to get it up the hill. It's dangerous after that."

"Why?" said Chad, thinking the cat was maybe waiting for them.

"Up is hard but safe, down is easy but not," said Ant.

Chad made no comment because now he was out of breath. Ant pulled the skate as if it weighed nothing and so quickly that Chad had trouble keeping up. Within an hour they had reached the main road without a single hiccup and stopped on the brow of the hill. And then unfortunately their luck ran out — probably because they were so pleased with themselves they weren't paying attention. The skate ran into a pothole and got stuck in the mud in the bottom and try as he might Ant was having trouble pulling it out.

As they rested for a moment, Chad noticed the water in the pothole vibrating. Little rings of water were forming. Chad and Ant looked at each other. And then they heard it. Grinding slowly up the hill was a very, very big farm truck with huge wheels. Chad knew enough about potholes from his journey in the milk float to know that potholes were made by wheels and where potholes are is where wheels will go again! And Henrietta was stuck on a roller skate in a pothole!

"We have to get her out," said Chad, "and quickly." Ant said nothing he just cut through the string tied to the skate with his teeth, ran around to the back of the skate and jumped in the pothole now knee deep in water and mud. With amazing strength he lifted the front of the skate up onto the lip of the hole. The ground was shaking a lot now as the farm vehicle rumbled and grumbled up the hill ever closer to them. The noise was now becoming deafening and black smoke was coming from a big pipe on the top and underneath it.

"Hold the front Chad, while I lift the back." Chad did as he was told, and Ant went around to the back dragging the strings behind him. This time it wasn't so easy. When Ant had lifted the front the back wheels had sunk further into the mud and try as he might the wheels just wouldn't come out. The truck was now so close they could feel the heat coming from it. Henrietta was frozen in fear and Chad was desperate and then there was a squelching sucking sound and the wheels came free. With an almighty shove, Ant pushed the skate out of the hole and it started to roll away towards the opposite road turning.

Chad grasped the red leather side to the skate and pulled himself aboard just in time to see the two big wheels of the truck roll over the hole with Ant in it.

chapter 16

C had could not believe what his friend had done to save their lives. The truck picked up speed and rolled away. There was no doubt that Ant was dead — nothing could have survived the truck's wheels. The roller skate with Chad and Henrietta on board picked up speed and Chad realised they now had another big problem. He had no way of stopping the skate and it was increasing in speed every second. Henrietta squealed with what Chad thought was fear, but when he looked she had a look of delight on her face and a huge smile. Seeing she was actually having fun, Chad decided to tell her about Ant later.

The skate was now going so fast Chad knew if they hit something they were finished, but although it bumped and swerved from side to side it continued going in a fairly straight line. It was then that Chad realised that if they both leant one way or the other they could influence the direction of the skate slightly, so Chad shouted in Henrietta's ear what to do and between them they steered the skate as best they could as it careered down the road. Chad was the first to notice they were slowing down. "The road must be getting flatter," said Henrietta.

"I don't think so," said Chad, a little puzzled by the reduction in speed.

Then Henrietta said, "What's that smell?"

Chad looked over the side and, in an instant, realised where the smell was coming from. "Er, we have a problem," said Chad,

"What?" questioned Henrietta.

"There is smoke coming from the wheels. I don't think it was made to go this fast so maybe that's why they threw it away in the first place."

"Oh," said Henrietta, "that is a problem then."

The smoke was getting was worse but now the road was beginning to flatten out and it was a dead end just like the opposite one they had come from. This time though the house was right by the road and the tree was on the opposite side of the road instead of behind the house.

"We're going to make it," thought Chad, as they were slowing down. Then one of the smoking wheels at the rear burst into flames followed quickly by a second on the other side.

"Whee!" shouted Henrietta. Chad turned to look at her in surprise and admiration, thinking what a cool mouse she had turned out to be. She turned to look at him, smiled, and said, "this is fun!"

"Yes," said Chad, "but it might kill us."

"Might," she replied, "but also might not!"

"Well," thought Chad, "you just can't argue with that."

The skate had slowed down considerably but Chad decided they had pushed their luck. It was literally getting far too warm for comfort.

"We have to jump, Hen," he said. Hen smiled at him. It was the first time he had called her that. She grabbed his hand and without another word jumped off the speeding skate. They hit the ground together. Chad found it easier as he had had the practice. They ended up in a heap in the grass next to the tree and the skate sailed on until the wheels gave out and it completely burst into flames and burnt itself out.

When Chad and Henrietta untangled themselves and stopped laughing Chad told her the bad news. "I don't think Ant made it Hen. I didn't see him come out of the pothole."

"I'm so sorry Chad," said Hen, "here we are laughing when you have lost your friend."

"I know," said Chad, but Ant would have understood and laughed with us.

chapter 17

Contrary to what Chad and Hen thought Ant was very much alive albeit wet, muddy and very, very dizzy.

When the truck went over the pothole the two wheels straddled the hole which saved Ant's life but unfortunately the string still tied to his body caught in between the wheels and that's where he was now, stuck between two wheels occasionally getting wet and muddy again when the truck drove through the next pothole. He simply wouldn't be able to get out until the truck stopped and he daren't cut the string that was keeping him away from under the moving wheels. He just hoped that Chad and Henrietta had managed to arrive somewhere safely. The last thing he saw before he was carried away was the two of them disappearing over the brow of the hill.

He was going to be a long way away when he finally got off these wheels and then finding them again would probably be impossible, he thought. Probably, absolutely, perhaps, maybe, definitely! It would just take him a very long time, he thought, as he went around and around and around getting dizzier by the minute.

chapter 18

C had and Henrietta quickly got off the road and hid behind the tree. The skate had burnt itself out, but Chad was worried that someone could come out of the house. The ground behind the tree rose up steeply and there were other trees higher up. Chad looked up at the tree and could not believe his luck. Just three feet off the ground was a large cleft. "Wait here," said Chad to Henrietta. "I will be back in a minute." He quickly climbed up the trunk like a seasoned mouse tree climber and entered the cleft. It was full to the top with leaves and to the left and right there were two other openings. "Perfect," thought Chad. He stuck his head over the lip and shouted down to Henrietta. "You want to come up? Or shall I come down for you?"

"I'll come up," replied Henrietta.

She followed Chad's route carefully as she was still sore from her fall and joined him in the pile of leaves in the cleft. "So, what do you think?" said Chad, "our new Home."

"Well," said Henrietta, "fine. There's plenty of room, but just one problem."

"What?" said Chad defensively.

"It doesn't have a roof."

"Ah, yes," said Chad. "No problem, there is something I learnt from staying with a beaver." So Chad set about building a timber roof with branches. It took him a lot of work over three days. It wasn't a big roof, but he wasn't a beaver or a big mouse. Henrietta helped him where she could and under his instruction very quickly learnt to move around the tree as quickly as Chad. Within a week their new home was complete and for the first time in his life Chad felt content. A house in a tree with a partner he loved. She was equally content and never imagined that from the first day she saw Chad she would end up with him.

Spring came and turned into summer and they had their first child, a daughter they called Mot, followed by a second daughter they called Fidgit, and they could not be happier.

They had a few leaks in the roof they had built but with the splendid supply of new leaves that summer brought, repairing it was easy.

Shortly after Fidgit's birth Henrietta complained to Chad about being very tired all the time. "Oh it's nothing," said Chad with great authority. "You have just had two children." But what he didn't mention was that he too was feeling very tired and finding it hard at times to climb the trees. Their two daughters who when they were born were full of energy and quickly learnt to climb trees just like their parents now no longer left the nest but sat or lay together very quietly for days on end.

Henrietta who now too hardly had the strength to leave the nest told Chad she was expecting another child and was concerned about whether she would be strong enough to give birth. "Don't be silly," said Chad trying to be strong, but he knew now something was wrong with his family and he also knew they would not survive long as he himself was getting sicker by the day.

It rained for several days and the roof leaked, but Chad did not have the strength to repair it. He knew now he only had a matter of days left. Henrietta was better than he, as were the children but not much. Each day he went to sleep and wondered whether he would wake the next day to see his family.

One afternoon it started to rain heavily. The skies grew darker by the minute. Dusk turned into night, the rain grew heavier and started to come in through the roof and their home began to get very wet. And then the storm intensified. The wind increased and the tree swayed and shook. Lightning and thunder followed, at first in the distance and then moving ever closer by the second.

Chad surveyed his family. He loved them all so much. "At least we are all together," he thought. When the lightning finally arrived it hit the tree. It was so powerful that as the power coursed through the branches and trunk on its way to the ground everything in its path was electrified. Chad witnessed it all. He witnessed the white lights as he and his family were electrocuted. Small leaves burst into flames and were instantly extinguished by the torrential rain. The hum of power flowing uncontrolled through wet wood on its way to earth filled the air and then the white light turned green and then bright green and from beneath their nest huge shafts of green burst out and for the first time in his life Chad felt so powerful and so powerless at the same time. Then it was gone and the white light was gone too, and Chad watched his family breathe their last as one by one they died. Then he too took his last breath.

chapter 19

The storm began to move away. The dying wind had wreaked havoc in its path. The animals of the night hid – no matter how strong they were they hid away from this invisible hidden force. But although the storm was dying it had one last gasp before it moved on and expired, and lightning hit the tree where Chad and his family lay dead. The electricity once again travelled through the tree and all of its lifeless occupants, and it was gone.

The wind died just as quickly and left only the sound of trickling water. In the almost dead still of the night there was a small cough, and then another. Chad opened his eyes. He was wet, very wet. Before him lay his daughters and Henrietta as still as stone. A huge wave of pain and grief swept through his body. He had survived, and they had not. And then they moved. First Mot coughed and then Fidgit and then Henrietta. His body ached from head to toe, his fur had turned white, but he and his family somehow were alive.

Dawn came and with it the warmth of the sun. With his whole family alive around him, Chad was in a daze. He knew what he had witnessed last night. He also knew that somehow he had been brought back from the dead; it was beyond his comprehension. His children were wide awake and chasing each other around as if they had never been ill at all but now with huge amounts of boundless energy. And Henrietta's beautiful smile lit up their home – well, what was left of it anyway.

However, the tree they resided in had not been as fortunate. The force and power of the storm had taken the life out of the old tree. Hardly a leaf remained and nearly all the branches were black and burned. Chad could hear the tree weakening by the minute. Its branches were creaking and groaning under their own weight and

Chad knew it was only a matter of time before the tree fell over. As if the tree had been listening, a huge branch broke away from the main trunk and tore a huge hole out of the side of it. The branch crashed to the ground right onto the road outside the house and because it was now so dry and brittle it smashed into a thousand pieces.

With this branch gone the tree was no longer balanced and Chad felt what remained start to move in the opposite direction. "Time to move," he shouted at Henrietta.

"I agree," shouted back Henrietta, but where to? Mot and Fidgit had of course now stopped playing and were looking at their parents for instruction.

The sound of the tree crashing into the road had woken the old couple who rushed out of the house into the road to inspect the damage. Chad saw the open door to the house and in an instant decided it was time to find his family a safer place to live.

"Quickly," he said, "follow me, we won't have much time." Chad knew he had to move quickly. He was going to move his family into the house and it had to be before the front door closed. The old couple were out in the road. The women had her hands to her face in dismay and the man had one of those funny black boxes to his ear which Chad had seen the milkman use.

Chad shot down the back of the tree with Henrietta and their daughters close behind. The tree was shaking now and starting to move. The storm's power it seemed not only destroyed the trees branches but its roots as well.

They ran straight into the road. Chad had decided the direct approach was the best as the old couple were preoccupied. They jumped off the small kerb such as it was one by one and ran in a straight line towards the front door. Chad could not believe how fast he could run now and turned to see if he had left the others behind, but they too were moving very quickly right behind him.

The kerb on the other side was much higher. It was made of

granite and was very smooth. It was too high for them to jump. Without thinking Chad grabbed a branch ready to drag it to the kerb, but much to his surprise he picked it up as if it weighed nothing. He laid it up against the kerb and his family were up and onto the top of the kerb stone before he had a chance to tell them what to do.

As they approached the door they slowed down, the front door now they were nearer was enormous. There was a small threshold to climb over and then they were in. The floor was polished so when they went to stop they slid along the floor. The children thought this was very funny and giggled with delight as their mother told them to be quiet.

Right in front of them was a long hallway; to the right an arched doorway and to the left a larger one.

In the room on the left was a large table with several chairs around it and underneath a big red carpet. But at the end of the room Chad had instantly spotted what he was looking for: a small hole in the wall by the floor. With some slipping and sliding Chad headed for the hole and his family followed.

chapter 20

Over the next few weeks Christopher spent almost every day with Slippers but never Sundays because the new owners of the house were at home all day or if not at home certainly in and out and Christopher couldn't take the risk of getting caught in the open. He made sure he came out of his home after his parents left and before they came home.

Since his first meeting with Slippers there had been no sign of Blanket, but Slippers warned him it was only a matter of time.

He realised very quickly, with Slippers' help, that he had inherited some of his father's strength and speed and the fact that he could read and write too. The television helped a lot as well and he had an insatiable appetite for knowledge.

And then one afternoon he discovered that his sisters had hidden powers too that they didn't even know they had. Having never met any other mice they just assumed what they had was normal and took it for granted. He had discovered that the television above Mot and Fidgit's room was on a different station to his so to learn about worldly things and humans would be his television as he now called it and Mot's was on science geography and space programmes which Christopher didn't really understand.

One morning before he went to meet Slippers he went to his sisters' end of the house which was rare as nothing they said or did interested him, but he was curious to see if they too could read like he could. As he approached where they lived and slept he could hear Mot laughing behind him, but when he turned around the laughing stopped and there was no sign of her. Christopher could see extremely well in the dark, so it was not possible for her to hide from him anywhere in the open. Christopher turned back to continue, and he heard her laugh behind him again, and she said,

"I can see you!" Now irritated by the silly game she was playing he turned around just as she appeared out of a wall as if from thin air and said "Boo!!" Christopher jumped back defensively. The issue with Blanket had made him very wary. "How did you do that?" said Christopher.

"Do what?" said Mot, nonchalantly pretending she didn't know what he was talking about.

Christopher tipped his head to one side as if to say very funny. "Well I have always been able to do this," said Mot defensively. "I spent hours practising in the mirror I have in my room."

"Oh," said Christopher, "I thought you were just vain and liked looking at yourself." Mot then disappeared back to her room in a huff literally!

Christopher decided any interest he had in his sister's abilities wasn't worth the trouble, so he decided to go and see Slippers. If he had just looked up as he turned back, he would have seen right above his head Fidgit stuck to the floorboards of the floor above and grinning like mad. He had neither seen her nor heard her which she was both pleased and disappointed with at the same time. Having witnessed her sister showing off to her brother, Fidgit had wanted to do the same. So still clinging to the floorboards she watched her brother head back to his room but much to her surprise he turned right towards the front of the house and the forbidden zone!!

Fidgit dropped gracefully to the floor and landed in a crouch. She stood up and as quietly as she could she followed her brother. She reached the corner that led to the front and craned her head around the corner. There was nothing to be seen except a pale arch of light at the far end. Christopher was gone.

"What are you doing?" said a voice right behind her which made her jump.

"Mot, don't do that, you scared me," she said instantly recognising her sister's voice.

"We are not allowed down there," said Mot.

"I know," said Fidgit, "but Christopher's gone down there and disappeared."

"What!" said Mot, "you mean he can do it too?"

"No, I mean he's gone somewhere, silly."

"Oh," said Mot.

"I am going after him," said Fidgit.

"We're not allowed," said Mot again.

"Well, Christopher's gone!" said Fidgit.

"Me too then," said Mot, and they both crept around the corner and nervously worked their way towards the faint light.

They carefully stuck their heads out of the knot hole. There was no fire today, so the only light came from the windows. "Over there," said Fidgit, nodding in the direction of the front door.

"I'll go first," said Mot.

"Why?" complained Fidgit.

"Why do you think?" said Mot disappearing in front of Fidgit's eyes.

"I'll wave to you if it's safe."

"Very funny," said Fidgit, "how am I supposed to see that? Stupid."

"Good point," said Mot temporarily reappearing. "I'll do this again when I get over there," and off she went.

Fidgit waited 30 seconds and followed. "This was my idea not hers," she said to herself. As soon as she got to the arch, she bumped into her sister. "Sorry," she said laughing quietly, "I didn't see you."

"You are not taking this seriously, are you?" said Mot. They looked around the corner of a big arch and there was Christopher talking to a big dog. Neither sister could believe their eyes.

"You'd better come over here and meet Slippers," said Christopher smiling. "I heard you coming from the moment you came into the first room." The girls came over and Mot reappeared in front of Slippers. "Now that!" said Slippers, "is impressive!"

"My sisters," said Christopher, "Mot and Fidgit."

"Nice to meet you both," answered Slippers. Slippers warned the girls about Blanket and they exchanged worried glances. "Come on," said Slippers, "I will show you around the house." Needing no second invitation the girls followed with Christopher up front with Slippers.

"He thinks he's in charge," whispered Mot to Fidgit.

"I heard that," said Christopher, without looking round. Everything was fine until they arrived at the stairs.

"This bit's more complicated," said Christopher, "Slippers can give you a lift if you hang on to his fur or you can climb up the carpet."

"I don't think so," said Fidgit and crouching down on her haunches she leapt up the flight of stairs in one bound landing on the top step. "Ha!" she said, "easy."

"Impressive," said Slippers for the second time.

"I'll take the lift," said Mot grabbing hold of Slippers' fur, and everybody laughed. There was nothing much to see upstairs but in one of the bedrooms at the front was a big bay window and all the mice stood up at the glass enthralled with the view. Slippers stood quietly behind them.

"So this is what the outside looks like," said Christopher.

"It's beautiful," said Mot.

"It's fantastic," said Fidgit pinning her face against the window, "how do we get out there?"

"There is only one way out," said Slippers who was now sitting beside them quietly, "through the front door. Blanket comes and goes through the cat flap, as do your parents. The humans call themselves people and use the front door to come and go and I can only go out if they let me or take me as the door has locks which I can't open," he said sadly, holding up one paw as a way of explanation.

"Come on," said Slippers, "we'd better go back downstairs. I'm not supposed to come up here; I'll get into trouble." Using the same method as before Christopher and Mot hitched a ride on Slippers, while Fidgit rolled herself into a ball and bounced all the way down the stairs.

"Show off," muttered Christopher, and Slippers laughed.

chapter 21

Over the next few days Christopher, Mot and Fidgit made their way out to the front of the house as soon as they heard their parents leave. They would spend hours questioning Slippers about the outside and about their parents' travels and well, just about everything. But of course, Slippers didn't know everything. He was only a dog after all. He explained to them one day, "you can learn from hearing and talking but nothing beats experiencing it yourself," he said sniffing the air. "When I go for walks there is so much to see and smell!"

"Smell?" said Mot, turning her nose up at the thought.

"Yes," said Slippers, "dogs can smell lots of things from a long way away."

One day Mot didn't come out with the others to see Slippers. "Where's Mot today?" he asked.

"She said she wanted to work on some chemistry experiments she heard about."

"Chemistry?" said Slippers.

"Oh, we don't know," said Christopher, "something she heard about."

They had not long engaged in more questions and answers when there was a huge bang and the whole house shook! Slippers was on his feet and moving towards the sound almost as quickly as the mice. As he turned the corner a huge puff of smoke and dust shot out of the knot hole which of course was the mice's front door. Christopher and Fidgit didn't hesitate. They ran straight into the hole because they knew their sister was inside. As it turned out there was dust everywhere but very little smoke. They found Mot in a pile of debris in her room and a big hole in the ground at the rear of the house. The air was cloudy with tiny particles, so much so it was hard to see anything, and just like everywhere else the dust was on everything. Mot, however, was fine.

"What on earth happened?" said Christopher.

"Don't ask," said Mot.

"Look at our room," said Fidgit.

"Really," said Mot, "the way you tidy up I think this is an improvement! Don't worry I will clean it. It's one experiment I won't be trying again until I know a bit more about it."

"Is everything alright?" shouted Slippers through the knot hole.

"Yes," said Christopher and Fidgit, returning to the dining room. "Mot's fine but she has a lot of cleaning to do."

Mot popped out of the knot hole. "Sorry Slippers, didn't mean to worry you."

"You better stay there now," said Slippers, "time to go back anyway. The owners will be home soon and you don't want to get caught. If they find out you live here, they will try to get rid of you."

"Why?" said Fidgit.

"I told you before, most people don't like mice."

"And mice don't like people then," said Christopher.

"Sometimes, sometimes not. Come on, enough. Hurry up."

The next time the cleaner came she just couldn't understand where all the dust had suddenly come from!

Christopher, Mot and Fidgit just made it back through the knot hole when the front door opened. They watched as Slippers' calm behaviour changed to one of great excitement and he followed his owners towards the kitchen and out of sight.

As they all made their way back inside the same conversations about outside began again. Mot usually started it, but today it was Christopher and this time he was more adamant. "I'm fed up with talking about this we have to plan a trip." His sisters this time remained silent. "Well?" said Christopher, surprised by their lack of response.

"It's safe here," said Mot, "we have everything we need so why risk it? You know what Slippers said, if they find us, they will get rid of us."

They reached the end of the dark passageway and parted left and right not exchanging another word little knowing that once again their lives were just about to change course again.

chapter 22

Christopher woke first as he always did, waiting to hear his parents leave. But today something felt wrong. He got up and instead of waiting he went straight to the place where they all ate. There was no food set out on the table; it remained exactly as it was when he went to bed. He felt a little lost. He had gone through this routine for several weeks now and didn't know what to think. The people in the house wouldn't have left yet so he couldn't go and see Slippers. So he decided to go and wake his sisters instead. He needn't have bothered as they were both up too.

"Something's different," said Mot. "I woke up very early." This was some statement because Mot never woke up early.

"Me too," said Fidgit. "There's no food," she said, looking at the bare table. Her parents should have called her stomach as she was perpetually hungry.

"Maybe they are in their room," said Mot nervously, her imagination running wild. "Maybe they're sick, maybe they're..."

"Oh, shut up," said Christopher, "there you go again thinking of everything negative."

"I think we have to look," said Fidgit quietly. They all looked at each other and then Christopher said, "but we have never been allowed in there."

"I know, but we still have to look," Fidgit said nervously, speaking the unspoken. Mot was just nodding her head.

"Alright," said Christopher, "let's look." Christopher went first and approached the large wooden door which was very wide and as high as it could be. This was the only place the children were not allowed to go. Christopher did not remember, but his sisters told him their parents had built this out of old wooden floorboards they had found lying around under the floor as soon as they moved in.

He knocked gently.

"Louder than that," said Mot who was hiding behind Fidgit and just peeking over her shoulder. Christopher knocked again only this time louder. The only response was a faint echo but nothing else. Having never entered their parents' room before and it being the only closed off part of their home, they had absolutely no idea what to expect.

Christopher gently turned the handle and pushed the door. At first it did not move but when he pushed a little harder it then gave very easily. He had expected it to creak, but it opened completely silently. Whatever ideas the children had had for what the room behind the door was going to look like none of them would have imagined what they were now seeing.

In the centre of the room at the end was a small bed with two little tables one either side but that was not what took their breath away. On the right-hand side there was a shelving system with rows of boxes. They were labelled with their contents such as sunflower seeds, hazelnuts, walnuts and so on.

"It's food," said Fidgit, "lots of it. They have been storing it for some reason. I thought they got it for us every day."

In front of the shelves sat a large two wheeled cart. The wheels were spoked, five to each wheel, and made from wood with a metal band around them to hold them together. The cart had four sides that could be opened downwards with wooden pegs to keep them closed and metal hinges at the bottom. In front was a long pole with a bar at the end in the shape of a tee which was obviously for pulling it along. In the bottom of the cart were two boxes with half a dozen books in them.

Fidgit said, "why on earth would father build that in here?" But the others weren't listening because on the left-hand side almost completely covering the wall were rows and rows of bookshelves with a desk underneath. The books on the bookshelf were tiny – small enough for a mouse to hold and read. Mot squealed and clapped her hands with delight. Christopher was pretty impressed as well as he too loved to read, but didn't want to show it. But as to their parents, there was not a sign.

They all moved over to the bookshelf and desk feeling very uncomfortable as you would going into your parent's room without permission. On the desk were lots of notes and several books lay open. Christopher picked one up "the theory of worm holes," he read.

"Didn't Slippers say something about worm holes when he was telling us about our father's travels?" said Fidgit, who had been completely silent up until now.

"Yes, he did," said Mot, picking up another book that lay open, **Travelling through worm holes**.

"What's a worm hole?" said Fidgit.

"No idea," said Christopher.

"A worm hole is a shortcut though space and time according to Einstein's theory of relativity, and would allow you to find new planets and minerals that are sparse here but plentiful there," said Mot, as if she was talking about the weather. Christopher and Fidgit's mouths had fallen open in surprise.

"How do know all that?" said Christopher.

"Oh, that television thing above our room, it's on almost all the time and it's very interesting." Christopher and Fidgit looked at each other in surprise.

"So you're not always concentrating at looking in the mirror," laughed Christopher. Mot just scowled back.

A week passed and still no sign of their parents returning. They discussed it with Slippers, but he too had no idea where they could have got to and was more than just worried, but he didn't tell the children that.

As per usual every morning they heard the televisions come on. "The people are leaving," said Christopher.

"Ok," said Mot, "let's go."

"No, not yet," said Christopher, "wait till you hear the front door close." They waited a few minutes, heard the front door slam, and then went in search of Slippers. They followed the usual route and arrived at the fireplace and there, looking pleased with himself sat Blanket licking his lips with anticipation, there was no sign of Slippers at all.

chapter 23

"Well, well, well," said Blanket, "the cute little children all alone left to fend for themselves by their parents. I couldn't have chosen a better time to come and visit."

"And who are you?" said Christopher, knowing full well who was sitting in front of him and pushing his sisters behind him. "And where is Slippers?"

"Slippers was dragged out of the house by his owners. He wanted to stay and protect you — he told me all about how your mother and father left a week ago and you were very vulnerable and couldn't manage without him and that every morning you came out of your home to be with him for safety and begged me to not hurt you, but he knows," said Blanket with venom, "that I have an issue with your father and mother and you will have to pay for it. I have looked forward to my revenge for a long time. I will thank him later for making this so easy."

Christopher now knew that Slippers had very cleverly misled Blanket into believing they could not protect themselves and that the end result of this forthcoming fight was a forgone conclusion, well at least to Blanket.

Christopher did not respond immediately, but indicated to his sisters to sit beside him which they did and then he sat himself. "I have no interest in any issues you may have with my father or mother," said Christopher, "that is for you to resolve with them, but I do require a favour."

Blanket was a little puzzled. He had known that the mice were going to come to him because Slippers had rather foolishly told him what they did each day and he had waited impatiently for them to arrive. He also expected them to run as soon as they saw him. So far things had gone to plan, but not quite as he expected.

"A favour?" asked Blanket, repeating Christopher's question and doing his best to contain the anger that was bubbling inside him because he was more curious at this stage to find out what the favour was that the mice wanted. The way he saw it he would indulge them for a while and then kill them afterwards. That would be a wonderful unpleasant surprise for Chad when he came home.

"Yes, a favour," said Christopher again. "As you already know my parents are not here, they leave every day in the morning and return in the evening."

"Yes, I know that," said Blanket irritably. "I lived here before he did!" referring only to Christopher's father.

"Well," said Christopher, completely ignoring Blanket's outburst, "they have been missing now for over a week and we," he said, nodding at his sisters in turn, "intend to go looking for them. So, I would like your help."

"You want my help?" said Blanket with an incredulous tone.

"That is correct," said Christopher, preparing for what he believed would be the end of Blanket's patience and his inevitable attack.

"And how could I help you find your father?" said Blanket, raising himself on all fours and beginning to arch his back.

Christopher sensed the nervousness of his sisters, but he was still in control of the conversation and so far, was very pleased with himself. Slippers would be proud of me, he thought to himself.

"You travel a lot do you not?" asked Christopher, and continued without waiting for an answer, "and I understand you also may know where my father's old friends come from or are located now."

"I don't care," said Blanket, getting ready to attack.

"And also," said Christopher taking a step forward yet still unbelievably calm, so much so his sisters couldn't believe it, "has it not occurred to you that the issues with my father that you referred to, which originally I didn't want to talk about, related to him being strong enough to beat you up and then throw you across the room, after which you ran away! They may be inherited, which means that his son has these powers too! And that you may also know something about the worm hole in the woods?" Blanket's anger had been about to explode, but at these last words he froze and visibly shrank back to the floor. Any anger he had shown was gone in the blink of an eye. "I, I don't know what you're talking about," he said, backing away.

Christopher took another step forward and then there was a noise from the front door. It flew open and Slippers came running in followed by one of the people living in the house. She fetched some water, said hello to Blanket who hadn't moved, plonked the water on the floor and ran out of the door obviously late.

Slippers looked at Blanket first who still hadn't moved and then looked around for the mice. Christopher emerged from behind a plant flower pot, Fidgit bounced back down from the ceiling where she had gone as soon as the door flew open and Mot reappeared, which produced a sharp intake of breath from Blanket. Slippers looked around expecting carnage. "Impressive!" he said.

The mice and Slippers sat down in front of Blanket who hadn't moved or said a word. Then suddenly he got up and ran out through the cat flap so fast he must have hurt himself. "What happened?" said Slippers.

"I told him about my strength," said Christopher proudly, "and he became very frightened."

"I don't think so," said Mot. "It was when you mentioned worm holes; that's when he stopped being angry and wanting to fight." Christopher went to argue but before he could Fidgit said, "She's right. As soon as you said worm holes he became terrified. Anyway," she continued, "he's gone now and I'm very hungry, what are we going to eat?"

Slippers laughed. "Well, what a surprise! I expected to come back and find the house in a mess. I don't know what I was more worried about you lot, my home or Blanket."

chapter 24

Sid the seagull was bored! He had been quite happy with his life eating, arguing with other seagulls, resting in the park then flying a bit, more eating and arguing. A simple life really, who could ask for more? And then he met a mouse called Chad, instinct told him more food and he was quite put out that the mouse was eating his berries (even though they were not his favourite food).

And so he had made it very clear that all the berries were his and his alone. Much to his surprise the mouse disputed his ownership and there followed a long discussion which, much to Sid's puzzlement, he began to enjoy as he had never had a real conversation with anything before least of all a mouse! So when Chad tried to leave, Sid had begged him to stay.

One thing led to another and Chad ended up giving him his name, Sid! They had flown together, and the last time Sid saw his new friend was when he saved his life after the big flood. Sid had gone back several months later after realising that on the whole seagulls are not interested in talking but Chad was nowhere to be found. I guess he thought to himself I'm never going to see him again.

And then one day Sid was resting in the park when he overheard two seagulls complaining about a moody beaver that had chased them away. Now, the fact that two seagulls were discussing anything at all was unusual in itself! Sid continued to listen. "Anyway," said one of the seagulls, "there I was at the water's edge looking for something to eat when I knocked over a pile of wood and before I could blink this beaver rose out of the water and started shouting at me saying 'it's my wood, it's my wood,' which was very silly because everybody knows that it all belongs to me—"

"No, me," said the other seagull

"No, me," said the first seagull getting angry.

"Anyway," said the first seagull who was telling the story, "the beaver suddenly said the only creature allowed to touch my wood is Chad and with that he dived back into the water."

"What's a Chad?" said the second seagull now completely forgetting they were in the middle of an argument.

"Absolutely no idea," said the first seagull, at which point they both lost interest in the story altogether. Sid quickly waddled his way over to the two seagulls who looked at him expectantly.

"That water, where was it?" he asked.

"What water?" replied the first seagull.

Sid sighed. "The water you were talking about."

"Oh that, er, I don't remember," said the first seagull. "Anyway, it's mine." Sid let out another weary sigh and thinking it couldn't be too far away, he decided to try and track down his friend. With that he soared into the sky with new purpose in his life.

chapter 25

Blanket was a very selfish self-centred independent grey cat that belonged to no one and travelled around a lot. He had no memories of any siblings or for that matter his parents, which of course he must have had. It would seem he was born to be selfish! As a result, he had never cared about anything else but himself. He had no fixed abode unless you counted one place where an old couple spoilt him whenever he visited. In fact they even gave him his own door called a cat flap, so he could come and go as he pleased. But of course, he didn't care about them either; he just pretended to.

His home as far as he was concerned was the wood and wherever he chose to roam. Fortunately, he had no natural enemies to speak of. He had had fights with local foxes – lost two, but he had won the last with a fox cub that he chased away.

When I say no natural enemies, he did in fact have one: a mouse, believe it or not! Every time Blanket thought about him his blood would boil. His first meeting was in a tree. Blanket had ended up with a torn ear which was still droopy to this day and even though later that day he had cornered him and another mouse he was after in a tree trunk they had both somehow still managed to escape.

Blanket would come and go and then one day found the house empty. The old couple had moved away, but he continued to come and go when it suited him as the cat flap had not been locked or closed off.

Several weeks later he had all but forgotten about the mice when, returning home one day, he found out that a white mouse had moved into his home! Or at least what he considered to be his home. Just as he arrived the mouse climbed out of the cat flap and disappeared into the wood. He was living under the floor and the only access was a small hole in the skirting which of course Blanket could not get through. There was no other way in or out so, determined to finish off any mouse that had the cheek to move in, Blanket sat and waited for him to return as he knew he would have to.

The ensuing outcome of the mouse's demise did not go as he had planned. As a cat Blanket knew how to fight and when not to, so a mouse was nothing. But not only did the white mouse turn out to be the same one that plagued his memory, the long and short of it was that he was thoroughly beaten and had to flee. He simply could not understand how something as small as a mouse had beaten him and somehow, one day, he was determined he would get his revenge.

During Blanket's travels over the next few weeks he heard more and more talk of a "worm hole". None of the other animals had any idea what it was and as Blanket was not particularly friendly with anyone he couldn't be bothered to ask.

It was on one of his return visits to part of the wood that he found the normally populated area deserted. There was not a single creature to be seen. Even the birds in the trees were missing or they had stopped singing. It was then that he stumbled on the rotting corpses. Now death was not uncommon in the wood, but the dead animals were in a pile all from this one area. There was a mole, a weasel, two squirrels, and some that were so badly decomposed he could not identify them. Only people he knew killed like this for no reason, so he moved on indifferently as any selfish cat would.

But when he moved further into the wood and found another pile of bodies like the first, he began to get nervous. The bodies were very thin as though they had starved to death and now he thought about it, so were the first ones he had seen. This was a part of the wood that humans never came to as it was too dense. Just like the earlier part he had been to the wood was completely silent and nothing stirred.

There was plenty of food around so why had these animals starved? Not that he cared about them, since he was only worried about himself.

He travelled further and further into the wood. Here the trees were so tall and close together very little natural light penetrated so he was surprised when up ahead he could see a bright white glow. He crept forward very slowly. Only people created this kind of light and unless you knew them and vice versa they were dangerous, although it seemed sometimes some of them actually liked cats and dogs.

The source of the light was a tiny hole not much bigger than a cherry, but the light was so bright it hurt his eyes and he had to look away. As he watched, the circle of light gradually got bigger and bigger and the brightness dimmer the larger it became.

It continued to grow and as Blanket watched it began to crackle with energy. Blanket became very afraid but as with most cats, curiosity for now overcame his fear and budding terror. The white hole continued to grow. Blanket could now look directly into it and inside a hole was forming. It looked like a cave or tunnel, but that was impossible, he thought. It was about two inches above the ground and about a foot in diameter and it appeared to go on forever.

And then, suddenly, out of the hole poured hundreds of ants, some quite large, and these ants were carrying dead animals and they started to dump them in piles. Finally fear overcame curiosity. Blanket had seen enough. Self-preservation kicked in and he turned to flee, but unfortunately he knocked over some stones as he turned. He had just enough time to see the ants stop briefly and look straight at him. He needed no more persuasion; cats were not good at running but Blanket ran and ran and ran. He knew that if the ants got him he was as good as dead, so he headed to the only place he thought he would be safe: back to the house.

Blanket arrived back at the house early the next morning having hidden up a tree for the night. He had waited for Chad and Henrietta to come out as they did every morning, but they didn't appear which puzzled him a bit. So, waiting until he was sure the owners were up, and the mice would be out of sight, he entered though the cat flap. Slippers was there waiting for his daily walk and was surprised and alarmed to see him.

"Er hello Blanket," he said uncomfortably.

"Hello," said Blanket not really meaning it and looking around sensing something was wrong.

"I hope you're not here to cause trouble," said Slippers.

"Why would I?" said Blanket suspiciously.

"Well," continued Slippers, "Chad and Henrietta are not here and have been gone for a week and their children are alone and very nervous they come out of their home every morning to be with me and I protect them so please leave them alone."

"Really," said Blanket with an evil smile appearing on his face, all thoughts of the dead animals, ants and the strange bright round hole suddenly forgotten.

At that precise moment and before Slippers could say another word, one of the owners appeared, clipped a lead on his collar and they were out the door a moment later. Blanket sat down by the fireplace to wait.

"Well, well, well," said Blanket. "The cute little children all alone, left to fend for themselves by their parents. I couldn't have chosen a better time to come and visit." Blanket, of course, had already assumed the outcome of his first and final meeting with Chad's children. He was at first surprised that the boy was brown not white like his father and the girls were grey.

The following conversation also surprised Blanket and as his anger rose and he got ready to attack them, Christopher finished what Blanket thought would be his final speech, "...and that you may know something about the worm hole in the woods."

Blanket's anger had been about to explode, but at these last words he froze and visibly shrank back to the floor. Any anger he had shown was gone in the blink of an eye. "I, I don't know what you're talking about," he said, backing away.

With these last words everything he had witnessed in the woods came flooding back into his mind and the terror of it too. It was then that he realised that the round white hole he had seen and the worm hole that all the animals had been talking about for months and he had shown no interest in were one and the same and somehow Chad and his family knew about it and perhaps controlled it!

At this point the door flew open and Slippers came running in followed by one of the people living in the house. She fetched some water, said hello to Blanket who hadn't moved, plonked the water on the floor and ran out the front door obviously late. Slippers sat down quietly in front of Blanket and waited.

The mice, who had magically disappeared with incredible speed, reappeared. Chad came out from behind a flowerpot, Fidgit bounced down from the ceiling where she had bounced to and Mot reappeared right in front of him which terrified Blanket even more. Slippers nodded his head and said, "Impressive!"

Fear overtook Blanket's quest for revenge and without another word he shot out the cat flap and fled from the house having no idea where to run to. All those ants in the wood which he was sure were now looking for him and a dangerous mouse family in the only place that he could remotely call home.

chapter 26

After Blanket's dramatic exit Mot stopped joining her brother and sister every morning with Slippers. Slippers asked once where she was but the other two just shrugged and he didn't mention it again. Mot in fact was fascinated by the books in her parents' room and her insatiable thirst for knowledge drove her back there every day. She studied every book she could and sometimes fell asleep with a book in her hands.

It took her a very long time sometimes reading day and night with very little sleep and when they were finished, she started on her father's notes.

Occasionally Fidgit or Christopher would come looking for her, but she was so engrossed she would wave them away.

Her father's notes fascinated her. They were largely devoted to the theory of travelling to another place and time and the more she read the more she learnt, taking notes and developing her own theories. The only interruptions would be when the others would come to get some food which they had noticed was beginning to run down.

chapter 27

Ant thought his journey would never end. He had lost count of how many times he had gone round and round. Eventually after the truck had travelled many, many miles, it came to a stop and the driver got out and walked away.

It took Ant quite some time to chew his way out of the string which he had used to pull the roller skate. It had wrapped itself around the wheel and bound Ant tightly to it. It had saved his life, but the rainwater in the puddles that the truck had driven through on its long journey had soaked the string and it had swollen.

Finally he broke free and dropped to the ground just in time it seemed. No sooner had he escaped, the driver returned and drove away in a cloud of black smoke which belched from the back of the truck.

Ant looked around. He now had an almost impossible journey to undertake to get back, a sense of urgency was driving him, but he had no idea why. He was a big ant, but it was a long walk. He would have to try and find a quicker way if he could.

With that thought in mind he set off down the road in the direction he had just come from.

chapter 28

"Well we will have to raid the kitchen," said Slippers. "I have never done it before, but I know they have some bread because the cleaner eats it for her lunch when she's here. It's very strange, it's white when she starts then she puts it in a machine that burns it brown and then she eats it. Come," he said, "follow me. We must do it now so when the cleaner comes she will think it's the owners who made the mess." They followed Slippers into the kitchen. "The bread's up there," said Slippers, standing on three legs and pointing up at one of the worktops.

"Whee," said Fidgit and before anybody could move she bounced up in the air and landed on the worktop.

"Show off," said Slippers with a smile.

"Where?" said Fidgit, looking up and down the confusing array of cupboards and machines. Slippers jumped up so his front paws were on the worktop which meant he could just see over the top. "You see the silver round thing over there," said Slippers pointing at the bread bin with his nose, "that's where they keep the bread. You will have to lift up the front."

Fidgit went over to the bread bin but try as she might she couldn't lift the door open. "It's too heavy," she cried, "I can smell the bread I am so hungry."

Christopher laughed. "Leave it to me," he said. "Slippers, stay there a minute," grabbing hold of the hair on Slippers' leg, Christopher quickly climbed up, ran along his paw and onto the worktop. Mot followed him and did the same.

Christopher flicked open the bread bin as if it weighed nothing. Inside was a large loaf of bread which Christopher proceeded to pull out onto the worktop.

Fidgit went to bite into it. "Wait a minute," said Slippers, "if you bite into it like that they will know there are mice in the house."

"What then?" shouted Fidgit whose stomach was rumbling so much she was sure it could be heard miles away.

"You will have to cut off a slice with that knife over there," said Slippers. All three mice looked at him. "Yes," said Slippers, "come on, Christopher, it should be easy for you."

Christopher shrugged his shoulders. "Yes," he said, "I think you're right." He went over to the bread knife which was very large and with a little struggle at first managed to pick it up.

"I don't think this is a good idea," said Mot.

"Shut up, said Fidgit, "you're hungry too, aren't you?"

Mot said nothing more because she was probably hungrier than Fidgit but didn't complain.

Before Slippers had a chance to explain how to use the knife Christopher slammed it down onto the bread with such force that the bread exploded into two halves with bits of bread flying off in all directions. Slippers rolled his eyes. Meanwhile Fidgit was running around grabbing bits of bread and swallowing them as quickly as she could. Mot was more sedate and just went over to the bigger pieces and ate quietly.

"If we are going to keep your presence here a secret I am going to have to take the blame for this," and with that said Slippers knocked what was left of the bread onto the floor. Christopher put the knife down as Slippers said, "remind me next time to tell you how to use a knife before you pick one up."

Christopher looked away rather embarrassed.

"Oh," said Slippers, "one more thing."

"Yes," said Christopher looking up, expecting more of a lecture. "Impressive," said Slippers with a big smile.

The cleaner came in as expected and couldn't believe the mess in the kitchen. Slippers behaved suitably humbly when told off. She then fed him and warned him not to do it again.

"If only you knew," thought Slippers. "Somehow I have to help these mice to find their parents and get them some real food that they like and can eat."

chapter 29

Ant had walked for so many days he had lost count. He had
stuck to the road when he could, but he was quite a large
ant and the road had a constant flow of trucks and cars which
sometimes changed direction without warning. Ant knew he had
had a lucky escape with the last truck in not getting squashed, so
he had to be careful.

There were very few people around on the road which helped.
He had found out that humans called themselves people when they
didn't know their names, not humans, so now he had adopted the
new word.

It had dawned on Ant pretty soon into his journey that it was
going to take him weeks to get back. This was the first time in his
life he wished he was a flying ant.

As he trotted along the road avoiding various bits of rubbish,
paper cups, empty tins, bottles and plastic bags, each slight
diversion was slowing him down and increasing his weariness. To
make matters worse it began to rain and the gutters each side of
the road began to fill with water.

As he progressed, now even slower because of the weather, he
reached a steep hill going down into a valley. It was now becoming
almost impossible to continue because each time a vehicle went
past he would be blasted by its spray and on several occasions when
he had the bad luck to be next to a big puddle when it happened
the force would knock him over.

The water in the gutters began to rise as the rain became
heavier. The small trickle had changed to a torrent moving at
great speed taking the rubbish left there with it. Ant seized his
chance and as a floating tin began to shoot by he jumped on it. It
temporarily sunk and stopped, and he nearly fell off. It quickly

began floating again and he was off at breakneck speed down the hill. The ride was exhilarating but what energy he saved not running or walking he more than spent riding the can down the hill, keeping his balance and trying to stay on as it got faster and faster.

Ant could see the bottom of the hill in the distance because there was a large pool of water spreading across the road. "Time to disembark old chap," he thought to himself. Next to this puddle was a glass frame with several people inside. He had no idea what it was, so he assumed it was for sheltering from the rain. As his can rocked from side to side and occasionally spun completely around making it very hard to stay on, Ant knew the time had arrived to get off. Another large truck went past rocking his can from side to side but this time it had glass windows all around it and it was very tall with windows both up and down. It continued down the road ahead of him and then it began to slow. He noticed all the people under the glass cover suddenly stuck their hands out and he wondered whether they were checking to see if it was still raining. The big glass truck slowed down and pulled to a stop. All the people stepped inside and then it was gone. Ant arrived at the glass frame and jumped off just in time to see the can he had been on swirl around and around and then sink into the middle of the pool of water. It immediately got crushed by the next vehicle that sped past, spraying water everywhere. The wave it created swept Ant over to the verge and onto a small area of grass under a bush.

Ant had enjoyed his ride and was pleased by the extra distance he had covered but was exhausted so decided to rest awhile. Within a few minutes more people began to collect under the glass frame. Ant looked up at the post in front of it which said 'request bus stop'.

"I see," said Ant to himself now understanding that the vehicles with lots of windows in were in fact buses. He had read about them but never actually seen them. Before long another bus arrived; some people got off and walked away and the ones at the bus stop got on.

Ant had watched this flow of people back and forth for several hours. He had concluded that the quicker way he needed was a bus. But this was easier said than done. The bus had a very big step which at any other time he might have been able to jump up, but with all these people around there was no way. He would be seen in seconds and, knowing the general reaction people had to insects, the outcome would be a foregone conclusion: "no more Ant".

He considered climbing up the glass shelter and jumping off the top! Same old problem though – he would be seen and, in any event, the slightest bit of wind and in all probability "no more Ant".

He soon realised that any attempt he made to get on the bus had to be done by climbing on a person first, but again he would definitely be seen. The next bus came and went but still he had no idea what to do about getting on one. And then things changed as from time to time they invariably do.

Two women crossed the road towards the bus stop. One of them was holding the hand of a child and she carried with her a small satchel. Ant's hopes rose but there was a flap over the top and no way to get in. In his excitement he had come out from under the bush and as they approached he shrank back under it.

The two women stood facing away from Ant and started to talk. He was well out of their sight, but not so much that of the little girl who was of course considerably shorter and could see right under the bush. She crossed over to the bush and said to him, "Hello, little dog, how are you?" Ant could not ignore her. He needed her help somehow and knew sooner or later she would point out his presence to her mother.

So, taking a chance, he said, "Hello, little girl, I'm not a dog I'm an ant." Completely unsurprised that an ant could be talking to her the little girl said, "I'm very sorry Mr Ant, what's your name?"

"Well actually it's Ant," he replied, and the little girl giggled.

"What are you doing here?" she asked.

"Waiting for a bus of course," said Ant, "but I have trouble getting on because I'm too small."

"I can help you if you like; you could get into my bag."

The other woman turned to the mother and said, "who's she talking to today?" nodding at her friend's daughter.

The girl's mother laughed. "It's another of her invisible friends, she has lots of them."

"Oh I see," she laughed. And they resumed their conversation.

The little girl bent down and unlatched her bag to let Ant in which he quickly did. Just in time as the little girl's mother called "Josie, come on, the bus is coming." Ant scrambled down to the bottom of the bag which was a little difficult because he was a big ant and it was a small bag full of various things that little girls collect, but just big enough to hide under.

All the people at the bus stop got on and Josie sat behind her mother because she wanted to talk to her new friend some more.

chapter 30

Blanket fled from the house into the road and then stopped. For the first time in his life he simply didn't know where to go or what to do. Having been a loner and selfish cat all his life he had no friends he could turn to for help or advice. He knew he couldn't go back to the woods as it was too dangerous. He was convinced the ants had seen him and were going to hunt him down. Many times, he had seen the remains of some unfortunate animal that the ants had stripped to the bone. Admittedly the animals were dead already they hadn't killed them, but these ants were different. He was sure they were bigger and were dumping bodies not eating them and the way they had looked at him when he turned away and ran sent a shiver down his spine. And he certainly couldn't go back to the house. The only safe path away was to stay on the road. So he set off up the hill while he pondered what on earth he was going to do.

At the top of the hill was a road junction where the buses stopped and people got on and off on a regular basis. He knew from experience that if he hung around long enough someone would stroke and pet him and occasionally give him something to eat. The milkman also delivered daily and he usually gave him some milk.

"That's it," he decided, "I'm jumping on the milk float and it will take me away from here forever. I'll find a new home and a new wood away from the ants and everything will be fine!"

So, with a new determined bold step to his stride he started up the hill towards the bus stop and what he thought would be the start of his new life.

chapter 31

The bus took a long time. It stopped frequently, and people of course got on and got off. Ant knew he was going in the right direction but of course being in the bag he had no idea how far he had to go. He heard a scuffle and the flap of the bag opened and a little voice said, "Hello Mr Ant, are you there?" A silly question of course because he had nowhere else to go, but he thought better of saying that in case Josie got upset.

Ant carefully poked his head out from under the collection of bits in the bag to see Josie was looking down at him. "Hello Josie," he whispered. Talking to imaginary friends was one thing but nobody else was supposed to hear but you if your friend spoke back.

Ant could see the roof of the bus and the backs of the heads of her mother and her friend deeply engaged in conversation.

"Well," her friend said. "You know that house I clean every day down the end of the road?"

"Yes," said Josie's mother.

"And that lovely dog – the red setter – who's as good as gold."

"Yes," said Josie's mother again.

"Well yesterday for the first time ever I got to the house and you wouldn't believe the mess in the kitchen. Somehow he had got into the bread bin and there were bread bits everywhere. He gets fed every time I go there and in the evening he's such a good dog. It took me ages to clean it up and when I told the owners they wouldn't believe me at first."

"Must have been upset by something," said Josie's mother.

"Yes, you're probably right. Well we will see today if he's done it again. I hope not."

"Josie," said Ant, "can you lift your bag up to the window, so I can try and see where we are?"

"Of course," said Josie and she lifted her bag up so that the flap was towards her and Ant could look out with nobody else seeing, but he did have to duck down every time the bus stopped in case anybody outside could see in.

Try as he might Ant didn't recognise anything going past the window. It didn't help that the window was all misted up because of the rain. It depressed him a little bit. "It's alright Josie," he said with a weary sigh, "I've seen enough."

"Where are you going to?" said Josie.

"Well I don't really know," said Ant. "I'm trying to find a friend called Chad who I just feel is in trouble. The last time I saw him he was tearing down a hill on a roller skate."

Josie laughed. "Sounds like fun."

"Maybe," said Ant, but I nearly got squashed under a truck.

"Oh," said Josie and sat back for a moment.

"Will you come and live with me?" said Josie suddenly, "you would be much safer, and I have a ready-made home for you."

"I can't," said Ant. "I told you, I have to find my friend."

Josie was quiet again for a moment. "I used to have a friend, you know."

"Really?" said Ant, not really paying much attention. He was trying to work out when and how to get off the bus. He had been very lucky to get this lift but if he got off too soon he was unlikely to get another ride and if he got out of the bag now he might go too far and in any event Josie was sure to get upset and make a scene if he tried to get out of her bag. The whole thing was giving him a headache. He would have held his head in his hands but of course he didn't actually have any – hands that is!

"She was a lovely grey mouse and I used to play with her every day and then I made a silly mistake," continued Josie.

"Really," said Ant now giving Josie his full attention and hardly believing where he thought this story was going.

"Well she lived in a cage by my window and I loved her so much so I put the cage outside to give her some fresh air. That's when she was attacked by a nasty horrible cat that knocked her cage off the windowsill. It broke when it hit a tree and we never found her. I think the cat ate her. It was a terrible day and it was all my fault," said Josie, now looking tearful as she relived the moment in her head.

Ant could not believe his luck. If he stayed with Josie, at least for now, he would get back to roughly where he parted company with Chad. "Well," said Ant, "I will stay with you for a little bit but I must go and find my friend soon."

"Alright," said Josie, now visibly cheering up.

Josie's mother looked over her shoulder and Ant ducked down just in time. "We're almost at our stop Josie. We have to get off soon. Is your friend coming too?"

"But of course," replied Josie and her mother smiled and winked at her friend.

Ant of course had no choice but to get off now. He hoped he would recognise where he was and then go on from there. Josie's mother got up and held out her hand for Josie and they walked down the aisle of the bus to the door.

chapter 32

It had stopped raining now which Blanket was pleased about. Most cats don't like water in huge amounts and Blanket was no exception. As he looked up the hill a bus pulled up. It was going away from the wood towards the main town, which was exactly the direction he wanted to go in, but even if he ran he would never catch it. He didn't worry though. He knew from experience that another one would be along soon. The best time really was the morning or late afternoon when the people were going out or coming back from wherever they went almost every day.

He intended to give his best performance ever of meowing and leg brushing and purring so that either the bus conductor or a passenger would feel sorry for him and maybe just maybe take him home. Blanket had rehearsed his performance over and over in his head so many times that he had convinced himself that it was guaranteed to happen.

The sun had broken through the clouds and Blanket was getting too warm. He knew he should stop for water, but he just wanted to be ready for the next bus that came along so he picked up his pace. The best place to be would be just inside the bus shelter. It would give him some shade and everybody who got off could see him straight away.

When he reached the bus shelter there was nobody waiting for the bus which was a disappointment to him as it meant people were only going to get off not on. They would definitely be going in a direction he did not want to go. He heard the rumble of the bus engine in the distance as it climbed up the other side of the hill to the brow where the roads met. It duly pulled up right where he expected it to. He arched his back, cleared his throat and prepared to start the "hey, take me home" performance of his life.

chapter 33

Two people had come down the stairs and stepped onto the exit platform of the bus in front of Josie and her mother, just as the bus pulled up to the bus stop. Josie was looking down at the floor as they prepared to leave as she still wasn't big enough to be confident about going up and down steps without looking down at them. So when the two people in front of her stepped off the bus she looked up and there in front of her was a grey cat.

Josie couldn't believe her eyes! Right in front of her was the cat that had eaten her mouse. She let out a huge scream. Everybody on the bus turned to look in concern, thinking she had fallen and to see what had happened. She screamed at her mother, dropping her hand and pointing, "That's the cat that ate my mouse, look!"

Blanket froze. This was not quite what he had planned. In fact, it was absolutely nothing like he had planned. Josie screamed again and completely forgetting Ant was in her bag whipped it off her shoulder and threw it with all her might at the cat she had almost forgotten about but hated for so long.

The bag flew through the air, the shoulder strap curling into a loop as it flew towards Blanket. He was frozen in place by the shock of it all — so much so he didn't have time to avoid the bag, and the twisted strap wrapped itself around his neck as it landed.

The force of the blow knocked him out of his trance and he took off in the only direction he could, towards the wood and away from Josie and her mother. One thing was certain; he would not be finding a new owner today.

Ant had no idea what was going on. One minute he was planning his escape, the next Josie was screaming and he was upside down flying through the air and hanging on for dear life. He felt the bag land on what he thought was the ground and then he was moving again.

Blanket raced away with the bag wrapped around his neck and as he ran it began to tighten so much so he was beginning to have trouble breathing. He ran into the wood, one fear temporarily overpowering the other. The strap now pulled tighter the more he ran and dragged it behind him. He could still hear Josie screaming behind him in the distance as he raced away.

Ant was bouncing and banging all over the place. He knew now he was somehow attached to an animal by the sounds of the breathing and the movement of running. It also sounded in great distress as its breathing had become ragged and coarse.

In his haste to get away Blanket jumped over a fallen tree. There was a large drop on the other side, the bag caught on a broken stump and the strap completely tightened around his neck as he fell to the ground, but the strap was too short, and Blanket was suspended only inches off the ground and began slowly to choke to death.

chapter 34

The bag finally stopped moving much to Ant's relief and all was quiet except for a faint gurgling sound. Ant had ended up on his back. He turned himself upright and crawled out of what was left of Josie's belongings – most of them had fallen out during his bumpy journey. He headed for the bag's flap which thankfully was now lying open and came out onto a tree lying on the ground in a wood and apart from a few bumps he was none the worse for wear. In the distance he could still hear Josie sobbing and crying.

However, the gurgling sound which he had heard earlier was much quieter now, but he could still just hear it, so he looked over the edge of the tree to see where it was coming from.

Blanket knew he was dying. He had no energy left. He had struggled briefly but the run from the bus stop had exhausted him and, in any event, the more he struggled the tighter the strap became. He could see the strap going over the fallen tree and just out of reach was a catch that would have released him, but he knew he could never reach it now. Then over the edge of the fallen tree appeared a large ant and Blanket realised then he was right; they were looking for him, this was the first of thousands and it was all over. The last thing he saw was the ant crawling down the strap towards him. He made one last weak attempt to get free and then he lost consciousness.

As soon as Ant looked over the edge, he knew he had to do something. The cat he was looking down at was in serious trouble and close to death. When Ant looked him in the eyes, he had never seen an animal so totally petrified. The strap around his neck was now so tight it had almost disappeared into his fur. About halfway up there was a catch on the strap which Ant knew was for adjusting the length; it had almost broken because of the strain that had been placed on it as Blanket had dragged the bag through the wood.

Ant proceeded to climb down the strap to the catch. He realised that with a good pull he could bend it open and the cat would fall to the ground. As he drew closer the cat tried weakly to struggle free and then his eyes closed.

Ant was sure he had just seen the cat die. But he continued down the strap to the catch and as he had thought with a few hard tugs the catch finally burst open and the cat fell to the ground. The strap was firmly embedded in the cat's neck, so the first thing Ant did was yank it free. He put his head to the cat's chest and much to his surprise there was a faint heartbeat. The cat suddenly shuddered and started to breathe again but still remained unconscious.

Ant looked around for some water. Not far away was a puddle left over from the heavy rain and close to that an old discarded drinking cup. He grabbed the cup, picked it up easily and took it over to the puddle dragged it through it and managed to half fill it up. Now of course it was not quite so easy to handle but with a bit of manoeuvring he manage to get it on top of his head and carry it back to the cat. He set it down on the ground and gently tipped the cup until some of the water trickled into the cat's mouth.

The water had an immediate effect and the cat started to revive and opened one eye. Ant said, "Hello old chap, looks like you got yourself into a bit of trouble. Can I help?"

chapter 35

When Christopher came out the next day to see Slippers, he was immediately sent back to fetch his sisters. "Tell them it's 'Meeting time'." Christopher dutifully collected his sisters. He was as interested in what Slippers had to say as much as he was sure his sisters would be.

The three mice sat down in front of Slippers and politely waited for him to speak. Slippers was amused, but he didn't show it. Here in front of him were three of the strongest, cleverest mice ever born and they were sitting patiently waiting for him to speak, and it was obvious they trusted him implicitly. He felt he had become their unofficial guardian. They were very important to him and had become his friends as had their parents of whom there was still no word. He was seriously worried about them.

Slippers began, "Well I have decided you can't stay here any more!"

The calm expectant expressions on the mice's faces instantly disappeared except perhaps Mot's; she was the eldest and probably the wisest.

"Why?" said Christopher.

"Yes why?" said Fidgit.

"Because there is not enough food and you will have to go and search for it and more importantly your parents have not returned. I believe they are in trouble and need our help, so we have to go and find them."

Christopher nodded and so did Fidgit as Mot said, "We?"

"Yes," said Slippers, "you can't do this on your own. I will have to come with you, but there is a problem."

"What?" said Christopher, waking up from the shock of Slippers' announcement.

"I'm locked in every day. You can go in and out of the cat flap, but I can only go out the front door. On top of that I have to be honest, your parents never divulged to me where they went every night, where they go to get the food or anything else they did – they were always very secretive about it."

"We found some small books," said Mot suddenly. "I have been thinking for some time where they came from. Christopher asked our father but all he said was 'Ah but that's another story', which is pretty much what he would say every time we would try to find out anything about their past, or for that matter what they do in the present."

"I believe it may have something to do with their powers but I'm not sure," said Slippers. "I know you have them but apart from your father's strength I have no idea what else he and your mother can do."

"The lock is easy," said Fidgit, nearly interrupting Slippers because an idea had popped into her head and she couldn't wait to share it. "I can bounce up there and turn it."

"Right," said Christopher, "how are you going to turn it? You don't have my strength." Fidgit fell silent.

"It's not that simple," said Slippers, "there is a second lock that requires a key and only the owners and the cleaner have one."

"Oh," said Christopher and Fidgit almost together, "that means we are stuck before we've even got started."

"Possibly not," said Mot, who had been silent during the conversation.

"How so?" said Slippers curiously, knowing that Mot was the thinker and possibly the cleverest of the three of them.

"Well one day when the television was off I heard one of the people talking to the other. He said he had lost their keys and so wanted to get some more made and he said in case it happens again he would put one in the top drawer in the dining room, wherever that is."

"I think I know where that is," said Slippers, "where the tables and chairs are."

"So where are the drawers then?" said Fidgit.

"Good question," said Slippers. "They moved them somewhere else some time ago."

"So where are they now?" said Christopher.

"I think they went upstairs," said Slippers.

So they all went upstairs and spread out. Most of the doors were closed but being an old house with a very thin carpet, the mice could slip in and out of the rooms under the doors. Slippers had explained what they looked like and shortly they re-met on the landing to confirm there was no sign of the chest of drawers anywhere.

"So much for that plan," said Christopher glaring at Mot who just shrugged her shoulders.

"I have an idea," said Fidgit. "When the cleaner comes in we all rush out, she gets scared and Slippers escapes out the open door before she puts his lead on." Fidgit smiled with satisfaction.

"That's a good idea," said Slippers, which made Fidgit smile even more, "but there is a catch."

Fidgit's smile disappeared as quickly as it had appeared, "What?" she said.

"Well," said Slippers, "as soon as I run off the cleaner will call everybody she knows and more, and then everybody will be looking for me. Since I am very red it's not as if I can hide easily and it will all be over."

"Oh, I thought it was a good idea," said Fidgit, sounding very disappointed.

"It was a good idea, but we have to get away without any human knowing until we get deep into the woods. That's where your parents went and that's where we have to start."

"So," said Mot, "we are back to finding the key plan I think? And I have another idea."

"What's that?" said Slippers.

"Well," said Mot, "we know they hid a key somewhere, yes?" Everybody nodded. Mot was quite pleased with herself because she had everybody's attention. Mot continued, "and we also know that when they come home they both hang their keys on the hooks by the front door and take them again in the morning when they go out. Correct?" Everybody nodded again.

"So, we wait until they go to bed, and we steal one set of their keys!" Silence followed. Then Christopher said, "and?"

Mot sighed. "Well, if we take one set of their keys—" and before she could finish Slippers smiled and said, "they will go looking for the hidden one."

"Correct," said Mot, feeling very pleased with herself.

"Actually," said Fidgit, "I think that's very clever Mot."

"So do I," said Slippers, "so tonight that's the plan." They all nodded in agreement.

Mot and Christopher headed back to their home and Slippers went to lie down. Fidgit was sitting in the hall looking at something. "What's up?" said Slippers, noticing that Fidgit hadn't gone back to her home. "Oh, just looking," she said.

Fidgit had noticed something that none of the others had. There were eight hooks beside the front door in two rows of four with two prongs on each hook, just as you came in. They were quite high and Fidgit knew that almost every time the keys were left on the bottom hooks and that only two of them were strong enough to lift the keys – Slippers and Christopher – and neither of them were tall enough.

She could bounce up there, but couldn't lift them, and so with that problem in her mind she went looking for two things she needed for tonight. She found the paperclip in the dust under a floorboard. The string was at first a little more difficult, but with a quick scout around the kitchen she spied it on a shelf, bounced up and pushed it off onto the floor. She went and fetched Slippers and asked him to move it and hide it somewhere until later. He looked at her quizzically, but obliged. She then went home to wait for the night.

chapter 36

Blanket was having the worst dream of his life. He had died and was now being held prisoner by a very large ant. He tried to move but he couldn't, and now the ant was talking to him offering to help!

"Would you like some more water?" said Ant. Blanket tried to reply but for some reason the only things he could move were his eyes.

As Ant moved around trying to make Blanket more comfortable, Blanket realised this was not a dream. He remembered his terrifying run from the bus stop and hanging from a tree, and his last thoughts had been that the ants had found him and it was all over.

But no more ants had joined this one and he was not behaving like an ant who wanted to kill him – quite the opposite. The ant continued to talk to him, asking questions that he couldn't answer but really wanted to.

What puzzled Blanket most of all was why this ant wanted to help him? Blanket had been a selfish cat all his life and had never helped or cared about a single other animal – or insect for that matter – even if they were in trouble. And now here he was, paralysed and completely at any creature's mercy and a lowly ant was trying to help him for no reason but just to help.

The ant had now sat down in front of him and continued to talk about anything and everything. He had completely removed the strap from around his neck and given him some more water. Blanket found the whole thing very calming and for the first time in his life felt the feelings of gratitude to the ant.

His heart rate, which at one stage after he had woken was so high that Blanket thought it would burst out of his chest, was now back to normal with the ant's help. Suddenly his left front paw wiggled and was quickly followed by the right. His mouth, which had been hanging open, now closed and seconds later he felt new energy course though his body and he was able to sit up.

"Well that's a relief," said Ant, not moving from his spot, which surprised Blanket because he thought he would run away. "I thought you were going to lie there for ever."

"Why are you helping me?" asked Blanket with a croaky voice, swallowing two or three times to try and clear the soreness that the strap had caused him.

"Well," said Ant, "I try to help all animals when I can, but I have to be honest I also wanted your help to find a friend."

"I don't have any friends," mumbled Blanket looking sadly down at the ground.

"Well you do now," said Ant, "I'll be one of your friends."

"Why?" said Blanket with a puzzled look on his face.

"Why not?" Ant asked, smiling. Much to his surprise, the reply brought a smile to Blanket's face too.

"Do you have a home?" said Ant.

"Yes and no," said Blanket, "not far from here is a house I lived in from time to time, but I don't think I'd be welcome there any more."

"Why?" said Ant.

"Well it's been taken over by some mice," said Blanket with a sneer from his old self.

"Oh!" said Ant, "would you happen to know their names?"

"What friend?" said Blanket, suddenly remembering what Ant had said previously.

"Well it has occurred to me that we might be talking about the same mice."

"Christopher, Mot and Fidgit! Those are their names," hissed Blanket as if the words had caused a bad taste in his mouth.

"Oh," said Ant disappointedly, but noticing that something

must have happened between them to cause such animosity. "No, they are not the same I'm afraid."

"They asked for my help to find their parents," continued Blanket as if Ant hadn't spoken, "and I refused because I hated their father, but now I feel ashamed. I have been so selfish for so long that now I'm in trouble I have no friends to turn to."

"Well you have me," said Ant again. "I will help you get back there tomorrow. It's going to be dark soon – you're not really well enough yet and it's not safe to travel. I will stay with you tonight and we can set off in the morning after the roads get quiet and find your house, what do you think?"

"I think that's a very good idea," said Blanket amazed with himself as he was about to settle down for the night with an ANT of all creatures!! Ant settled down next to him. "After that I will have to set off to find my friend," said Ant just as Blanket drifted off to sleep. "I wonder where you are Chad?" he said out loud, but Blanket was already asleep and didn't hear him.

As the sun set and darkness enveloped the wood Ant began to glow green as he always did, but here he was safe as there were no people to see the glow in the dark. Blanket slept on.

chapter 37

The house had fallen silent as soon as the people had gone to bed but there were other sounds that became predominant with their absence. The ticking clock in the hall, the sound of pipes cooling under the floor now the heating was off and, of course, the sound of mice coming out on a mission!

Slippers was awake and waiting for them with his head on his paws. He was just about to undertake a big new adventure in his life and theirs, but he knew in his heart that even with their superpowers they would be at risk and he had to protect them at all costs.

Slippers knew the mice could see at night even if it was pitch black — he couldn't, but tonight there was a full moon which shone brightly through the glass in the front door. It lit up the hall almost as if it was daylight, so he saw the mice as they rounded the corner of the door into the hallway. Slippers got to his feet terribly aware of the noise his nails made in the dead of night as he walked along the wooden boards.

"Well what's the plan?" he said to all of them even though it was really directed at Fidgit.

For once, Christopher was silent because he hadn't thought about it at all. Fidgit took charge and said, "Slippers, can you get the string please?" Slippers obliged and trotted over to his basket and dug the ball of string out from under his blanket where he had hidden it, brought it back, and placed it carefully in front her before he sat down. Fidgit went and retrieved the paper clip from behind a pot plant where she had left it earlier after finding it. She gave it to Christopher and said, "Can you bend that into a hook please and tie it to the string?"

Christopher quickly bent it and tied on one end of the string.

Fidgit started to roll the ball towards the front door and when she got there she turned around and rolled it back so there was a large loop stretched out on the floor.

"Christopher," she said, "can you pull it into a pile for me?" Christopher dutifully did as he was asked and pulled the string into a pile.

At that moment a door opened upstairs throwing a shadow of light down the stairs and then the lights on the stairs came on and one of the people started coming down the stairs.

Slippers couldn't believe it! But he moved quickly. He plonked himself down on top of the pile of string and pretended to be asleep, quickly whispering to the mice to hide. They needed no second prompting. For Mot it was easy; she just disappeared. Fidgit bounced up onto the coat stand and Christopher dived under Slippers. The woman of the house walked down the stairs coughing slightly, turned at the bottom, and went into the kitchen. Slippers watched her with one eye. He could see her making something hot because the silver thing was making bubbly noises and it only did that when they made something hot. He knew about hot – he had sniffed a cup once and burnt his nose!

She put something in a cup, poured in the hot water and stirred it. Slippers could hear the spoon clinking on the side of the cup as she did it. She came out of the kitchen and spotted Slippers in the hall not in his basket, but he had closed his eye, so she hesitated briefly, assumed he was fast asleep, and then went back upstairs.

The house resumed its silence but they all waited a little longer to be sure before they came out of hiding.

"That," said Christopher "was very close."

Slippers smiled. "Yes, you're right. It was. Come on, let's get on with it." Fidgit bounced down from the hat stand and before anybody could say anything else she grabbed the loop of string and bounced back up with it, looped it around the top hook over one of sets of keys on the hook below. She bounced down then up again and, hanging on the larger prong of the bottom hook, hooked the paper clip around the keys.

"Can you pull please Slippers?" she whispered. Slippers backed down the hall with the string in his mouth now understanding what he had to do but very conscious of the noise his nails made as he walked. The string tightened and with Fidgit's guidance rose off the hook they were on. "Now back," she said, and Slippers slowly let the string go loose as the keys were lowered slowly to the ground.

"Hide the string please Slippers," said Fidgit.

"Wait!" said Christopher, who grabbed the string and in the blink of an eye rewound it. Christopher took out the paper clip hook and Slippers hid it in his basket.

"Where are we going to put the keys?" said Slippers.

"We will have to take them home," said Mot, who had said nothing up until now.

"Why?" said Christopher "we will need them later to open the door."

"Yes," replied Mot, "but in the morning they will start searching and it's highly likely that wherever we choose to hide them, they may look there and we would be right back where we started."

Slippers nodded and of course Christopher reluctantly had to agree. They had a struggle getting the key ring through their front door (the knot hole), but with a bit of wiggling they managed. Slippers went back to his basket and waited for the trouble to start.

chapter 38

Blanket awoke just as the sun was rising as was customary at the time of year. Especially in the woods the morning was cooler, and Blanket shivered. He looked around to find he was alone, and much to his surprise he felt disappointed. The sun's rays were just beginning to penetrate the wood, but they caused strange shadows that appeared to move very slowly which unnerved him. On top of this, the wood was completely silent when it should have been alive with animals stirring and birdsong.

Blanket had just convinced himself that he had just had a bad dream when Ant reappeared from around a tree.

"Morning old chap! How are you today?" With all the problems swirling around in his head he had to admit he was pleased to see Ant and smiled. "You were fast asleep," Ant continued, "so I went to have a look around. Something's just not right. I can't find a single animal at all and there don't seem to be any insects either."

"There is something I must tell you," said Blanket, "and I am sure I will feel better when I do so."

"Really?" said Ant, "fire away then."

Blanket hesitated. He had been avoiding telling Ant anything. He was after all an ant too so he might be taking a risk but he had helped him so Blanket went on to tell him about his terrible experience in the wood and that he realised it had been going on for some time. He had noticed and didn't really care, but now he did and he thought the ants were looking for him and were up to something terrible but he didn't know what.

When he finished Ant stood still and he just stared at the ground, deep in thought. Blanket began to worry a little and then Ant said, "so there were lots of small ants and a few big ones. Was there anything else about them that you noticed that was different?"

Blanket thought for a moment. "Well," he said, staring into nothing and reluctantly remembering the moment, "I am pretty sure that when the big ants moved out of the light they looked a little green, like they were glowing in fact."

Ant shook his head. "I thought you might say that," he said, looking off into space and really talking to himself.

"It's time to set off now," said Ant, suddenly collecting his thoughts together. "I have to see you home as promised and get on my way. We will go through the wood – it's a little longer, but safer. We will be too exposed if we go down the road together.

"I'm not sure about safer," said Blanket, his newfound confidence swiftly evaporating and never thinking he would be accepting the help of an ant to go anywhere!

So Ant set off through the wood with Blanket reluctantly following. The sun penetrated through the trees almost everywhere which suited Blanket, but he was ever wary of a sudden white light appearing and the thought of it made him nervous, but he had told Ant all about it and he seemed completely unworried. He was moving through the wood at a great pace much to Blanket's surprise. He was a much bigger ant than normal of course but even then his speed and agility was unusual. Knowing the woods almost as well as Ant he realised they would be there very soon.

chapter 39

The household stirred as it did most days. The occupants usually came down together but today the man came down alone, had breakfast, and then took Slippers for his customary walk. He had grabbed his keys off the hook and made no comment about the missing set. This didn't surprise Slippers as they didn't both put their keys there every day. Slippers returned from his walk, the man went upstairs, there was a brief conversation and then he left. Still no sign of the woman.

The mice had appeared at the corner of the dining room and Slippers told them to go back because only one of the people had gone out. Things were not going to plan! As invariably they do not.

Slippers heard her talking to someone upstairs. It had to be that black box thing that people talk into from time to time. Her voice started to get louder and then it stopped. Then there was some banging and thumping then some doors slammed. "Somebody's not happy," thought Slippers.

There was a thump, thump, thump down the stairs and she appeared, obviously upset, sniffing and coughing and talking to herself, "Make me go to work when I'm not well, short of staff. Not my blasted problem, not fair." Slippers kept his head low and watched out of one eye as she put on her coat and reached for her keys. Next, she checked her pockets and then her bag, thought for a moment and took the black talking box out of her pocket. Slippers heard her say "have you taken my keys?" There was a brief silence. Slippers heard a faint murmur from the box. "Well they aren't here." Again a silence and then she asked, "so where are the spare keys?" There was a brief murmur of reply and she said, "in the loft. That's a lot of good. Look, I have to go to work. I'm not well, but they are insisting I come in. I will have to shut the front door without double locking it, but Mrs Smudgeit's coming today and Slippers is here." With that she abruptly hung up, petted Slippers on the head, said "look after the house boy," and flew out the door in a hurry muttering "now I'm late."

The house returned to its usual silence and the mice reappeared.

"Well," said Christopher, "let's go. There's only one lock on now and that's easy for me to turn."

"We can't," said Slippers.

"Why?" said Christopher and before Slippers could answer Mot said, "because if we are gone when the cleaner gets here Slippers will be too as he is helping us, and she will raise the alarm as soon as she finds Slippers missing and then everybody will be looking out for him. So we have to wait until she has left so we can have a head start." Slippers just nodded in agreement. Christopher sighed in frustration.

So they all waited patiently, or at least as patiently as they could. Even Mot who was the calmest had to admit the delay was frustrating. They heard the rattle of keys in the lock and a surprised exclamation when she found the other lock unlocked.

They watched her scoot round the house. She petted the dog and fed him and within an hour she was gone, double locking the door on the way out.

"Right," said Slippers, "come on. Let's get going before anything else happens. Christopher, bring the keys please."

chapter 40

Ant pushed on further into the deepest part of the wood. He was not following a beaten track and there were frequent obstacles which Ant navigated with ease because of his size and abilities. Blanket, of course, was considerably bigger and not nearly as flexible. Blanket knew because of his sense of direction that they were taking a direct line to the house, but he suddenly wondered how Ant knew where they were going.

"Hey Ant, stop please!" called out Blanket. It had become very dark where they were because the wood was so thick the sun's rays could not penetrate.

Ant stopped, turned back as requested and made his way towards Blanket. As he approached, Blanket's heart skipped a beat and he was filled with dread. Ant had begun to glow green, and any questions Blanket had had about their direction and how he knew where to go were frozen in his head.

"What's up old chap?" said Ant stopping right in front of Blanket who once again was frozen to the spot with renewed fear about the ants.

"You're, you're—"

"What?" said Ant, puzzled by Blanket's petrified look. "Green," he managed to blurt out.

"Oh, I see. Of course, now I understand," and Ant promptly sat down in front of Blanket. "Please sit," he said, "and I will explain."

Blanket sat. He had no choice really. His mind was in turmoil friend, enemy, friend, enemy, which? So he sat and waited, and Ant began.

"I used to live here with the rest of my colony." Blanket tipped his head in question. "Oh, a colony is an ants' nest where we all lived together with our queen, the leader. I was only a soldier ant. All I had to do every day was search for food, but I was born different. I could speak, which ants can't do, so from the very beginning I felt as if I was on my own even though I wasn't.

"Then one day something hit our nest and almost every ant fled leaving just a few behind. They eventually left too, except one who stayed with me a long time.

"We were like brothers," Ant said sadly, "but he couldn't speak like me. Then one day he went out and didn't come back so I assumed he was dead. I did search for him but found no trace."

Blanket had now calmed down and was listening to the story with interest.

"It was shortly after that I realised we had begun to grow much bigger than normal ants and could lift very heavy things. It wasn't until I looked at myself in a pond that I realised how big I had become and that I glow green in the dark.

"What worries me now, Blanket, is the green large glowing ants you told me about. I have a bad feeling that the ant I thought was my brother is not in fact dead, but is behind all these deaths in the woods and the worm hole, and that my friends are somehow in trouble because of this. I can't explain why, it's just a feeling. I understand you might be afraid of me now but soon we will part company. You will be home and I have to continue my search for my friends and save them if it is not too late."

Blanket sat in silence when Ant finished, and Ant waited for a response expectantly.

"Ant!" said Blanket, suddenly sitting up straight. "I am ashamed of myself. Since we have met you have done nothing but help me and be my friend. I have done nothing but doubt you. Travel to my house. I will make my peace with the mice and then I'm coming with you to help you find your friends or at least die trying."

Ant was shocked. It was the last thing he expected to hear. "Thank you, Blanket. I will accept your offer — I need all the help I can get — and you can show me where the worm hole last appeared."

With that they both turned to continue their journey Ant with a new friend and Blanket with a new bold step of confidence in his stride.

chapter 41

This time Christopher didn't struggle with the keys. He now knew the shape of the wood knot hole entrance to their home and the best way to turn the key ring to get it out. He carried the keys over to the front door.

"The long flat key with the oval end is the bottom lock," said Slippers, "just like the kitchen, you get on my back and walk up to my nose with the keys."

So Christopher tried to climb onto Slippers' back with the keys, but it was just impossible. He could hold the keys but couldn't climb and if he climbed, he couldn't hold the keys. Fidgit suggested bouncing up with the keys but with the extra weight she couldn't get off the ground. They then started to argue with one another as to how to do it, each one firmly convinced that they were right and the others were wrong.

Mot watched all this calmly and silently and then said loudly, "Slippers!" Everyone stopped talking or rather, arguing, and turned to Mot. "Slippers, go and get the string. Fidgit, go and get the hook. What's wrong with you? If we don't all work together, we will never get out of here." Christopher said nothing as the others did as they were told.

"Fidgit," said Mot, "jump up there with string like you did before and loop it over the handle of the top lock like you did to get the keys." Fidgit did as she was told. "Now the tricky part," said Mot. "Slippers, can you pull up the keys and hold the string tight while Christopher ties it to the leg of the hat stand?" Christopher and Slippers followed Mot's instructions, but it took three attempts before they succeeded as the string slipped out of Slippers' mouth the first time and the knot Christopher tied the second time wasn't tight enough.

The keys were now hanging just below the lock. Christopher climbed onto Slippers' back and Slippers lifted his head up level with the lock, but being so close made him cross-eyed. "Hurry up Christopher," said Slippers, "my eyes hurt." Christopher quickly ran to his head and onto his nose and easily lifted the key into the lock. But try as he might with all his strength, he couldn't turn the key around to unlock the door.

Christopher, who was now out of breath, had to admit defeat. "It's too stiff to turn," he sighed.

"Slippers," said Mot, "take Christopher to the kitchen." Christopher hung on as Slippers trotted to the kitchen accepting without doubt that Mot was in charge. "Fidgit, jump up there where you went last time to get the bread," which she obediently did. "Right Slippers, please pull open a drawer." Slippers did as he was asked. "Fidgit," said Mot again, "what's in there? Are there any metal things that are thin enough to fit through the key head?"

"No," said Fidgit. So drawer by drawer they worked their way along the kitchen. Then on the fifth attempt Fidgit said, "Stop." By now Christopher had worked out what Mot was looking for so as soon as Fidgit said stop he climbed up to Slippers' nose and stepped onto the worktop next to Fidgit.

They had found the cutlery drawer. "That is what I need," said Christopher pointing at a teaspoon, and with that he jumped into the drawer. Slippers was so keen to have a look he nearly squashed Christopher in the drawer. "Hey!" said Christopher, managing to stop the drawer before it closed on him.

"Sorry," said Slippers, backing off a bit and still frustrated because he wasn't quite tall enough to see what they were looking at.

Christopher picked up the teaspoon and waved it triumphantly. Mot rolled her eyes. "Come on," she said, "we have to get a move on." Christopher jumped onto Slippers' head and he carried him back to the front door. Christopher swiftly put the spoon through the end of the key and turned it now with ease. The door moved a fraction as it rested against the only remaining lock that was preventing their escape.

"Come on," said Mot, "put everything away first." The keys were still hooked onto the string, so they quickly lowered them to the ground, hid the keys behind the coat rack to make it look like they had been dropped there, put the string back in Slippers' bed and hid the paper clip.

"Ok," said Slippers, taking a big breath as Christopher ran up his back and along his nose. Christopher grabbed the gnarled knob of the lock. He heard the internal mechanism engage and the front door started to open. Christopher could feel Slippers quiver with excitement beneath him. The door unlatched. All that held it in place now was the friction of the door and the frame.

Christopher and the three mice looked at each other in anticipation when the door started to move inwards all by itself.

chapter 42

Blanket was now full of confidence and with a firm commitment to Ant his new friend (well only friend actually) and his mission to find his missing friend, Blanket had no trouble keeping up. From time to time they entered dark areas of the wood, but Ant's green glow made him easier to follow.

They soon came out onto a well-worn footpath through the wood. "We have to be careful now," said Ant. "People come through here quite often but no animals now I'm afraid." The path ran downhill parallel to the road and Blanket knew at the bottom was a gap in the wood where an old tree used to be directly opposite the house they were trying to reach.

They heard a sound, so they stopped but it was just a woman walking up the hill on the road. She didn't even glance their way, but Blanket recognised her from the bus. "She's the cleaner of the house," he whispered. Ant turned to look at him and smiled. Blanket realised Ant had recognised her too and he had to grin back. They waited a few minutes and then continued on their way. Now walking side by side Blanket said, "So what's the plan when we leave the house?"

"Well, my friend had help to get here originally so what I plan to do is go back to where he came from and from what he told me find the rest of his friends and see if they want to help. It's going to be dangerous because ants united are a powerful foe. But we have one advantage."

"What?" said Blanket.

"We can think for ourselves. They only think as a unity, not as individuals."

"I see," said Blanket, when in fact he didn't see at all. In fact he didn't really understand half of what Ant had said because he was too afraid to ask when in fact he should have.

"There were four friends he made on his journey: a fox, a beaver, a seagull and a dove. I think it's highly unlikely we will find the seagull and dove, but the beaver was by a river or pond and there's only one I know on the other side of the wood near a rubbish dump so we will start there. What do you think?"

"I think you're in charge, so I will just follow your lead." With that said, they continued down the path to the house and their next challenge.

chapter 43

S id had soared as high in the sky as he could. The higher you got, the further you could see, and he was looking for water. He knew it wouldn't be seawater because all the seagulls round here were for all intents and purposes land seagulls so really, they were called gulls. Sid was the same; he could find all he wanted to eat locally without flying too far but when every gull has the same idea there are a lot of arguments. "Anyway," thought Sid surprising himself because he was now having independent thoughts, "I like being called a seagull. Sid the gull doesn't sound so good."

Sid was looking for the shimmer of water. There were lots of parks, but he knew no self-respecting beaver would live in a park. He would be in big trouble with the humans as soon as he cut the first tree down. "I don't know how they do that," said Sid. "If I tried to cut down a tree my beak would break off!"

Sid swung instinctively to the east. He knew the land disappeared the other way as that's where lots of humans lived and the air was smoky and smelly and there were no trees in great quantities or running water.

Sid unfortunately suffered with what most seagulls did: a bad memory. There was simply no reason to remember what he did yesterday or for that matter what he did ten minutes ago. After all, he was going to do the same thing tomorrow, so why remember today?! Now of course he had a different opinion because he had made this new friend and without knowing it, it had changed his outlook on life. He would love to discuss it with his fellow seagulls but unfortunately, he knew now they would forget what he had said just ten minutes later.

He swung lower as he approached a large expanse of water. It was a river with a pool or pond near the highest point. Then he saw what he was looking for: several trees had been cut down and were lying across the river creating a small dam.

Sid swooped lower. He knew he was on the right track now. In the middle of this small pond was a small house made of wood. Sid remembered just enough about life's experiences to know that's where beavers lived and to stay away from them. Putting caution to the wind he swooped in low and landed on the bank.

He landed with a flamboyant whoosh and his big wings caused the leaves on the ground to fly everywhere. Unfortunately his chosen landing spot was very close to a pretty white dove that was standing very quietly next to the bank enjoying the sunshine. "Be careful please," said the dove, who had been blasted by his downdraft on landing, "there are others here you know."

"It's mine," answered Sid reverting to his old self without thinking and instantly regretting it. The dove just turned away. "My sincere apologies," said Sid, "I don't know what I was thinking. I'm just in a hurry to find my friend. Can you forgive me?" The dove nearly fell over with shock; a Seagull with manners was simply unheard of.

"Of course, I can," said the dove getting over her surprise. "Is your friend from around here?"

"I don't really know," said Sid, and then said nothing else.

"Oh, I see," said the dove, beginning to realise that having a conversation with this seagull was going to be almost impossible. "It unlikely he's here," she continued, "as all the animals have left the wood because it's too dangerous."

"He became my friend by accident," continued Sid suddenly as if the dove had said nothing so the dove assumed he hadn't heard what she was saying, "and we had some great conversations and then I went off to be a normal seagull again without realising that I couldn't any longer. All the other seagulls just want to talk about the same thing every day so when I overheard a seagull talking to another one about being told off by a beaver for knocking over his wood I wasn't really interested, but when the beaver said 'the only other creature allowed to touch my wood is Chad' I asked where they had been but they couldn't remember so I thought I would go looking myself, you know. Beavers, water, seemed a good idea at the time."

The dove had turned to speak to Sid with a big smile on her face when out of the woods appeared a fox. Sid instantly spread his wings to take flight, but much to his surprise the dove walked over to the fox and said, "Hello Freddie. How's your friend today? I haven't seen him out at all."

Sid was confused. Firstly, doves couldn't be friends with foxes, could they? And secondly, he was sure beavers couldn't be friends with foxes, or could they? Today was becoming very confusing! He had to be careful or he would forget what he was doing here in the first place.

The dove turned back to Sid. "Your friend," she asked, "what is he?"

"He is a very good friend and I miss him a lot."

"No," said the dove patiently, "not what is he to you, what creature is he?"

"Oh that, well a mouse of course," said Sid, very pleased with himself because he was now having conversations all over the place.

The dove and fox turned to look at one another. The dove then said, "Well, we think you may have come to the right place."

"What was your friend's name?" asked the fox, who until now had said nothing to Sid directly. Sid lowered his wings a little reluctantly because keeping them on standby for flight was an effort and they were starting to ache. "His name was Chad," said Sid proudly, "my first real friend!"

"Well, well," said Freddie. "I will fetch Beaver and he might be able to help" and much to Sid's surprise Freddie dived into the water and disappeared.

chapter 44

Ant and Blanket finally came out of the woods directly opposite the old house. All they had to do was cross the road and they were there. They looked around and there were no humans to be seen. They had discussed this just before they arrived. Blanket had explained that a dog called Slippers lived there as well as three mice who lived under the floor. "You'll see Slippers," he said, "but I am pretty sure the mice won't be around. To get in you will have to climb through the cat flap — it's always open, that's how I come and go."

They crossed the road together and stopped outside the front door ready to climb through the cat flap. The front door moved slightly and stopped. Then a small breeze suddenly came from nowhere and the front door slowly opened by itself.

It was hard to see who was more surprised Blanket and Ant, or Slippers and the mice.

Slippers, Christopher, Mot and Fidgit backed away from the door and it creaked slightly as a sudden small gust of wind blew it open completely and there, standing outside the door, was Blanket and a large ant. At first no one said anything. Then Slippers spoke. "Hello Blanket, this is a surprise. Who's this?" he said, nodding in Ant's direction.

"He has been helping me," said Blanket, "in fact he saved my life so now I'm going to go with him to find his missing friend, a mouse." Ant said nothing and neither did the mice.

Blanket continued, "I have come to make my peace with you, Christopher, and your sisters, and with your mother and father were they here. I am going with this ant to find his friend. I wish you luck with finding your father and I am sorry when you asked for my help, I didn't give it."

Ant spoke for the first time which made the mice and even Slippers jump because they had never heard an ant speak before. "It is nice to meet you all. Might I ask, what are your mother's and father's names?"

"Henrietta and Chad," replied Mot.

Ant sat down with a bump. "I don't believe it!" he exclaimed.

"Why?" said Christopher defensively. "That's their names."

"No, you misunderstand me," said Ant. "The last time I saw your father they were rolling down a hill on a roller skate, and now he has a family. So where are they?"

"We don't know," said Mot, "they used to come and go but we believe that they got involved with something called 'worm holes' and we are just about to set off and find them if of course we can."

"Then if we may Blanket and I would like to join forces with you, because what we were about to do required more help which I was about to seek from Chad's old friends that he met before he came here. But I must warn you, I believe it will be very dangerous and we may not come back alive."

Blanket's mouth had fallen open when Ant had just confirmed that his long lost friend was in fact Chad. "Are you saying," said Blanket when he finally recovered from the shock, "that Chad is the mouse that is your long lost friend?"

"Yes," said Ant, "incredible though it may seem, he is."

"Wow!" said Slippers. "Heavy. Outstanding."

Mot smiled. "Good speech Mr Ant. I believe I can speak for all of us when I say count us in!"

"Thank you," said Ant, "but please just call me Ant."

It was now midday and much warmer. Slippers pulled the front door shut and if anybody had been around, they would have seen a highly unusual sight of three mice, a very large ant, a dog and a cat all abreast, heading towards the wood as one.

chapter 45

C had and Henrietta were very warm, perhaps hot was a better description. After weeks of searching for the worm hole that they believed was somehow killing the creatures in the wood they were finally in the right place at the right time, but now in the wrong place at the wrong time even though it was by intent. They had said goodnight to their children without realising that it was highly unlikely they would see them again.

Chad, pondering on his predicament, thought about how it came to be while Henrietta slept restlessly.

When Chad first encountered rumours of the worm hole that all the animals in the wood persistently talked about, the woods were alive with life and although Chad was friendly to everyone he went out of his way to behave as a normal mouse. He had a family to look after and food was his main concern.

So, on each trip he would bump into various animals who in turn would tell him various versions of what they had heard about the worm hole.

"I heard it's full of worms," said one badger knowledgeably, "that's where they all live and come from."

"Really?" said Chad politely, because only the day before a Squirrel in the same vicinity had told him it was a trap to catch worms and rid the forest of worms forever.

Chad knew well enough to not even think of questioning the reasoning behind the rumours because, of course, like all rumours they were usually based on speculation and hearsay. Add in a little exaggeration and some embellishment and a story started on one side of the wood was nothing like its origins when it finally arrived at the other side of the wood having been passed on from creature to creature with each adding their own little bit to the story.

In fact, on two occasions Chad bumped into the same animals days later and, forgetting they had already met him before, they told him the same story with a different conclusion. Chad would nod his head as if in agreement, make his excuses and carry on with his day.

So each time he met an animal he would politely listen, make no comment for or against, and move on. However, the only thing they did seem to agree on was that it appeared apparently from nowhere, was round and brilliantly white. Now logic decreed from Chad's point of view that a full moon on a foggy night would cause the same illusion, but that had been happening for years so why had the animals started to call it a worm hole? What interested Chad was where the name came from rather than the so-called worm hole itself.

Henrietta, the love of his life, had recently given birth to their third child, a boy, which had pleased Chad greatly. He had two lovely daughters, but a son had completed their family. They now lived under the floor of a house where they had escaped to after their tree home was hit by lightning.

None of the children showed any signs of the powers that he and Henrietta were suddenly capable of, nor did they show any adverse effects from the lightning when they were in the tree — which Chad of course was very pleased about. Their son was now old enough to be left with their sisters, so Henrietta was due to join him on his nightly forages for food to feed their family.

When he first moved into the house there was food everywhere. It fell through the floor on a daily basis, but something changed and the food suddenly stopped because the house had changed hands. Chad made another friend call Slippers and remembered his first enemy called Blanket.

Slippers would see him go and come each night and morning and sometimes they would chat about Chad's past adventures, but he would never talk about his powers. Slippers had seen them only once when Blanket tried to kill him, but since then he had had no reason to use them and he didn't talk about Henrietta's powers, so Slippers assumed she didn't have any, but he did hope one day to meet her and the rest of his family.

Then, one evening Chad was searching for seeds when a section of the wood ahead of him was suddenly brightly lit. Chad knew immediately this was no full moon and for the first time he was close to the "worm hole" that everyone had been talking about. He set off towards the light. It grew gradually dimmer as he approached, but before he could get close enough to see anything, it was gone.

Chad's night sight was perfect so even when the bright light in the wood had disappeared, he could see perfectly and just ahead of him was a small green glow. It appeared in the distance through the branches of the trees as a mound.

Chad came out into a small clearing and there before him was a small pile of dead animals. They were all sickly looking and some had lost their hair. There was a squirrel, a badger, a fox and several types of bird. Some had wounds on them as if they had been fighting or beaten. The wood was unnaturally quiet, and Chad remembered he had seen this green glow before.

Ant his long-lost friend who had died under the truck wheels had glowed the same way – as did he from riding on Ant's back. But after a few weeks it had faded away so there was no connection there!

Chad headed home with what little food he had collected, full of concern that something bad was happening in the wood. He needed to discuss it with Henrietta. It didn't affect them at all, but he had a feeling very soon it would.

He climbed in through the cat flap. As Chad had returned very early, Slippers was still asleep, which Chad was pleased about for today he was in no mood to talk. He entered his home through the usual small knot hole in the skirting and went straight to his room and woke Henrietta.

They discussed it in some detail for several hours and Henrietta said from now on he would not go out alone. As they had planned to go out together, Chad couldn't argue. They told the children of their plans and as they never saw their parents in the evening there was no concern so that night they left together.

Although they were going out together on the pretext of getting food for the family which was a necessity, they both knew they were now on a mission to seek out the source of the worm holes, what was killing the animals, and why. As they left that evening Henrietta met Slippers for the first time. Slippers turned all sloppy and shy and both Chad and Henrietta laughed a lot, which lightened their mood, and then together they set off into the night.

If they thought their search would be short, they were mistaken. Night after night they worked their way through the woods, occasionally finding a living creature, but now the fear of death had spread and instead of theories of worm holes they refused to discuss the subject at all. In fact, Chad and Henrietta now found more animals dead than alive.

Chad and Henrietta sat together for warmth. It was a cool clear night and the wood was completely silent. They were tired; they had traversed the wood from one end to the other every night for weeks. They knew that if they did not find the source of the worm hole soon they there would not be a single creature left in the wood and whatever was killing them would not stop, which meant their family would soon be at risk.

On the same token – and they had discussed this at great length between themselves – although they had hidden strengths, they simply did not know if those alone were enough to defeat whatever was out there.

"Chad," said Henrietta quietly, "there is nothing more we can do is there?"

Chad was silent for a moment. "No, Hen, you're right. There is nothing we can do but keep searching, but we can't just give up."

Henrietta put her hands together in despair and hung her head. "Show yourself. Now! Now! Now!" she thought.

Chad sat up. He had heard something like a pop and crackle and then right in front of them a single spot of white light appeared no bigger than a tennis ball. It hovered just above the ground. Chad could not believe what he was seeing, finally! Henrietta had not moved. She was staring at the ground. He nudged her once and she didn't respond so he nudged her again. She sat up and, in that instant, the ball of light vanished.

"What?" said Henrietta wearily.

"Did you not see that?" asked Chad.

"See what?" she replied.

"A ball of light appeared. It just hung in the air a moment and then it was gone."

"Really," said Henrietta, "I think we are tired and you were wishing and willing yourself to see something."

"Hen, I saw it, but it was small like it was only just formed, and then it was gone." They sat in silence for a moment.

"That's what I was doing," said Henrietta.

"What?" said Chad.

"Wishing," she replied.

"Wishing for what?" he said.

Henrietta sat bolt upright. "The worm hole, I was wishing that it would appear now."

"Really? said Chad, "so now you think you can summon worm holes?"

"Actually, Chad, I think I can," and with that she put her hands together and said "worm hole appear now." They sat in silence and absolutely nothing happened. Chad, realising that Henrietta was deadly serious, said "Hen, try to think what exactly you thought."

Henrietta put her hands together again, thought a moment,

and said out loud "Worm hole appear now." As soon as she said it she knew it was wrong. "No, that's not it, oh! What was it? Wait! Show yourself now! Now! Now!"

Chad laughed.

"It's not funny, you know, it's serious."

"Sorry Hen," said Chad, and then there was a pop and crackle and right in front of Henrietta the white hole reappeared.

Chad's mouth fell open with shock. Henrietta got up and walked over to the small round ball of light that somehow, she knew she had conjured up. She walked right around it. "You can't see it from the back, it's like it's not there," she said.

Chad had stood up. Henrietta reached forward to touch it. "Careful, Hen," said Chad. As she moved her hands outwards to touch it, the white ball grew in size. Henrietta stopped and so did the ball. "I can control it Chad," she said. He had watched in silence. "You're right," he said, "you can. You have somehow created your own worm hole." She moved her hands again and spread them wide. The white hole grew until they could see into it. It extended forever and inside looked like a long tube or tunnel. It crackled and hummed quietly. Henrietta moved her hands from left to right and the hole obediently followed her movements.

"This is amazing," said Henrietta who now was enjoying herself. Suddenly there was a crack and a pop, and less than ten feet away another white hole began to appear. Henrietta dropped her hand and instantly the white hole she had created disappeared. They quickly scurried up a mound and hid on the other side to watch as the worm hole they had searched for for so long appeared in front of them. It expanded until it was about a foot in diameter and then out of the hole came several ants. They hopped onto the ground and looked around as if seeking something. "I think they are looking for us," whispered Chad into Henrietta's ear and she nodded silently. The ants looked around and came to where Henrietta's own worm hole had been. "No, they are looking for your worm hole — they know somehow?" The ants wandered around aimlessly for a while and then returned to their worm hole. Almost as soon as they entered it, it disappeared and the wood was plunged back into darkness. "Come on," said Chad, "let's get out of here. We have lots to talk about."

Chad and Henrietta made it back to the house well before the sun rose. Slippers was still asleep and today they did not disturb him. It had been a tiring few weeks for them both, but finally they felt they had achieved something. Although very tired they had no wish to sleep so once in their room they sat down to plan. "They knew we had made our own worm hole," said Henrietta, before Chad could say a word, "and something sent the ants to investigate."

"True," said Chad, "but making our own worm hole doesn't really help us. We need to go through theirs to find out what's happening at the other end."

"True," said Henrietta. "I think we need to go through our worm hole to see what's at the other end and maybe that will help us decide what to do." Chad was silent for a moment. "What if we can't get back?" he asked.

"I will just make another one. How hard can it be?" and she laughed.

"I wish Ant was still alive. If he was here, he would know how to distract the ants," said Chad.

chapter 46

Ant took the lead with Blanket as between them they knew the wood very well. Slippers followed on behind with the mice who had all hitched a ride on Slippers' back. Slippers had wanted to go first such was his enthusiasm for "the mission", but Ant had explained that he and Blanket knew the woods better than he and were better suited to lead. Slippers hadn't really argued as he knew they were right.

They followed the paths used by people, ducking out of sight when they heard any oncoming bicycles. The bicycles were hard to hear when they came — they moved very fast and invariably were upon them before they had a chance to hide, but fortunately the riders were so preoccupied with their machines and where they were going that in most cases they didn't even give them a second glance.

"Where are we going?" said Christopher to Ant on the second day, having spent the night in the wood nestled under Slippers with his sisters while Ant and Blanket took turns on guard duty. They need not have worried as any predators that once lived there were long gone. Or at least the ones that had lived there were!

"Your father once told me that he made friends with a beaver who lived by a pond connected to a small stream and he said if he ever needed help to go to him so that's where we are going. Maybe, just maybe, he has been there."

Blanket was a great help. He was of course bigger than Ant and so some of the shortcuts Ant wanted to take were fine for an ant but no good for a dog as big as Slippers. They were now off the footpaths and picking their way through the bush when Ant said, "I think we will have to stop soon, it's beginning to get dark, but I think we will get there by tomorrow. What do you think Blanket?"

Blanket had hardly said a word since they started because he was so pleased to be part of what they were trying to do he didn't want to spoil it by saying something stupid about the past. "Oh! I think you're right," he said, "we should be by the pond by tomorrow morning."

Once again they settled down for the night in a small clearing. It had just got dark when Fidgit heard something. "Slippers," she whispered, "there's something in the wood." Slippers sat up, waking Christopher and Mot as he did so.

"What's up?" said Mot. Before Fidgit could answer there was a distant pop and a crackle, and a white light appeared through the trees. It quivered and pulsed for a minute or so and then it was gone.

"Where are Ant and Blanket?" whispered Slippers looking around. They all looked around; there was no sign of them. They heard movement from the direction of the light. They knew the wood was dead, so this could only mean trouble. Slippers sniffed the air, but the wind was blowing the wrong way, so he couldn't smell what was coming.

"Maybe they got Ant and Blanket and now they are coming for us," Mot said. She heard Slippers growl slightly and they all tensed ready for a fight.

And then Ant and Blanket slipped into the clearing they were in.

"Where have you been?" said Slippers, "did you see the light?" Before Ant could answer, Blanket said "We have seen the worm hole." Ant said nothing.

"And?" said Mot. Blanket looked at Ant and then Ant spoke. "It is the first time I have seen it. Blanket has seen one before. It opened up almost in front of us then a lot of ants came out followed by bigger ones carrying dead animals." Mot took a sharp intake of breath and covered her mouth with her hands. "They were very thin and glowing green. They looked like they had been beaten and starved to death. And then they climbed back into the hole and it just vanished into thin air." Ant just stopped talking. He said no more and looked down at the ground.

Blanket looked at him. "Go on Ant; tell them what you told me."

Ant looked up. "Well you know I glow green in the dark."

"Yes," they all nodded, giving Ant their undivided attention.

"They were glowing green too – the ants I mean – but unlike me they can't speak so they communicate by smell or small sounds to pass on information or orders and to give warnings." Ant paused for a moment.

The others sat patiently waiting for him to continue. "Well as you know I am an ant," he smiled weakly, "and therefore I could communicate with them if I had wished."

"Had?" said Mot.

"Yes, I said had because as soon as they arrived I sensed total fear. You have to understand, ants aren't afraid of anything. They will fight to the death to defend their colony, but all of their conversations were about what He would do to them if they didn't do this right and what revenge He would take on all of them if they did not obey."

"I don't understand," said Christopher, "why does this matter?"

"You have to understand how colonies work, Christopher. The colony has a queen; without her the colony would not exist, she creates all of us in different forms – work ants, nursing ants for the young and so on, but everything revolves around a queen. But these ants are afraid for themselves because of a Him! There are no Kings in ant life. I was born different and as far as I know I am the only ant that can speak, but when my own colony was hit by something they all left with the queen and I and a few others stayed until there was only one other and me. We worked together for a while and grew much bigger – something I believe to do with the green ball that hit our nest, and then the other ant disappeared one day. I searched for him and didn't find him so I presumed he died."

"Presumed?" said Mot, picking up on what this meant.

"Exactly," continued Ant, "presumed! The creature behind all this death is I believe an ant. For what purpose I don't know, but worse I believe this ant is my long lost brother who is just like me but can't speak and by now he may be even bigger."

There was abject silence. "I guess this is not good then?" said Slippers.

"No," said Ant. "Not good. I am now sure that these ants have been taking the animals to do something for their "king", my brother, and your parents have been taken too. To find them and save them we will have to follow the ants into the worm hole."

"Then we have to find the others for help as soon as possible," said Christopher, "or we might be too late. Let's get going." So they set off again, but there was an unhappy silence among the children. They were all thinking reluctantly that they may already be too late, and they may never see their parents alive again.

chapter 47

C had and Henrietta had discussed their plan in depth and decided no one including Slippers was to know what they were about to attempt. Saying goodnight to their children as they went to bed was a little more emotional for Henrietta than normal. Mot felt it and didn't know why, Fidgit didn't, and Christopher was a boy anyway and didn't like being hugged.

They set off at their usual time and travelled as far away from the house as they could. They thought they knew that somehow from the moment the worm hole was created the ants would come to investigate. Hence they travelled the greatest distance from their home they could. However, this theory would turn out to be completely wrong.

During their planning they still didn't know if there were some magic words or if it was purely how hard and what Henrietta thought that made the whole thing work and as Chad had pointed out "it's not the kind of thing you can practice in your bedroom." They had both laughed about that.

They travelled for several hours and arrived at a clearing. Chad had no idea how long they would be gone but the plan was to go, see and return, and then plan again. But Chad knew from experience which Henrietta had not yet had that things almost never go to plan.

Henrietta sat on a log and composed herself. She had thought long and hard about how this worked and was of the opinion that there were no magic words. It had to be about her and what she thought, so bearing that in mind she had to choose her words carefully. She placed her hands together unsure if this was a requirement, but as she had only done this once before it was too early to try too many variations on the method, because if it didn't work how would she know which bit was wrong? "I wish to go to they who can answer why this all began."

Henrietta looked up. At first nothing happened. Chad looked around expectantly and felt the stirrings of disappointment, and then the familiar pop and crackle and the brilliant ball of light appeared obediently in front of her. It took all her self-control to contain her excitement. She expanded her hands as she did before, and the ball increased in size and the endless tunnel became visible.

"Time for testing," she thought, without moving her hands. She told the ball to move closer to the ground and once again it obediently obeyed. "Well let's see," she thought and lowered her arms to her sides. The ball remained exactly where she had positioned it flickering and pulsing with the same hum as before.

"Hen, it's now or never," said Chad. He reached over and grabbed her hand and then they both stepped into the hole.

As journeys go it was all a little disappointing. They had both discussed at great length what it might be like, but in any event it was over before it began. They arrived at the other end in less than a blink of an eye and the hole extinguished itself behind them. They looked each other up and down. Nothing appeared to be missing and they were none the worse for wear for the journey.

They found themselves in a large, long cave that was lit here and there by candles hanging on the walls which were made up of layers of rock ranging in colour from dark brown to bright yellow. It was obvious the cave was very old. "What did you think for?" asked Chad.

"I thought 'I wish to go to they who can answer why this all began'," she answered, a little puzzled by the outcome.

The cave curved to the right so, letting go of Chad's hand, she set off down the tunnel. She did not have to go far because almost as quickly as it started it finished. It widened out towards the end and there was a small counter with a sign above it which said "The Library" and just below that a small bell with a cord on it which said "Please Ring". Behind the counter were rows and rows of books all neatly stacked next to one another. To the left and right were more candles which made it much brighter. And right at the end was a four-wheeled cart with yet more books in it.

Chad and Henrietta looked at one another. Chad shrugged. "So ring the bell," he said, which she promptly did. Before the sound of the bell had finished echoing around the cave there was a thump and a crash and then the sound of muttering from around the corner of the desk. A flickering shadow fell across the books at the back of the counter. Chad and Henrietta backed up a bit in preparation for what was coming, and then two paws and a head appeared over the counter. It was a very old weasel. All his hair was grey, and he was wearing a very small pair of spectacles. "Yes, my lord," he announced with as much graciousness as he could muster.

The glasses he was wearing obviously weren't working very well because whoever he was expecting wasn't there. The weasel wasn't particularly tall and neither was the counter, but the mice weren't particularly big either. "Hello," said Henrietta. The weasel jumped back in shock and then lent over the counter.

"Well this is a very welcome surprise, a very welcome surprise indeed. I knew it would happen one day, well hoped actually, oh yes, oh yes, oh yes," the weasel could hardly contain his excitement as he hopped from one back leg to the other.

"Come in," said the weasel, lifting a flap in the counter and unlocking the little door underneath and pulling it open which was pretty pointless as there was more than enough room for two small mice to go underneath but they both politely said nothing. Chad and Henrietta hesitated, "Come on," said the weasel, "if he comes and finds you here it will all be over."

They stepped through the little door and the weasel quickly closed it back up again. "Follow me. Come, come." The weasel's haste was infectious, so they followed him quickly round behind the counter through another small door and into a large round cave.

Whatever Chad and Henrietta had expected to see when they entered the room what they saw was not it! Whatever you could think of was in there; yet more books, chairs and tables of all sizes, some beds and pillows and sofas and yet more books. "Please sit down," said the weasel, pulling out two small chairs for them to sit on and knocking a ladder over in the process.

"Thank you," said Chad. "Do you live here?" he said, looking around the cave and seeing there were no doors or windows or any form of opening anywhere apart from the way they came in.

"Yes, I live here," said the weasel. "This is my prison cell."

"I don't understand," said Henrietta, "you're in prison here?"

"Well please sit down and I will explain. I have been waiting so long for someone to come; you must of course have come by portal?"

"No," said Chad, "we came by worm hole." He was about to continue explaining when Henrietta nudged him in the ribs and nodded her head just once.

"Ah," said the weasel, "same thing really, I was just talking about the entrance and exit."

"You seem to know a lot about these things," said Henrietta guardedly.

"Well, er, yes," replied the weasel hesitantly, "I have studied much as did my twin brother and we created our first portal not long ago. Unfortunately if I had known all the trouble and grief that would befall everyone and myself, I would have left the ideas in my head."

"Is that how you got here?" said Chad.

"No," said the weasel. "There used to be an entrance but one of the earthquakes we have these days from time to time completely closed it up. This cave is at the bottom of a mountain. There is no way in or out except by the means you used, though I am curious as to how you came to find me."

Chad went to speak again, and Henrietta glared at him. "I will happily tell you about us, but first I need to know how you came to be here. What have you done to be locked in a cave forever?"

"Of course," said the weasel, "it's a pleasure to talk to someone other than myself. There are some chairs over there that suit your size, please help yourselves." With that he pulled up his own chair and began.

chapter 48

"**A**s I explained before my brother and I are twins. He was the practical one and I was the scientist. Well, sort of anyway. I had worked for many years studying the theory of travelling through two points in a universe. There are books here you can read if you wish, I have plenty to spare. So, the point is we finally succeeded in creating the first portal to another place. What we imagined was traveling to different places to gain new knowledge – at least I did – never considering rather foolishly that if we can go one way something can go the other.

"We were a small community of creatures and a large community of insects, mostly ants, and to the best of my knowledge certainly in my rather long lifetime we all lived in harmony.

"That, though, is where the similarities between where you come from and here finish. Your home is, I believe, full of lush green and is cool and a stable climate. You have plenty of clean fresh water and what volcanic activity you have is localised. You have safe minerals and unsafe minerals but none that are in sufficient quantities to make them life threatening. Is that a good brief description of your home?" said the weasel, leaning forward a little and looking at them over the top of his spectacles.

"Yes," said Chad, "I think so, apart from the bit about volcanic activity and minerals. We don't know what they are," he said, looking at Henrietta who confirmed what he had said with a nod.

"Ah, I see," said the weasel. "Well when you leave you can take some books with you. I have no wish to offend you, but I assume you both can read?"

Chad and Henrietta both laughed shyly. "Yes," said Chad, "we can both read."

"So, as I was saying," said the weasel regathering his thoughts, "unfortunately our home is nothing like that. We have water, but it is not very fresh, and it comes from a lake up in the mountains we think. Whatever greenery we had died a long time ago because of the heat and eruptions. Most of the trees still stand to this day but appear to have died. The volcanic activity over a very long period of time had brought radioactive materials to the surface which almost wiped out life although the insects were unaffected. Eventually creatures like me evolved enough to tolerate the normal harmful effects, but we are outnumbered by billions and billions of insects, so it is just as well we live in harmony. Well, we did anyway."

Chad and Henrietta sat in silence in awe of the weasel as he spoke to them eloquently and calmly as if they were guests in his home unaware of the fact he was a prisoner.

"The first portal was finally created using the machine we found in this very cave, we used the radioactive materials that had originally been spewed out from the volcanos and, combined with the vast amounts of electricity we needed again from the volcanos, we managed to get the machine to work. It was only open very briefly but after years of work we had also hoped that we might be able to bring back something to improve our environment.

"I have to be honest we could not have done it without the ants. My brother developed a simple way to communicate with them with small sounds. I don't know why they were willing to help, but they just did. Perhaps they too knew we would not survive much longer with our present environment.

"So, overjoyed with our success we created a second portal and left it open ready to use and that's when everything started to go wrong. Not long after we had opened it the portal started to fluctuate and expand. I must admit I thought it was all over and I had made a huge mistake and it was going to explode. The only way to shut it down was to move the two minerals we had found apart, but it was now impossible to get to the device I had reactivated as it had begun to meld into the rock face where it still remains today."

The weasel was silent for a long moment just staring at the cave floor. Chad and Henrietta looked at each other and shrugged. The weasel looked up suddenly. "I'm sorry," he said, "just remembering what terrible mistakes I have made. Anyway," he said, resuming his story, "it continued to expand and then out of the portal appeared a huge ant." This time Chad and Henrietta look at each other with concern "you think it was him?" whispered Henrietta. Chad looked shocked and confused and looked away.

Almost the moment the big ant appeared and stepped out of the portal the ants that had helped us for so long just stood still. More and more poured out of everywhere and in the blink of an eye he had taken control and, worse still, he communicated directly with my brother.

"Why worse still?" said Chad, recovering from the shock of hearing that Ant was still alive.

"Because," said the weasel, "we learnt to our cost that although he couldn't speak he could read our minds, so when he asked my brother about the portal he realised this big ant could be a threat and lied about everything."

The weasel went very quiet for a moment, Chad and Henrietta waited patiently. "I have never seen such rage in an insect before. From quiet enquiry the ant exploded into rage, he tore across the gorge we were in at the bottom of the valley, throwing ants aside without concern. Some died of their injuries. He grabbed my brother by the throat and squeezed so hard my brother could not breathe. I was powerless against this brute strength – all I could do was watch in horror as my brother began to die in front of me. And then he dropped him onto the stone floor barely breathing and he turned to look at me. I wanted to run away but my back was against the gorge wall. He came closer and craned down so his head was directly in front of mine. I could feel the evil coming from his eyes and the total hatred he felt towards me. I was sure I was going to die.

"And then my brother got up and said something I didn't understand. The ant turned away swiftly. I am sure to this day my brother saved my life. They communicated for several minutes and then the ant turned away and resumed his place. The other ants moved swiftly out of his way."

Chad and Henrietta had sat in silence with the shock of it all, but there was still more to come.

The weasel looked them both in the eyes. "I have not been totally truthful to you both," he said, "and as it was lies that got me into this mess I think I had better be honest now."

Chad and Henrietta sat back and waited patiently for the next revelation.

chapter 49

It was going to take another day and a half to reach their destination. Several times during their journey Ant had stopped and waved his head in the air. He would turn to the others and say just one word, "Wait." He would then disappear into the depths of the woods for some time and then return. It did not take long for the children to learn why. He was looking for bodies but not just any – he was checking for their parents. But each time he returned he smiled weakly which was at least positive for them but not the creatures he had found.

The night before they reached where Ant believed Chad's friends might be, assuming of course they were still alive, Christopher brought up the subject that everyone had wanted to discuss but didn't.

"Ant," said Christopher, "have you had any thoughts of how we are going to find the worm hole if and when we find help?"

"Yes," said Ant quietly, but did not elaborate.

"Well?" said Christopher, a little irritated because Ant normally couldn't wait to discuss anything and everything.

"Bait," he replied. The others looked at each other and Slippers just shrugged.

"I don't understand," said Mot.

"But I do," said Blanket. At this Ant looked up. "Shall I tell them," said Blanket to Ant, or will you?

"You don't have to," said Christopher before either one could speak. "We may be our parents' children, but we are no longer children! It is obvious that whoever is taking the animals and why is a mystery," Ant went to interrupt. Christopher waved his paw, "I know, Ant, of your theory and you may be right, but the truth is all the animals have gone and the wood is dead. So very soon whoever is doing this will start to look elsewhere and we will never find the worm hole, let alone my parents assuming they are still alive." At this Fidgit winced and Mot said nothing.

It was a particularly cool evening and Christopher's words had made it feel much cooler. Without a word Mot began to gather some wood to make a fire and Christopher continued. "So, I am assuming Ant that we are all going to gather together in one place as "bait" and hope the ants looking for us turn up, correct?"

"Well almost," said Ant. "I will leave some messages around in the form of a scent as we ants do," he smiled briefly, "and because my brother and I were from the same colony they will follow the scent and find me. You and anyone else we have to help will hide and I will get them to lead me to the worm hole. Once there I will send them in the wrong direction, and we will have to enter it. It should close behind us because I have watched them leave before. When they return they will be stranded. There is one minor problem though: I have no idea what will be waiting for us at the other end and how we will get back."

Mot had finished collecting the wood while Ant was speaking and lit it, but no one noticed how she did it.

"Only a minor problem then you think?" said Slippers curiously.

"Well," said Ant, "maybe that's an understatement, but if you can think of another way I'd be happy to listen."

Nobody spoke or commented. They just turned away and settled down for the night knowing that tomorrow they would know if they were on their own or not.

Mot awoke with a start which was unusual and a shiver ran down her spine. She wasn't particularly cold, so she was puzzled as to what had woken her and caused it. It was early morning, but dawn had not yet arrived and there was no moon present, so the wood was pitch black. This, of course, was not a problem for her as she could see quite adequately in the dark. She looked around.

Everybody she could see was asleep. There was a faint red glow, but it was just the remains of the fire she had lit the evening before. She stood up. The wood was completely silent – it shouldn't have been but with the absence of life only the wind could now let it make noise, except? There was something? The well-trodden path they had used to get where they slept ran in two directions; one slightly downwards and one up. The sound had come from the upward direction and it was there that she thought she heard something move.

She looked around again. Everyone was there except Ant. Ant was nowhere to be seen; was he on guard duty? She didn't remember them discussing that the night before. For the first time since she was born that she could remember she decided to confront something rather than avoid it or run away. She slipped into her invisibility and set off up the path. When she first tried it was impossible – she was trying to move without treading on anything that might give her away, but she found that was difficult to do when you can't see your own feet or legs! The best way was to look straight ahead and stick to the path. Then she heard the movement again. It was some way ahead and sounded like a faint rustling.

She moved steadily forward and as she did the sound appeared to get louder, but now it felt like it was moving towards her rather than she was moving towards it. She paused a moment. The rustling stopped.

Mot was not afraid. She had her invisibility, but she also had something that no one else knew about that she had discovered by accident. Some time ago she didn't feel like joining their usual morning chat with Slippers so told Christopher and Fidgit she wanted to work on some chemistry experiments. This wasn't true really – she wanted to listen to a programme through the floor above her room as she often did about matter and antimatter which was completely confusing to her. While trying to fathom out what it was and being totally engrossed in listening to the programme she unclenched her right hand, and there, much to her surprise, floating in the air just above her palm was a tiny ball of light no bigger than a pea slowly turning in an anti-clockwise direction.

Her curiosity was aroused and without a second thought, she thought about antimatter and opened her left hand. Sure enough, there in her hand floating just above her palm was an identical ball of light but spinning in the opposite direction.

Now she had learnt enough about matter and antimatter to know they can't exist in the same space, but here they both were in the palms of her hands. So, to test her assumptions she tried to move her hands closer together. Almost immediately the little balls of light reacted frantically, they started to spin erratically and as they got closer together started to spit sparks of electricity and small balls of flame. Mot rapidly pulled them apart and they settled down again to their calm spinning behaviour. By thinking about them individually she could turn them on and off at will.

She realised now that any experimentation with these two matters would have to take place at more than arm's length if she was going to keep her arms, or at least her hands, so she threw the little spinning ball in her right hand as far as she thought was safe. It landed on the earth beneath the house's floor at the opposite end to where she and her sister had made their room, by the rear wall of the house. Then, eyeing up her aim, she threw the ball in her left hand at the other one.

She didn't remember much after that apart from watching the two balls collide. When the dust settled both balls were gone, she was covered in dust and there was a large crater in the earth beneath the floor. She made her excuses to her brother and sister and decided any further experimentation would have to wait until another time and place, preferably outside!

Unfortunately, that time and place had never come! And apart from lighting fires she hadn't practised at all. Now with hindsight having boldly gone out on her own perhaps she should have done so.

She had stood still for several minutes now and had heard no further movement, but instead within the wood to her right a white light had appeared behind the trees. She knew at once what it was so without thinking she left the path and plunged into the wood in the direction of the light. She wanted to see this worm hole for herself. Within minutes she realised her mistake. If indeed something was rounding up the animals and taking them away she had rather stupidly done their work for them because now the worm hole was in front of her and whatever had been in the wood was sure to be closing behind her. She came across another fork in the path which led in the same direction as she was going in. She quickly decided she had more chance on the path than in the bushes and she could move faster. She was running now and the white light was getting brighter by the minute. She burst out of the bushes onto a small hillock and skidded to a stop. There, almost in front of her, was a beautiful spinning ball of light and just in front of it several small ants with a much larger one in front of them. It appeared to be instructing them and then it turned to face her. She knew she couldn't be seen but it appeared to be looking at her and to her horror, she realised it was Ant! She gasped in shock and Ant tipped his head to one side. She was sure he had heard her. She covered her mouth with her hands and slowly backed away. All this time they had trusted him but he was the ant behind all this. There was no brother; he was the leader, he was the killer! She had to get back and warn the others. She turned and ran back down the track the way she had come, past the fork where she joined it, running as fast as she could. She was sure Ant would come after her, but as she ran she heard the rustling she had heard before coming towards her. With no choice she ran towards it and as she rounded a corner in the path there in front of her was an open piece of land and the source of the rustling became clear: hundreds and hundreds of ants filled the area all moving towards her. She came to an abrupt stop, realising that she was hopelessly outnumbered and would soon be surrounded. Now was the time to fight.

Chapter 50

The weasel had sat in silence staring at the floor for some time until Henrietta decided to prompt him. "Lies, what lies?" she said, no longer in awe of him.

The weasel looked up very aware of the change in Henrietta's tone, Chad looked at her a little shocked.

"Well firstly," continued the weasel, "I am not a scientist. Everything I know about portals or worm holes as you call them, I gleaned from these books. As I already explained the very thing that we used to recreate them I found in this cave."

"Recreate?" said Henrietta questioningly.

"Yes, recreate. The previous civilisation long before me discovered and created the machine that destroyed our environment and most of their own civilisation. All of what you see here my brother and I discovered by accident. This mountain used to have a wide path right around it. Then one day my brother and I, long after our parents were gone, felt the ground shake which it does almost every day but this time it was particularly violent, and the entire path collapsed into the chasm below and we fled for our lives. When the dust had settled, which took several days, curiosity of course brought us back and now we found running around the mountain a small path that must have existed before but had been buried. But more exciting was a cave entrance had opened up which also must have been buried and sealed at the same time.

"The ants continued their daily lives as if nothing had happened even though many of them had died in the earthquake. We on the other hand couldn't wait to explore and what you see now is largely what we found except for the machine which we moved outside. We got it to work and then the ant arrived. He took over and forced me to work in here because the worm hole only goes to the same area every time: your wood, and the ant wants to expand his domain — he calls himself King Ty Rant. I have been forced to stay in here to keep my brother alive to try and find a way to alter how it works but I do not understand enough and then a second violent earthquake sealed the tunnel and so unfortunately, I will be trapped in here until I die."

"That's very sad," said Chad.

"Yes, it is" said Henrietta, nudging Chad in the ribs again, "but we have to leave. I'm sorry we can't help you."

"So," said the weasel, "there is no chance I could travel with you then?"

"No," said Henrietta quickly before Chad could say anything, "we really don't understand how it works either. It is not big enough for you to travel through. But we could study the books and try to find a way."

"Good, it's settled then. Take what you need and please come back as often as you can, I have no idea how long the air will last although it's a very big cave and I do have water and some dried food."

Chad and Henrietta loaded up the cart with as many books that related to worm holes and portals that they could and the weasel gave them several journals that had been written about the disasters that had befallen the previous inhabitants of this land. "Is there anything else you would like to take?" said the weasel.

"Yes," said Henrietta without thinking. "Can we take the small bed and tables too?"

"Of course," said the weasel, "they are of no use to me. Would you like a hand to put them on top of the cart?"

"No thank you," said Chad without thinking and lifted the bed up on his own and placed it on top of the books.

"Let me open the counter for you," said the weasel, lifting up a second flap and opening a second small door in the front of the counter to make it wide enough for the cart to go through.

"Thank you," said Chad and pushed the fully loaded cart out through the gap without any effort at all.

"Well, have a safe journey," said the weasel, "can I watch you leave?"

"Not really," said Henrietta before Chad could say a word. "There is a very bright light and it could seriously hurt your eyes."

"Very well," said the weasel moving back towards where they had sat and talked before. "Oh," he said turning back slightly, "you never told me your names."

"Chad and Henrietta," said Chad before Henrietta could stop him.

"Nice names," said the weasel. "Have a safe journey, Chad and Henrietta, please come back soon I really could do with your help." With that the weasel turned and left.

"Come quickly Chad!" said Henrietta quietly. "Let's get out of here I know he's lying about something. Quickly, before he sees how we leave." With that Henrietta thought about home and their bedroom and the worm hole appeared. She expanded it enough to get the cart and the furniture in and Chad pushed it in. They jumped in after it and they were gone.

The weasel watched them go just as he had watched them arrive; he knew it was not the so-called King Ty Rant that he had woven into his story. He did exist of course, but the Ant – oh no! That he was not or so he thought! Neither Chad nor Henrietta had noticed the mirror high on the wall above the library counter. "So, it would seem I am not the only one who has been lying here," he said to himself.

chapter 51

The weasel came back from where he had been standing when the mice left. He walked around in front of the counter just to confirm that they were no longer there even though he had witnessed it with his own eyes.

He stared at the wall and thought, "Brother, are you there?"

"Yes brother, how are you?"

"Frustrated, what do you think?" he thought in reply. "How is the tunnel clearing?"

"Progressing slowly. We have cleared the larger boulders so now it is proceeding quicker but the animals we bring here do not live very long in our environment and the ants are finding it harder and harder to find more. The portal as you know only appears within one location and no other creatures are returning to the wood because they sense the fear. I could send more ants, but I don't think that would work as the portal could close before they come back. Plus—" his brother hesitated.

"Plus what?" said the weasel.

"Well some of the stronger creatures manage to escape up to the hills on the far side of the mountains. It's too far for the ants to seek out and bring them back and the Queen is being uncooperative in producing more soldiers. I think she has been told you are trapped inside the mountain."

"Don't worry," said the weasel to his brother. "I think I have another plan. You will need to send out what ants you have to find two mice who live in a house I think. Their names are Chad and Henrietta. I believe what they have will be able to solve all our problems. Concentrate on that and nothing else."

"And the digging?"

"Nothing else, was that not clear?!"

"Yes of course," replied his brother. "Consider it done."

"The queen I will deal with when I get out of here. But be warned brother, I have observed them and they are not normal mice so make sure when the ants find them they are prepared."

"Observed them when?"

"Just do as I say. All will become clear!"

"Very well, brother, very well." The weasel's brother broke contact or perhaps he should say his brother had broken contact with him. His headache returned worse than ever as it did every time his brother communicated in this way.

chapter 52

Mot was concerned. She knew what she was about to do would slaughter hundreds of ants and having never killed anything before it was a difficult decision to make. But she also knew what their sole purpose was and if she did not act, she in the end would be dead.

She raised her right hand and repeating exactly what she had done previously, she unclenched her hand. The little ball appeared just as before and cast a strange shadow around the wood and over the ants. They seemed unperturbed by the light or shadow. She then opened her left hand and more conflicting light and shadows appeared. Something about the appearance of the second ball of light must have changed something in the air that Mot could not sense, because the ants stopped moving and stood stock still.

Mot moved them together slightly as she had done before just to make sure they still worked, which of course they did, and then without further hesitation she threw the right hand ball towards the centre of the ants.

Much to Mot's surprise they moved amazingly quickly and moved apart before the ball landed, which technically it hadn't because it stopped just above the ground and floated there. Now at this stage Mot knew she could stop what she was planning to do, but as the ants had shown no indication they were planning to leave she took careful aim and threw the second ball at the first and covered her ears for the inevitable explosion and destruction.

Unfortunately, or fortunately from the ants' point of view, her entire plan was based on bringing the two balls together but it became quickly apparent that although her theory about the destructive force of bringing antimatter and matter together was correct, her lack of practice in throwing things meant that the second ball landed some 18 inches away from the first.

The ants again deftly parted company around the second ball as well as the first. Mot knew she was now in trouble. She could turn the balls of light on and off when they were in her hands but not when they had left. She also knew that while the balls of matter and antimatter still existed she couldn't make any more or at least she hadn't succeeded in doing so yet.

The ants began to move again in her direction and she started to back away. She inadvertently stepped off the path and backed into a tree realising that even if she climbed the tree the ants were more than capable of coming after her. She prepared to go down fighting.

Until this point the two balls of light had not moved at all, but Mot noticed the change in light as did the ants and they stopped moving. The two balls started slowly at first to spin around each other in a clockwise direction as if they were suspended on an invisible ring, they spun like two boxers sparring in a boxing ring sizing each other up. The ants had now turned to face the balls as they began to spin faster and faster. At first each spin could be followed but as the speed increased, they began to become a blur.

Mot heard the leaves move first towards the ever-accelerating light, and then the ground began to sink beneath them. She felt herself being pulled towards them, so she grabbed hold of the ivy on the tree to stop herself being pulled into the ever-increasing indentation in the ground that the balls were creating apparently in their quest to dominate one another.

The ants were less fortunate: they attempted to crawl away, but the force was too strong, and Mot watched in shock and awe as the ants started to slide into the hole in the ground that the balls had created and were slowly sinking into.

Her arms began to ache. The force was so strong now she was not sure if she could hold on much longer. Then there was a sudden large pop and a flash, the light was gone and the earth had returned to normal. The earth was bare in a wide circle around where the balls had been as every leaf, blade of grass and ant had disappeared.

The sudden disappearance caught her by surprise, and she bounced back to the tree on the ivy and dropped to the ground. She hadn't understood what had happened or why, but she knew Ant was right behind her so without hesitation she resumed her run back to where the others were subconsciously circumventing the hole in the ground where the balls of matter and the ants had disappeared.

It only took minutes to return to where she had been sleeping. She jumped behind the log and lay down with only minutes to spare, because Ant came rushing into the glade where they slept almost immediately after her.

He looked around. Mot knew what he was looking for, but no one was missing. Mot watched him in the dark with half-closed eyes. He stayed a few minutes and then left again. Much to her surprise, maybe because of exhaustion and having succeeded in escaping, she fell asleep.

When she awoke the others were awake already and Ant was there. She wondered who she could tell about what she knew and who would believe her.

Before she could decide what to do, Ant spoke: "Hello everyone, I have some news." The others turned to listen.

"Last night I found the worm hole and met the ants. They are returning in two days, but they cannot let me know exactly where because the worm hole never returns to the same place. They are still looking for animals to take and they think I am working with them."

"You are," thought Mot.

"So, the plan is to come back here with or without more help and then enter the worm hole." Mot could not believe what she was hearing. It was a perfect trap and everybody was falling for it. And then Ant continued. "I also thought I had some good news. I went to my old colony and managed to speak to my queen — she is aware of the problems in the wood and has lost a great deal of the colony's ants. She was very much aware of the rumours and has greatly increased the amount of soldier ants she is producing as queen ants can do to protect the colony. I have told her what we know and what we are attempting to do. She agreed to let me have 10,000 soldier ants to help us. I had brought them with me and they were going to travel with us, but last night I left them in a small clearing and I don't understand how, but they all disappeared." Mot let out an involuntary squeak and covered her mouth. "Something wrong Mot?" said Ant. Mot shook her head. She couldn't speak now she knew what she had done.

"Well that's it," said Ant, "there is no more to be said. We will reach the stream this morning." That said, he turned and headed off down the track.

Mot was the last to leave. Fidgit asked her "are you alright Mot?" She just nodded and said nothing. She had no one she could tell about this. She missed her parents sorely — they would have told her what to do to ease the pain she felt about killing all those ants that were there to help her and the others. How could she have known? But she still felt it was unforgivable.

chapter 53

C had and Henrietta arrived in their room in the blink of an eye. "I could get used to this," said Chad. Henrietta laughed, but the experience she had had with the weasel still played on her mind because it was all too easy, and she felt she had missed something. They sorted out the books and the furniture in no time and then started to read the journals. They were painful to read — they spanned several decades and recorded a dying society brought about by interfering in nature without fully understanding the repercussions of their actions. By the time they understood what they had created it was too late to reverse the damage. And then the journals stopped. Chad and Henrietta assumed it must have been because the cave had been closed off by the earthquake, but something just didn't feel right.

They both spent time going through the books about portals and read the journeys over several times again. But between them they still couldn't find what they felt was missing. Then one evening Chad said, "I can't see what you're looking for Hen, I'm sorry."

Henrietta sat up straight. "You're right," she said, "we can't see it because it's not here."

"Eh, sorry?" said Chad.

"The weasel gave us these journals, correct? But we chose the books. There is nothing missing about how this happened but there is about what happened." Chad looked at Henrietta a little puzzled. "There is another journal Chad and the weasel didn't give it to us for a reason; he's hiding something."

At first Chad said nothing and then, "Hen, on the subject of the weasel, are we going to leave him to die?"

"I know," said Henrietta, "we have to save him, but I can't help thinking he is behind all these problems in the wood."

"But why? What for? What is so important that you need animals from the wood and why are they dying?" said Chad.

"We have to go back Chad," Henrietta said suddenly. "We have to go back!"

"What, to save him?" said Chad.

"Yes and no," said Henrietta. "I believe the missing journal holds the secret of why this has come about and that the weasel if not behind it is part of it. We set off to find the worm holes and that we have done for all intent and purposes, but that's not enough. Now we have to go directly to the other end but through our worm hole not theirs, otherwise they will be expecting us perhaps?"

"Well," said Chad, "the one thing we are not sure about is everything!" And they both laughed.

chapter 54

As Ant had predicted they arrived at the brow of a hill overlooking the river and lake late in the morning. Ant stopped at the top and looked down. Unfortunately, since his last visit a section of the hill that used to lead down to the river had collapsed and taken the footpath with it. Although large, Ant would have no trouble climbing down and perhaps too the mice, but for Slippers it was too steep and definitely too wet and muddy for Blanket who, as most cats do, hated wet and muddy things.

Mot had lagged way behind the others as they all gathered at the brow of what was left of the hill. "We will have to go down the other path," said Ant nodding his head to the right, "that leads back into the wood. It's much longer, but it eventually comes out down there." He pointed down at the riverbank.

The mice had sat down either side of Ant with Slippers and Blanket either side of them. "It's very quiet down there," said Christopher, "are you sure we are in the right place?"

"Yes," said Ant, "see the lodge in the middle? It's where beavers live—"

"Or perhaps lived," said Blanket.

"I can see a seagull," said Fidgit.

"Yes," said Ant, "not a good sign. I'm sure if the beaver was there, he would chase him away. Come on; let's go down the other way. There is only one way to find out, but it looks like we wasted our time and will be going back alone."

They all turned away down the path still not noticing that Mot was not with them. Mot had looked up the path and seen them all at the top of the hill and seen them come away from the top and turn back into the forest. It was not until she got to the top that she understood why.

Sid stood on the edge of the riverbank waiting for Freddie to return, still getting over the surprise of Freddie's disappearance into the water! He was getting a little worried because, being a seagull he might just forget why he had come here. He looked over at the dove, but she was behind a tree preening herself. Just then, Sid saw movement on top of a cliff, which was once a hill, because Sid could see what was left of the footpath after it had for some reason collapsed. Much to his surprise a large ant appeared followed by two mice, a cat and a dog. Now seagulls have very good eyesight so, blinking several times to make sure he could really see them and wasn't imagining things, he turned to the dove and said, "I thought you said there were no animals in the wood?"

"There aren't," replied the dove.

"Oh! What's that then?" said Sid, nodding his head in the direction of the hill. The dove came out from behind the tree and of course Ant and the others had turned away and disappeared out of sight. "Where?" said the Dove.

"Er, they were on the hill," said Sid, now a little puzzled because perhaps he did imagine them being there after all. The dove went back behind the tree and continued preening herself. Sid looked up at the hill again and now there was a solitary mouse instead. "Enough of this," thought Sid, "I'm going to look for myself," and without warning he spread his wings and took off.

Mot had seen the seagull take off and was just about to turn away when she realised it was heading straight for her. She was on open ground and knew it would be difficult to escape. Since she had no wish to become a seagull's dinner, she instinctively balled her hand ready for a fight which she knew from her point of view, not the seagull's, was going to be very one-sided. But much to her surprise, instead of attacking her, the seagull landed right in front of her and said, "Hello, I'm Sid the seagull."

More than a little surprised by the arrival of the seagull and it not attacking her Mot said, "Hello, I'm Mot," still keeping her guard up.

"You're a mouse," said Sid.

"Yes," said Mot hesitantly. The last thing she had expected was for the seagull to start talking to her, but since he had stated the obvious she replied, "and you're a seagull."

For a moment Sid said nothing and Mot waited. "he noticed he had tipped his head to one side as if thinking, which of course he was, as having conversations was something very new to Sid and still took some thought.

"So, what can I do for you?" said Mot.

"Actually, I am looking for a mouse who I met around here – my first friend ever, we went flying together. I saw you and thought you might know where he lives."

Now Mot had heard of a story about her father flying with a seagull from Slippers and had always had her doubts about whether it was true, surely this couldn't be the same seagull, could it?

"Er, what was the mouse's name?" she said slowly.

"Chad, his name was Chad," replied Sid without a moment's hesitation and quite impressed with himself by his prompt response.

"I don't believe it!" said Mot.

"Why ever not?!" said Sid, quite offended.

"No, no you misunderstand me," said Mot, "it's just a saying meaning wow! I can't believe that's possible, but it is." Sid tipped his head from side to side as he usually did when he was thinking a lot.

"Why didn't you believe it?" said Sid, still trying to digest the complicated answer and Mot's explanation.

"Well," said Mot, "I am looking for Chad too."

"Why?" said Sid.

"Because he went missing with my mother. My brother and sister and I are trying to find them with the help of some friends."

"I don't believe it," said Sid.

"See?" said Mot, "I could get upset but I know you don't mean it." Sid burst out laughing and Mot joined in. "So, the dog, cat and Ant I saw at the top of the hill before are your friends?"

"Yes," said Mot, her sombre mood returning. "We are looking for all the help we can as all the animals have disappeared from the wood now including my parents, so we have got together to try and find them and rescue them, which is a bit difficult as we actually don't know where they are, but Ant has a theory."

"I see," said Sid, which of course wasn't entirely true as most of what Mot had said had gone over his head. He had only just managed to absorb the fact that Chad had a whole family the rest of whom he couldn't wait to meet.

Mot was staring down at the floor her previous mood returning because the death of the ants was on her mind again.

"What's wrong?" said Sid, sensing the sudden change.

"Well," said Mot, "I don't know who to tell but as you know my father I feel I can trust you." So she went on to tell him about her powers and how she had thought the ants were attacking her and they had disappeared down a hole she had created and now they were all dead. She finished her story with a small sob, as she was still feeling terribly sad.

Sid was silent for several moments, as he usually was when he had a lot to think about. "How do you know they are dead?" he said.

Mot looked up. "Because they all went swirling down the hole," she replied.

"Yes, but you didn't actually see them die, did you? So if they went down a hole they could theoretically come back up again!" Sid was very proud of himself. He had put a lot of thought into what he considered his most brilliant answer to a problem ever! Mot hesitated before she answered, and Sid nodded his head as if to say, 'well I'm right aren't I?'

"Well," said Mot, "if they are not dead, where are they?"

"You tell me," said Sid, sort of shrugging his shoulders even though he didn't have any, "you're the one with the powers."

"Well," said Mot, now warming to the theory. "If I created the hole—"

"If?" said Sid.

Mot smiled. "Well when I created the hole it was spinning in one direction, so I supposed if I recreated it to spin in the opposite direction they could come back."

"Sounds good to me," said Sid rather smugly as it was, after all, his idea.

"There's only one problem," said Mot.

"What's that?" said Sid.

"I don't know how."

"Oh," said Sid.

At that moment they heard a dog bark and they both looked down. Ant and the others had arrived at the edge of the wood not far from the river having found the other path.

"I am supposed to be with them," said Mot, "but I lagged behind."

"No problem," said Sid, "hop on my back and we'll fly down there."

"Really?" said Mot.

"Well yes," said Sid, "your father did when he was about your age – you just have to hang on tight to my feathers."

Mot smiled and with the prospect of flying for the first time needed no second invitation. She hopped onto Sid's back and as with her father before her she nearly fell off as Sid launched himself into the sky. They flew up high into the sky and Mot whispered into Sid's ear, "I want to try something." She had had a theory in her head about invisibility – whenever she tried it if she picked up something it too became invisible, but the question was, what were the limits of her power? So, hanging on to Sid as he climbed she chose to turn herself invisible. Within seconds she could see through herself and as she watched, Sid began to disappear in front of her. Now she realised the dangers. With Sid not visible she could not see where to hang on if she lost her grip.

"What?" said Sid somewhat belatedly in response to what she had said.

"You're invisible now, look," she said, pulling herself tighter and waiting for the shocked response.

At first Sid did nothing. He looked down his beak and then it began to dawn on him – it wasn't there! He brought his wings slightly forward and looked left and right and his wings weren't there either. Mot hung on waiting for the panic she expected but nothing happened. "You know," said Sid after a long silence, "that's the most amazing thing I have never seen! You are really clever you know Mot, really clever. I know my wings are there because I can feel the weight of my body as I fly, and I know my beak is there because I can feel the wind blowing into it."

"No," said Mot, "you are the really clever one," now full of admiration for Sid's calmness. "Come on, let's surprise the others. Just as you land I will make us visible." Sid laughed and Mot felt him turn into a dive and she could see the land approaching at incredible speed. With Sid invisible the view took her breath away and made her heart race with excitement. Just as the bank approached beneath them she could feel Sid's body change as he prepared to land.

chapter 55

Freddie surfaced inside the loft with ease having lived there since his injury which had now completely healed. "Beaver, you have a guest."

"So what?" said Beaver. "I have been watching. What would I want with a seagull?" he said in his usual abrupt gruff tone.

"He is looking for Chad," said Freddie.

"What! Well why didn't you say so in the first place? He has just flown away."

"Well I'm sorry Beaver, but it's not my fault you don't want to know anyone. I came as quickly as I could." Beaver nodded. "You're right, sorry Freddie." With that he dived into the water through the hole in the floor. Freddie sighed and immediately followed him back into the water.

Beaver shot out of the water with such speed and enthusiasm he would have knocked Sid over, if of course he had been there. "Where did he go?" said Beaver to the Dove. "I don't know, one minute he was there and then suddenly without warning he took off in that direction," said the dove, nodding in the direction of the hill.

"This is very frustrating," said Beaver. Freddie, who had not made it back nearly as quickly as the Beaver which was understandable as he was only a fox, was surprised. He had never seen Beaver so worked up before.

"Well that was a waste of time," said Beaver turning back to the water's edge and then stopping before he dived in. "You hear that?" he said.

"What?" said Freddie and the dove simultaneously.

"I hear movement in the wood." They all turned towards the path leading from it to the water's edge. The sun was now fully up, so it cast dark shadows over the entrance.

"It's probably a human," said Freddie nervously. "I hope it's not the dogs again they haven't been here for a long time. Maybe they are back." As if they had heard him, a dog barked.

"Oh great," said the dove. Freddie and Beaver quickly turned to the water's edge and out of the wood came the dog they had heard, a cat, two mice and a large ant. Together they calmly strolled down the path towards them. Only the dog was agitated.

Beaver waited, as did Freddie. They knew they had an escape route and anyway they didn't feel threatened yet! The dove could fly at a moment's notice and curiosity held her there.

The dog calmed down when they reached the river's edge and sat down, appearing to sulk. The ant spoke, much to Beaver's surprise: "Hello, my name is Ant. This is Slippers," he indicated with his front leg, "and that is Blanket, Christopher and Fidgit. There is another mouse their sister who will be along shortly." Slippers snorted. "We should go back to look for her," he muttered quietly. Ant ignored him. "We are looking for help," he continued.

"Why should we help you?" said Beaver before Ant could say anything further.

"Well we are looking for help to find their missing parents – the mice, that is. We think they have gone missing with all the other animals from the wood."

Beaver looked at Freddie. "You know about that?" he questioned.

"Yes," said Ant. Before Ant could say any more, they all heard a swishing sound coming from above. They all looked up towards the sky but there was nothing to be seen.

Mot had never felt so excited in her life! The first mouse to fly on the back of a seagull, and then she remembered actually the second mouse, but the first girl! The flight was finishing as quickly as it had begun and as she looked, she saw that the others must have heard them as they were all looking up with puzzled expressions on their faces.

Sid and Mot landed and reappeared simultaneously in front of the others with a flourish and then Mot proudly hopped off. Fidgit clapped her hands with delight. Christopher's mouth fell open with shock and Slippers of course with a big smile on his face said, "Outstanding, I think!"

Ant just looked. "This," said Mot, "is Sid, my father's first real friend and he too is looking for him." Mot saw from the corner of her eye Sid lifting himself up with pride.

"Hello," said Beaver, "I am Beaver the builder. I got my name from a mouse called Chad."

"So did I," said Sid, "but it's Sid the seagull." Freddie had by now joined them at the water's edge and said, "he gave me my name too, Freddie the fox."

"He never gave me a name," said the dove sounding disappointed.

"Perhaps you never asked him to," said Beaver.

"Actually, you're right, I never did."

"There you go then, your fault not his," he said defensively as if Chad could do no wrong.

"I can't complain," said the dove. "Chad saved my life; without him I would not be here now." Everyone was very quiet for a moment.

"So, you're looking for Chad," said Beaver addressing Sid directly, ignoring Ant and the others and swiftly changing the subject, but before Sid could answer he continued, "well I haven't see him for some time actually, not since the last time," which of course made no sense but none of the others was prepared to correct him least of all Sid as he would probably say the same kind of thing. "I do expect him though. He told me if he went exploring he would come and get my help. I'm bored now stuck inside most of the time ever since I lost my partner to those dogs, probably," he said with a sad heavy sigh.

"I saw him last," said the dove. "He used to live in a tree before and just after the great flood, but he's not there now. I've been back since. I think he lived in the woods for a while."

"Does he live there now then?" asked Sid. Beaver, Fox and Dove looked at each other nervously and although Sid wasn't very clever, he sensed something was wrong. "The wood is dead," said Freddie. "Something has happened we don't know what. Some time ago there was much talk about worm holes, but no one knows what they are or what they do and then bit by bit animals started to disappear. I have found some of them dead in piles, so now I stay here with Beaver. It's safer."

Ant spoke indignantly, fed up with being ignored. "I told you, we are all looking for Chad. These are his children and we are his friends," again waving a front leg in the direction of Slippers and Blanket.

"I don't like ants," said Beaver rather rudely. "All the rumours are that it's the ants that are taking the animals. I couldn't understand how but if they are all as big as you maybe now I can."

There was a stunned silence. Beaver just glared at Ant, Ant just looked back. All the others just looked on uncomfortably.

"I came here to get help," said Ant, "to try and find my friend Chad and to find out why the animals are being killed and try to stop it. Chad's children are with me and so are Slippers and Blanket. We don't know if Chad is still alive but the only way to find out is to follow the ants through the worm hole to where they take the animals and then for some reason bring them back when they are dead!

"We all," he said, waving his leg in the direction of the others, "have to be in the wood tonight and no later. The worm hole does not appear in the same location each time it comes. I have spoken to some of the ants who come from it and whatever is at the other end they are too afraid to speak about, but I fear it is my brother and he is bigger than me. Somehow, he is controlling everything for reasons we cannot understand. We may not succeed but we will certainly die trying. So yes, to some extent you were right the ants are involved, but they are not from here. They come from another place we have yet to see and understand."

"You!" he said, pointing at Beaver, "can stay here Mr Beaver with your friends safe in your house made out of wet and rotten wood in the middle of a pond and watch your life go by, but we intend to try and save Chad and any other animals we can. I have nothing else to say to you. Come on everybody, we have to leave now if we want to make it to the worm hole in time tonight."

With that Ant turned away and one by one the mice followed. "I'm coming too," said Sid. Slippers was next. He looked at Beaver and Freddie and said, "Impressive, isn't he?" Blanket followed on behind. Beaver and Freddie stood and said nothing.

They had not gone far when Beaver shouted "Wait!" Ant turned to look. Beaver looked at Freddie and he nodded. "We are coming too. But I still don't like you," and with that they fell into line and followed the others into the wood.

chapter 56

Henrietta stirred in her sleep. She was not well which was unusual for her. Chad came back from where he had been pondering about their predicament. Certain words were echoing around in his head, "what if we can't get back? I will just make another one how hard can it be?"

Unfortunately, much harder than they thought it would seem. Henrietta had attempted to create another worm hole to get them away from where they had arrived, but it had proved impossible. Henrietta woke with a start and smiled. "Hello Chad," she said.

"Hello Hen," replied Chad, "are you feeling any better?"

"Well no," replied Henrietta, "and I won't for a little while," she said quietly.

"Why?" said Chad with concern.

Henrietta was quiet for a moment, "well I should have told you before we left but then you would not have gone."

"Told me what?"

Henrietta smiled. "We are having another son or daughter soon."

"Well of course that's wonderful news and a big surprise, but you're right, I would not have let you come if I had known which means we really do have to find a way out of here."

"You would not have let me come," said Henrietta.

"Yes," said Chad emphatically.

"Well," said Henrietta with a smile, "how exactly were you going to create a worm hole on your own?"

"Er, good point," said Chad smiling back. "I hadn't thought of that."

'Here' was in fact a rock ledge just above the portal that the weasel had spoken of and where they had arrived. No one had seen their arrival, but it was stiflingly hot where they were located and they assumed that the heat was coming from the portal. The rock face projected out on the right, left and above where they were. It must have been a small cave at some time. It had been dark when they arrived and still was. They had no idea how long a day was where they were or for that matter if they had daylight at all. A small breeze occasionally passed them, but it was almost as hot as the air around them. "Are you sure we are outside?" said Henrietta, "we might be in a cave."

They watched for some time the comings and goings. Ants went out sometimes alone sometimes with corpses and then returned with animals of all sorts, but they were mostly very small.

The portal, however, never closed. It remained open continuously irrespective of who or what came and went. Chad and Henrietta had discussed this at length. When they leave to come here the portal closes, they agreed as they had witnessed it themselves. So why did the portal stay open here? There was only one answer: they must now somehow have created simultaneous connections to other places. "Which means," said Chad, "that they, whoever they are, are expanding whatever they are doing with the animals because as soon as the wood is empty, they will move on until there are no animals left anywhere."

"Chad," said Henrietta, "this is my fault. I will have to be more careful in future about what I wish for when I create these worm holes. I wished to find the source of theirs," she said, nodding in the direction of the portal. "We are lucky we landed here! There is only one way I can think of to get us out of here quickly."

"How?" said Chad, moving back from the rock edge he was contemplating climbing down, and turning to face her.

"Easy, we go through their portal!"

"And?" said Chad.

"Well when we arrive wherever that is it must be somewhere in the wood; we move away from the worm hole and we will be able to use our portal again if we have to, we might even get lucky and arrive somewhere we recognise."

Chad thought for a moment the plan had so many ifs and buts in it they would take forever to discuss it. So without any further hesitation, Chad said, "Let's go."

Chad moved over to the edge of the rock ledge they were on. "It's a long way down Hen. We can climb it, but doing so without being seen is another matter. You're the right colour being grey, but I will be seen easily." Henrietta picked up some rock dust from the floor and started to rub it into Chad's fur. It quickly lost its white sheen — it wasn't perfect, but he looked a lot less bright in the dark. "Thank you," said Chad only half meaning it and coughing at the same time, "just what I needed, a rock dust disguise." Henrietta laughed, and Chad grinned. "Come on, let's go."

They both slipped over the edge and began to climb down the sheer rock face. It proved to be easier than they thought as the rock face had many fissures for hand holds and they were quite small.

Within minutes they confirmed they were outside and not in a cave. Once clear of the ledge and its overhang they could look directly up above them and there appeared a beautiful dark black sky with thousands of stars twinkling and a moon that was much larger than normal.

They moved slowly downwards and away from the portal. The slope of the rock face was easier to scale that way and they hoped that they would be less likely to be seen. They had expected it to get cooler but much to their surprise the rock beneath their feet was getting warmer. "The heat is not coming from the worm hole Hen," said Chad. "It must be all the volcanic activity that the weasel told us about — that's where the heat's coming from."

As they moved further up the valley away from the portal it was getting darker without its light, but seeing in the dark was not a problem for either of them and in any event they felt more comfortable as they were less likely to be seen.

Occasionally a pair of ants would pass by in one direction or the other. Never alone, they were always in pairs unless they were carrying something.

Chad whispered, "Someone is definitely controlling them Hen. They are patrolling somehow; I think they are expecting us."

"How?" said Hen. "Nobody knows about us except the weasel and he is locked up."

"Really," said Chad, "there is something very strange about this thing. Everybody has a theory or a story, but the question is who's telling the truth?" Henrietta said nothing.

Although the rock face was solid, here and there, there were little loose pieces of rock and as they were nearing the bottom they now had to take extra care not to dislodge anything. The portal was now out of sight because the valley it had been set up in had a very slight curve, but they could now see clearly the opposite way but unfortunately only briefly as suddenly it had become shrouded in a fog or mist that was moving very slowly towards them.

They scrambled to the bottom just as it enveloped them. It had a strange smell that irritated their throats and they had to strain not to cough. "Sulphur," said Henrietta, "I think it's sulphur from the volcanic activity."

"You're probably right," said Chad, "but we are going the wrong way now. We have to go back if we want to travel through the portal."

They were about to turn back when they heard a small click of metal on metal. They both stood very still and waited. After what seemed like forever, they heard it again. Chad and Henrietta looked at each other. They both knew in an instant they would have to investigate. So instead of doing what common sense decreed, they continued to travel up the valley. The sound now became more frequent as if whatever it was knew they were there.

"We have to be careful Hen," whispered Chad, "another ant patrol will be along soon." Henrietta just nodded. They knew they were getting closer to the source of the sound; it had become more frequent as if trying to attract their attention. "If we have to run for it," said Chad, "run straight up the cliff face. They won't expect that." Henrietta nodded silently again.

Out of the mist as they drew closer shadows of a shape began to appear. It looked like some kind of platform made out of thin pipes with a large pipe in the middle.

And then it moved and turned towards them with more clicking and clacking of metal which sounded like chains. The mist cleared partially and there in front of them was a huge, giant ant staring right at them getting ready to attack, or so it seemed. They were almost frozen to the spot waiting for the ant to move, but it just stared at them.

"How did you get here?" said a voice, but the ant hadn't moved. Chad turned to Henrietta and asked, "Who said that?" while looking around for yet another threat that was about to appear from somewhere.

"Said what?" she replied.

The fog came and went as it gently drifted down the valley, so the ant disappeared and reappeared intermittently. "I said it," said the voice. "I'm right in front of you. I can't speak, but I'm in your head." Chad looked at the ant who nodded imperceptibly.

"You're the ant the weasel spoke of, aren't you?"

"Which weasel?" said the ant's voice in his head.

"Hen, this ant is talking to me in my head." Henrietta just looked at him.

"I can talk to you too," said the ant.

"I heard that," said Henrietta.

"There is something different about you both. I cannot see what you are thinking. I have not met a creature here before who can prevent me from doing that. Why do you suppose that is?"

The question the ant asked previously had just sunk in. "What do you mean which weasel?" said Chad, ignoring the last question evasively.

"Well," replied the ant, "there is the weasel trapped in the cave and there is the weasel responsible for all this." He waved one of his legs with lots of clanking of chains to indicate the surroundings.

"I don't understand," said Chad. "We were told you were responsible for all of this," and he waved his arm as the ant had done.

"Hide," said the ant suddenly and looked away from them. Chad and Henrietta slipped into a small cleft in the rock face as two ants went past, but they need not have worried as they paid no attention and disappeared into the fog as quickly as they had appeared.

"I am imprisoned here," said the ant, "over-curiosity was my downfall. I came across the worm hole that had been the talk of the wood for months and foolishly ventured into this domain. It is controlled by a weasel called Mustelee – or at least he thinks he controls it – who in turn controls the ants. He has the same ability as me and can communicate with any creature this way. Their queen is imprisoned and has been for many years; they know no other life but this. Successive generations have grown up loyal only to Mustelee he calls himself King Ty Rant. They fear him because he will kill anything that gets in his way. I was captured and overpowered. The weasel now wants the secret of my growth and will go to any end to find it. With that he can build an invincible army that will be unstoppable.

"I have watched every day the poor animals brought here and forced to work for him and when they die they carry them away to dispose of the corpses back where they came from, but over time less and less have been found and he is getting desperate. There are other empty chains here that must have held other creatures, but I believe from a long time ago, before him. He thinks about 'what the journal says' frequently." Chad and Henrietta looked at each other.

"I believe some animals escaped to the hills on the other side of that mountain," he said, waving in the opposite direction up the valley.

"Something terrible happened here that destroyed this place and left it barren. Mustela was so obsessed with trying to reverse it using the information in the journals and the machine, although there is apparently one journal in particular that is important." Chad and Henrietta looked at each other again. "He was completely unaware that his brother had taken control of everything. Mustela is now trapped in the mountain, ironically with the journal that could apparently help save this place or give Mustelee the power he wants. Neither of them has managed to work out what it is and so this place is slowly destroying itself. The earthquakes have become more frequent since I came."

"But we were told by the weasel inside the mountain that you were behind all this, not them."

"Interesting," said the ant, bending down and looking closer. "How, might I ask, did you speak to the weasel in the mountain when he has been trapped in that cave for quite some time? And as I have already asked, how did you get here? You cannot have come through the portal. They know – the ants that is – the moment something arrives."

Chad looked at Henrietta as if to say 'shall I tell him?' She nodded, so Chad began.

chapter 57

The weasel was irritated by all this my brother stuff! It all started when the ant arrived, "we have names," he thought, "I am Mustelee and my brother is Mustela."

He knew his brother was completely mad and had been for many years and now it seemed he was suffering from delusions – being trapped in there so long was finally getting to him. But mad or not, he understood science and he had been a great help in getting the machine they found to work. But as with all things though, Mustela wanted to do things for the environment. He, however, had much grander plans. He already controlled the ants. His brother was sympathetic about the ant queen but he was not, so when one day the cave entrance collapsed and trapped his brother inside, he was overjoyed.

His brother believed that they were working non-stop to dig him out. He, however, had made no attempt to try and release him and knew his brother would eventually die in there from suffocation. It was unfortunate his brother could contact him as they had similar abilities (but not as good as he when it came to mental communication), and Mustela contacted him on almost a daily basis which was very irritating. Fortunately Mustela could only communicate with him, whereas he could communicate with almost every living creature and in turn, control them.

The giant ant that had suddenly arrived had been his biggest challenge yet. When he had tried to imprison him for "research", the ant, mistaking Mustela for the leader who was talking to him, nearly killed him for trying to do so. By telling him he would send back hordes of ants through the worm hole to seek out his colony and kill his queen, he very quickly allowed himself to be controlled, but the burning hatred he felt for Mustelee was constantly in his eyes and although they had him chained up if he passed by him would follow him with his eyes. Mustelee knew there was only one safe outcome for him and for the ant: the ant would have to die soon.

Having read his thoughts he knew there was another ant back there that came from the same colony, had been exposed to the same thing at the same time and also glowed green. He had grown larger but not as large, but he could talk too. He had been exposed to the radiation that existed here naturally by accident there, but it seemed it did not create huge growth so what was the difference between them?

But after many trips into the woods through the worm hole not one ant had found any trace of him and neither had the few remaining animals they had captured.

And then there was something his mad brother who still thought he was in charge said. He had ignored it initially, but it had dwelt on his mind if he remembered correctly, he had said, "you will need to send out what ants you have to find two mice who live in a house I think. Their names are Chad and Henrietta. I believe what they have will be able to solve all our problems. Concentrate on that and nothing else." And then, "But be warned brother, I have observed them. They are not normal mice so make sure when the ants find them they are prepared."

Had his brother gone so mad that he was now imagining mice with names?! Well, better to be sure. He would send out several groups of ants to search, but the wood was a big area and there were no animals or very few left to ask. Birds! That was the answer. Birds were useless to him – they were hard to catch anyway and most of those they did invariably died quickly or escaped and were never seen again and totally unsuitable for the work that needed doing, but they went everywhere. So where to start? Ah yes, the river birds are always by the river: fish, insects, worms, food of course. He summoned one of the soldier ants and instructed him to take

100 of his best soldier ants and split them up into groups. If his brother somehow was telling the truth and they were not normal mice he had no idea what they would be up against. The only clue he had was they lived in a house, so he told them to ask the birds if they had seen them or find a house near the woods. Mustelee knew what he was asking was almost impossible, but they were to try.

The other problem he had was the worm hole. It no longer closed itself after the ants returned and he could not understand why each time the ants used it they arrived in a different place. It might mean it was connected to other places simultaneously which was convenient, but also dangerous. It left them permanently open to attack without warning. Mustelee had assigned his best soldier ants to guard the entrance just in case, there was no longer a problem with the ant escaping – he was far too big now to go through the portal.

He remained chained up though for Mustelee's own safety. Mustelee looked up at the mountains. He knew hiding up there somewhere were some of the animals that had escaped, but he had no idea how many it could be they were massing together. As this thought ran through his mind a shiver ran down his spine and a foggy mist suddenly descended on the valley. It did from time to time due to the volcanic activity that was increasing day by day but today something was different. Something had changed but he just couldn't sense what. He decided to increase the guard on the portal tomorrow. The question was, he asked himself, if there was going to be an imminent attack was it going to be this side or the other?

chapter 58

It was going to take Ant and the others a little longer to go back to where they had rested the night before because it was mostly uphill, and Sid could not walk as fast as he could fly but flying in the wood was out of the question for a bird of Sid's size. At times the wood was so dense it all but blocked out the light. The path was only wide enough for two of them at a time, excluding Slippers who had to trot along in single file. They found their natural order of position with Ant at the front followed by Christopher and Fidgit side by side then Blanket, Freddie and Beaver, with Mot and Sid at the rear.

Sid brought up the subject of the ants again. "So, when are you going to see if you can bring them back?" he asked. Mot looked at Sid for a hint at what he thought or meant literally, but he had a blank expression on his face that Mot could not read so she looked away again. "No help in making a decision there then," she thought. She had got over the shock of what happened by now and had been giving what Sid had said some thought. She was now firmly convinced that she could reverse what she had done, but was a little nervous about making things worse and she told Sid this.

Sid of course was silent for a while as usual and Mot waited patiently for his answer as they followed the others along the path.

"Why," said Sid, "don't we stop at the next clearing? I will find something that you can make swirl into the ground, maybe a log or branch which you will feel happy about because you can't hurt it and then try bringing it back. Besides, I can't wait to see you do it," he said excitely.

"Sid, that is a very good idea," said Mot and once again Sid seemed to grow a little taller with pride. The path turned and twisted for a while and then they entered a small clearing. "What about here?" whispered Sid, getting excited again.

Mot slowed her pace and Sid matched his to hers. The others continued on without noticing and disappeared into the next opening in the wood. They both stopped and waited to see if anyone had in fact noticed, but of course they hadn't, and they were alone.

Sid hunted around and found a small log and two small boulders. Using his wings and pushing with his feet, he managed to arrange them in the centre of the clearing. "Well come on then," said Sid, trying to contain his excitement.

Mot looked at him apprehensively and opened her right hand. The clearing they were in was not very big and the tops of the trees had grown over it in an attempt to close it up. As a result, although it was daytime, the clearing was quite dark and full of shadows so when the first ball of light appeared in Mot's hand the effect was quite dramatic and caused a sharp intake of breath from Sid. He tried to bring his wings together to clap as if they were hands. This brought a small smile to Mot's face and made her relax a little. She had done this many times but of course this was important because if successful she would be able to bring the ants back at will. She threw the ball and it landed just outside of where the boulders and log had been pushed to by Sid, she then raised her left hand and again as before made the second ball of light appear spinning in the opposite direction. Then she very carefully threw the ball to the opposite side of the log and boulders making sure they did not collide and warning Sid at the same time not to get too close because if her aim was wrong there would be a big explosion and if it was right, he could be sucked into the hole when it was fully formed. For once Sid responded immediately and backed up to where Mot was standing.

At first, just as before, nothing happened. It was as if the two balls of positive and negative energy were sizing themselves up for a fight, and then they began to spin. There was a rustling of the leaves and what felt like a small breeze. The log wobbled and the boulders started to move closer to the centre of the circle of light the balls were making. And then they began to sink into the ground. Sid was absolutely mesmerised. Although he had believed what Mot had told him, part of him had still found it hard to imagine what she said she created, and yet now it was happening before his very eyes. Mot, however, was now more of an observer. She knew what she could create but what was important this time was to see how it came about and to make the balls of power and light behave the opposite way in order to reverse it.

The balls began to spin faster. Mot knew from her past experience that this was a dangerous moment and told Sid to stand behind a tree with his wings wrapped around it. He broke out of his trance and did as he was told, as did Mot – just in time it seemed. As the leaves began to slide towards the ever-increasing hole the balls were making, suddenly, just as before there was a pop and a flash and the logs and boulder were gone leaving a bare patch of ground remaining.

Sid was silent for some time and only moved when Mot moved to the centre of the now non-existent hole.

"That," said Sid, "That, that, that was outstanding," copying Slippers' second favourite word. He walked around the non-existent hole nervously and dabbed at it with his foot. Mot smiled, "but now is the hard part," she said, "come on back over to the trees."

She had a theory of how this was going to work, but it was only a theory. After all, she had done this twice quite successfully and reversing the direction of the balls she believed was about making one slightly bigger than the other so that it became the dominant one, but – and it was a big but – how was she going to determine what she brought back? If this worked it proved she could do it but this is where the log and the boulders disappeared. Did she have to be in the exact place that the ants went down to bring them back or was it about thought?

"We have to catch up with the others. They will eventually wonder where we are, but what about bringing the log and boulders back?" said Sid.

"I will try to explain my predicament on the way." Sid cocked his head. Mot immediately knew he didn't understand. "Come," she said and Sid joined her as they hurried to join the others.

chapter 59

C had sat down, as did Henrietta and the Ant with some rattling as the chains settled on the ground. Chad began to tell their story.

He kept it as brief as he could. He began with his leaving his parents and knowing that they now were gone he went on to tell of his meetings with Ant and all the others and how he met Henrietta.

He told of their tree house being hit by lightning and their lucky escape and then finding they had powers. He purposely didn't mention their children and then he hesitated, but only briefly. If this ant that was chained up was Ant's brother, which he assumed he was, then logic decreed that he was a friend so he told of their powers and the fact that Henrietta could create her own worm hole at will — well, almost anyway, and they had travelled here before and that's how they met Mustela inside the mountain. Again, he avoided mentioning the books they had taken, but he explained that they understood the principle of travel through worm holes and that's why they came here to try and put a stop to all the killing.

He explained that they now knew that Henrietta could not create a portal or worm hole, whichever you wanted to call it, when located next to an open portal. This puzzled him a little bit as he said it because he remembered Henrietta opening two at once before, but he carried on without saying anything. He would discuss that later with her when they were alone.

He told the ant of their plan to escape back to their realm by using the open portal even though they now knew it was guarded, but he didn't mention why they could not wait long to do so.

The ant listened to this story without a word, except to warn them when a patrol was approaching.

Chad finished their story and although it was as brief as he could make it had taken some time and over the horizon the first cracks of dawn had begun to appear turning the mist or fog a golden orange.

At first the ant said nothing and sat quietly. He then stood up with the rattle of noisy chains. "You must go, and swiftly," he said in their heads. "The guards are talking. Tomorrow, which is now today, Mustelee is increasing the guard to the portal and he is sending out some soldier ants to look for you. Somehow he knows you exist but obviously he does not know you are here already."

"But how does he know of us?" said Henrietta.

"It can only be Mustela," thought the ant.

"But he is trapped in the mountain," said Chad.

"He is," said the ant, "but his brother communicates with him on a daily basis as if he was in charge. He has no idea his brother wishes he was dead and cannot wait for him to die."

"So for the sake of your little one you must go now," said the ant, nodding towards Henrietta.

"You know?" said Henrietta.

The ant smiled. "Babies think too, you know."

Chad said, "Yes, we'll go, but not before we set you free," and before the ant could say another word Chad's clenched fist came down on the first of the four shackles that held him secure and it instantly burst under the blow. He swiftly moved onto the other three and burst them open too. "For the first time in many weeks," thought the ant, "I am free."

"You must flee up to the mountain and find the others," said Chad. "We intend to come back. This tyranny must come to an end before Mustelee finds the secret to this growth and creates his army."

The ant nodded. "I will try," he thought to them. "If the animals are alive I will find them; you have set me free, it is the least I can do. I will create a diversion for you. Chad, please break off that piece of chain," he pointed at one of the chains that moments before had held him prisoner. "Run quickly when I start, before it gets any lighter." Chad instantly obliged.

The ant picked up the chain and with relish started to lash the sides of the rock face that led to the portal. Such was the force he applied the sides of the rock face started to crumble and large pieces of rock began to roll down the sides. Even with the sound-deadening effect of the fog, the noise of the rocks falling echoed up and down the valley. He dropped the chain, waved goodbye and disappeared into the fog just as the ants came running from the entrance of the portal. Chad and Henrietta waited for them to pass and quickly ran the other way. They dodged around two more ants who were slower than the others, but then no more. They entered the unguarded portal without hesitation and just like before they were back in the wood before they knew they had left.

They quickly looked right and left. To the left Chad saw movement. He grabbed Henrietta's hand and pulled her with him to the right. She didn't hesitate and they both ran immediately in case the ants had tried to follow, but they hadn't gone far when the light from the worm hole extinguished and they knew they were alone.

They hadn't run for more than two minutes when Henrietta skidded to a stop and Chad, who was almost right behind, nearly ran into her. "We are idiots, you know that," Henrietta said.

"What?" said Chad. Suddenly in front of them was a portal.

"We have our own shortcuts, don't we?"

Chad grinned in understanding and together hand in hand they stepped into the portal which Henrietta had just formed and of course it closed instantly behind them.

chapter 60

A nt arrived with the others considerably quicker than he thought. It was late afternoon, so they had time to waste. He told them he had to go off and leave some messages so the ants could find him. He would be back as soon as he knew the location of the worm hole. He then disappeared into the undergrowth.

There was some tension in the air. For all the talk, the time had now come for them to fight and not one of them had any idea if they would succeed. They were ill-prepared and not a firm fighting unit. Since Beaver the builder and Freddie had joined them there had been an atmosphere, mainly because Beaver didn't trust Ant and the truth was he wanted to be in charge.

The children were unaware of the tension because they were more worried about their parents and really had no comprehension of what a fight was going to be like — except Sid and Mot, Sid because seagulls squabble and fight over food from the moment they can walk and Mot because of the confrontation with the ants, which it now seemed hadn't been a confrontation at all. What was interesting was that they had sort of divided into pairs: Christopher sat with his sister Fidgit, Slippers was with Blanket, which really was to be expected, and Beaver was with Freddie which was also to be expected. The dove had decided she didn't want to come, and Mot and Sid sat together on a log, which of course suited them both as they were about to sneak off and continue their experiment.

"Come," said Mot, "now's better than later," and with that they drifted off down one of the paths. No one paid them the slightest bit of attention.

It didn't take long for them to find another clearing which was little bigger and more like a glade. Mot said it was better to find somewhere smaller as they would not be disturbed, so they went down one of the smaller paths which had obviously been made by animals and not humans and found a small bare patch of ground. Sid began to get excited again. Although he had seen this once before, he couldn't wait to see it again. Mot made herself comfortable, as did Sid, and then once again she formed a small ball of light but this time in her left paw and she allowed it to grow fractionally bigger before she threw it on the ground where of course it floated just as before. She then used her right and repeated the process but made the ball slightly smaller and then threw that on the ground so they were slightly apart as before. All the time she was thinking stones, logs, logs, stones.

The two balls of power did their usual dance for superiority and then began to spin, this time anticlockwise. Mot pressed her hands together in anticipation. Sid looked at Mot and said, "Is it happening?" It would seem Sid didn't know the difference between clockwise and anticlockwise, so she said "yes, this time it's spinning the other way, but we might bring up something we don't want."

"Oh," said Sid, "I didn't think of that," now looking rather nervous.

The balls of light picked up speed until they formed a continuous circle which glowed and pulsated violently unlike before which was rather unexpected. The ground beneath them began to shake as did the trees around them.

"I'm not sure I like this," said Sid, looking rather anxious. "Is it supposed to do that?" he asked, looking at Mot. Mot laughed. "I don't know," she said, "I've never done it before, but it's too late now isn't it?" Sid thought for a second and then laughed too, "Yes, you are absolutely right."

Just as they thought it was going to get worse and maybe explode, out of the ground in front of them appeared the log and two stones. The moment they appeared the circle of light disappeared and then everything went quiet. The trees settled down and the ground stopped shaking. If it weren't for the dust in the air you would have thought nothing had happened.

Sid looked at Mot. They were both covered in dust and, perhaps a little too close to the process for comfort, unaware who started it first they were soon both laughing hysterically – a combination of satisfaction about success and the fact they were both still alive and in one piece!

"Come on," said Mot, dusting herself off. "We had better get back. They are bound to have missed us by now." But they were wrong. No one had missed them at all. Slippers, however, smiled when they returned – he had obviously seen Mot leave with Sid and considered her in safe hands. Satisfied now she was back, he decided to snooze.

chapter 61

Three dung beetles were sitting on a log when Mot and Sid turned up in the clearing and of course they paid them no attention. When the balls of light appeared, and the ground began to shake they certainly did. In fact, they nearly fell off the log they were on.

When Sid and Mot left, and the clearing returned to its usual humdrum silent normality except for all the dust hanging in the air one of the beetles said to the other two: "Did you see that?"

The other two looked at him as if to say 'how could we miss it?'

Just prior to Sid and Mot's arrival, the beetles had been discussing the shortage of dung. They too had heard the rumours going around the wood about the ants taking animals and at first they had been indifferent to it. But with almost all the animals gone, it was getting very short on the ground and on a daily basis they met to have a grumble about it.

The three beetles sat still for a moment as the dust settled. Then the first beetle said, "Do you remember when the ants came around and tried to talk to us about animals and if we knew any that were hiding out? They offered dung supplies as a reward and we weren't interested because at the time there was plenty to go around?"

The two other beetles turned to their friend and said, "Yes, so?"

"Well now there isn't plenty to go around and we have seen two animals."

"What makes you think they are going to be interested in a mouse and a seagull?" said one of the other beetles.

"Well, they are animals, aren't they?"

"True, very true, but they don't come around here very often now do they?"

"What, the animals?"

"No, the ants," replied the first beetle.

"True, very true," replied the other one and all three of them returned to looking at a log and two stones that hadn't been there a few hours ago, slowly getting covered in a layer of dust.

chapter 62

Mustelee was in his secure compound and heard the crashing sounds echo up and down the valley, but he was unable to work out what it was or where they came from because the fog muted and distorted the direction it was coming from. In any event it didn't bother him. The mountain and land around it was making more and more strange noises as the earthquakes had become more frequent.

Technically it was not his compound. It had been built many years ago by past inhabitants and then abandoned. It had been built against the mountain and was surrounded on three sides by sheer cliffs many feet high with jagged ridges – so high in fact that no creature alive today knew what was on the other side.

The two sides of the cliff had been enclosed by a high wall apparently built from lava, but how the previous inhabitants had handled such a hot and dangerous building material was beyond his comprehension. In the face of this wall were two gates that could be secured.

Within the compound was what can only be described as a palace, but when he and his brother had first arrived it was derelict and deserted. They had spent some time – again with the aid of the ants – to restore it to its original condition.

Mustela spent more and more time in the mountain cave reading in what he eventually called the library. He finally moved in there permanently, calling the palace extreme. It was around then that Mustelee realised that his brother had become obsessed with his quest and was gradually turning mad. Mustelee of course had become unaware of his lust for power and his own oncoming madness – he became totally ruthless and began to call himself King Ty Rant.

His ability to control the ants, and then the arrival of the giant ant after his brother managed to activate the machine they found, convinced him that he could do no wrong and would be king of everything. So, he set in motion his plan to build an army of giant ants by finding the magic material that made the big ant grow.

At first, he had sent out ants to find bigger ants and quickly learnt that his prisoner was not lying and that there was only one ant like him, but although they searched he was not to be found. Mustela had told him that the growth was due to the material that naturally came from the volcano where they lived and though they were unaffected by it, creatures from where the ant came from were.

Unfortunately, he found out very quickly that ants from the other place did not grow when exposed to their environment and animals instead became very sick and died. He pushed his brother to search through the books in the "library" to try and find the secret, but to no avail. He began to believe his brother was conspiring to "overthrow" him; he was of course becoming paranoid.

He heard more noise coming from the valley and some soldier ants rushed through the gates into the compound. Within seconds, Mustelee knew his prize experiment and the key to expanding his domain and reign, albeit delusional, had escaped.

The rage that began to flow through his veins was overwhelming and the ants, sensing the violence and usual carnage that followed, began to back away from him preparing to get out of range.

But suddenly the information that two mice, one white and one grey, had escaped through the portal became more important and his temper instantly began to cool much to the relief of the ants – particularly those at the front!

He had realised in seconds these must be the mice that his brother had spoken of and they were apparently real and had been here already! But how? Anything coming in through the portal he would have known about because of his soldier ant guards, so how did they get here? Time, he thought reluctantly, to speak more with his brother. In normal circumstances he would wait for his brother to contact him asking about pointless updates on things he thought were happening but in fact were not. But this was urgent!

"Hello, Brother," thought Mustelee, cringing at the address which he hated. "How are you?" he asked, of course really not caring how he was but for once hoping he was still alive.

"I am still alive," his brother responded, "but not for long. I fear the candles are beginning to flicker and dim, so I know that my air will soon run out." For several seconds Mustelee heard nothing and was about to ask the most important question when Mustela thought again, "what news of the mice?" he asked. Mustelee, controlling his keenness to know about them and not telling his brother they had in fact been here already, thought casually, "how do you know of them?"

"They came here to visit me, and we had long discussions about the history of this place and the problems it has." Under normal circumstances Mustelee would have thought his brother was suffering from delusions, but he knew the mice had been here, so he let him drone on until he could no longer contain his patience, "but how?" he asked. "There is no way in or out is there?"

There was no reply for nearly a minute and Mustelee thought he had gone, but then his brother responded again: "why are you so interested in this when you were not before?" His thoughts were clearer now and obviously the questions and the fact that his brother had made contact and not the other way around had aroused suspicions.

"Because," replied Mustelee, gritting his teeth and thinking in the most servile way he could, "you asked me to find them. You never told me why and any information that could help find them would be useful."

The ants had waited for their orders after Mustelee nearly exploded and without doubt would have killed some of them in a fit of rage as he had done many times before. He was now sitting and rocking back and forth with gritted teeth but whatever he was thinking of they had not been allowed to be part of it, so they continued to sit awaiting the outcome hoping it was satisfactory for their sakes.

Mustela could sense something had changed. His brother's usual indifference to his orders and opinions was not there, so he knew that his brother knew something he did not, but Mustela knew also that his only chance of getting out of the cave was the mice and so, with no choice, he told his brother: "The mice can form portals on demand and at will with no machines or power sources. It is beyond my understanding, but they are the only chance I have of getting out of here. They told me they cannot expand the portal but I saw them do it. They have total control to travel from one realm to another and more importantly I am sure were in that realm, which means even we could leave this place and travel to another realm too."

Mustelee could not believe what was going through his head. If he could travel to anywhere at will there was nothing he couldn't do.

Because he and his brother were twins and had the ability to communicate without speech they could see each other's thoughts and memories, but Mustelee had the ability to keep his own memories private from anything he communicated with including his brother. However, such was Mustelee's keenness to see the mice create a worm hole and vanish through it he delved into his brother's memories without a second thought.

There in his head he saw the mice create a worm hole and travel through it and to his dismay it appeared they had taken the books and journals that related to the creation of the machine he and his brother had found. "My brother is a fool," he thought, but then Mustela spoke. "You have lied to me, brother." Too late, Mustelee realised his brother had seen the truth and everything he had done and not done.

"You have not tried to save me; you have left me here to die. We were brothers how could—"

Mustelee had heard enough. He had made a mistake and allowed his brother to see the truth, so he cut him off from his mind in mid speech. His brother was no longer of any use to him; the books and journals were now outside of the mountain and his brother in and on his last breaths. He laughed, "ironic really," he said to himself out loud that his brother's last acts actually helped rather than hindered him. The ants looked at each other and just watched and waited for their next instruction from their very strange and unpredictable leader who appeared to now be talking to himself.

chapter 63

C hristopher was a little bored and so was Fidgit. They had slept a little and now the sun was setting and hopefully the big moment was drawing near. Ant had not returned, Slippers had gone to sleep, and the others were keeping to themselves. There was nothing to do so they both decided to have a look around on their own. The best place they felt to explore was the track that Ant had taken to leave. The sun was now tipping over the horizon and the wood gradually became darker, full of oddly shaped shadows and although they were frightened a little bit it was also exciting.

As they ventured into the wood it became darker and darker, but seeing in the dark was not an issue for them.

Just up ahead a small pale light began to appear just on the right side of the path. Christopher stopped and Fidgit bumped into him. "What?" she said, because she hadn't really been looking where she was going, but looking nervously around the wood. Christopher had one finger up against his mouth to say shush and of course now she had turned around she too could see this small ball of light that was appearing.

Any minute they expected ants to appear. Ant had gone looking for the worm hole and here it was appearing almost right in front of them. It suddenly reached full size and they were just about to hide when out of the hole shot two animals. They hesitated briefly, and then tore down the path in the opposite direction.

It took them a few seconds to realise that they were both mice. One was grey, the other white, and the grey one looked very fat. Christopher and Fidgit looked at each other. Surely not! Had they just seen their parents?

By the time it had dawned on them who they might be the mice, who were moving very fast, had disappeared around the next corner in the track. So without another thought they set off in hot pursuit.

As fast as they ran, they didn't seem able to catch up. They knew the mice they were chasing were still running on the path and had not turned off because there was dust hanging in the air in front of them, kicked up by the speed they were running at. They rounded a corner in the path and there in front of them was another worm hole. They had just enough time to see the two mice, hand in hand, step through it. Then it disappeared, and the wood returned to darkness.

"That was definitely not our parents," said Fidgit, skidding to a halt again.

"Why?" said Christopher.

"Well the grey one was too fat and the white one was holding her hand and our father wouldn't do that with another mouse," she said indignantly.

"Well yes, I see your point," said Christopher, but not really as holding hands seemed quite innocent and normal to him. "We had getter get back and tell the others we have seen not just one worm hole but two! And two strange mice who are using them." With that they turned around and ran back the way they had come.

chapter 64

The ant had no trouble finding his way towards the mountains. He had watched them appear out of the mists of dawn every day and disappear again at dusk.

Apart from the rumours about the animals that had escaped there, there had been talk that fresh running water still existed there as well where it once had below.

But rumours were rumours, and to get there you had to cross an extinct volcano that at the end of its eruption had collapsed in on itself and created a perfect bowl of rock that was many, many miles across and still so hot that to walk on it you would burn to death before you got very far. It was this that prevented the ants from searching for these escaped animals that the big ant believed no longer existed and had died trying to escape.

But a promise was a promise. He laughed to himself; he had absolutely no intention of keeping it. Chad and Henrietta had believed everything he said and set him free, but he had to search for these lost creatures even though he believed they no longer lived because if they did, it would affect his future plans. He had to get well so he could return and regain his rightful place.

At first, he struggled. He had not walked free for a long time and his limbs were stiff from inactivity, but the further he got from the valley the cooler it became which made it much easier for him. This was also a surprise because if the stories about the collapsed volcano were true, it should be getting warmer. He travelled at night and slept by day as the wounds on his legs healed. After five days he reached the cliff face that led to the rim of the volcano and with great apprehension started to climb up the side. It was not particularly high as over the last few days he had climbed higher with his journey.

That evening, just as the sun set and the moon rose, he pulled himself over the edge of the rim not knowing if shortly he would fall to his death, burn to death or die from the gases that he was sure would come from the crater, but in doing so he could satisfy his curiosity before he returned to the palace.

chapter 65

A lmost as soon as Henrietta and Chad arrived home, Henrietta gave birth to a little boy who they named James. Chad went looking for the children to tell them the surprising good news. But the children were not at home. Assuming they were talking to Slippers, Chad went looking for them to find no sign of them anywhere and both Slippers and Blanket were out too.

Chad looked at the coat rack. Slippers' lead was hanging there so he hadn't gone out for a walk. Chad noticed his water and food bowls were no longer where they were usually kept. So when the cleaner turned up and didn't look for him, Chad knew something had changed.

He reluctantly returned to their home and told Henrietta the bad news.

James by now was running around. Being the son of a couple of super mice he was of course growing very quickly and soon would need real food, not just milk. They had some food in the store, but he would need something fresh.

"I have a theory," said Chad.

"What?" said Henrietta, trying not to show her concern as she was hoping the children were with Slippers. She knew he would protect them with his life.

"I think they went to look for us after we went missing and didn't come home and they are with Slippers and Blanket."

"Who are Slippers and Blanket?" asked James, who had started talking almost from the moment he was born.

"They are two of our best friends," said Henrietta, "and helped to look after your brother and sisters." At the mention of Blanket being one of their friends, Chad's eyebrows shot up, but Henrietta smiled and Chad shrugged as if to say, "alright, if you say so."

"So where are my brother and sisters?" asked James.

"Well," replied Chad, "they have gone looking for us because they thought we were missing, and we weren't." However illogical this answer sounded James appeared to accept it and decided to chase his tail.

"We have another problem," said Henrietta.

"What?" said Chad.

"The weasel in the mountain," she replied. "We can't just leave him to die and if we are to resolve anything at all we need the missing journal. There is no doubt that his brother will work out who we are and come looking for us. With the ant gone it's the only chance he has of becoming the 'king of everything'." Chad laughed. "I'm serious," said Henrietta, "you know what the ant told us, many animals have died in his quest for power and he will stop at nothing to achieve it. If the children come across a worm hole I am sure they will enter it and if the weasel has enough ants waiting at the portal they will easily be overcome. The weasel does not know we have children and I would like to keep it that way."

Chad nodded in understanding. "I agree Hen, but how can we travel with James?"

"I know," said Henrietta, "that is a problem. If Slippers were here I would leave him with him, but unfortunately he's not. If we wait long enough he will be able to look after himself, but I think it unlikely the weasel will still be alive by then."

"I could go on my own as I am the only one who can make worm holes," ventured Henrietta, already knowing what the response would be.

"Absolutely not," said Chad in such a loud voice that for several moments James stopped chasing his tail and looked at them both in concern. Chad, realising he had frightened his son, lowered his voice and smiled at James who, happier now, went back to chasing his tail. "I almost lost you once and I promised myself I would never lose you again so it's either together or not at all, unless by some miracle Slippers turns up."

"Yes, you're right," sighed Henrietta, "besides which sooner or later the ants are going to find us, so we may have to move but if we do and the children come home, how will they know where we are?"

"It's a problem Hen and somehow we have to solve it."

"Solve what?" said James.

"Nothing son," said Chad, "it's nothing."

chapter 66

Ant returned later that evening and although Christopher and Fidgit had told the story about the mice and the worm holes several times to the others, they couldn't wait to tell it again.

Ant listened patiently and then said, "I think you were dreaming."

"Why?" said Chad and Fidgit simultaneously with an irritated tone.

Ant smiled and then changed the subject. "I have found the ants and the worm hole," he said, which immediately caught everyone's attention. "I have told them I know of a place where animals stay and that when I come back I will tell them where, but they won't wait forever. We have to be quick. They will not be expecting this so when we get to the other side there might be a couple of ants on guard but otherwise no more than that."

"How do you know this?" asked Beaver who still didn't really trust Ant but since everybody else did and he had been with Chad almost from the beginning, he felt he had no choice. "The ants I spoke to told me they only have two ants on guard at what they call the portal."

Beaver grunted as if to say "and you trust them."

"Come," said Ant, "I will take you there. When we get near you will have to hide and then I will misdirect them. We can all enter the portal and it will close behind us leaving them stranded." Ant set off quickly with the animals behind him in the same order as before. They knew when they were near the portal before Ant told them because of the bright light emanating from the forest in front of them. Ant stopped, and they all caught up. "Wait here," he said, "I will call you."

Through the bushes they saw Ant approach the portal guards.

After several minutes of apparent discussion the guards headed off down the path and Ant waited by the portal until he was sure they had gone. He called to them quietly, "all clear," and everyone emerged. "Are we ready?" he said. Everyone agreed except Slippers. "I'm too big," he said with dismay looking at the very small spinning ball of light. They all looked the portal that hovered just above the ground and it was obvious that Slippers was right. He wouldn't fit.

Blanket and Beaver were the next smallest and they would just but Slippers? Not a chance.

"You're not going," said Slippers quietly to Mot. "Neither you nor your brother or sister, not without me."

"Shush," said Mot, "no one knows we have these powers. We will be fine. Go back to the house and wait for us. Maybe our parents are back," she smiled weakly knowing this was highly unlikely.

"Blanket, I cannot come," said Slippers, "please look after them for me in my place. They are important to me."

"I will," said Blanket, who rarely said a word. "You have my word on it."

"Quickly," said Ant, "it's time," and with that one by one they filed into the worm hole and about a minute after the last one went in the portal just disappeared.

Slippers wasted no time. Without thinking he just ran. He knew exactly where he was going – home. He almost smiled at this thought but with no one he loved there it would not be the same, but he was too upset at not being able to go with the mice. He had watched them grow up and spent so much time with them his only hope was that somehow Ant could pull this off, get there, rescue Chad and Henrietta, and get back here so the family could be together again.

He thought this as he ran without knowing that things had become a lot more complicated than he could ever imagine and were going to get even more complicated very soon.

chapter 67

As was usual with experienced portal travellers the Ant and his fellow travellers arrived in a blink of an eye, but they were not experienced travellers and contrary to Ant's opinion, their visit was not a surprise. They had been expected.

The moment they appeared out of the portal they had no time to think and were immediately surrounded. Ant tried to fight but he was quickly overpowered, Beaver in his usual negative critical way was heard to say as the ants grabbed them "so much for that plan."

Christopher whispered to his sisters "do nothing yet" and Mot whispered to Sid "Fly now!!" Sid needed no second bidding and took off. Several ants tried to grab his feet but quickly fell off as Sid accelerated away. "Reconnoitre" Mot shouted at him as he flew away and hoped he knew what it meant.

Ant was chained up where his brother had been only a day or so ago, but they couldn't use the same chains as Chad had broken them.

The others were herded down the valley towards a fork in the rock face. The valley continued on into the distance to the mine and the entrance to the cave under the mountain, now completely blocked by fallen rocks. But their destination was Mustelee's palace. It was a very steep climb out of the valley towards a plateau and it took some time. Just outside the palace there was a small compound totally enclosed apart from a small window in the roof with bars and a steel door. Fidgit smiled when she saw it, but said nothing. The door was slammed behind them and locked.

"Well not a good start," said Freddie.

"Yes, you're right there," said Beaver, but less aggressively. Seeing Ant chained up had changed how he thought about him.

"Oh, I don't know," said Christopher, "sometimes things are not as bad as they seem," looking at his sisters who both smiled back.

"Well," said Beaver, "I never thought I would be locked up with three crazy mice who seem happy about it."

Christopher turned back to them. "The ants are nothing; they are just servants or slaves, they are not the ones behind this. If we are to succeed we need to find who it is and where and if our parents are here and still alive." Fidgit winced at this. "Sooner or later we will be summoned or visited. We were expected – I don't understand how they knew we were coming, but nevertheless they did."

"We will wait one day only and if no one has come by then we will break out and find them ourselves. We also have to set Ant free." Freddie had listened to the conversation going back and forth and was a little puzzled at how Christopher could speak so positively about what they were going to do when they were surrounded by four solid walls with a steel door and only one window with bars on it high above and out of reach. And so he said, "I don't understand how you think you can escape from here. It has four solid walls, a steel door and a window with bars on it well out of our reach, let alone set Ant free." Beaver had folded his arms and nodded in agreement.

Christopher smiled again and said, "we are not quite what we seem." Freddie put his head in his hands, "What have I done?" he thought. "I was having a happy life, well sort of. I learnt to swim, and I was safe, well sort of, and I had plans! Well sort of, well actually not I was bored which is why I have joined up with three crazy mice and it would seem as if Beaver and I are going to die here." Blanket said absolutely nothing and settled down in a corner which completely confused the both of them. "Well," he thought, "I'll just have to wait and see I suppose."

chapter 68

S lippers ran as fast as he could but it still it took him all day and by the end of the day he was almost down to a walking pace, but his nose had not let him down and soon he was on the last path in the wood that reached the house that was his home. He hadn't realised how much he missed it, but not as much as he was missing Chad and his family.

He came out of the wood late in the afternoon – too late for the cleaner and too early for his owners, so he lay down in front of the front door and wondered how the others were getting on. A car came down the road and a person stepped out, patted him on the head, and said, "Hello Slippers, welcome home. Your owners are going to be really pleased." He then put one of those funny black boxes to his ear and drove away. Slippers had absolutely no idea who he was, but obviously he knew him. Not long past and another car came down the road and skidded to a stop and out jumped the cleaner. She was overwhelmed to see him, "Oh Slippers, where oh where have you been? We have been looking everywhere for you." Slippers was tired, but he was just as pleased to see her and as soon as the door opened he raced to his water and food bowls which, much to his surprise, were not there.

"Well boy, you have been gone a long time. Your owners were so upset they blamed me for letting you out of the house, but I never did."

"Well I know that," thought Slippers, "but you will never know how I got out," feeling a little guilty that he had caused so much trouble and sorrow.

The cleaner hugged him and then said, "Phew you need a bath," ran to the kitchen and got him some water and food and then ran him a bath. Slippers had forgotten what it was like to be looked after and loved every minute of it. She washed and brushed him and then said, "Do you want to go for a walk?" Slippers looked up at her and thought, "if only you knew. I don't want to go for a walk for a month." He just flopped down in his usual place so glad to be home, while the cleaner rang his owners to tell them Slippers had returned.

Chad had heard an unusual noise coming from the house at an unusual time of day but after listening carefully he heard the murmur of a human voice and relaxed. He was on his guard. If the ants found them in all probability they would come from under the floor and with little James here it made him and his family more vulnerable. He would have to talk to Hen about moving sooner or later, but he still hadn't solved the problem of who could look after James when they went back for the weasel. Chad knew they had very little time left to save him from suffocation.

The front door slammed, and it was quiet for a while and then it slammed again. More voices, very excited. He recognised them – the owners, probably back from a holiday or something, and then he heard a bark. He sat up instantly. Was Slippers back, or perhaps another dog? Surely they hadn't got another dog already? He had to go and look.

Henrietta had heard the noise too, as had James. Chad told them to wait while he made his way to their front door, the knot hole in the skirting. He carefully looked out without showing himself. The last thing they needed now was to be spotted by the people in the house. There was no chance of that however. It was the owners – both of them – they had come home early because of Slippers' return. They were so occupied with spoiling him that Chad was sure he could have gone out there and danced in front of them and they would not have noticed. Slippers had calmed down a lot and he suddenly turned towards where Chad was, smiled and then lay down. "He knows I'm here," thought Chad, the power of a dog's nose – wow!

Slippers' deliberate calmness was a clever move. He had in fact smelt Chad and needed to speak with him urgently, so he needed to calm his owners down quickly. He realised if he lay down quietly, they would calm down quickly too.

Chad, who had worked out what Slippers was up to smiled to himself, thinking what a clever dog Slippers was. Chad felt a nudge beside him and without looking he said, "James, what did I say?"

"I know what you said father, but there is so much happening, and I just had to come and look."

Chad sighed, "Better now than later," he thought and he went on to explain that Slippers the dog was a friend, but not all dogs were, and people could be friends but most were not and that the owners didn't know they lived here, and it was best it stayed that way, or else they would have to leave quickly. He thought that they would have to leave quickly anyway if the ants came.

"Why quickly if the ants come?" James asked suddenly. Chad stopped talking in mid-sentence. "How did you know that?" he asked in shock. He knew perfectly well that he hadn't spoken out loud.

"I hear lots of things people are thinking all the time, and ant told me lots of things too. You set him free and he was very grateful."

Chad sat in silence for a moment contemplating what he had just learnt. James looked at him quizzically tipping his head from side to side not realising of course the amazing ability he been born with.

At that moment there was a puff of breath at the knot hole. "Chad, it's me, Slippers. It's all clear. We need to talk it's urgent." Chad stuck his head out of the hole. "Hello Slippers, it is good to see you. Just one minute while James gets Hen."

Slippers looked puzzled. "Who's James?"

Chad asked James to run and get his mother. She quickly returned and then all three came out to meet Slippers together.

Henrietta made the introductions. "Slippers, this is James our son. James, this is Slippers, one of our best friends and one of the dogs you can trust."

Slippers smiled broadly. "Well this is a big surprise, a big, big surprise," he said as he looked at Henrietta and Chad. And then the smile faded and before Chad or Henrietta could ask, Slippers said, "The children have gone through a worm hole looking for you as you had gone missing. Ant is with them, Sid, the Beaver and his friend Freddie."

Henrietta sat down with a bump and covered her mouth with her hands. "Oh no," she said.

"Are you sure?" said Chad. James looked from his mother to his father realising something was wrong.

"I wanted to go too," said Slippers almost apologetically, "but I was too big. So, Ant told me to come back here in case you returned."

If the people in the house had walked into the dining room they would have seen a very sad dog, two very upset mice and one very inquisitive young one sitting in a semi-circle having a serious discussion as to what to do next.

"We have another problem," said Chad after a prolonged period of silence while nobody spoke, and James just kept looking from one to the other waiting for something to be said. "There is a weasel trapped in a cave who is dying. We have to go back and get him, also a missing journal that may well tell us what happened to start all of what has happened off."

Slippers looked confused. "The point is," said Henrietta, "I have to go with Chad and someone has to look after James. Will you?" she asked, looking at Slippers. "We should only be away a day at most." She said this while crossing her fingers behind her back. Portal travel could be a very hit and miss form of transport as she and Chad had found out to their cost.

A huge smile lit up Slippers' face. "Absolutely. No problem," he said, "I would love to."

"I trust you're happy with that," said Chad to James.

"Yes, father, no problem at all," said James thinking this was going to be fun.

"But remember, James," said his mother, "you can only come out to be with Slippers when the people are not here. Understood?"

"Come," said Chad, "we have to go." With that the mice returned back through the knot hole and Slippers returned to his usual place by the fire to wait for his duties to start when the people left for work in the morning.

Chad and Henrietta put their son to sleep in their room in their bed and told him he could look at any of the books if he wished while they were gone. They showed him where the food was kept and told him to help himself as and when he felt hungry. They also told him if there were any problems, he was to go to Slippers immediately, especially if he saw any ants!

Once James was asleep Henrietta smiled and composed herself. Chad smiled too and said "Here we go again. Go for it Hen."

Henrietta out of habit raised her hands in the air even though she didn't have to and said "I wish to go to they who can answer why this all began" which seemed funny considering that they knew most of it now, but it was important that they went back to exactly the same place. The portal obediently appeared and with one look at each other they stepped into the portal.

Fortunately they arrived as planned in exactly the same place as last time. However, it was not quite the same the library they had left. It was very dark and there was only one candle alight. It was very small and struggling to stay lit. The moment they stepped out of the portal they found it hard to breathe. The air was foul, and they realised they may be too late.

Chad coughed. "Hen, can you bring some air in here?" Henrietta nodded. She looked up at the ceiling and visualised a portal to clean air and sky. She repeated the same thought to her right, but it must have wind, she thought. Both portals opened at her command almost simultaneously and as soon as they opened the fresh air rushed in and as she had planned, the stale air left through the portal above her head. The candle on the wall flickered slightly because of the sudden draught but stayed alight and as the air improved it brightened considerably. Chad and Henrietta left the portals open and went in search of the weasel. The door to the counter was closed but there was sufficient room for them to squeeze underneath.

They found the weasel very quickly. He was on the floor surrounded by pieces of a table which it looked like he had broken when he had fallen or perhaps in a fit of rage. He was sprawled on the floor and his spectacles lay on the floor next to him. It looked like they were too late. Henrietta stood back while Chad checked him, "He is alive, Hen," he said, "but he is unconscious." The draught they had created with the portals was swirling around the cave and occasionally picking up bits of paper which floated briefly until they fell out of the draught and then floated back down to the ground.

The air had improved considerably so Chad suggested that Hen close the portals just in case they got something they didn't want. Henrietta closed the draughty one first and of course the wind stopped. She looked up at the ceiling and as she closed the second portal briefly for a moment was sure she saw a large ant and a bird looking down the hole, but before she could change her mind the portal closed.

She heard a groan and hurried back to Chad. The weasel had recovered enough to sit up and Chad had picked up his spectacles and gave them to him. Fortunately they were not broken. When he put them on, he was shocked to see them, "you can't stay here," he said, "you will die."

"I think Henrietta's fixed that," said Chad, smiling, "at least for now. We came back to get you."

"What?" said the weasel.

"We came back to save you," said Henrietta. "We knew you would die soon without air, but not just you; we also came for the missing journal that you never gave us."

The weasel was very quiet while looking down at the floor. "I kept it back because I believe it has the secrets of the machine and what went wrong with it, but it is in a language I cannot understand, and neither could Mustelee. He has left me to die, you know."

"Who has?" said Chad.

"My twin brother. He lied to me; he was never trying to save me. I was a fool; I thought I was in charge. I wanted to change our realm back to the way it once was, but he is more interested in ruling everything he beholds! He has gone mad."

"He is not the only one," thought Chad.

"Where did the air fresh air come from?" said the weasel, suddenly realising he was breathing normally.

"We brought it with us," said Chad, "where is the missing journal?"

"So that's why you came back, not to save me but to get the journal."

"Both actually," said Henrietta somewhat ruthlessly, "we felt that both you and your brother were as bad as each other, but at least you had a basically good reason for what you did even if it wasn't quite right."

"What do you mean by that?" said the weasel indignantly.

"Turning a blind eye to what your brother was doing and doing nothing about it. All those poor animals dying for your brother's quest, whatever it is." The weasel's attitude changed at this and he slumped down. "Yes, you're right, I did ignore it. I thought once we found out how we could put everything right he would change, but I was so wrong. I will get you the missing journal and I suppose that's the last I will see of you. You have given me a brief period of extended life, so I can die later," he said, feeling sorry for himself.

"No," said Chad, "we came to get you and perhaps you can help us defeat your brother and if we can decipher the journal, try and reverse whatever happened to your realm."

"You are going to take me with you?" said the weasel, not believing what he was hearing.

"Yes," said Chad, "so we have to go so please get the journal!"

"Well that's going to be a problem," said the weasel. "Since I regained consciousness after the lack of air I can't remember where I put it."

Henrietta put her head in her hands. "I knew it," she said, "I knew this had gone just too easily."

chapter 69

The white dove waited on the riverbank every day after Beaver and Freddie left. She felt a little guilty about not going with the others, but the truth was she didn't want to die, and she had heard all the rumours about dead birds.

Not long after the others had left a small group of ants had appeared on the riverbank and came up to her. They had tried to communicate with her but as only one could generate sounds anything like speech after much grunting and frustration and drawings in the mud she understood that they were looking for two mice in a house. Without thinking she explained, "Oh, you must mean Chad," and then went on to tell them they lived on the other side of the wood. It was only later in the day she realised her stupidity and of course by then it was too late.

The ants had followed the rough direction and met up with some of the others. By the time they met the dung beetles they were almost all together nearly 100 strong. The dung beetles, promised never-ending supplies of dung, told them where the nearest house was and one of the beetles added a warning to watch out for logs popping out of the ground! The ants had absolutely no idea what they were talking about, but thanked them anyway and set off, full of confidence set. They were sure they would find the mice, overwhelm them and take them back.

Chapter 70

Sid had soared very high in the sky while still keeping an eye on where Mot and the others were being taken. The air was filthy and he wanted to cough. He saw them being locked up but was not too worried because he heard Christopher telling them to do nothing and shortly afterwards Mot had said "reconnoitre".

Now this posed a problem as Sid had absolutely no idea what this word meant, or whether it was two words, or maybe even three?

He had run it through his head several times: Wreck a notor? Reck a noy tur? Rec a notor? Maybe wreck an oyster? No definitely not that. He finally settled on Wreck a Notor because he knew what wreck meant but not notor so all he had to do now was find the notor and wreck it but that was going to be very difficult as he had absolutely no idea what a notor was, where to find it, and why Mot wanted him to break it. This was giving him a headache, if not that then certainly the air he was breathing. But he had felt a wind blowing slightly from the opposite mountain and it was a lot fresher, so having confirmed where Mot and the others were from his lofty viewing point and noticing that nothing appeared to be happening, he decided to swing over to the other mountain and take a look.

This of course was exactly what Mot had wanted Sid to do generally, but unfortunately, he didn't know that. "Oh well," he thought, "this is why I am a stupid seagull."

This of course was nowhere near true either. No other seagull had amassed so many different friends, learnt so many new words and indeed so many new things: setting out on a mission to find Chad on his own, then setting out on another mission to save Chad and Henrietta, help the animals from the wood and to top it all, in this adventure he was in now in another realm (whatever that meant). Sid knew that if he had not met Chad none of this would have happened and he would still be sitting somewhere with other seagulls talking repetitive rubbish and promptly forgetting most of it and insisting that anything he could get his beak on or for that matter anything he could see was "mine".

He was, however, a little sad. He knew now there was no going back and it would be highly unlikely he would ever meet another seagull that would be like him, so he was destined to be single forever.

All these thoughts had run through his head while drifting on the thermals that allowed him to fly with very little effort towards the other mountain.

It was now completely dark or would have been but for a huge full moon that appeared to rest over what was once an active volcano several miles across.

The inside of the volcano was a beautiful silver colour with occasional green flashes here and there and glistened and glittered in the moonlight arousing Sid's curiosity. Sid dived down for a closer look, very conscious that he would need to swing back to the other mountain and valley soon to see if anything had changed, although he thought it unlikely before dawn.

chapter 71

With one last heave the ant crawled over the rim of the volcano. Whatever he had imagined, it was not this. There was no gas or fire or the huge bowl of hot dust that he had expected to die in trying to cross. Below him was a huge lake glistening in the moonlight. Somehow the volcano had filled with water almost to the edge in some places, but there was no indication as to where it had come from. He knew it didn't rain any more, at least not on the opposite mountain and valley.

He sat to rest and ponder what to do next. The only way to get to the other side was to walk around the rim and that was a very long journey. Unfortunately, the rock he had chosen to sit on was not stable and as he sat down it began to roll down the side of the volcano, throwing him head first into the water and knocking him unconscious on a hidden rock. He then slowly began to sink, completely unaware that all his efforts to supposedly fulfil his promise to Chad and Henrietta for setting him free and his plans for the future were irrelevant. This would now be his last resting place and all the plans he had so carefully made would amount to nothing.

chapter 72

As Sid flew down he realised that what he was looking at was a huge lake of water. He was just preparing to land on it then quickly remembered that he had to be careful; he was not in his usual place and what he saw here was perhaps not what it seemed. As he flew lower he thought he saw movement at the edge of the crater slightly further away, so he changed direction slightly to have a look. Much to his surprise it was a very large ant. At first he thought it was Ant and then realised that he could not possibly have escaped and got here before him, besides which he noticed as he got nearer this ant was considerably bigger but much thinner than Ant. As he watched, the ant pulled himself over the side of the rim and then sat down.

What happened next happened so quickly that at first Sid thought he had imagined the ant being there. One minute he was there and the next he was gone. Sid only had the light of the moon to see by, so it was only the rippling of the water where he had been that made Sid realise the ant had fallen in. Without hesitation Sid turned into a steep dive. He arrived just as the ant's body started to disappear beneath the surface. Wrapping his webbed feet around the ant's body, Sid pulled him out of the water. He was very big but weighed almost nothing – certainly not compared to a fish that Sid of course being a seagull was a master at catching, but not with his feet!

He quickly gained height. The ant didn't move – unlike fish that even when out of water would still try to escape. Sid hoped, because he had had no time to check, that what he had dipped his feet into was in fact water and looked down just to make sure that his feet hadn't dissolved or fallen off. No, everything was fine; his feet were still there with the ant, but glowing green slightly which of course was very unusual, so he flew to the nearest flat piece of land he could, gently laid the ant down and sat next to him, wondering if he had been quick enough getting him out of the water.

Sid had a dilemma: for some reason he couldn't fathom he felt an obligation to stay with the ant he had saved, but on the same token he had an obligation to look after his friends and of course Chad's children – although he had a feeling they were more than capable of looking after themselves.

The ant hadn't moved, and Sid couldn't tell if he was breathing or not. He vaguely remembered something about ants not breathing like he did, but if not, he wondered how they did? This thinking thing was hard work sometimes!

After much deliberation he decided to wait until dawn. If the ant hadn't moved by then he would find something to cover him up with and return to check on Mot and the others and ask her what to do. With that firmly out of the way he drifted slowly off to sleep.

What Sid hadn't noticed was that the ant had regained consciousness and was surprised to do so. His last memory was falling towards the water and hitting a rock just beneath it, so when he woke up on dry land at first it didn't make sense. He couldn't move yet but hoped that would change, so he had lain there and heard every word that Sid had thought and was grateful for what he had done to save him and would tell him so as soon as he could in order that he would continue helping him, but only because he needed his help. But he was even more amazed at the concern felt for him and all the others. As an ant he had fellow soldier ants, but they would never be considered friends; ants just didn't have them. He now knew from reading Sid's mind that his brother (it felt strange thinking that) was now chained up instead of him and the mouse family was locked up too. The thoughts he got about Sid's affection for them confused him, but his heart was made of stone and he decided there and then that once the weasel was gone, he would capture them all and use them for his own purposes and plans.

He would wait for the sun to come up, when Sid would make his next move. Hopefully he would be able to walk by then and he could use Sid to carry on with what he had planned.

chapter 73

Mustelee was very pleased the so-called assault by the mice that he had feared was a failure. As far as he was concerned, the mice who had just left through the portal had returned with their pet ant and his animal friends, apparently a beaver, a fox, and a bird that got away as usual. The ants very rarely caught one and some time ago he had told them not to bring any more as they could not do the hard work that was required in the mine.

The ants he had sent out to find the mice were wasting their time but he had no way of contacting them, so they would eventually come back even though they may fear for their lives because of failure. He would get great pleasure from chastising them even though he now knew they had no hope of succeeding.

He was considering abandoning work on the mine now that he had enough of the mineral that gave the machine its power, but he still hadn't worked out how it made some creatures strong and others weaker until they died. Even his clever brother hadn't worked that out. Well, too late to ask him now.

The ant was now chained up and apparently he could speak. This must be the one that his previously imprisoned ant referred to as his brother. He was of course now dead, which was a huge relief. Mustelee did not believe any of the rumours about escaped creatures living on the other side of other mountain. To reach there you had to cross the volcano basin which no creature could do. It was boiling hot and would never cool otherwise he was sure some would have returned.

So, with these so-called special mice (according to his brother anyway), now his captives and their ability to create portals at will at his disposal he was looking forward to seeing a demonstration of their powers – if they really existed. He was somewhat dubious about what his brother had told him. If they could travel at will why did they escape through the worm hole and then come back again the same way? And why hadn't they already escaped again? Very puzzling, but he had had enough excitement for one day with his brother soon dead and an army of thousands of ants to protect him he felt totally in control, and tomorrow was another day.

He would go to the compound in the morning to meet his new captives. The beaver and fox would go straight the mine where of course they would very quickly die. The mice, if they proved as useless as he suspected, would follow soon afterwards and he could look forward to long conversations with the ant to get to the truth about his very unusual growth.

chapter 74

The ant drifted off to sleep and was woken up by what sounded like a wind blowing. He opened his eyes and was pleased to find he could now move his legs, so he stood up. Sid was still asleep and there was no wind but still the low whistling sound of air moving persisted. As he turned around trying to see where the noise was coming from he knocked over some stones and the noise woke Sid up. Sunrise was a few hours away but thankfully the moon had not fully set so they could see each other. "Hello," thought the ant, "thank you for saving me."

"You're welcome," said Sid, cocking his head because he too could now hear the sound of the wind.

"I think it's coming from over there," said the ant and together they moved over to investigate. There was a column of pale light coming out of the ground. Edging closer and peering over the edge, much to their surprise they could see right down inside the mountain, but it didn't make sense because the tunnel or tube ran at an angle straight through where both of them knew was the extinct volcano and that was full of water. So what they were seeing was well, just impossible. Just then, at the very bottom, they both saw a small grey mouse with its arms up in the air and then the hole just vanished, and they were in darkness. Sid and the ant looked at each other and then back at what was now solid rock. Sid pecked it and then the ant put one foot on it. "Definitely solid," thought the ant.

"I can't argue with that," said Sid, pleased that there was something the ant couldn't understand as well as himself.

"Well what are your plans now, Sid?" thought the ant.

"I am going back to see if my friends are alright as soon as the sun comes up."

"Can you do me a favour first?" asked the ant.

"Yes of course," said Sid, without thinking of asking first.

"Could you fly me to the other side of the volcano? I promised Chad I would try and find the other animals that escaped like you did to help with the fight if there are any."

The ant was too big and too light to safely stay on Sid's back. The wind would no doubt blow him off and he would get in the way of Sid's wings, so the ant suggested he stand on his feet and hang onto his legs. This meant of course that Sid would have to fly with his legs down instead of tucked underneath him. He had never done this before and had no idea how it was going to affect his flying.

Sid stood up and the ant stepped on. Sid had two legs and feet and the ant of course had six, so with a bit of scrunching up the ant managed to get all six legs on Sid's because Sid's feet fortunately were webbed and much bigger.

Sid had a little trouble taking off as he usually used his legs as thrusters to launch himself into the air. Once off the ground it was wobbly at first but a bit like flying when you are getting ready to land.

They flew directly over the extinct volcano using what was left of the moon's light. For the ant to have walked it would have taken forever but with Sid's help they arrived in what seemed like no time at all, just as the sun began tipping over the horizon.

Sid landed somewhat clumsily which really wasn't surprising and the ant jumped off. Beneath their feet was grass which surprised them both.

"I have to go," said Sid and they agreed to meet back there in a few days' time to see if the ant had found any other escaped animals that had made it around the volcano.

Sid was in a hurry now to get back, but with light to fly by and his legs tucked away he made very good time. He circled the place where Mot and the others were held. Nothing had changed so he found a perch not far away and waited to see what was going to happen next.

chapter 75

Christopher had woken at sunrise and quietly called over his sisters and asked Blanket to join them. They went over the plan and Mot made it very clear she could take care of the front door, but from the outside because it would be safer. Christopher was puzzled as to how, but Mot assured him it would be fine and the ants couldn't see her, but she warned them to stay away from the door until it fell over.

Beaver and Freddie were still asleep but pretty soon they would be awake. Blanket said he would wake them up and explain how they were going to escape. They wouldn't believe it, but they would just have to wait and see. So, wake them up he did. Now fully awake and standing next to Blanket in the corner furthest away from the cell door, Beaver and Freddie looked on in confusion and somewhat dubiously.

"Right," said Christopher, "time to go!" Fidgit stood under the bars high above their cell. She put her arms around her sister and jumped. Mot and Fidgit flew up in the air through the bars and landed outside on the roof. Beaver and Freddie's mouths had fallen open and Blanket had to smile. Mot and Fidgit ran to the edge of the roof and Fidgit again put her arms around her sister and jumped off the roof. She landed by the door and immediately jumped back onto the roof. Mot backed away from the door and disappeared.

So far no one had seen anything except Sid, who was watching with great interest. Mot of course was now an old hand at this. She produced one small ball in her left hand and placed it by the steel door, then backed away and produced the second one, all the time remaining invisible except from the spinning balls.

There were two ants on guard duty at each end of the cell they had been in that were both asleep. However, the pop and snap of the first ball sitting on the ground and another one floating in mid-air had woken them up. They both stared at the floating ball completely unable to understand what they were seeing.

This time Mot made absolutely sure that the second ball hit the first; she was not trying to make a sinking hole in the ground. The ball hit the first and exploded, taking the cell door clean off its hinges which was exactly what she had planned to do. The ants had been knocked unconscious, but the sound echoed around the compound and very soon every ant in area would be after them.

Before the dust had even settled Christopher picked up the bent and battered steel door now shaped like a banana and threw it outside, so it landed flat on the ground (well as flat as it could be anyway) with a big bang and another cloud of dust and then he shouted, "everybody out and jump on the door."

Beaver and Freddie thought he had gone mad, but having been suitably impressed so far did as they were told and ran out of the now open cell doorway and jumped on its door. Blanket followed them and jumped on too.

Christopher stood behind the door, grabbed the edge and said, "Hold tight." The compound was at the top of a hill above the valley and the path or road leading to it was well worn rock. It had taken them over an hour to walk up to where they were, but Christopher had no plans for it to take that long going down.

The bottom of the valley near the portal once again was shrouded in fog but the top where they were had bright sunshine. Fidgit and Mot were the last to jump on, Mot having returned to her normal visible self.

Beaver and Freddie turned around to look at this mouse just about to attempt to push them down the hill and just shook their heads, but seconds later the steel banana shaped door took off down the hill being pushed by Christopher. Freddie and Beaver nearly fell off and hung on for dear life to the bars over the window of the door which was now a sledge not believing what they were seeing. Blanket, who was normally very quiet, laughed a lot — he really was enjoying himself.

"We have to get off at the bottom if we are going to find Ant and then return," shouted Christopher above the noise of the screeching metal sliding down the hill. It was now sliding under its own momentum, so Christopher jumped on too. There was of course a problem: how were they going to stop? But as it was too late to do anything about it, Christopher decided not to mention it as they all hung on and hoped for the best.

Sid had watched all this unfold in front of him from his vantage point and he was really impressed, but when he looked down the valley and saw the fog he realised he would have to be quick otherwise he would quickly lose track of them, so he immediately took off and hastily followed the careering sliding door hoping to land on it before it entered the fog. As he swooped down the valley after them, exhilarated by the danger of it all, he was really excited — every day was just so interesting! And different!

chapter 76

M ustela was full of apologies. Chad and Henrietta had to accept that this time it wasn't his fault for forgetting, but of course it was his fault for hiding it in the first place. Henrietta assured him that what was done was done but they had to find it. At first Henrietta suggested that they all split up and search separate areas, but Chad shot her a look which of course she immediately understood "how did they know they could trust Mustela?" Well the truth was they couldn't, so Chad suggested that he go around with Mustela looking together in the hope he might just remember something, and Henrietta would search on her own.

The cavern they were in was part of a large cave, so it was agreed that they would search the library and Mustela's living area first. As the most obvious but unlikely place to hide something it took them all day and turned up nothing although of course being in the cave days turned to nights and they were completely unaware of it.

Chad watched Mustela carefully while searching and he appeared to be genuinely trying to find the journal, but of course he had an ulterior motive: they were his only way out.

They rested very briefly and then Henrietta had an idea. They discussed with Mustela who he thought he was hiding the journal from. He answered without hesitation "his brother".

"So," said Henrietta, "where do you think you would hide it that your brother would not think to look in view of the fact you are twins and think the same way?"

Mustela was quiet for some time and then he said, "High, somewhere high. My brother knew I was afraid of heights."

They spent the next day searching every high point they could in the cave. Chad did most of the climbing even looking in places it would have been impossible for Mustela to reach but checking anyway just in case and frequently asking Mustela did he remember anything but every time getting the same shake of the head, no. So after the second day they had achieved something: the journal was nowhere to be found!

Mustela was very unhappy. He was sure that if he didn't find the journal the mice would leave him here and not come back, but try as he might he just couldn't remember. Henrietta and Chad weren't happy either, but they of course had absolutely no intention of leaving Mustela behind journal or no journal.

Henrietta suddenly sat up straight and she said, "The library."

"We have searched the library twice, Hen," said Chad, "what's the point of searching it again?"

"But have we searched high places?"

"There aren't any," said Mustela, "the ceiling is curved and there is nowhere to hide anything."

"What about above the mirror above the bookshelves?" Chad and Mustela looked at each other and then in an instant they were up and almost running to the library.

The door and counter flap was still open from their last visit and they all turned to look at the very long mirror that ran from one end of the bookshelves behind the counter to the other. It was in fact not one whole mirror but divided into three pieces by dividers similar to the frame itself. The frame was very ornate and protruded slightly all around and formed a very small narrow shelf above it, but in no way big enough for the missing journal. They were all immediately disappointed.

Chad was very quiet then said, "Mustela?"

"Yes," he answered.

"How do you get to the top books on the shelves if you need them?"

"There is a long ladder, but I took it down. I hated going up it and just looking at it made me dizzy." Chad looked at Henrietta and before anything more was said he had jumped onto the counter and then the shelves and was climbing up the side. He swiftly reached the mirror, climbed up the side and onto the top of the frame.

Chad had expected the frame to be made of wood but in fact it was some kind of silver metal. As he climbed along he disturbed small granules of gritty dust that had fallen slowly over the years from the curved cave ceiling above and onto the bookshelves below. The frame was only just wide enough for Chad to crawl along and it hadn't been disturbed in years. He relayed all of this to Henrietta and Mustela below, who could barely look at Chad's progress because of his fear of heights.

As Chad travelled along the top of the frame, he passed the first divider and then stopped. Something was different; the top of the frame was now much cleaner. There was a small straight line above the divider. Chad looked over the edge to have a closer look. Mustela covered his eyes and thought he was going to faint and he wasn't even up there!

The joint travelled right down the front of the mirror in the centre of the divider. It appeared now that was how it had been made so no mystery there. What was strange was why the top was now clean.

Chad called down to Mustela, "have you ever been up here?"

"Absolutely no way," said Mustela without hesitation and Chad laughed. He continued across the top of the frame and then again noticed a second joint and now the dusty granules were back. But with some disappointment he realised that nowhere was there a place to hide a journal. He turned to look back the way he had come and felt something under his feet. He crossed back over the joint again onto the cleaner section to have a closer look. There was a small round black button in the frame. He cleared away the dust he had disturbed. Just in front of it were four faint letters "P R E S S". He hadn't seen the other S, so in fact it was five. "This must be some code," he thought, and then he realised, "Oh of course, press."

"What is it?" said Henrietta, noticing Chad was scrabbling around in one place.

"Well there is nowhere to hide a journal up here," he said, "in fact nowhere to hide anything really except a button."

"Why on earth would you want to hide a button up there?" asked Henrietta. At this Mustela uncovered his eyes and said, "yes, why?" completely misunderstanding what he meant and thinking of a shirt button rather than a push button.

Chad decided to push it. At first nothing happened and then he felt a small vibration and the crack between the frames moved slightly, then without warning the mirror frame he was on suddenly swung open with him on it and he nearly fell off.

Mustela witnessed this happen and fainted there and then. Henrietta checked to see if he was alright and then looked back up. Behind the mirror were more bookshelves almost completely empty apart from two books – actually it was one book and something else. Chad climbed down and picked up the something else; he was sure this was the missing journal.

"Can you catch these, Hen?" said Chad.

"Certainly," said Henrietta, climbing onto the counter and one after the other Chad carefully dropped them into Henrietta's hands and she placed them on the counter. As Chad turned to leave, he noticed three more buttons inside above the top shelf. They too were labelled, but this time strangely. One said P R E S S, another said C L O S E, but the third said L E A V E.

He climbed up to the top of the shelf and as he did so, the mirror started to close and apart from the missing dust it now looked exactly the same as before.

Chad climbed down the same way that he had climbed up and then helped Henrietta get the book and what they believed was the missing journal down onto the floor. Just then Mustela began to stir. He sat up and looked around.

"Are these what we were looking for?" Chad asked.

"Yes! Yes, they are the missing journal and guide."

"Guide?" asked Henrietta.

"Yes, you need the guide. Well I think so anyway. It's very complicated I went over it for a long time and, in the end, I gave up."

"It's time to leave," said Henrietta. "Much as I trust Slippers, he and James have been on their own long enough and it's only a matter of time before the ants come and I don't think they will able to fight them. Slippers is too big, and James is too small."

"Who are James and Slippers?" asked Mustela.

"You will find out soon enough," said Chad.

"Where are we going to go?" asked Henrietta. "Mustela is too big for our home; he would never be able to leave."

"This is it," thought Mustela, "I knew it. They have what they want and now I am being left to die." Mustela was close to tears. Having nearly died once to go through it all again would just be too much.

"We will have to arrive outside the house," said Chad, "and then find somewhere for him."

"But what if we are seen?" said Henrietta.

"It's a chance we will have to take," said Chad. Mustela had perked up now. The fact they were talking about finding somewhere for him was positive.

"Are you ready?" said Henrietta to Mustela. He nodded frantically, unable to speak in anticipation of his imminent escape. Once again Henrietta raised her hands, she didn't need to but with a new audience it looked so much more dramatic. Mustela had of course seen this before but only in a mirror. To see it in front of his eyes was fascinating and exciting all in one!

The little ball of light formed once again and expanded at Henrietta's bidding to a size big enough to accommodate them all. Come on then," she said, "we must all go through together," and

Mustela needed no second bidding. They stepped into the portal, the candles on the wall flickered and they were gone.

chapter 77

On the first day Slippers saw nothing of little James at all. He checked on him regularly, but James would call back that he was fine. It was strange because every time he called back it sounded like he was in his head. He thought he was perhaps shy but when he thought this the next time he spoke to James, he assured him he was not shy, which was strange again because he hadn't actually asked him.

James was in fact studying. He had worked out that although he could read another creature's thoughts, he could not read their memories unless they happened to be thinking about them at the time.

He couldn't wait to meet his brother and sisters and he knew from what his mother and father had thought and his brief time with Slippers that they were a special family of mice, but they were in danger from ants coming. For what, he could not understand. He also knew enough from his father's reaction that being able to read other's thoughts was unusual and he assumed that none of the others had this ability. The question was, how many other skills did he have that he didn't know about or for that matter they didn't know about too?

One thing for sure was his ability to read from birth, but again he had nothing to compare it to – after all this was the first time he had been born, so he didn't know what was normal and what was not! He laughed to himself at this silly statement.

He had gone through all the books very quickly and absorbed all the knowledge therein. However, absorbing it was one thing and understanding it was another. Having very little experience of life a lot of what he had learnt simply didn't make sense yet because he could not apply it to something he hadn't seen or experienced.

Slippers was the answer, or maybe part of it. If he spent time with him, he was sure a lot of what he had read would make more sense.

So, putting down the last book he headed for the front door — the knot hole as he knew it was called. Poking his head out carefully to see if it was safe, he found his way to Slippers' usual resting place. Slippers was very pleased to see him and immediately asked him what he wanted to do. "Talk, then play," he replied.

So to oblige Slippers told him everything he knew about his parents, siblings and friends. Of course there were lots of things he didn't say but that he thought about, which helped James tremendously.

After a few hours James had learnt enough. "Let's go outside," he said. "You find a ball and we could play catch or go into the woods to explore."

"I don't think that's a good idea," said Slippers, thinking about keeping this young mouse safe for his parents' return. "Besides which I can't go out. I am locked in — I'm only a dog. Only people can open doors and their locks." He smiled to himself because this wasn't strictly true remembering how Christopher and Fidgit had in fact opened the front door for them all to escape.

Unknown of course to Slippers, James now knew this too. "A lock," he said out loud, "I have read about them," and flicking through his memories he came to the part about locks. "Levers, tumblers, latches, and handles, seems fairly simple to me." He moved over to the front door and Slippers followed. Looking up at the lock, there followed a clicking noise and much to Slippers' amazement, the handle pulled down seemingly all by itself and the front door opened.

"That's amazing," said Slippers.

"Ah," said James, "I guess that's not normal then."

"No," said Slippers, "not normal, but impressive! Very impressive." Impressive was now of course Slipper's favourite word of the moment.

So now with free access to the outside they could play and play and of course they did. James would throw the ball with great strength and speed and Slippers would tear after it and bring it back. When they tired of this James would ride on Slippers' back and they would run through the wood at great speed with James screaming in delight, but they would always watch out for people in the wood and never leave until the cleaner had been and gone. If outside the house and they heard a car coming or a delivery, James would open the door again and they would quickly duck inside.

Slippers, of course, was wary. In the back of his mind was the fear of the ants' visit. One time while they were resting and he was worrying about it, James asked him, "why are you worrying about these ants coming to get me all the time?"

Slippers didn't answer immediately. He thought back over previous conversations he had had with James and was sure he had never mentioned it to him. Before Slippers could reply James smiled and said, "No, you have never mentioned it before."

Slippers said, "You know what I'm thinking, don't you?"

"I guess that's not normal either then," said James.

"No," said Slippers, "it's not." So for the rest of the day they played a game. Slippers would look at things but think about something else and every time James got it right. "Outstanding," said Slippers, using his second favourite word.

Later they discussed the ants. "Why are my parents so worried about these ants and why are they coming for me?"

"Actually, I don't know why the ants are coming. Something happened on the other side of the worm hole and so ants are being sent here to get your parents back, but they are not here – you are, and that puts you at risk. But your parents will be back soon I'm sure, before the ants get here so you don't have to worry."

Slippers didn't realise how wrong he was going to be.

chapter 78

The makeshift sledge hit a bend in the valley but was showing no signs of slowing down. Amazingly they had all managed to hang on and Sid had made a very impressive landing on a moving target just before it entered the fog. The sledge rose up the valley wall as it turned down towards the portal entrance and although it was foggy they could still see the glow of it in the distance. The sledge now picked up speed and Beaver shouted out above the noise, "How are we going to stop?" Christopher of course had been thinking the very same thing but knew that it was too dangerous to stop it at this speed or to try to get off.

"We don't," he shouted back.

"I see," said Beaver, but of course he didn't really but there was nothing else to say.

Sid had heard the exchange and realised that at this speed they would either hit a cliff or go straight through the portal again, but he knew Ant was still chained up and the other ant was on the other side of the mountain and was expecting Sid to return. Suddenly the fog cleared, and the sledge shot past the place where Ant had been chained the day before, but there was no sign of him. He had gone. "He's escaped," thought Sid, "that's it then, and my mind's made up. Mot and the others will have to go through the portal and since Ant's safe I will have to help the ant in the mountain." Without a moment's hesitation, Sid stretched his wings and launched himself into the sky and swiftly rose out of sight.

Moments later the sledge had reached the portal. It had lost a lot of its momentum but was still moving very fast. The ants guarding it had no chance to stop them. They braced themselves in case they hit the opening but luck was on their side and they flew straight in and of course in an instant they were gone.

chapter 79

Mustelee had had a good night's sleep in anticipation of today. He was very positive and most importantly He! would have been pleased, not that it mattered as he now considered himself in charge.

When he heard the explosion echo down the valley he knew, just knew, it had gone wrong. He tried to summon his soldier ant guards, but there was no sign of them. He knew then he was once again not in control.

He went out onto the roof. He could see part of the valley from here and the compound. The bottom half of the valley was shrouded in the fog again — soon it would be permanent he was sure. The top half was still visible. A terrible screeching noise reached his ears and echoed back and forth and then he saw the prisoners unbelievably sliding away down the valley on a metal sheet. He could not understand how the mice and creatures had escaped. Just as they were about to enter the fog a large white bird flew down and landed amongst them. It was impressive to watch; it was the first bird he had seen in flight in many years and would probably be his last.

He went down the stairs to the courtyard. There was not an ant to be seen but soon he knew he would not be alone. He had seriously underestimated the skills and abilities of his enemies. Perhaps 'enemies' was too harsh, combatants, yes, better, but he felt he was not totally to blame. He had been led to believe they were harmless, helpless animals and at first, they had been, but these mice and the others with them — they were seasoned fighters. They had to be, but they can't have come from the other realm no such creatures existed except the ant and of course him! He would be here soon he was sure of it.

He had played a role just as he had been instructed and then tried to take over and at first succeeded. If the ant had not escaped he would have done so and now he knew it would be over soon, he was not sorry. He had betrayed everyone in the end, even his own brother. "We all have to choose sides," he thought, "I thought I had chosen well, but it seems I have not." A shadow fell across the courtyard. He knew who it was and he was about to turn around and ingratiate himself one more time when his feet left the floor. The last thing he remembered was his body smashing into the wall. He was sure he heard his neck break, but he felt no pain and it was a blessed relief.

chapter 80

They finally found the house they thought they had been sent to find. They were now 100-strong and all were firmly convinced this was it. Of course, not one of the ants had discussed what if it wasn't? Failure probably meant a violent death, but despite this they would still loyally return home as there was nowhere else to go.

They had arrived late one afternoon and observed the house for the rest of the day, but there was no sign of the two special mice they had been sent to find. Their knowledge was limited as all they had been told was that they were special! With absolutely no idea what the difference between a normal mouse and a special one was they were well, stymied.

The following morning the humans left the house and hurried up the hill. A little later another one arrived and then left again. They discussed with themselves what they should do next and it was agreed they would enter the house and find out just how many mice if any lived there, but if they caught them and they were not the ones wanted the outcome for them was inevitable.

Just as they had finally agreed a plan the front door opened again, and a dog came out. Expecting another human, they all stopped communicating amongst themselves and waited. But what followed was a very small mouse holding a ball. The dog began to get very excited and the mouse threw the ball down the length of the cul-de-sac outside the house.

Now the ants were paying attention. They knew enough about their own abilities to know that for their size they were much stronger than other creatures and could lift big leaves and twigs, but this ball was three times bigger than the mouse and he threw it so far and so fast they could not even see it leave his hand.

The dog tore after it, brought it back and dropped it at his feet, whereupon the mouse threw it again. Having observed this several times they all agreed this would be classified as a special mouse and even if they could take back one that should be good enough. Just one problem though: they all agreed that if he was as strong as he looked it was unlikely that only 100 of them could overpower him without help.

James had just raised the ball to throw it again for Slippers when he lowered his arm without throwing it. Instead, he beckoned to Slippers. Without hesitation, Slippers obliged, expecting a new game. As soon as Slippers was close enough James indicated he wanted him to lie down. Though a little puzzled, Slippers obliged. "They are here," whispered James into Slippers' ear.

"Who?" said Slippers, looking around.

"The ants," said James, "they are in the wood across the road."

Before James could caution him, Slippers looked straight into the wood and stared. "Don't look, silly," said James.

The ants were puzzled. It looked as if the mouse and the dog were having a conversation. This was all becoming stranger and stranger, and now the dog was looking over or at them – did he know they were here and if so, how?

Slippers looked back sheepishly, but of course too late. "I think it's time for an invitation, don't you think?" said James.

"An invitation to the ants?" said Slippers incredulously.

James turned to face the ants and thought "I think you better come out and join us to talk. Good idea, yes?" The ants looked at each other and with much nodding they all agreed; they had heard the same thing. But what to do?

One of the ants, who over a period of time had sort of become the leader, stepped out onto the road and walked towards James and Slippers. The others of course followed. They lined up behind their leader, waiting for instructions and thinking that this was now even stranger!

James stepped away from Slippers and smiled. He was just about to start an in-depth conversation with the lead ant when just above them there was a crackling, a popping sound, and there on the road out of nowhere appeared his parents and a weasel, complete with a pair of spectacles.

The ants backed away. They instantly recognised the weasel and a wave of fear swept over them. But with a second look they realised he was wearing spectacles; it was in fact the twin brother who they had been told had died in the mountain. Fear turned to confusion and they struggled to decide what to do.

James was disappointed that he had not had a chance to engage with the ants, but was very pleased to see his parents back safe and sound. Slippers' mouth had dropped open. He had never been on the receiving end of portal travel before and it was amazing. When he recovered his voice and shut his mouth he said just one thing. "Outstanding" and then he laughed. He too was very glad to see Henrietta and Chad back.

The weasel had just stood and said nothing. He looked all around at what he was seeing and smelling. It was overpowering – there were trees, there was greenery, the air was sweet and smelt of perfume from the flowers. The sky was clear and the air was cool. "So this is what the other realm is really like," he thought.

After the excitement was over, Chad introduced Mustela to James and Slippers. "This," he said, "is Mustela. He has been stuck inside a mountain for some time and we went there to rescue him." Underneath his arm were two books one big and one small. James looked at them curiously but said nothing.

"Thank you," said Mustela still amazed at how fresh the air was and thinking that it must have been like that once at home.

The ants just stood and waited, not knowing what to do. They had been instructed to bring back the mice. At first there was one with a dog, and now there were three with a dog and a weasel who was supposed to be mad and even dead and was the twin brother of the twin who was definitely mad and persecuted them and in turn was ruled over by Lord Ty Rant who without doubt was also definitely mad and persecuted everybody! It was just so confusing.

Ninety-nine ants waited patiently for their naturally nominated leader to make the next decision; it was much, much safer that way. Their natural leader of course was no nearer to deciding what to do than the others. Who was in charge here anyway?

The situation was confusing; if the mice were to be brought back as instructed, why were they with Mustela and how did he get here?

James had been listening to the confusing thoughts the ants were having and decided to speak, "Father, these are the ants that came to attack us, but they are confused," he said, pointing behind them. When they had all arrived through the portal they had done so facing the house, so they were completely unaware of the ants' presence, so they turned around to look, including Mustela.

With Mustela now facing them the ants became more nervous. "I'm afraid I can't speak to them, you know. Only my brother could do that; he had a mental ability to communicate with just about anything."

"I can speak to them," said James. Mustela just looked at the young mouse he had just met with amusement. Chad, however, knew better. "James, can you ask them why they are here and what they want?" James turned to the ants to communicate with them as his father had requested when there was a huge boom and a banging noise in the wood. Everybody turned to look. What now they all thought, what now?

chapter 81

After launching himself into the sky Sid quickly cleared the fog and almost immediately could see for miles. He had assumed that Ant, having escaped, would follow his brother towards the other mountain so he flew in that direction.

Once again as he flew the air became cleaner and the wind was blowing in the right direction, so he made good speed.

He flew over the extinct volcano and although he had good eyesight decided to fly lower to see if there was any sign of life. There was none; no sign of Ant or his brother.

In the distance he could see flickering light just like the water in the volcano, so being a seagull and spending most of his time by water he headed in that direction. As he flew he realised that for some time now he had in fact not spent most of his time by water, but what a great time he had been having instead.

The flickering he had spotted was in fact a lake or perhaps a pond he wasn't too sure of the difference only that one was much bigger. "That's probably why they have different names," he said to himself. As he drew closer he spotted a small river running into it.

And then, much to his surprise, he spotted a small beaver's lodge in the middle. He swiftly swooped down and landed on the bank. There was not a sign of life anywhere, but he called out all the same, placing his wings to each side of his beak to make his voice carry further. "Hello, anybody home?"

At first there was no response and then he was sure he saw some movement behind the twigs and logs that the lodge was made of.

But then, nothing. He waited a little longer and decided it was his imagination or perhaps the wind and was just about to launch himself into the air when a head popped out of the water right in front of him and made him jump.

"You're a bird," said the beaver in a strangely guarded way, as if not believing what she was seeing. She hesitated then said, "there aren't any birds around here. You're the first bird I have seen in a very long time, did you escape too? Are you alone?" The beaver looked along the banks to see if he was before Sid had a chance to answer.

"Yes, I am alone. I sort of escaped but I wasn't really a prisoner anyway." This of course made no sense to the beaver as at times what Sid didn't anyway, but she carefully came out of the water.

"Oh," said Sid, "you're a girl. Are you alone too?"

The beaver shook the water off her back still looking nervously around. "Yes, unfortunately I am. I had a partner once a long time ago but I was brought here to work in a mine by the ants with other animals. I managed to escape by chewing through a door and some of the other animals came too but unfortunately a lot died. There is something in the mine that hurts us — not the ants, but still their evil leader tries to get more animals to mine the mineral he needs. It kills us but makes ants grow bigger. He is very big and wants to rule everything with an army of ants. He controlled the ants here by threatening to kill their queen. Now so many generations have passed by they no longer have loyalty to the queen, only loyalty to him, but through fear and nothing else."

Before he came there were two weasels — they were bad enough, but the big ant is totally ruthless and can fool almost anyone. When he is violent nothing stands in his way.

Every day we fear he will succeed and come looking for us, but the extinct volcano is full of water and difficult to cross and the ants believe it is boiling hot, as does their leader. While that myth remains, we will be safe.

Sid was very silent for a moment. "He's here already," he said reluctantly.

"What do you mean already?!" said the beaver, frantically

looking up and down the banks of the lake and backing up slightly to the water's edge ready to return to her lodge, the only place she felt safe. So Sid went on to tell her of his flight over the volcano and seeing him fall into the water and of saving him and then bringing him here to try and find you all for help.

By then end of the tale the beaver had calmed down. At first she had thought he was working with the ant which of course he was, but unwittingly. The ant had fooled Sid and used him as he did with everything and everyone. She now felt very sorry for him because it was apparent he was deeply upset. He had tried to help and now things were worse.

Sid suddenly looked up. "Have you seen him at all? I dropped him off several days ago; you should have seen him by now."

"No," said the beaver, "I watch every day from my home. There are some other animals, but we do not visit each other. We agreed it is safer that way and that we would only contact one another if there was a threat. So far that has not happened, but it is a lonely life."

Not wanting to make things worse than he already had done, but curiosity winning, he had to ask, "Your partner died in the mine then?"

The beaver smiled. "No he didn't. I am glad to say I went out one day and the ants caught me — just me. They are immensely strong when they work together, and I was of course much smaller and much lighter." Then she smiled again. "We are partners for life — all beavers are, so he too will be living alone."

"Then the answer is to go home," said Sid firmly. "We all came here to fight the ants, but it's not the ants! It's the weasels and one ant, that's who we have to beat. The others have gone back and I now know how as well, but I am sure they will come again. If we can join them we can all fight together. It's better than living the rest of your life here in fear. He knows now there is no hot volcano; it's only a matter of time before the ant army comes."

The beaver hesitated. Having dwelt on Sid's statement it made sense, but the odds were overwhelming.

"And," said Sid, sensing he was on the verge of actually winning an argument or point without being rude for the first time in his life by using logic, "I think I have met your partner and he is living with a fox and is just as lonely as you!"

The beaver's head snapped up. "Really, you're not just saying that?"

"Yes really, I have met your partner I am sure of it."

"Then I will go," she said without further hesitation, "but I am not calling the others. This is one risk I will take on my own – well with you, anyway," she said smiling again.

"We will have to go now," said Sid, "it's a very long walk around the rim of the volcano."

"I thought you said it was full of water," said the beaver.

"It is," said Sid.

"Well I can swim then, can't I?" she said.

Sid closed his eyes briefly. "Er, well yes, of course you can," he answered, feeling a bit embarrassed. With that she went back to her lodge to get some things and they hastily set off in the direction of the volcano.

As Sid walked away from the bank a young solitary pair of eyes watched them leave; she had in fact been watching since the moment Sid arrived. She had followed the rules and not shown herself. Better to be alone than risk the safety of the others whom she knew hid here and there. She had in fact befriended the beaver and from time to time she came to visit when the loneliness became intolerable – it had suited them both.

She had been on the way there when Sid had arrived. She walked all the time. Her previously injured wing had healed but she had still not made any attempt to fly so walk she did. It didn't bother her, and she had become quite proficient at it. That is, until today when she had seen Sid glide beautifully to a stop on the bank, shake his wings and put them away in one fluid movement. It was the first time she had seen one of her kind since she had been captured and she nearly broke the rules and came out of hiding.

But fear for the others made her hesitate and now she had missed her chance to end her loneliness and, to make things worse, she had heard overheard their conversation and she knew the beaver, her only friend, would not be coming back either.

chapter 82

The three dung beetles had waited several hours after the ants had left. They watched the rocks for a while, but it was pretty obvious they were not going anywhere, when one of them said, "You know what?" The other two turned slightly towards the one that had spoken and said together, "What?"

"I think we have been had. I don't think the ants are coming back." The other two said nothing for a moment. Dung beetles have fairly simple lives and thinking about things was not that high up on their agenda.

"I think we should follow them. If they find the mice or any animals, we have a chance of getting hold of some dung."

The other two needed no further encouragement and hastily agreed. With that they hopped off the log and followed the ants in the direction they knew they had taken.

Dung beetles are not normally fast movers, but with the promise at least in their heads of finally getting hold of some dung they did their utmost to catch up with the ants.

In this endeavour they succeeded. Somehow they managed to get to the house before the ants, just in time to see James and Slippers playing ball. Now the dung beetles knew nothing about how the other animals lived but had gradually become more and more interested about the world around them and less and less about dung! Suffice to say they knew that normal mice didn't and couldn't throw a ball, or any object for that matter, as hard and fast as James was! So they decided to retreat back to the last clear patch of the wood just before they had reached the house and wait for the ants to arrive. Ants, you see, were almost invisible on the ground, but dung beetles because of their size and colour would be vulnerable out of the wood so all three agreed they had gone as far as they should and decided to wait in the clearing. They found a suitable log in the shade and side by side settled down to wait. The one thing dung beetles definitely had was patience!

chapter 83

Contrary to what Sid had thought the ant was going to do, the moment he was out of sight the ant turned around and headed back towards where he had come from. He knew that Sid had expected him to go searching for the others and originally that had been his intention. But having had access to Sid's thoughts, such as they were, he now knew things were out of control. He was worried that the mice and those helping might succeed in their plans, but unfortunately he had no idea of what they were because Sid didn't know either. What he did know though was his so-called brother was here and had escaped and it was very clear whose side he was on. Therefore there was going to be only one outcome when they finally met again!

It was unfortunate that he would now have to walk back around the rim of the volcano to convince Sid he was going to look for the others, but he of course hand no intention of doing so; falling into the lake was just an unfortunate accident while faking his escape.

His anger rose as he remembered arranging for Mustelee to put him in chains so that whoever came would think he was a captive, never thinking that Mustelee would leave him there and take over. His very presence in chains was enough to convince the ants that he really was a prisoner and allow Mustelee to take back over their control.

The ant was moving swiftly now, his anger overruling any residual pain. No longer limping he was ever watchful in case Sid should return and spot him before he reached the other side. Once there and down the other side he would be hidden by the fog that always hovered at the base of the volcano.

He emerged out of the fog to find the ants in disarray. He

quickly and violently reasserted his authority and took over to learn that the mice had in fact escaped with several other animals through the portal. This much he knew from Sid's mind, such as it was. But he didn't know that Sid was still here or where his brother was and if he had escaped through the portal too?

The ant summoned all of the ants and made it very clear that they were soon to do battle, and nothing was to go through the portal under any circumstances. He then headed for the compound. The ant did not reach out ahead with his mind. He knew where Mustelee would be and with no ants to protect him he was defenceless.

When the ant entered the compound or "the palace" as Mustelee would call it he was in the courtyard with his back to him. As the ant approached, his shadow fell over Mustelee and he saw his shoulders move in resignation. The ant could no longer control his rage and swiftly picked Mustelee up and smashed him into a wall with such force the ant was sure he heard something break. Mustelee fell to the floor and no longer moved.

The ant knew he must prepare. They would come back. The ant cursed his own spontaneous actions – he could have obtained so much information about the mice from Mustelee's mind, but too late now.

The ant turned, now to go see and threaten the queen, he thought, I need more soldier ants; many, many more.

chapter 84

The three dung beetles sat patiently on their log. This was something they did on a regular basis so prolonged periods of silence were not uncommon. The ants had come and gone, and it was late in the afternoon. The clearing was beginning to cool when one of the dung beetles suddenly said, "I think something is going to happen soon." He was of course referring to the reappearance of the ants with, they hoped, some dung producers. However, before the others could respond to his statement the ground began to shake. The dung beetles looked at each other as if to say, "Oh no, not this again". But in fact, it was not this again, but it was something similar. Suddenly to the right of the clearing just above the ground a large bright hole appeared. Although it was daylight it still lit up the clearing even more, seconds later a huge sheet of curved metal shot out of the hole. It looked a bit like a large bent cucumber only bigger, flat and not the same colour! (So technically not really like a cucumber at all!)

But if this was not amazing enough, sitting on it and hanging on for dear life was a beaver, a fox, three mice and a cat!

The sheet of metal ploughed into the ground as the bright hole extinguished behind them. However, the sudden halt was too much for the passengers and they all flew off the front into a heap.

The dung beetles would confirm later amongst themselves that perhaps they just might give up collecting and rolling up dung because following ants around just might be considerably more interesting.

The beaver, a fox, three mice and a cat untangled themselves and all of them were laughing – even Beaver for the first time.

Blanket was looking around and said, "I know this place. We are near the house," and when the others had finally stopped laughing and sorted themselves out said, "follow me," and set off down one of the paths. The others looked at each other and dutifully followed Blanket. Minutes later they all emerged onto the road in front of the house.

What they were expecting to see was not what they saw! As they stepped out of the wood there in front of them was a large group of ants sitting in a neat row. In front of them was one solitary ant – and then the mice saw their parents with Slippers, not alone, but with another small mouse and a weasel.

Even Blanket was confused. The mice rushed up to their parents and were promptly introduced to their brother, now that was a big surprise! Slippers, of course, was very relieved to see them back safe and sound with Blanket and then the introductions were made. First the weasel was introduced to them, and then the fox and the beaver. There was much talking and excitement and for a while everybody had forgotten about the ants.

The ants heard and saw all this confusion and happiness and for the first time since they had been born they understood what it was like to belong, be missed and care about one another. They had spent their lives being pushed around and now for the first time realised if they wanted to, they could have a choice.

chapter 85

The ant sat now calm and fully in control. Well, in control of what? That was the question. He had the ants remove Mustelee's body as its presence irritated him and kept reminding him of his mistakes.

The ants asked nervously whether they were to return his body to the other realm through the worm hole as they had done with all the other corpses.

"Good question," thought the ant, "but Mustelee was not from that realm." But did it matter? He had had all the other animals returned from whence they came, partly because there was nowhere to put them here, but mainly because they too reminded him of his failures. "Yes," said the ant on the spur of the moment, "take him through the worm hole and dump him in the wood well away from the worm hole and I mean well away, understood?" The ants nodded in reply, relieved that for once they had asked the right question, but also disappointed. Mustelee was quite heavy and it was going to be long walk.

The ant resumed his deliberations.

One thing was sure: the mice would return. They were a force to be reckoned with and the information he had gained from Chad who he had fooled into thinking he was on their side by being chained up would be useful. The ploy had worked, but whether the suffering would be worth it remained to be seen. Mustelee had paid the ultimate price for crossing him.

The open portal was now a danger to him purely because it would not close, besides which he could not use it as he had simply grown too big. So he decided he would get the ants to build a wall in front of it. Any creature trying to use it would die in the attempt. He was sure that there were ants out there looking for what remained of the animals in the wood and of course when they returned they too would die, but it was unimportant to him.

He informed the queen of what she was required to do, and it amused him that every time she made a feeble attempt to resist he would just randomly kill several of her workers and she would instantly capitulate.

With the queen now producing the soldier ants he needed it was time to plan, but time was what he was short of. He was sure that the others on the other side of the portal were doing exactly that, "planning".

He knew they would not attempt to use the portal. After all, Henrietta could produce them at will as long as they were not near to the unclosed one the now deceased twin weasels had opened. So it stood to reason that any attempt to attack would come at the compound, or palace, depending on what you wished to call it. He did not require palaces, so compound would suffice.

He had spoken to several soldier ants who had witnessed the escape and confirmed that on the door to the secure compound which they had somehow removed and turned into a makeshift sledge, there had been the three mice, a fox, a beaver, a cat and a seagull who had joined them at the last minute. This of course had to be Sid, who had saved him from drowning in the volcano, as no birds existed in his realm.

But something didn't add up. Three mice, three mice, he kept saying it to himself. If two of these mice had been Chad and Henrietta, who was the third and why did they need to escape through the worm hole when Henrietta could make her own at will? It came to him in a flash. Family! They have family. It wasn't Chad and Henrietta that came here; it was their family with help!

He needed Henrietta for the worm hole creation, and he'd thought he needed Chad too in order to force her to work, but a whole family – even better! What he could inflict on a whole family, especially in the mine. Henrietta would do whatever he asked whenever he asked, it wouldn't need to be a fight as they had no resources, but he had the soldier ants. They will be overwhelmed no matter how many animals come. So, the answer is a trap. He was sure they would appear in the compound, for where else was there to go? He decided therefore to make the compound their self-made trap. The ant was giddy with the planning of his success.

He had of course at this point completely put out of his mind that there was one other player still at large: his brother Ant, who somehow had escaped the chains and was nowhere to be seen or found. He assumed that he too had escaped with the others and the ants had just not noticed.

chapter 86

As instructed, enough ants gathered together to move Mustelee as they had been ordered to do. They had expected him to be as stiff as a board as he had been dead some time but surprisingly he was not, and his body sagged all over the place which made him much harder to carry.

"Is it me," said one younger ant to another older one, "but he feels warm."

"Yes," replied the other ant, knowledgably, that's because he's been lying in the sun.

"Oh, I see," commented the younger ant, but not really seeing at all because they picked his body up from the courtyard and he was definitely in the shade.

The journey was tortuous. Although they had the rocky road down the valley to follow it was still full of large rocks (well, large to ants anyway) which were difficult to negotiate when you were all trying to carry something heavy that kept flopping all over the place.

It took the best part of the day and the sun was setting when they approached the worm hole. The light it was emitting helped them see but already the ants had created part of a wall across the entrance. The leader of the carrying party told the others to rest and then engaged in a long conversation with the leader of the wall building team. At one point it looked like it became quite heated.

Their leader returned obviously disgruntled. Nobody wanted to ask but after a prolonged silence one of the ants had the courage to do so. "Well?" he asked.

The leader ant, relieved that he could now share his conversation, explained. "King Ty Rant has told them to close off the portal. It is difficult because if you get too near it sucks you in;

several ants have disappeared already when sections of the wall they were building partially collapsed and went with them, they didn't return!" Their leader let the last words hang in the air and they all looked at each other. "We can go through but when we come back, they may have built more of the wall and we will be crushed against it! I asked them to stop and they refused because it meant disobeying Lord Ty Rant."

One of the ants silently moved to pick up Mustelee and the others quickly followed. The decision had been made. They heaved the body over the mound of accumulating rocks, entered the portal and were gone.

chapter 87

Sid didn't have problem with walking generally but up hills and through bushes, well that was different. The beaver on the other hand had no problem at all and swiftly made her way towards the extinct volcano. Having struggled for a little while Sid made his apologies and said he would fly on ahead and wait. The beaver said she had no problem with that, and they temporarily parted company.

Once again Sid soared into the sky, very grateful that he could fly. He circled twice and then landed where he could watch the beaver's journey up the hill. Most of the time he could not see her, but with the occasional movement of bushes here and there he could track her progress.

And then he noticed some movement further down the mountain. A bush moved slightly and then again shortly afterwards. Sid became concerned as there was no wind at ground level to account for this brief movement in the bushes – was something following her? Sid stood very still, focusing on the bushes just above where the movement occurred, but it did not happen again, and he relaxed.

The beaver appeared out of some bushes and Sid flew down to join her to see how she was getting along.

The young injured seagull had dwelt on her future alone and had watched with anguish as the beaver disappeared into the foliage with Sid. Then later she saw Sid take flight and in that instant, she made up her mind to follow them. She had no idea what had convinced the beaver to leave, but she decided her time here was done and better to follow and see where her life would lead than die here alone. She knew really the sight of another seagull had swayed her decision and she couldn't wait to find out where they were going.

Having gone part of the way up the hill she noticed through a gap in the bushes that Sid had landed and was staring down the hill. It appeared he was staring straight at her and she froze on the spot! Sid continued to stare. The seagull was sure he could not see her, but her heart was pounding, she just didn't know why. After all, if he was helping the beaver, he had to be on their side perhaps then it was something else that made her feel this way, but what?

Sid turned away and took flight and then landed out of sight. The seagull presumed it was to join the beaver. She then started to breathe again only aware that all this time she had been holding her breath. She quickly resumed her climb. If she lost them, she knew she would never find them again and would be resigned to spending the rest of her days alone. In her heart she knew what she really meant was she would never find "him" again.

Chapter 88

The ant's assumption that the others were planning could not have been further from what he was thinking. True they were planning, but not their return. Once all the excitement had died down it was time to go home, but Mustela had no home and although he could have climbed through the cat flap there was nowhere in the house where he could successfully hide without being found. Beaver and Freddie of course were quite used to living outside in the wild which of course Mustela was not, but he was not complaining for if it were not for Chad and Henrietta, he would not be here at all or, for that matter, alive.

"We can make a camp," said Beaver, "in the clearing back there," nodding his head in the general direction.

"You won't be able to," said Slippers, "humans go through there every day on the two-wheel machines they ride on."

"Bicycles," said Blanket, who rarely said anything. "They are called bicycles and they go through there every day in the morning and all come back again in the evening. They call it a 'short cut' whatever that is."

"Not if we stop them," said Beaver, and with that he jumped up and entered the footpath that led to the clearing. They all looked at each other, apart from the ants who were still observing, debating and deciding whose side they now wanted to be on because this life seemed to be much better and interesting than the one they had left. All of them that is, except one. Lord Ty Rant had his favourites and throughout his ant army he had placed secret observers who were to report back to him any dissent or potential mutiny. Well, the ant had observed, and it was obvious to him that none of the others were considering going back, so while they were all watching the animals he quietly snuck away. The only creatures to see him go were the three dung beetles who had heard all the noise and had come to join the party the mice and animals were having.

They had taken up a new position overlooking the cul-de-sac in the shade on a much smaller log, when one of them noticed the solitary ant leaving. "I wonder where he's going?" said one of the other beetles.

"I guess he doesn't like parties," said one of the others as he disappeared quietly into the wood.

The ant knew he had to report back to Lord Ty Rant quickly. If more ants came and did the same there would very soon be no ants left in the army. His only way back was through the portals which appeared here and there around the wood and what the ants had only recently learnt was although the appearances seemed erratic, they were not. They appeared in one of seven places on a regular basis, so the ant knew that if he waited in one of these places he was guaranteed a journey home in seven days or less, so he hurried hoping it would appear sooner rather than later.

There was suddenly an almighty crash and a small tree fell right across the footpath entrance to the wood. Moments later there was another crash and a second tree followed it. The animals decided to stay out of the wood for now and if they could have put up a warning sign it would have been something like "danger, beaver at work". After much crashing and banging, Beaver's face reappeared through the bushes with a big smile. "That should do it," he said, "I enjoyed that."

The rest of the animals cautiously approached the pile of tree trunks that Beaver had felled quite cleverly to form an interwoven barrier to the footpath, but made no comment.

"There," said Beaver emerging from the wood covered in bits of bark and leaves and repeating what he had previously said, "that should do it!" And the general agreement was yes, it should. With that done they set about building Mustela somewhere to live. Everybody joined in, including the ants. They couldn't carry much, but everything helped and soon it was done. The sun was setting and Mustela could not believe what everyone had done for him and could not thank them enough. "Right," said Chad, "tomorrow morning meeting here. We have to plan. Remember Sid and Ant are still missing and the big ant is still planning. We must return and put a stop to this once and for all." There was much murmuring, and everybody drifted off.

The mice returned to the house with Slippers and Blanket. Chad stopped at the door. "Oh!" he said, looking at Slippers and then the front door.

"No problem," said James and before anything more was said the front door silently opened.

"I see," said Chad with a smile. "What more surprises are we to expect, James?" James bounced into the house with glee.

Beaver and Freddie were invited by Mustela into his new home and they decided to except Beaver was missing the cleanness of the water and surprisingly so was Freddie even though he was a fox.

"They are good friends to have," said Beaver suddenly. "It's at times like this I wonder what happened to my partner."

"Why, what happened?" said Mustela without thinking.

So Beaver told the story of her disappearance once again and his assumption that the fox hunt dogs had got her. When he was finished Mustela said, "I'm so sorry. You all know now what really happened. I feel it was my fault because of the ant and my brother."

"So," said Beaver, suddenly changing the subject, "are you going back with us to join the fight and put an end to this?" Mustela hesitated. He knew he liked what he had found, but he also knew that he was now obligated to return with all of them to bring this tyranny to an end. He hesitated only briefly. "I have to," he said, "I have no choice."

chapter 89

The ant had a conundrum and it was extremely frustrating. He knew the mice would soon return, but the question was when and what forces would they bring with them? He knew the wood was empty of animals, but he also knew having lived there once that there were other creatures beyond the boundaries of the wood. But he also knew that they would not believe whatever the mice told them as without first-hand experience of what happened it would be just impossible for them to imagine — as it would have been for him had he not experienced it himself.

Satisfied that they had limited resources, he spent a week searching the 'palace' as he now found himself calling it having admitted defeat on a rare occasion because every time he called it "the compound" it caused confusion.

The palace consisted of three floors: ground, first and second. The ground floor was made up of three large rooms at the rear and two at the front. The front two had windows which at one time must have had wooden windows, because some remnants of them remained.

There were two very high walls with two steel gates in the middle outside of which stood the prison. It too had a steel door which of course was no longer there thanks to the mice's brazen escape — he still hadn't worked out how they had blown the door off! Stacked against one of the walls were the remains of several boats which puzzled the ant; it never rained, and the valley was bone dry.

The first floor consisted of seven rooms; three at the front with windows and four at the back without. The second floor was mostly the roof with one large room at the rear and a huge balcony all around from which you could see right down the valley. The whole structure had been built into the mountain which towered above it. The ant stood on the roof looking down the valley. "Whoever built this," he thought, "knew what they were doing, but of course they would never have expected an enemy to appear from nowhere, or did they?"

As he pondered this, the mountain shook and groaned again. The ant was sure that sooner or later these frequent earthquakes would turn into a volcanic eruption; he had learnt that the earthquakes had only started after the weasels had begun digging the mine. It was almost as if they had disturbed something and upset a natural balance.

With the aid of the ants he searched it floor by floor; every nook and every cranny, every drain hole, crack or joint he saw he would instruct the ants to crawl down or into to find out where they went. The ants were puzzled by all this. After all, a crack was a crack, a joint was a joint, and a drain was a drain, but of course they all wisely did as they were told and dutifully reported back that the drains went where they were meant to but had not had water flowing through them for many years so were mostly blocked up and the cracks and joints got smaller and smaller and didn't go anywhere at all! This, of course, is what was expected.

And then on the ground floor the ants discovered two square frames one inside the other with a large square of flat rock in the centre of the frame like a trap door.

The ant was sure this was some kind of door, but no amount of prising, pushing, or levering could change the position of the two frames in relation to one another. So, after spending a day on this the ant finally gave up, deciding it was some designated mark of a meaning long ago lost, much to the relief of the other ants who thought that everything they had just done for the last few days was pretty pointless, but not one ant was stupid enough to say so.

chapter 90

C had too had a conundrum: life had appeared to return to normal, but Chad knew it was very much temporary. His first concern was that they were missing two of their friends, Ant and Sid. Ant had presumably escaped but had disappeared and Sid was last seen taking flight just before they returned, but why?

The question was had they been captured and if not, where were they?

In any event, Chad knew he had to return to finish what they had started. Without question he knew somehow that the ant or his influence would forever affect all of them and the wood would never return to normal unless they acted first.

Foolishly he realised that because he had assumed the ant was a real prisoner, he had given him information that he could use against them and inadvertently put Henrietta's and his family's lives at risk. The ant knew how he and Henrietta could travel from one realm to the other almost at will and enlarge or shrink the worm hole to suit, which the permanent portal the ant had could not. As a result, he was trapped there but his army of ants were not. He therefore realised it was only a matter of time before they would come for Henrietta and possibly his family as well or worse!

Chad was sure at this very moment the ant was fortifying the palace and would have many ants waiting at the portal to defend any invasion. But of course, the ant also knew they could appear almost anywhere and that they didn't have to use the worm hole and he wouldn't expect them to. Chad tried to think where the ant would least expect them to return to. But then again, they could maybe use the worm hole and surprise him. No, perhaps not even with the element of surprise – the palace was at the end of the valley on high ground and they would be trapped at the bottom, so that was a bad idea.

Ideas went round and round in Chad's head until he thought his head would explode! And then it came to him. The one place he would not expect them was the mine! The mine contained large amounts of the very material that helped create the portal and the ant knew it prevented Henrietta from creating her own; therefore it stood to reason it was the last place he would expect them to arrive!

So, he started to plan. He would of course have to get agreement from Henrietta mainly because the planning meant their children would go with them. He knew they would be safer with them than being left behind and in any case, he doubted they would agree to stay. His plans revolved around their powers as much as his and Henrietta's!

The following afternoon he called everyone together. Much to Chad's surprise the leader of the ants had approached Chad and through James confirmed they had decided to join with them in an attempt to overthrow Lord Ty Rant. However, there were now only 99 of them as he confirmed that one of their number had mysteriously disappeared overnight.

James confirmed to his father that the ant was telling the truth and none of them had any idea where the missing ant had gone.

Chad had a pretty good idea where the missing ant was and said so: he had returned to inform Lord Ty Rant that you have changed sides. The ants looked nervously at one another. "Yes," the leader ant communicated to James, "but the portal is probably closed by now."

"Why?" questioned Chad, "have they manged to shut it down?"

"No," replied the ant, and went on to explain about the rock wall.

Chad listened, truly shocked by the ruthlessness of the ant and his complete lack of regard for any life but his own, but it strengthened his resolve to carry out his plans to the bitter end.

It was a cool afternoon and the animals and creatures had gathered around including the dung beetles who had several days ago asked to join them. When asked what they could contribute they told James and he immediately said yes, and asked if they could start production as soon as possible. They had agreed and had not been seen until today.

Overlooking the animals and insects that had assembled together Chad realised that even with their powers, it was going to be a dangerous mission as they were heavily outnumbered. As he began to explain what he planned to do, he noticed the ants line up in three rows and he hesitated. Remembering his mistake of divulging too much information, he waited one moment and without further thought changed the plan and told everyone that they were going to invade the palace and would be leaving quite soon. He cut his speech short and with a puzzled look from Henrietta went back inside.

A solitary pair of eyes peering from the bushes watched the assembly and when it broke up it disappeared into the undergrowth. "Father—" said James.

"I know," said Chad, "I know," and looking at James he put a single finger to his lips as they returned home.

chapter 91

Lord Ty Rant had confirmed himself there was no other way out of the palace apart from the entrance gates. And he was sure that Chad and Henrietta would come through a portal straight to the palace and then escape again the same way. But he knew that they couldn't reopen a portal next to the existing one because Chad had told him so. It was at the bottom of the valley and he had absolutely no idea how to turn it on or off, let alone move it. Even if it was possible, but he was sure the green mineral that glowed in the dark that was used to create it in the first place could disrupt it so then it could be used to prevent Henrietta creating a new portal to escape. Not that he wanted to but if his plan was to work, he would need to test his theory out.

There was a considerable amount of the green mineral piled up in the mine brought up by the animals of which there were none left alive — at least not here anyway. It was not a place the ant liked to visit because of the constant movement of the mountain which he believed one day would collapse on the mine burying it forever. Mustela had — unfortunately for him! — succumbed to the effects of a previous earthquake and paid with his life.

The problem, thought the ant, was moving it all. He had plenty of labour with hundreds of ants, but it would take each group of ants a long time to move each lump of rock and time was not something he had.

But ants could work as a team and as part of their nature they could form chains and hand whatever they wanted to move from one to another. But rocks? All the way from the mine to the palace? That would take some serious teamwork. The ant made up his mind it was the only way, but first a test: he told a small group of ants to go down to the mine and to bring a small piece of the green mineral up to the surface and wait for him there, so he could have it transported to the entrance of the portal. The ants looked at each other. Every time some new and unusual instruction came along it usually did not work out well for those who undertook it but what choice did they have? Turning away, they scuttled off wearily to the mine to do Lord Ty Rant's bidding yet again.

chapter 92

The seagull had seen Sid fly off and she had expected him to return shortly but he had not so far. So, putting all her fears away she stretched her wings as far as she could and decided to try and fly to join the beaver. She looked at the outstretched broken wing that was bent at a strange angle where it had healed badly, and then shrugged. She turned around to face down the mountain and launched herself into the air. The gradient of the hill had helped but almost immediately she felt herself falling, the bent wing dragging her in the wrong direction. But with some clever manipulation of the twisted wing and help from the other she managed to stay in the air and gradually began to climb. Her flight was ungainly but it was flight and within a few minutes she had managed to master a happy balance between one wing and the other and she soared even higher.

She was angry with herself now. Why had it taken her such a long time to try instead of waddling around on the ground like a wounded duck? She laughed at this and her mood lifted. She banked sharply looking for the beaver and scanned the skies. There was no sign of Sid but now she was flying again for some reason her fear had faded away. She saw some movement on the ground it was the beaver so for the first time in a very long time she prepared to land.

It was not as smooth as she had planned but with a crash and a few bumps she hit the ground right next to the beaver. Showering her with dirt she stood up, folded her wings as best she could and said, "Hello!" The beaver was of course extremely surprised both by her arrival and the fact she had flown.

"I have come to join you," said the seagull bravely. "I overheard your conversation and I know you are not coming back, and I have no wish to spend the rest of my life alone." At this the beaver smiled. "I see," she said, "nothing to do with seeing another seagull then?" The seagull became a little shy and if she could have blushed, she would have done so.

"Come," said the beaver, "we have a long way to go. Sid will find us when he returns." With that they resumed their journey up the hill, the seagull reluctant to leave her friend again even though she now knew she could fly.

chapter 93

Sid had become a little impatient because of the beaver's slow progress, but didn't tell her so of course he just told her he had decided to fly over to the palace and worm hole entrance to see how the land lay so they could plan their escape. He took to the air in his usual way and swiftly rose above the volcano.

Dusk was just arriving and in the slowly fading light Sid could just make out the odd twinkling green spots of light at the bottom of the volcano's lake as he flew over it. The journey of course took him almost no time at all and he intended to use the worm hole's light to guide him, but as he drew nearer the light seemed subdued.

He circled around past the palace and then down over the valley keeping as low as he dared, but as the light was fading away having to sink lower and lower. The worm hole now appeared as a faint ring as if it was dying. Perhaps now the ant had found a way of turning it off. If this was the case, he and the beaver were in trouble; there was no other way of getting back home.

As he flew over the valley, stretching from the mine down towards the worm hole entrance there appeared a huge line of marching ants and another line stationary stretching up to the palace. Right in the centre of the line moving towards the worm hole was a group of much larger ants and in the centre of them without doubt Sid knew this had to be Lord Ty Rant, but what was he doing and where was he going?

Sid noticed just along the valley wall ahead of the ants was a small crevice just big enough he thought to hide in, so he could look down over the procession. It was risky, but he had to know what was going on. So, gliding quietly in the fast-approaching night he flew into the crevice to wait, not unfortunately noticing that he had disturbed some small pieces of rock which had all but silently fallen onto the rocky ground of the valley floor.

The ant had become paranoid. The constant thinking about the imminent attack was driving him so crazy that he could almost not think rationally. There were so many unknowns it was almost impossible to plan. He had made a plan and was now having doubts. Everywhere he looked he was suspicious of spies within his own army working against him. The queen had done as she had been told and produced more soldier ants but there was something about them that bothered him. Ants were supposed to be loyal to their colony, but for all intents and purposes there was no longer a colony, just Lord Ty Rant's ruthless regime.

So these ants should be totally under his control and when he ordered them to do something his wishes should be their command and obey they did, but only what he ordered. When that was completed, they just stopped and waited, incapable of making any moves without instruction. It was as if there was something missing from them and he was sure that the queen had done this deliberately.

He knew the time had come to eliminate the queen, but without a replacement he could not proceed. His own queen was still in the colony in the other realm; if he could return and take over his problems would be solved, so again everything came back to capturing Chad and Henrietta alive.

Such was his paranoia he had surrounded himself with a group of the largest ants and they were there to protect him at all costs even with their lives. Such commitment would normally be reserved for the queen, but such loyalty no longer existed. He constantly looked everywhere, unable to feel safe, and so when he heard the slight disturbance up ahead, he lifted his head up just in time to see Sid land and move out of sight. "The seagull," he thought, "the escaped seagull, so you are the spy! Well I know where you are." Without sensible thought, he commanded the whole section of ants that were guarding him to leave their formation around him, scramble up the side of the valley and kill the seagull, leaving himself completely unprotected.

The crevice Sid had landed in was not very deep and narrowed down to nothing at the end. He had just enough room to turn around once he had landed and folded his wings. Then he edged forward to look down on the procession. He had just shuffled two steps when the crevice was invaded with ants. They attacked Sid with an aggressive vengeance, covering his head and body. He just closed his eyes in time, but he could feel them biting and tearing at his eyelids and any part of his exposed skin. They tried to worm their way in between his feathers to try and bite him there. Sid had no room to take flight and was quickly overwhelmed. He blindly staggered to the entrance with the ants all over him and fell off the ledge onto the valley floor, knocking himself partially unconscious on a loose rock. Some of the ants died in the fall but still they attacked him and as Sid lay there totally overwhelmed, he realised that one silly miscalculation and decision was going to cost him his life. He began to fade into unconsciousness; the last thing he heard was a terrible, horrendous screaming sound so loud and so near that he assumed it was himself and if he could, he would have covered his ears.

chapter 94

The ant had waited patiently in one of the expected worm hole locations and sure enough, on the third day, out of nowhere the hole appeared. He moved quickly because he knew that unless he used it, it would quickly extinguish itself, but as he prepared to enter out of the hole came a group of ants carrying what looked like a weasel. He took several steps back in surprise and before he could react the portal closed behind them and he had missed his chance to return and report to Lord Ty Rant.

He began to remonstrate with the ants who, having put down the weasel's body in order to rest, listened quietly until he had finished. The lead ant then explained that they had been sent here to dispose of the weasel's body.

"Well dump it and lets go to the next worm hole. I have things to report – urgent things," said the ant, drawing himself up as if he was a superior and very important.

"Well," said the lead ant, "we could but Lord Ty Rant made it very clear that we were to dispose of the body well away from here and if we don't, you know as well as I do, he will know! Besides they are blocking up the other end. If you go back you will surely be crushed to death when you get to the other side."

"But they can't," said the ant, "we all knew about his plans to block up the worm hole, but he wouldn't do it until we return surely?"

"He knows we are here, and we were planning to come back, yes," replied the ant, "but that is Lord Ty Rant for you," and then he said no more.

The ant was silent for a moment and then asked, "So what are you going to do?"

"We are going to stay here; we have no choice. We will dispose of the body and try to make a life here but it's only a matter of time before he finds a way through the worm hole to here, so we must just wait and see. Come," he said, "help us carry the body. At least then we have done what we were supposed to do so if he does come sooner rather than later, we have a chance of surviving." The ant hesitated, and then nodded his head in agreement and understanding, and with that they all lifted the weasel's body to continue their journey into the wood, but it would now take some considerable time to travel the distance they had been instructed to because travelling through a thick wood full of trees, bushes and tall grassland was much harder than travelling over rock.

chapter 95

The seagull trundled uphill with the beaver. It was slow work because now the ground was rising rapidly and was very steep. Sid had been gone a very long time and she was beginning to get concerned. "I'm going to look for Sid," she said, and before the beaver could reply she turned around and launched herself down the hill in her ungainly but effective way. Turning back quickly and mastering her new method of flight she quickly rose higher. It was now nearly dark as she crossed over the volcano and, looking down, she saw the twinkling green lights for the first time. She knew which way to go for she remembered the terrible journey she took with a broken wing to escape never thinking she would be going back. A tiny shiver of fear coursed through her for she now had a sense of foreboding and felt that something was terribly wrong, and Sid was in trouble.

As she approached the valley from a great height, she too could see the column of ants stretched up the valley from the portal to the mine and from the mine to palace. However, there was no sign of Sid, so she swooped lower, content with the fact that as darkness approached she was for all intents and purposes invisible. It was then she noticed Lord Ty Rant surrounded by larger ants and all the memories of his tyranny and persecution came flooding back. Oh, how she and so many animals had suffered and died! She at least had got away with her life. Then she saw Sid. It had to be him because there were no other seagulls but the two of them, nor for that matter any other birds at all but only briefly for he suddenly entered a small cleft in the rock face and disappeared. She was instantly relieved that he was safe and considered herself foolish now for worrying over nothing. Her relief, however, was very short-lived. Suddenly all the ants surrounding Lord Ty Rant left him and tore over to the valley wall and quickly climbed it straight into the cleft she had just seen Sid go into. With horror she watched as Sid struggled out of the cleft and fell to the valley floor completely overwhelmed by ants. In that instant she realised that they had been ordered to kill him by Lord Ty Rant and all her hopes of being with him and finding final happiness where fading very quickly before her eyes. An overwhelming rage overtook her; she had never ever felt this way before and without hesitation she knew and understood the only chance of saving Sid was to attack the perpetrator of this act: Lord Ty Rant, now undefended. If he was attacked she was sure the ants would be ordered back to his defence and would leave Sid alone. So without hesitation and channelling this new-found rage into hate she had coursing through her body, she dived at great speed towards the ant that had caused her so much pain and screamed out so loudly she could hardly believe the sound came from her. The joint on her right wing had healed with hardened featherless skin and bone and as she dived, she aimed this at the ant's head, pleased for the first time that she had found a use for it.

She swooped down on Lord Ty Rant at an insane speed. With no thought for herself, she approached him from behind. The scream had attracted his attention as she intended, and as he turned towards her, her bony wing caught him in the neck completely by surprise and with such force it knocked him off his feet. At first, she thought she had killed him which was not her intention although she would have liked to, but with him dead there would be no one to call off the ants and Sid would certainly die.

She turned back to swoop down on him again just as he attempted to get up and started pecking him, but only half-heartedly while looking towards where Sid lay. Sure enough, the ants suddenly stopped attacking him and came rushing back to Lord Ty Rant. Just as she had expected, he had called them back to protect himself.

She waited until they were almost upon her and she half hopped, half flew over them to land next to Sid and immediately gave him a kick in the side. "Wake up quickly, get up," she cried, "you have to fly. Please Sid, please!"

Sid stirred a little, so she kicked him again and winced when she did it. On the second kick, Sid open his eyes. "You," he said, "are the seagull that was following us."

She was surprised. "You knew?" she asked.

"Yes," said Sid, "I knew," as he rather unsteadily raised himself to his feet.

"Sid, you have to fly now before Lord Ty Rant knows he has been tricked."

"What?" said Sid, still woozy from the attack.

"If we don't fly, we will both die here together!" Something about the way she said 'together' stirred Sid to action. His mind cleared and although he was bruised and bleeding, he knew nothing was broken. He stretched his wings and launched himself into the sky with the seagull right behind him, he almost hit the valley wall and then they were away and clear.

Just in time it would seem. Lord Ty Rant had turned in time to see Sid get up. Two seagulls, not one – how many more were there? In that second, he realised he had been tricked and played. He turned to the ant next to him to vent his anger, but the ant didn't flinch, it just stared straight back and before he could say anything the ant spoke firmly and without hesitation, "we obeyed your instructions, my lord. We left your side to attack the seagull and we returned to defend and protect you, as instructed." The ant let the last words hang in the air. From the corner of his eye he saw the two seagulls disappear into the night. It was then and only then that he realised how big the ants surrounding him had grown and that perhaps he had better take action before they began to get ideas of their own and threaten his reign. He said nothing, just instructed them to continue to the worm hole with the mineral. As he did so he looked up into the sky realising now he simply had no idea what he was up against. He had assumed the attack would come from without, but now it seemed it might be within. He had no idea how many hundreds of creatures were waiting out there ready to attack. He regretted now not completing his journey around the volcano; he was sure he would have known the answer if he had.

Of course, the ideas he had of what was waiting over on the other side of the volcano could not have been further from the truth and in different circumstances if Sid and the seagull had known they would of course have laughed. But they said nothing to each other as they climbed into the night sky together using instinct to find their way back, but not for long as a full moon had slowly risen illuminating the night as only a moon can. As they approached the volcano, instead of the dull green glow of the minerals lying in the bottom, once again the lake glistened and glittered beautifully in the night sky. It was the first time the seagull had flown over it at night and she was in awe.

Sid just flew silently without uttering a word. He had said nothing since they had taken off and the seagull was concerned, had she done something wrong or something to upset him? But try as she might she couldn't think of anything that she might have done.

Soon they approached where the beaver had been last, and they prepared to land, and by the light of the moon together they did so. The beaver was still awake and came to them almost as soon as they arrived. "Where have you two been?" she said anxiously, "I had no idea if either of you were coming back."

"I am afraid it was my fault," said Sid, speaking for the first time since they had escaped and turning to the seagull. He smiled. "If she had not come to help me I would surely now be dead." The beaver took in a sharp breath for only now she noticed Sid's bloodstained feathers and face.

"She bravely attacked Lord Ty Rant and as a result I managed to escape from a horde of ants that were attacking me. I foolishly got too close and that was nearly my downfall." The seagull now had become very embarrassed by Sid's statement, but Sid turned to her and said, "I will forever be in your debt. If there is anything I can do for you I would not hesitate to help."

The beaver glanced from one seagull to the other. She was fascinated; she was sure she was watching true love blossom in front of her only the other two didn't know it yet. "There is something," said the seagull, taking the biggest risk of her life because the wrong answer would devastate her, "two actually: can you please give me a name?"

"And the other?" said Sid.

Without hesitation the seagull said, "I want to stay with you forever!" Sid showed no immediate reaction to this which, of course, for Sid was not unusual, both the seagull and the beaver were unaware they were holding their breath.

"Charlotte," said Sid, "I will call you Charlotte." There was a brief moment of complete silence. None of them spoke and then Sid smiled at Charlotte and said, "I will gladly stay with you forever. There is not a better thing I could do with the rest of my life."

Charlotte was overwhelmed and for that matter so was Sid, but he wouldn't admit it. The beaver was happy for them but of course seeing them together reminded her of her own loneliness.

"Sid," she said, "can you give me a name too?"

"Lottie," replied Sid immediately, amazing himself at the speed of the answer without having to think about it.

Lottie laughed. "Thank you so much, but what now? When can we head for the worm hole or portal and go home, or whatever you call it?"

Charlotte and Sid looked at each other and went very quiet. "What?" said Lottie, looking from one to the other.

"The ants have built a rock wall over the portal entrance," said Sid, "I presume to prevent anyone or thing coming or going. Lord Ty Rant must have ordered it."

"Oh," said Lottie. "Oh." And with that and the realisation they might never get home their happy euphoric mood evaporated, and they fell into silence.

chapter 96

James timidly knocked on his father's door and heard a curt reply. "Yes?" Without hesitating for what he had to say was urgent and important although he knew he would have to convince his father of it, he pushed open the door and entered.

Chad was sitting in a chair staring at the ceiling so when he turned to see who it was, he was little irritated that it was his young son. "Yes, James, what is it?" he said, "I'm very busy," which from James' point of view he did not appear to be, but he was not about to say so.

"I have had a dream, Father," he started, but before he could continue his father interrupted, "Oh really, James, this is not the time for this!" James had known what his father's reaction was going to be, and he had considered several ways of starting a conversation he knew he had to have, but no matter what he said he expected his father's reaction to be the same. What he knew was so important that he had made up his mind to be assertive in order to get his father's attention.

"Father, please don't start. I know what is coming and how difficult the next few days are going to be, so I can assure you I would not have bothered you if I had not considered it important."

James' assertive statement had stopped Chad in his tracks. He had briefly forgotten that although James was young and played like a very young mouse, he had abilities and knowledge well beyond his years.

"Come, son," said Chad, "come, sit and tell me what you want to say." So James sat and began.

"Several days ago, Father, I began to dream something was talking to me. His name was Paradeigma. I couldn't understand what he was saying but over three nights in my dreams he spoke to me again and again until finally he spoke in English and I could understand." By now James had his father's attention and he was listening without any intention of interrupting.

chapter 97

Lord Ty Rant resumed his journey to the worm hole. He then instructed the ants to carry the piece of mineral they had salvaged from the mine to the edge of the pile of rocks, the only part of the worm hole that was exposed and emitted light. No sooner had they begun to move the mineral closer to this edge it began to glow a brighter green enveloping the ants carrying it in green light. Simultaneously the worm hole's light began to pulse and oscillate and the ground beneath began to shake. Some of the rocks on the edge of the pile fell into the worm hole taking several unfortunate ants with them.

"There," thought Lord Ty Rant with absolutely no concern for the ants he had just lost and probably died, "I was right. It will stop the mice in their tracks," and he immediately ordered the ants to remove every single piece of green mineral they could find in the mine and move it up to the palace.

Lord Ty Rant was by no means a scientist and the testing out of his theory regarding worm holes and the green mineral left a lot to be desired, but such was his obsession to win the coming battle at all costs the slightest indication that he was right was enough to convince himself that he was. Unfortunately, in this case he could not have been any further away from the true facts.

It took two whole days of torturous hard work and several ants died fulfilling Lord Ty Rant's wishes, but eventually every piece of the green mineral that could be found was removed and transported to the palace. Then, on Lord Ty Rant's instructions, it was distributed around room by room and area by area so that there was not a place that didn't have a least one small or large piece of it somewhere.

However, the mountain was not happy. The more they

removed on a daily basis the more the mountain groaned and shook. Lord Ty Rant ignored it because the mountain had been grumbling for ages, but rumours were rife amongst the bigger soldier ants that what they were doing served no apparent purpose and put their lives needlessly at risk.

At last Lord Ty Rant was ready. He brought every single ant into the palace – some 8,000 of them in total – it should have been considerably more, but the queen was still being very difficult and as soon as the battle was over which Lord Ty Rant was overconfidently sure would be a matter of hours if not minutes, the queen was to be executed. He had positioned lookouts everywhere. By his calculations, when Chad and the others arrived, they would be overwhelmed within seconds and, with no chance of creating an escape route, imprisoned in minutes. With a form of transport in and out of this realm to anywhere he wished at a moment's notice, nothing could stop him. So with the battle won in his mind before it had even begun, he sat and planned, completely oblivious to the dissent within his own army or to the fact that he had made certain assumptions that were completely and utterly wrong!

chapter 98

C had had listened quietly as his son memory by memory, dream by dream, repeated everything that Paradeigma had told him in his dreams. James remembered very clearly that he had asked many questions and Paradeigma had answered every one. Chad interrupted him only once to ask if he knew who or what Paradeigma was. All James could say was that he was a traveller who lived a long time ago. Chad was overwhelmed by James' clear, precise recollection of everything that had been relayed to him.

After several hours of speaking through the night, during which time Henrietta joined them, James was done. Chad thanked him and told him not to worry. Reassured, James left a lot happier.

Chad, however, was worried. What James had told him could put their very lives at risk, so he decided if there was going to be a time to do this it had to be now. He told James before he left to tell the ants to be ready; they were leaving in the morning. He called Christopher, Mot and Fidgit and told them today was the day. As soon as it was light, they were to go into the woods and find Beaver, Freddie, Mustela and the others, and tell them the same. They were all to meet outside the house as soon as the cleaner left. Henrietta went off to tell Slippers and Blanket.

The sun rose as it did every day. The owners went to work, and the cleaner came and went saying goodbye to Slippers and Blanket as she did every time she left, but noticed this time they were wide awake and waiting patiently by the front door without getting excited (only Slippers of course Blanket never got excited about anything usually). It was as if they were waiting for her to leave (which of course they were). It was unusual, but of course she quickly forgot about it after she left, little knowing that Slippers would once again be gone when the owners returned. And of course, she would be to blame again as the last one to leave as there was simply no other way Slippers could leave the house – or so they thought, of course!

Freddie, Beaver and Mustela had arrived first and waited in the woods as instructed until the cleaner left. They heard her say goodbye to Slippers and Blanket. She shut the front door, locked it and double checked and then got in her car, did a sharp U-turn and drove away up the hill.

Once the car had crested the hill, they waited a little longer to be sure and then stepped out onto the road. As they did so the front door swung open and they hesitated, but it was James working his magic again! Out came Slippers, Blanket and all of the mice. The door shut behind them and there was a sharp click as James relocked it. Chad looked up the hill and into the wood; although the footpath was now closed after the beaver's construction work, the occasional cyclist came down the hill because they didn't know there was no longer any access.

Chad knew that with all of them out in the open like this about to travel, anyone who witnessed what was about to happen could cause problems for them later, although it would be unlikely they would be believed! James was carrying a strange harness he had made out of several plastic carrier bags which he proceeded to fit over Slippers' head and around his body. He had a much smaller version for Blanket; he had not discussed this with his father or mother, so they were a little bemused.

Out of the woods came the three dung beetles followed by the ants. Each one was carrying a small black ball with what looked like dotted paper wrapped around it. One by one they began to fill the bags on either side of Slippers and Blanket. Slippers had six bags, three either side, and Blanket had two, one either side because he was much smaller. Unable to contain her curiosity any longer and just beating Chad who was going to ask the same question Henrietta asked James what this was all about. James smiled.

"Well," he said, "the dung beetles came to me and said they had seen me throwing things and they could roll up things for me to throw, but I said I can pick up anything to throw so why would you need to make it? The dung beetles looked at one another and smiled, saying, 'because we once made a big mistake' and then they told me what it was."

"As you know," continued the main spokes beetle with additional bits thrown in here and there from the other two, "we love to roll up dung, but after a while we started rolling up anything we could find. Well, one day we found these boxes in a thing that humans call a garage, and stacked up inside were loads of pretty coloured boxes full of long tubes. They had been all squashed up and out of the tubes black powder was falling out."

"We had never seen anything like them before," joined in the other two beetles before the first beetle could continue. "So we started to collect the powder. At first it was difficult to roll together, but after some practice we managed it and rolled several of them into the road at the back of the garage. We had a fine collection built up in a pile, but it was very smelly, and we were beginning to get bored when one day a human came along as they do from time to time and dropped one of those white smoking sticks that glow red that they stick in their faces for some reason and it rolled against our pile of balls. We were just returning to the garage to get some more but it was getting a bit boring and we were about to move on and do something else when there was a huge bang and a flash of light that blew us through the air. Luckily we were only singed and landed safely, but when we returned the balls had gone and there was a small black hole in the ground. It was exciting, but dangerous so we decided not to make any more of those balls!"

"So they took me to where the powder was," James continued, "and also there was some paper with little dots on the packet. It said they were called caps so I adapted them and, well, now we have exploding balls in our armoury," said James proudly "thanks to the dung beetles of course," he said quickly. It was, after all, their original discovery or invention albeit by accident.

"James, I know you mean well," said Chad, "but these seem quite dangerous to me."

"Yes father, they are," he agreed readily, "in the wrong hands, but they are not in the wrong hands; they are in my hands. They have to be thrown very hard to ignite and must be kept away from fire and fire is the one thing ants can't fight and fire and explosions are what these can make in an instant."

Chad hesitated briefly as once again he had underestimated his son's intellect and abilities because of his actual age. "Very well," said Chad after a moment's thought. "You're in charge, and I see you have some very able helpers," pointing at Slippers and Blanket.

The ants had now finished loading the bags so Chad with James' communication skills for the ants began to put everyone in order: Slippers and Blanket together at the front, then Mot, Fidgit and Christopher and the ants in the middle, and the others at the rear. Chad and Henrietta stood at the front at one side.

Once again hidden in the wood, a solitary pair of eyes watched in anticipation.

James turned around to speak to his father, but there was no need. He too had sensed this presence again. Chad turned to speak to Henrietta and whispered in her ear, "We are being watched you know, but there is another problem: we will have to go first to check where we are going to arrive. You will have to create the portal, we will go and return, and then bring the others."

"What if we can't return?" whispered Henrietta.

"Then we will have done our best and protected everybody else." Henrietta nodded. Chad spoke to James, explained and told him to wait. In any event the portal his mother was about to make would only be big enough for them initially. James nodded in agreement.

Without moving from her position Henrietta thought about the portal and as always it appeared on her command. This time she did it with no hand movements whatsoever as she and Chad had intended, so there was no indication to any observer exactly who had created it. The portal was very small; Chad and Henrietta stepped forward and were gone. James sat and waited patiently for his parents to return.

chapter 99

The milkman was running late. There had been a fault on the batteries of his milk float and by the time he located the service engineer and had it fixed he had lost two hours. (What he couldn't have known was that in the engineer's haste to fix one fault he had inadvertently damaged the connection for the handbrake and although working, it was not working fully – it would be fine as long as he didn't park on a hill.) Determined to make up the time he rushed around his round. He had made up more than an hour by the time he got to the entrance of a small cul-de-sac at the bottom of a hill. After that he had to go around the wood and the rest should be easy.

The delivery was very small – only three bottles of milk and a loaf of bread. As he crested the brow of the hill and commenced his downward journey, he had to apply the brakes frequently. The milk float was powered by electricity – batteries to be precise, and they were extremely heavy. He looked down the hill and much to his surprise at the bottom was a small group of animals in a line in the middle of the road and just in front of them if he was not mistaken a small bright light just winked out. He brought the milk float to an abrupt halt causing all the milk bottles to bump together noisily with all his thoughts of making up lost time temporarily forgotten.

The noise from the milk float was very loud, but the animals didn't appear to hear, or they weren't bothered. He was at a loss as to what they were doing so overtaken by curiosity he inched slowly down the hill to get a closer look. His windscreen was not as clean as it should have been as it had been raining earlier and the country roads were very muddy. So he stepped out of his cab very quietly for a better look. With a clear view he could now see better and looking down the hill he could now recognise the dog standing quietly in the front of the animals. It was the red setter that had gone missing a few weeks ago from the house he was just about to visit, with what looked like a plastic bag on his back. The milkman heard a squeak from behind him. He turned to see his milk float starting to very slowly roll down the hill. He must have forgotten to put the handbrake on fully. He jumped forward and grabbed the door handle, but the door was locked and he watched in horror as his milk float gradually began to increase in speed as it rolled down the hill straight towards the group of animals waiting in the road for something. He didn't know what they were waiting for, but one thing was sure: if they didn't move they would surely be crushed to death.

chapter 100

C had and Henrietta arrived as usual in a blink of an eye. It had been a wise decision to come before the others. Henrietta had thought of a secluded space to arrive in the mine and that was what she got, but it was barely big enough for them let alone the other animals. It quite simply would have been a disaster. The air was full of fine dust and pale light was coming from several places, so it was not completely dark, and as they arrived the mountain shook slightly. Chad looked at Henrietta and whispered, "It looks like James' dreams might be true." Henrietta said nothing because she heard some movement. They looked around a boulder and there were three ants lifting a green piece of rock that glowed slightly. They raised it above their heads and were gone.

Chad and Henrietta waited a little longer but there was no more movement, so they came out from behind the boulder to find themselves in a large cavern. There were obvious signs of major activity at some time, but they could tell by the dust that it was not recent. A shudder ran up Chad's spine. "This is where all these poor animals died," he thought. Chad checked carefully and confirmed they were alone. "Now is the time," he said to Henrietta. "They have been left in the road too long, someone could come." With haste Henrietta opened a portal this time much bigger to accommodate everyone and of course once again they were there in an instant. But when they arrived they did not quite expect to see what they saw. Directly in front of them of course was James and all the others, but the first thing that Chad saw over their shoulders was a milk float tearing down the hill with a human running like mad after it. It was obvious that it was going to run straight into everybody with dire consequences. James was very pleased to see the portal reopen in front of him again, but was more surprised to see his parents suddenly start waving frantically while shouting, "Move, move now, now!"

They were looking past him, so he turned briefly and immediately spotted the danger. By now the man running down the hill was close enough to be heard and so was the milk float, which had picked up even more speed, the bottles of milk banging loudly against each other and the odd loose items beginning to fall off.

The milkman was now close enough to see the animals clearly and had almost caught up with the milk float, although it was getting faster by the second, when much to his surprise a huge circle of light appeared right in front of the animals and two small mice appeared out of it, one white and one grey. They were standing on their hind legs and began waving frantically. As he watched all of the animals including what appeared to be some insects moved into the circle of light. One by one they rapidly disappeared. The milkman could not believe what he was witnessing and nearly tripped and fell twice.

By now the milk float had accelerated beyond the speed he could run at and was heading for the white circle of light at great speed. The milkman stopped in his tracks and placed his hands on his head in despair. The animals had disappeared into the white hole and it looked as if his milk float was going to as well! And then the white hole just blinked out. The milk float continued on its way past where the hole had been now on flat ground and rapidly losing momentum. By the time it reached the end of the cul-de-sac it was back to a walking pace and just crashed gently into the hedges, spilling milk bottles everywhere.

Just before the circle of light closed something ran past him – a creature of some kind – and tried to enter the white hole, but it was too late and just ran on back through where the hole had been into the bushes.

There was silence. No hole, no animals, just the milkman and his float. What on earth was he going to say to his bosses? If he told them what he had seen he would without doubt not be believed and they would think he had gone mad. So he set about cleaning up the mess and trying to think of a way of explaining away the damage to his milk float. He knew one thing; he would never be able to get the image of what just happened out of his mind or for that matter, begin to understand it.

The solitary ant awoke. His last recollection was being called and told today was the day and then something hit him on the back of the head. He rose unsteadily to his feet to find he was alone. Recovering his senses quickly he trotted back to the camp, but there were no ants and no animals either. He heard a sound in the distance; he knew it was coming from the direction of the house, so he followed, but all he found was a milk float stuck in a hedge and a milkman cleaning up broken bottles. It was then the ant realised everyone had gone and he had been left behind alone.

chapter 101

The moment the last ant crossed into the portal, with a swift wave of her hand even though it wasn't necessary, Henrietta closed the portal and only just in time. She cringed as she did so as the float was so close, a second later and it would have followed them into the cave. It was unbelievably warm inside the mountain, and it shook almost as soon as they arrived, causing small spirals of dust to drop periodically from several places in the rocks above. The air was thick with dust and there were layers of it almost everywhere.

Chad took charge immediately as he was the only one who knew what their plans really were. He instructed James to speak to the ants and have a head count. James came back and confirmed all 99 ants had arrived safely; no one had been left behind or lost. The dung beetles had taken the easy way and ridden on Slippers' back next to James.

Chad then spoke to Mustela and now told him the next part in the plan. He knew from their previous conversations that he knew the mine very well having been down there several times and that Mustela also knew the correct way out, so with Mustela leading next to Chad and the ants behind them, they slowly worked their way to the surface.

"It is strange," said Mustela to Chad, "I never expected to be back here again or for that matter out of my 'prison'. You know that when we reach the surface Lord Ty Rant will very quickly know that we are here because all ants communicate with one another."

"Yes," said Chad, "that is part of the plan," and quickly changed the subject. "Where does the light from the rocks come from?" he asked.

"I don't know," said Mustela, "it was like this when we

discovered it. To be honest we called it a mine, but we didn't dig it. This cavern and all its caves were here already; a huge landslide exposed the openings and one of the journals in the place I called the library pointed us in the right direction. The mineral in fact was buried here, as was the worm hole machine in the other cavern you have already been to, we just found it and began to unearth it again.

Chad turned to look at Henrietta with a grimace and with James' story fresh in his mind said, "so why was it buried here?" He in fact already knew the answer but wanted to know if Mustela knew what he had started by unearthing it all, and if so, whether he was going to be truthful.

"I don't know," replied Mustela. "The journals I read never gave me an indication as to why it was buried here. The other two journals I gave you might, but I have never been able to translate or decipher them."

At this point they rounded a corner and much to Chad and Henrietta's surprise in front of them was a steep stone staircase so long they could not see the top. "Ah yes," said Mustela. "I had forgotten about this. This is why my brother and Lord Ty Rant brought the animals here. The steps are so high and smooth that they are difficult to climb. I believe whoever created them must have been very large beings. However, the sides are sloped and that is how we managed to drag everything up." The ants, obviously familiar with the routine had hopped onto the ledge without instruction. The animals could manage the steps, but the mice couldn't. Fidgit of course bounced up them three at a time and James muttered, "show off" under his breath. Once on the sides though they made good progress, but it was hard work, so it was difficult to talk. In any event Mustela told them the top of the stairs was near to the entrance, so it was wiser to be quiet.

The air began to get fresher and cooler. There was less dust falling and the mountain appeared not to shake so much at the higher level. They finally arrived at the top which opened out into a large cave. Again there was no sign of any ants at all. "Right," said Chad, "this is what we are going to do next," and everyone gathered round to listen.

chapter 102

As soon as the sun came up Sid, Charlotte and Lottie set off again. They were very close to the water's edge so Lottie dived in heading straight across the lake and Sid and Charlotte took to the air. In daylight Sid looked a little worse for wear; there were small blood spots here and there and Lottie was concerned, but Sid assured her he was fine, and he was because for the first time in his life he had someone who cared about him and someone he cared very much about.

They had decided to return to check on Lord Ty Rant and his troops. Sid was sure that Chad was returning sooner rather than later and given the amount of ants that had been amassed, Chad was going to need all the help he could get even with his secret advantages. Lottie of course knew nothing about Chad or his family so when they met, she was in for a surprise. Sid told Lottie what he was going to do and agreed to meet her back at the water's edge later.

The two seagulls circled the mountain several times but nothing was happening apart from a huge amount of ants encamped in the palace. "If Chad arrives there," thought Sid, "it will all be over in minutes," but try as he might there was just no way he could think of to warn them, so he and Lottie flew along the valley towards the mine and where the ant colony and the queen were located to see if anything was happening there.

A sharp-sighted ant had spotted the birds high in the air and reported back to Lord Ty Rant. By the time he came to look they had circled twice and were leaving, but of course his paranoia controlled his mind and he was sure they were planning something even though they were not!

chapter 103

C had had explained that they were going to attack the colony and rescue the queen. He had no idea how heavily protected it was, but they knew she was a prisoner so only the ants guarding her would be a problem, not the workers who looked after her. They were all now assembled in the entrance to the mine. The entrance to the colony was another cave slightly higher up the valley but clearly visible from where they were.

"First, we need more information," said Chad to Mot. "Can you get over there and see what we are up against?"

"Yes, Sir," she said and saluted smartly, then laughed. Chad had to laugh too. Mustela was confused as to why was Chad sending one of his daughters to do something so dangerous and then, before his very eyes, Mot disappeared. He took a sharp intake of breath with the surprise of it and Slippers laughed. Not a sound was heard as she slipped away, but Henrietta warned her, "Remember the ants will still be able to sense you, but they will be confused."

"Got it, Mother," said a voice from nowhere and she was gone.

It seemed like forever but suddenly she reappeared in front of them again making Mustela jump. "I have been in the cave, father, there are only five ants guarding it and I managed to get right up to the queen. I would have liked to have told her what we are going to do, but only the ants or James could do that."

"Right," said Chad making an instant decision. "We go now, everybody straight to the colony cave." So on Chad's instruction everybody in broad daylight moved up the valley towards the colony cave except one solitary ant who hung back and nobody noticed. He waited until they had all moved away and as quick as he could, he headed to the valley. He was on a mission to find Lord Ty Rant and report back exactly as he had been told to do. He was quite proud of himself that he had surmounted all the odds and made it back.

There was no fight at all. The moment the ants arrived the five ants guarding the queen gave up; they weren't very keen on doing what they were doing anyway so in some ways it was a relief and they were very happy to change sides.

Sid and Charlotte had just begun their flight along the upper valley prior to going back to the lake when out of a cave on the left which Sid knew was the entrance to the mine came a group of ants which surprised them both. But a bigger surprise was to come: following behind and moving very quickly were Slippers and Blanket and some other animals and then Sid spotted Mot. With an excited squawk he dived down and Charlotte followed. By the time they arrived they had entered the other cave. Sid was ecstatic to see everyone again, especially Mot, as they had become quite close.

"What's happening?" said Sid to Chad. "I see you made it back. Is this all of you?" he said, looking around with some dismay as he knew what Lord Ty Rant had waiting for them in the palace.

"Yes," said Chad, "but we have a few surprises and now you are here you can tell us what's happening in the palace and what we are up against." It was then that Chad spotted the marks of blood on Sid's feathers. "Sid, what happened to you, did you crash or something?"

Sid smiled. "Er, no, I just had a little run in with some ants and I owe my life to Charlotte here whom you have not met." Charlotte became very shy as she was introduced to everybody and just for a brief time the oncoming battle was forgotten.

"Father," said James suddenly, "the ant queen wishes to speak with you. Can you come?"

"Yes," said Chad, "it would be an honour." With several ants as guides Chad and James were led deep into the colony's caves and there, right at the end was the queen, surrounded by her workers.

James then began to translate for his father. "She says thank you so much for what you are trying to do. I know that if you fail Lord Ty Rant plans to execute me, but I hope you succeed – not for my sake but for the sake of what's left of my colony. I wish I could produce some soldier ants for you, but there is not enough time and they would be no match for the ants that he has as they are tougher and larger than anything I can give you. But I have to say while he lives there will be no peace in this realm and from what I have been told of the worm holes and the mineral that was found, there will be no peace in other realms either if he succeeds. He plans to capture you and your family as hostages to force Henrietta to create worm holes so that he can travel anywhere at will."

Chad was deeply shocked. He knew Lord Ty Rant was evil and would go to any means to achieve his aims, but this was just too much. He was now extremely upset and very angry. He knew by coming here he was putting his family at risk, but now his resolve was even stronger. He had had qualms about the plans he had for Lord Ty Rant, but now no!

"How do you know this?" asked Chad, recovering from his shock.

"Lord Ty Rant thinks he is clever," replied the queen. "He shields his mind and thought from other ants so they don't know what he is thinking, but his unusual growth and his belief that he is powerful have made him paranoid and he cannot make rational decisions. While he goes over and over every possible outcome in his head he loses control of the ability to keep his thoughts secret so bit by bit, thought by thought, slowly his plans for me, the colony, you and himself have leaked out. Some ants are still loyal and relay this information back to me. I am of course powerless to do anything about it except one thing: you should know I have been forced to supply him with soldier ants, some 8,000 of them, but I have created them with an inability to think instinctively for themselves so if he is removed they will do nothing to harm you as they will take instructions from no one else. The bigger ants, however, have grown bigger still and they in turn are now beginning to have grand ideas of their own so they are the truly dangerous ones.

"I wish you and your family luck, Chad, but if you cannot succeed then take your family home safely as what happens here will be as it is – it is not really your fight."

Chad thanked her for the information and he and James turned to leave. "The problem is," said Chad, "that it is 'our' problem – if not now then certainly later. Come, son," he said, "time to put our plan into action."

When Chad and James got back to the cave there was more bad news. The ant leader said one of their number was missing and he had a bad feeling the missing ant was in fact a spy for Lord Ty Rant and was at this moment returning to the palace to report. "Well," said Chad, "that is good news" and that answer surprised everybody.

chapter 104

The ant spy was very pleased with himself and was making good time. He would be at the palace soon and could not wait to impart the information he had learnt. There were brief stops at the gate, then on inside. At each floor he was questioned, which irritated him as he had made it clear each time why it was so important that he report back, but the bigger ants he spoke to were unimpressed and the smaller ants like himself just didn't react at all to the urgency of it all! Very puzzling.

Finally, he arrived on the roof where Lord Ty Rant was sitting overlooking the valley. The ant quickly informed him of what had happened and that all of the ants sent to search had gone over to the other side except him, but he had managed to come through the worm hole created by the mice to return here with the other ants and several animals. At this point Lord Ty Rant showed more interest. "How many animals and how many ants," he asked.

"Ninety-eight ants and," hesitating slightly while he thought about it, "six mice, one beaver, one fox, a cat, a dog, and a weasel. Oh yes, and three dung beetles."

At this Lord Ty Rant shouted out loud, "Is that it? Is that it?" he exclaimed. The ant backed away, fearing for his life and the guards on the roof looked over nervously. He then started to laugh maniacally which was worse.

"So," he said, starting to strut around, "that's it. One hundred ants, six mice and a bunch of animals — they have no chance against my ant army."

"Actually, it's 98 ants," said the ant politely trying to correct him, but Lord Ty Rant was strutting around madly waving his arms in the air already celebrating victory, so it was at this point he decided to keep his mouth shut and not mention the round balls they were carrying as he didn't know what they were anyway.

Finally, he calmed down and stared at the ant: "So what are their plans?"

"I don't know, my lord," he replied nervously. "I left them at the mouth of the mine but there were going to free the queen and that's where they are now." At this his paranoia kicked in again, "Why would they go there? She can't possibly make enough ants to defend themselves, perhaps he is tempting me to attack. Well, that's not going to happen, nice try Chad, nice try. I'm staying here and are you in for a surprise when you arrive!" With that, he dismissed the ant who was greatly relieved to have survived the encounter and was now beginning to think that perhaps the other ants had had the right idea.

chapter 105

C had assembled everybody such as they were and outlined what he had planned. Sid and Charlotte were there as well. As Chad went over everything and during his outline, he pointed out that they were outnumbered several times. Sid was sitting next to Mot and he lent closer and whispered in her ear. "Don't you think this is a good time to tell your father about the ants?"

"What do you mean?" said Mot, really knowing exactly what he meant.

"The ants you sent underground that Ant arranged for us. You could bring them back."

"That was another place, not here," replied Mot.

"True," said Sid, "but the stones came back in another place so why not here? Your father needs your help Mot, we all do. You have these powers and now is the time to use them." Mot was surprised at how Sid talked now. He was so confident and calm it made her feel good.

"You're right," she said, "now is the time," and without another thought she stood up and interrupted her father. "Father, I need to speak to you right now. It's very important and relevant to what you are planning to do." Chad nodded his head in acceptance. By now of course, because of the things that James could do, he was sure that Mot had something similar that she could do that he knew nothing about. They shuffled over to a quiet corner and Sid joined them. She then went on to tell her father what she could do and what she had done and also believed she could bring the ants back here and if so, it would completely change the odds of succeeding as these ants were made for fighting. She also told him about her ability to make huge explosions at will almost anywhere.

"Why didn't you tell me about this before?" said Chad. "I don't know father," she replied, "I just didn't have the confidence in myself until Sid persuaded me, he was there when I brought the rocks back and he thinks I can do the same with the ants, but we are in another realm after all."

"Yes, you're right," said Chad, "but your mother can create portals wherever she goes, so assuming you have very similar powers you should be able to do the same."

"Well," said Sid, "there is only one way to find out: try!"

"What, now?" said Mot.

"Why not?" said Sid.

"What, here?" said Mot.

"Well no, not here, as there is not enough room. We will have to go outside. If this works it will change everything." So Mot, Chad and Sid went outside. Mot and Sid agreed that because of the hole it would make they would have to go to the very top of the valley where there was a large flat area. "We will need James too," said Chad.

"Why?" said Mot.

"Well, he is the only one who can talk to them except other ants, but they are from a different colony, remember?"

"Yes of course you're right, Father," so she fetched James and the four of them walked to the end of their part of the valley.

The day was almost gone again so it was getting dark, but it was perhaps the best time to do this almost under the cover of darkness. When they reached the top Chad, Sid and James stepped back. James had not been told what was about to happen, so he was a little bemused. Mot raised her hands and now feeling a lot more confident created the small balls exactly as she previously had.

"You're going to like this," said Sid into James's ear.

"We are going to need your communication skills in a moment." James was very puzzled but impressed and Chad just calmly waited and watched. The balls began to chase one another the correct way and then the vibration in the ground started.

The ground opened up just as before and sure enough out of the hole crawled thousands of ants. They circled the hole in lines and it was an impressive sight. The last ant climbed out and with another shake and a bump, the hole disappeared.

There before them standing neatly in rows stood the ants, exactly as they were before they disappeared. Chad was very impressed. Sid was proud and James was ecstatic. Mot was very relieved they were still alive. Rocks are one thing but living creatures another.

"James," said Chad, "can you tell them where they are and what we are up against. Ant is still missing so you really are the only one who can explain everything."

It took James a little while, but at the end everything had been made clear. "It's alright," said James, "they understand. Ant had explained to them who we are and what we are trying to do so they are with us." James turned to his sister. "Mot," he said, "that was really cool." Mot smiled.

"Right," said Chad, "time to attack the palace." He turned to Sid. "We are going to need yours and Charlotte's help if that's alright."

"I can't wait," said Sid enthusiastically, and they all returned to the cave leaving the ants together patiently waiting at the end of the valley.

chapter 106

As dawn approached Chad got everyone ready. They had now been told the plan and the object which was quite simply to get rid of Lord Ty Rant forever with as little bloodshed as possible. At this statement the animals went very quiet; the ants apparently were not bothered.

They all left the cave together, but the 10,000 ants remained at the top of the valley out of sight as instructed, awaiting their orders. They all moved slowly down towards the worm hole that had been closed off, it still emitted a small amount of light from an opening at the top that the ants were unable to close. When they reached the point just before they could be seen from the palace, Chad called a halt.

"Right," said Chad, "time for the diversion." He had hoped that a diversion was not going to be necessary as just about every morning there was a fog that would cover the lower valley, but as luck would have it there was no sign of it today and the air was completely clear. But it did have one advantage: when everything started Lord Ty Rant would see it all. Chad just hoped he would react the way he wanted.

Chad spoke briefly to Henrietta. She, Christopher and Fidgit were standing together and beneath their feet were several small boxes. He went over their plan again. They all nodded to confirm they understood, and Chad hugged Henrietta. Fidgit too, but not Christopher — he just didn't do that kind of thing as he considered himself too old. Chad and Henrietta smiled to each other, said goodbye once more and seconds later a small portal appeared next to them, created of course by Henrietta. "You're getting very good at this aren't you?" commented Chad. Henrietta smiled. Fidgit and Christopher picked up the boxes at their feet and with one last wave from Henrietta, they were gone.

Chad turned back to the others. Slippers and Blanket came forward with the bombs that James had made. He had changed the design of some of them, so they had little handles for carrying – these were for Sid and Charlotte. On Chad's command, Slippers and Blanket started to run uphill towards the palace. The dung beetles were in Blanket's bags which were the bombs with the handles. Sid and Charlotte swooped down, the dung beetles rolled out a bomb for collection and first Sid then Charlotte collected one and soared into the sky above the palace. Their target was the roof where Lord Ty Rant sat.

Chad told Mot to head for the worm hole as quickly as possible, so she jumped on Freddie's back and the ants who came back with them climbed on the back of Beaver the builder. They then raced down the valley across the junction leading up to the palace and down towards the worm hole. For the first time, Mot was totally lacking in nerves. In fact, she was excited as if she was leading an army albeit a very small one. Unfortunately, she had no idea of what danger she was soon to be in and if Chad and Henrietta had known too, they would never have sent her and the others.

Chad had told her it would be guarded and wanted to get the ants away from the worm hole before Mot did what she had to do. He told her the ants would deal with this and he expected little resistance as they were from the same colony, they simply would not survive if they did not.

Mustela had told Chad that when he and his brother had reactivated the machine to create worm holes, they had used the journals they found that explained how it worked and used some of the mineral they had found to power it. But either they had used too much or did something else wrong because foolishly they started it up without finding out first how to stop it. The machine become so powerful that it melded into the cliff face next to the worm hole and it was now impossible to turn off unless it was destroyed or ran out of fuel, but there was nothing in the journals anywhere to explain what to do and the other two that Chad and Henrietta had taken back were in a code or language that, as yet, they had been unable to translate or decipher.

So Mot had to first destroy the rock wall that Lord Ty Rant had built and then, when the time was right, the left cliff face with the machine inside it so that the link between the two realms would be broken forever.

Mustela had reluctantly agreed — not that he had any choice as the machine of course was irreplaceable and the only one of its kind, even though the journals had indicated there were once two. Chad told Mustela he would have to hide in the colony.

"Why?" he asked, somewhat relieved not to be involved in any of the action. "Lord Ty Rant thinks you're dead and died in the mountain. If news spreads that not only are you alive but free, it would not be good for what we have planned." Mustela went to ask why but before he could Chad just put up one hand to silence him, so he didn't ask.

James set off first. For Slippers it was easy with his longer legs, but not so for Blanket, so Slippers set his pace so that they could stay together. The ground was very rocky of course and neither of them were used to it. From time to time as they ran, they were slipping and sliding all over the place. It was fortunate that the dung beetles were inside the bags because they would definitely have fallen off.

And then James suddenly called a halt. "Blanket, please stay here," said James. "Slippers, we have to go back to the ants quickly I forgot something." Slippers obediently obliged, turned around and tore down the valley. He was moving so quickly James nearly fell off. "I have to go back to the ants," said James hanging on for dear life as Slippers tore around the bend and back up the valley towards the ants, passing a surprised Chad who thought as he passed "is this in the plan?"

Slippers skidded to a halt by the ants that, as instructed, had remained where they were. James quickly changed their instructions and told them to come down to where the two valleys joined, where his parents were when his father called. He waved his arm to demonstrate what waving meant and then said, "Wait out of sight until called." They nodded in acknowledgement.

"Go, Slippers," said James, "stop by my father and then back to where we were." Slippers wasted no time in turning around and tearing off back the way they had come. He skidded to a halt by Chad. James told him about the ants and then they were off again, he hadn't had this much fun in ages! The ants would follow on at a far more sedate pace. Slippers quickly arrived back with Blanket who raised one eyebrow in question. Slippers just laughed and they continued their journey towards the palace.

Here and there Lord Ty Rant had placed ants as lookouts. James of course had sensed their presence and was aware they had informed him of their imminent arrival.

chapter 107

Lord Ty Rant's paranoia had all but faded away. He stood at the front of the roof of the palace with the largest single room at the top against the cliff behind him, surveying the valley below and because of the strange change in the weather although some way away he could see most of what was happening and what he couldn't the team of lookouts he had placed along the valley leading to the palace and worm hole were keeping him informed. He had, however, neglected to place any lookouts leading to the mine and colony so firmly convinced was he that Chad would come to him that it never occurred to him to do so; he had no idea what was there.

His calmness had come from more sensible deep thought. He was an ant and ants from time to time had enemies – usually other ants or the odd ant or ant egg-eating creature and they were well prepared for such eventualities: protect the queen, protect the eggs and fight to the death if necessary while the workers moved everything. But during his lifetime which of course had been considerably longer that the average ant, nothing like this had ever happened in this colony, but it had in his own and the queen just moved.

The animals, however, were different though they had many enemies most of the time it seemed stayed away from each other including humans who on the whole seemed to leave ants alone as long as they stayed away from them, he thought.

So, because of this he realised their fighting strategy was vastly different. We are defensive when we are attacked whereas they are defensive when attacked and have the ability to plan defences and attacks. He felt the beginnings of a headache. As he watched the mice move what little troops they had, he realised they were planning something, but with all his increased mental ability and experience he simply lacked the knowledge to work out what. He was fundamentally alone. His so-called protectors, for all their size, were almost unable to think for themselves or when asked an opinion didn't have one, or didn't want to have one for their own safely should their opinion be the wrong one!

A dog and cat were coming up the valley. They appeared to be carrying some kind of bags. As he watched two seagulls swooped down and appeared to take something from the bags and then soared up above the valley and were circling the palace. He knew now they were the same seagulls that he had nearly managed to destroy, but they had escaped and there were simply no others.

The dog and cat had now stopped some distance away, but clearly in view. Lord Ty Rant moved closer to the roof's edge in an attempt to see more. There appeared to be sitting on the back of the dog's back a small mouse and he had what looked like ball in his hand.

He suddenly raised his other arm and waved at the sky. Lord Ty Rant involuntarily looked up. The seagulls had stopped circling and were now diving down towards the roof. They pulled up and away and flew back down the valley, but not before dropping two small objects. Seconds later they hit the top roof behind him and exploded with such a huge noise that it reverberated around the valley several times. The explosions were loud but not particularly forceful but were still strong enough to blow small bits of the roof into the air which fell onto the ants guarding Lord Ty Rant. He nearly fell off the roof with the surprise of it all and his guards started to back away in confusion towards the access doorway which was the only means of access to and from the front roof.

Lord Ty Rant looked back down. The seagulls had swiftly returned to the back of the cat and had become airborne again. This time he knew what was coming so he too started to back away when he noticed the small mouse throw the ball in his hand. For what purpose he couldn't imagine as he was way too far away, but much to his surprise the ball arrived almost as soon as it was thrown and hit the rock face above the main roof. Whatever was in the previous balls the seagulls dropped wasn't in this one. It hit the rock face and created a huge explosion and blew out a considerable amount of debris which rained down everywhere.

This was enough for Lord Ty Rant's so-called ant security and they fled the roof. He had one last look down the valley as the next airborne barrage arrived and noticed the mouse was preparing to throw another bomb and he too decided to leave seeking the safety of the floor below, or so he thought!

As he hurried to the floors below, he was sure he had heard an even bigger blast and felt the palace shake, but nothing fell on them as they hurried to safety.

chapter 108

Henrietta, Christopher and Fidgit arrived at the designated destination in an instant. It was completely dark, but Henrietta had expected this. Quite capable of seeing in the dark she opened one of the parcels they had brought with them and inside were several packs of candles that James had made prior to their journey.

They were back in the library inside the mountain! Henrietta told Fidgit where to put the candles and with some controlled bouncing she managed to light the library completely with fresh candles only extinguishing two while bouncing up and down. Both she and Christopher were curious and wanted to explore but Henrietta told them this was not the time and they only had a very brief amount of time to complete what they had to do. Henrietta set about refreshing the air as she had done before with two portals. Christopher and Fidgit were impressed as they had never seen her do it before.

Then came the hard work, fortunately a lot easier for Christopher because of his strength. They set about building a barrier across the library from the counter to the cave wall to divide it into two. It had to be quite high and difficult to get over but only for a short period of time. It involved moving a considerable amount of the old furniture in the other cave and piling it up to create a wall higher in fact than the counter. They then had to do the same along the counter to close it all in. There were gaps everywhere but only very small which they needed to get from one side to the other.

Christopher stood back when they were finished and looked at their handiwork. He had moved all the big stuff with help of course and his mother and sister had filled in the gaps with smaller items.

It in fact was made up of everything they could find – planks, small rocks, boxes which they filled with rocks, cupboards, even piles of old books.

"It's not very stable," remarked Fidgit.

"It doesn't have to be, dear," said her mother, "it only has to last a minute or two." Fidgit and Christopher looked at their mother in surprise, but she made no further comment and they knew better than to ask. "It's time to go," she suddenly said, "we must get back. It's important we are not too late," and with that she opened a portal, beckoned to her children and they were gone just leaving the candles on the walls flickering and casting strange shadows created by what they had built.

chapter 109

James was enjoying himself. He was pleased that his father had allowed him to participate, particularly his contribution of the explosive devices.

They had succeeded in driving Lord Ty Rant off the roof, but the plan was to get his troops and protection to leave the palace. So Sid and Charlotte continued to bomb the roof and James now started throwing bombs at the window opening, deliberately not throwing them through the windows. It was important that they thought that soon the bombs would come through the windows and that James was just a bad shot, which of course was not the case.

James raised his arm to throw yet another missile when the voice he had heard before but only in his dreams spoke to him: "James, it is Paradeigma. Your sister is in great danger; what she is about to do will surely kill her if she is too close."

James lowered his arm and looked around, "Where are you?" he said out loud. "How do you know this?" But there was no reply even though he asked again and again. James didn't know what to do but the decision was made for him. There was a loud boom followed by a weird whining groaning sound and then silence.

chapter 110

M ot was half way down the valley and as they rounded the curve of the valley walls the pile of rock that had been built over the worm hole became visible. At this point Mot told everybody to stop. There was no sign of any ants guarding what was left of the worm hole, but the ants did as they were instructed and returned, nodding their heads to confirm there was nothing to worry about.

Mot then told Freddie and Beaver to wait there for her; she would go on alone. Beaver objected the most, but she was adamant that when the explosions happened – and there would be two – it was better that only those who had to be there should be there. She also told them when the second explosion happened they were to run as fast as they could away from it. Beaver objected, but Mot interrupted him, "I know what I'm doing," she said, when in fact she really knew she didn't. Once again Beaver and Freddie agreed to do as she asked but very reluctantly. They both sat down to wait as agreed and the ants stayed with them.

The moment Mot left though Beaver said, "I know what she told us, but I'm not moving until she's back," and Freddie nodded in agreement.

Mot being a mouse of course was quite small and it took her some time to work her way over the rocky surface to get near enough to the worm hole to launch her magical explosive spheres. She was almost there when she heard the first boom echo around the valley; she knew that meant James had started his attack, which meant she was already behind schedule. She hurried on until she knew she was close enough and composing herself raised her right hand and thought about a large sphere. As always it appeared in her hand, but it was much heavier than normal, and she almost dropped it. At that moment some rocks fell into the valley from the cliff face and Mot hesitated. She felt someone was watching her. She looked up at the cliff edge where the rocks had come from but could see nothing; whatever it was had moved away or was hiding. The sphere was by now getting heavier by the minute, she had learnt now through practice that not only could she create and throw these spheres, she could also control their flight so with some concentration she was able to make the sphere appear lighter. She launched it and landed it exactly in front of the pile of rocks covering the worm hole. The second sphere she created she launched immediately and threw it with all her might at the first.

The explosion was outstanding as Slippers would say and in the first instant Mot thought too outstanding. The pile of rocks lifted off the ground and started to travel towards her. She had enough time to think, "Oh, too close perhaps," but because of the blast the other side of the rock pile was caught in the worm hole's force and everything followed. Then with a terrible grinding howling sound like something was overloaded the force of the blast was sucked back into it and within seconds was gone. "Where?" thought Mot as she watched from where she had ducked down behind some small rocks and also realising that what she was hiding behind would have been no good at all if the rocks flung out had come her way, "I hope no one is on the other side when that lot arrives."

Thinking about the lucky escape she had had Mot backed down the valley but not too far. She knew there was a limit to how far she could throw anything. "I wish I had James's throwing arm," she thought. Then an idea occurred to her. She changed her mind and went back down the valley and stood next to the left side of the worm hole. She then created the largest sphere she had ever produced and carefully placed it beside the rock face on the left side of the worm hole. The worm hole fluctuated and whined slightly as if it knew Mot's intentions and then settled down again. Its reactions unnerved Mot a little bit and she was glad to back away from it. She retraced her steps back up the valley as far as she could and prepared to make the second sphere.

chapter III

James was very concerned about Mot so when Sid returned, he asked him to cease the bombing and go and check on her as he knew they had grown very close. He would keep up the barrage for as long as they could with Charlotte if that was fine with him. Sid readily agreed, said goodbye to Charlotte, and hastily flew away in the direction of the worm hole.

James now changed his aim to the lower window opening in the hope that would be enough to drive the ants and Lord Ty Rant out, but he was getting concerned as his ammunition was going to run out soon and there were no reserves.

Lord Ty Rant and his so-called security ants were now on the ground floor camped out with the entire ant army and he didn't like it. He had heard the explosions on the upper floors and each time fine rocky dust rained down. So they had now managed to get the bombs through the windows! It was fortunate they had moved to the ground floor. He was at a loss as to how simple mice had created such things obviously not so simple! But they were only small animals and although they could fight, insects could overwhelm them simply because we are small, he thought, even bigger creatures if there are enough of us. "Well there are," he said out loud, looking towards his ant army. "There are five mice, one dog, one beaver, one fox, one cat, two seagulls and 99 ants against 8,000 small biting ants and the only thing they can do to stop the biting is run and jump into water but," he thought gleefully, "there isn't any."

Lord Ty Rant edged to the door. There was very little to see as the ground floor was surrounded by walls with only the ungated entrance to look through. At that point another bomb arrived and landed right above his head, or so it seemed, and larger chunks of the ceiling fell down amongst them. In that instant he made up his mind and instructed his entire ant army to attack with the sole purpose of wiping out the animals, "but you must capture the mice at all costs." The ants looked blankly at their leader and immediately began to leave the palace and head down the valley to fulfil their orders.

It was an impressive sight: the ants marching down the valley, filling the width of it, straight towards James, Slippers and Blanket.

James was just about to throw another bomb and was wondering what he was going to do soon as he could now see the bottom of the bag which meant he was nearly out. Charlotte too had noticed she only had five left and mentioned this to James when over the brow of the hill came the marching ants, thousands of them. James smiled with relief. "Well, time to go I think," he said to Slippers and Blanket. They quickly turned around and tore down the hill with the marching ants not far behind them. Lord Ty Rant knew something had changed as the bombings had stopped almost as soon as the ants had left and then word came from one of the lookouts: the dog and cat were fleeing down the valley.

"Well now," thought Lord Ty Rant with great satisfaction, "how are you going to stop them now?"

chapter 112

Henrietta arrived back at where she set off from with Christopher and Fidgit at the perfect time. Chad was relieved to see her back and quickly asked, "Everything set?"

Henrietta replied, "yes."

"Perfect," said Chad. Christopher and Fidgit looked at each other puzzled, set for what?

At that moment Slippers and Blanket appeared coming over the brow at the top of the valley running as fast as they could which could mean only one thing; the attacked had started and the ants were coming. Chad could not wave his ants into battle until James, Blanket and Slippers were clear because they had to meet halfway down the valley. Chad had no idea how fast the ants would be travelling. He and Henrietta watched nervously as they got closer and the ants appeared over the brow of the hill behind, but not far behind James. "Come on James, faster," thought Chad, but he already knew that he was going as fast as he could.

The ants filled the width of the valley and poured down it like a black undulating flowing carpet. They were not moving nearly as fast as James but of course that was understandable as Slippers and Blanket had longer legs.

With the ant army gone Lord Ty Rant could now move outside and his so-called security followed him. He moved to the crest of the valley with excitement: he wanted to see this one-sided battle for himself.

Sid reached the other part of the valley very quickly and soared over it at a high level. He knew that Mot's mission was to blow up the worm hole and the machine buried within the rock face, so he had been very careful to have a good look first from high up as he had no wish to be blown up with it.

He had arrived just as Mot was walking back from the cliff face and he saw her turn and make the second sphere. Even from the great height he was at he knew Mot was too close so without hesitation he started to dive down towards her.

He plummeted as fast as he had ever done before, far faster than was wise. He knew at the speed he had accelerated to it was going to be very hard to pull up. He saw Mot raise her arm and throw the sphere with all her might and then start to run back up the valley. Sid's heart was pumping with fear Mot was so small he knew already that if the blast was going to be as big as expected Mot had no chance. It was impossible now to save her; there was just no time – unless?

Chad waved his arm just before Slippers, Blanket and James tore past him and the ants without hesitation swiftly moved off and turned the corner rapidly moving up the valley to meet the oncoming attack. They were far more experienced than their opponents and filled the valley from side to side as they had, but they were seasoned fighters with great loyalty to their queen from their own realm and knew that a defeat here would mean certain death for her later. They rapidly rose up the valley as the ants from above rapidly descended.

Chad was not happy with the certain death the thousands of ants on both sides would suffer, but he knew this was the only way peace in both realms could finally be achieved.

By now all of the ants were in the valley both coming down and going up. It was at this point a clear section of valley appeared above the ants just as Lord Ty Rant crested the top of the valley. Chad called to Henrietta, "Get ready, Hen, it's time."

Sid realised by now the only way to save Mot was to grab her in flight and at this speed it was going to hurt both of them. He had dropped now until he was almost level with the ground but still flying at a ridiculous speed he had just one chance to grab her, but his feet were webbed so there was no other way but to use his beak. He was seconds away from grabbing her when the spheres exploded. The explosion was nothing compared to the blinding white light that came soaring down the valley. Parts of the cliff face either side of the valley shook and crumbled with the force of the explosion and seconds later the sound of it caught up with him. It was so loud that Sid thought he would never hear properly again. Sid grabbed the back of her neck; she squealed in pain and struggled. At first Sid could say nothing, knowing that if he tried to he would surely drop her. He could taste her blood in his beak where he had nicked her and then she relaxed. She had realised that she was flying and it was not the blast of the explosion carrying her along. Sid thought his beak was going to come off. With all the power he could he at first tried to climb, but Mot was quite heavy so he quickly changed his mind and decided to try and outrun the force of the explosion which was rapidly bearing down behind him. As he swung round a slight turn below him he could see Beaver and Freddie already running as fast as they could and Freddie looked up as he passed them. He thought he had almost made it but the blast of the explosion caught up with them and they disappeared in the cloud of dust and fine rubble it had created. It was then that Sid accepted he had tried and failed, but he had done his best. The white light got brighter so much so he could no longer see anything. He suddenly felt lighter and a wave of disappointment swept over him and his memory faded away.

chapter 113

Lord Ty Rant crested the brow at the top of the valley and stopped immediately. So abruptly in fact that the ants behind him ran into him, but instead of erupting in anger he said nothing, much to the relief of the offending ants. He could not believe what he was seeing. Instead of his ant army invading the lower valley there was a matching army of ants rising up the valley to meet them. His mind was overwhelmed; his ants were brown the others were black, so he knew immediately they had not come from the queen, so where? This was impossible, surely not another realm. How?!

Chad, without looking at Henrietta, said, "It's time, Hen." She in turn without turning produced a portal right behind them much, much larger than normal. Chad turned to Christopher, Fidgit and James and said, "We will be back soon. Help Mot and the others when they get here. If all is well, we will be going home very soon." With that he and Henrietta stepped into the portal and it closed behind them.

"I wonder where they are going," said Christopher.

"I have no idea," said James in reply even though the question wasn't directed at him, and Fidgit was very quiet.

Lord Ty Rant continued to stare down the valley in disbelief. The remaining ants behind him, realising now that defeat was imminent, looked nervously from one to the other. Not a stone's throw in front him a circle of light appeared — it was a large worm hole that blocked the view of the valley. As it appeared it settled down into a large perfect circle as always and out stepped Chad and Henrietta. And then the portal closed. They appeared not to have noticed the ants and when they did, they jumped. Henrietta started to frantically wave her arms and Chad was frantically urging her on.

Lord Ty Rant could not believe his luck; they had finally made a fatal mistake and arrived in the wrong place at the wrong time. As he watched, Henrietta reopened the portal and it was obvious they were going to escape. Without hesitation or rational thought he ran down the hill towards the spinning white light, just as Henrietta and Chad began to enter it. The remaining ants not wishing to be left behind followed immediately.

Chad and Henrietta appeared to hesitate at the portal entrance, but such was the need for Lord Ty Rant to catch them he gave it no thought, nor for that matter why the portal was so large when they were so small. Just as he was close enough to grab them they entered the portal, but he was right behind them, as were his so-called security ants now more worried about themselves and what the army of ants would do to them than their fleeing leader. Lord Ty Rant's thoughts as he entered the portal were that by pure chance victory would be his and Chad and Henrietta would be his slaves forever. The ants followed him in, and the portal closed behind them.

chapter 114

As their parents vanished into thin air a large boom reverberated down the valley and James and Christopher turned to look at the far end of the valley where the worm hole was. A huge beam of white light shot into the sky in all directions. Although they could not see directly down it, the walls were lit up with white light. Christopher looked at James and his look said it all. Mot was down there, this was not good. The light got brighter and brighter and the noise was horrendous almost as if some creature was dying but fighting to survive. Then, coming up from the valley they could see Freddie and Beaver running as fast as they could. Right behind them a huge cloud tore out of the valley. It reached them in seconds and enveloped them, small pieces of rock rained down everywhere and almost as soon as it had arrived, it was gone. The white light blinked out and all that was left was the sound of the explosion echoing around the valleys and the pitter-patter of small rocks falling to the ground like rain.

Freddie and Beaver appeared out of the dust and Christopher looked past them with dread. But there was nothing. No sign of Mot, no sign of Sid, no sign of any life at all.

"Sid grabbed Mot," said Freddie, "he flew over us just before the blast hit us, we were lucky we were behind a rock. We ran around and he was flying towards you. He must have got here surely?" Christopher's face said it all. "No Freddie," he replied, "they are not here, neither of them, they're gone."

Slippers came over to them with Blanket. They had been at the bottom of the other valley leading to the palace, so were completely unaware of what had just happened to Mot and Sid. "Look," said Slippers, "the ants have stopped fighting. As soon as Lord Ty Rant left, they just stopped." Sure enough, just as Slippers had explained the moment Lord Ty Rant stepped into the portal the ants had just stopped. Whatever influence he had had over them was gone and they just stopped and stood still. The black ants had fought on for a moment until they realised that the brown ants were no longer a threat and they too stopped fighting.

James was still in shock that he had just lost his sister and his good friend Sid, but he told one of the ants near him what to do and he in turn dutifully scuttled off to tell the others.

Slippers suddenly noticed how sad everyone was. "What's up?" he said, cocking his head to one side.

"Mot and Sid are gone," said Christopher sadly.

"What?" said Blanket.

"They are gone," he said again, "they got caught in the blast and they are gone."

The animals gathered together all thinking the same thing: who was going to tell Chad and Henrietta they had lost their daughter and a very good friend who gave his life trying to save hers?

Just then Charlotte landed and Christopher had to give her the bad news too – that she would never see her beloved Sid again.

chapter 115

C had and Henrietta arrived exactly where they planned in the second cave where the furniture used to be. The candles were still burning but the white light from the portal was of course much brighter. They knew Lord Ty Rant was right behind them, so they hurried over to the doorway in the counter that led to the other cave where they had built their barrier. Seconds later, Lord Ty Rant arrived. They waited long enough to let him see them and then scurried under the door beneath the counter hatch and into the other cave.

The other ants arrived right behind him and as they did so the portal closed. It was now much darker and harder to see. He had spotted the mice as soon as he arrived and seething with rage went after them. He rounded the corner, saw them go under the hatch door and, unaware of where he was threw himself at the hatch and flap nearly taking it off its hinges as it flew back. Chad and Henrietta had again waited by the barrier they had built and once they knew they had been seen ran underneath it.

Still as yet unaware of where he was Lord Ty Rant threw himself at it. It completely blocked the cave from side to side and in a frenzy, he attempted to climb over it, but as he did so it began to move and collapse. His long legs began to get entangled in the various pieces of junk that Henrietta, Christopher and Fidgit had put together, but he managed to climb high enough to see over the top – just enough to see where the mice had gone.

The answer was nowhere. Chad and Henrietta had stopped at the end of the cave and there was no way out. For a moment Lord Ty Rant thought he had them trapped, but it didn't make sense.

He looked around the cave he had never been into, but Mustelee had told him about the cave his brother worked in and where he was eventually trapped and had died. He saw Henrietta lift her hand and seconds later a tiny portal appeared behind them, just big enough for them to pass though and in those seconds, he realised he had been very cleverly fooled. His rage increased as he struggled to get over the junk, he was entangled in it and his frantic efforts began to make the whole thing collapse with him entangled in it. Now he knew where he was. This was the cave where Mustela died and as he struggled more and more to reach the mice he saw the two of them begin to turn towards the portal. Henrietta waved once and Chad bowed. They stepped into the light and were gone as was the portal and the light that came from it. Lord Ty Rant in those few seconds realised that he was trapped forever and would die here. If he could scream he would have done so, but there was nothing he could do. His plans and any chance of escape had disappeared just as the mice had and he was left staring at a blank cave wall in the flicker of candlelight.

chapter 116

C had and Henrietta returned from whence they had gone full of euphoria from their victory. However, as soon as they arrived one look at the others was enough to know something was seriously wrong. Christopher told his father what had happened and he said nothing at first, but Henrietta immediately started to sob and Fidgit hugged her as much as she could.

Chad took charge and told everyone to go back down the valley to look in case there was a chance they had found shelter. They all knew it was pointless but complied any way.

Several hours later they all came back with the same news: there was no sign of them at all, not even a feather.

James told his father that the queen wanted to talk with him. Mustela was still there and they told him that Lord Ty Rant was gone and would never return. The queen thanked Chad for what he had done and gave him her sympathies for the loss of their child and friend.

As Chad walked back down the valley with Mustela and James he told them they would be returning home the following day. He asked Mustela whether he wanted to stay or go, and he replied he wished to stay. With Lord Ty Rant gone, the place would be at peace.

Charlotte had told Beaver about Lottie and Beaver set off to find her. Freddie agreed to go too. He asked Chad if he could either wait or come back to fetch them and Chad said he would come back.

The mood in their little camp should have been good, but the loss of Mot and Sid had affected everybody including the dung beetles.

As the sun set Chad and Henrietta walked down to the end

of the valley where the worm hole used to be and where their daughter had died. Apart from the rubble scattered here and there the cliff face where the portal entrance used to be had returned to what it had been before the worm hole had been created. It was hard to believe that everyone had escaped through this rock face before. They turned away sadly walking back the way they had come to sleep and get ready for their return, but they both knew they would remember Mot and Sid for a long time to come.

As the sun rose everyone got ready to go. Beaver and Freddie had already left for the mountains the day before to search for Lottie, Beaver's long-lost partner.

The ants wanted to return to their queen, so Henrietta sent them first. She then travelled back to the road outside the house to check if the coast was clear. She was gone for quite a while and Chad started to worry. But when she returned, she explained she had waited for the owners of the house to leave before coming back. They said their goodbyes to Mustela and then she opened a bigger portal for them all. The dung beetles climbed onto Blanket's back much to Slippers' surprise and then Chad, Henrietta, Slippers, Blanket with the three dung beetles, Charlotte, Fidgit and James stepped into the portal and were gone.

chapter 117

They all arrived of course as planned right outside the front door of the house. James quickly unlocked the front door and everybody went in. The dung beetles returned to the wood, as did Charlotte, but not before they made Chad promise that if another adventure came up, he would count them in.

They all entered the house in a solemn mood. Slippers and Blanket returned to their normal place by the fireplace and the mice went to their home. It felt very strange and lonely without Mot.

Chad and Henrietta returned to their room and a little later James heard his mother sobbing quietly. The day wore on. They heard the cleaner come and her surprise that Slippers had returned and her puzzlement as to how he got into the house. Then, later, the owners and their excitement at his return and eventually of course evening came, and the house went quiet. The mice went to bed the expected first of many without Mot, but Fidgit appeared to be suffering the most as she used to share a room with her sister.

James was so tired that he fell into a deep sleep and while asleep the dream returned. Paradeigma spoke to him again.

"James, this is important, your sister and her friend are not dead. When the machine was destroyed they created a ripple. The machine makes them anyway from time to time; it was one of the biggest problems of consistent travel not always arriving where you were supposed to. They are in a different realm, but the climate is so severe they will not survive long without your help. The journals your father has will help you find them. I will help you translate them.

"When you are awake think of me, and I will return."

James woke with a start. At first he couldn't believe what he had dreamt and would not have done if it weren't for the fact that Paradeigma had once spoken to him while he was not dreaming. Now fully awake he rushed to his parents' bedroom and without knocking rushed in. They were both awake and looked as if they had had a sleepless night. "Father, mother," shouted James. "I have had another dream and Paradeigma has told me that Mot and Sid are still alive, but they are in danger. We have to help them. The journals you have hold the secret."

By now James had cried out so loudly that Fidgit was awake and came to join them. "What did he say?" said Chad without hesitation and now accepting that Paradeigma existed, but not knowing where outside of his son's mind.

So James repeated what he had been told and when he had finished Chad carefully carried the journals to their dining room table and opened the first one. "Well, son," said Chad, "it's up to you now. You're the only one it seems who can help us rescue Mot and Sid. It looks like we are all going on another adventure sooner than we thought, so let's get started."

The end

Epilogue

Several months ago, a cyclist reported to his local paper that some vandal had cut down trees in his local wood and blocked an access point through the wood that many cyclists used. Upon investigation by the paper an expert said that they had definitely been cut down by a beaver, but as there were no lakes or rivers anywhere nearby it still remains a mystery as to where the beaver came from.

Since then several other people have reported strange pools of light popping up everywhere in the wood, mostly at night. This has been put down to methane, an underground gas, but there is no record of natural underground gases in the area.

The latest discovery has been a pile of broken scorched rock three metres high and almost as wide. It is estimated it weighs several tons and has completely blocked a main footpath. The rocks are not indigenous so where they came from, how they got there and for what purpose still remains a mystery.

A local woman who cleans a house near the wood was interviewed. She said she knew nothing about anything in the wood, she had her own problems. She cleans a house locally which has a dog and somehow even though she locks him in he finds a way to get out and sometimes back in. She has been told if it happens again, she is out of a job.

CHRISTOPHER, MOT, FIDGIT AND JAMES

A story by
Michael Bread

chapter 1

Lottie watched Sid and Charlotte fly away and began to swim across the lake. She noticed when she dived under the water that in several places there was a green glow emanating from the bottom so, curiosity getting the better of her, she swam down to look, but it was of no interest just some green rocks that glowed. After a couple of hours, she reached the other side and sat and waited patiently for some time for them to return. As dusk came and went and darkness descended, she realised they were not going to make it back today.

Dawn came and still no sign of Sid and Charlotte. She remembered the way back to the valley but she also remembered that when she came the first time she went the wrong way around the volcano and found there was no way completely around. However, that route took her past the edge of the valley so she decided to go that way again so she could look over the edge and if possible try and find out what was happening and see if there was any sign of Sid and Charlotte.

chapter 2

M ot awoke. It was pitch black; well, almost. There were thousands of stars above her but no moon. She sat up and spat as she had a mouth full of warm sand. The sand she sat on was warm, but the air around her was bitterly cold. She began to shiver so she lay back down where it was warmer, but she was a little puzzled as to where she was and why.

Her last memory was flying into white light with Sid hanging on to her and her neck hurting. She put her hand up to feel the back of her neck. There was a small scab there and it felt sore but no blood which meant at some time it had stopped bleeding. So how long had she been here? Then she thought about the stars again. She had studied the stars in one of the books she had read at home. She sat up again, wrapping her arms around herself to try and keep warm. Trying to ignore the cold she looked around her and despite no moon with her night sight she could make out row after row of dunes rolling away from her as far as the eye could see.

She looked up at the sky again. There was no constellation like the one she was looking at in the books she had read nor in the other realm they had just been in. She was not at home nor anywhere she knew and it would seem all alone in what appeared to be a freezing desert with warm sand, which could only mean one thing: soon it was going to get very hot and there was nowhere to hide or take shelter. Very hot meant no water and no water meant swift death with or without the sun rays. "How long was a day here?" she thought, "or for that matter a night?"

She jumped. Something had moved in the dark; it had rustled quietly. Snakes, snakes live in the desert. She had read about them and how they could take the heat and some of them came out at night to hunt. Me! She heard the sound again and she stood up. There was nowhere to hide and she didn't have Christopher's strength or Fidgit's bouncing skills, not that there was anywhere to bounce onto. She did have the magic balls but for them to work they had to collide, and she had to see what she was throwing them at!

There was only one thing for it; she would have to find open ground, or open sand, in order to see her enemy. "Let's hope it's only one." She raised her hands in the air to be ready as she knew she would have to move very fast and only had one chance. Her invisibility would be no good. The snake could in all probability see her body heat outline as it was and she thought she would probably freeze to death before she was even thirsty enough to die. This thought made her realise that if she was freezing then there was a chance of getting water from the air. She knew the science as she had of course read about it. She carefully backed away from the sound which was coming from behind the dune she was behind until this dune sloped down and faded into the sand. She backed away and then as quietly as she could she passed between the gap between this dune and the next and approached the snake from the other side. It was white and a strange shape.

******

BV - #0021 - 071220 - C0 - 234/156/21 - PB - 9781914195044 - Matt Lamination